TESTING
LIBERTY

Theresa Linden

This is a work of fiction. Names, characters, businesses, places, events, and incidents are products of the author's imagination or are used fictitiously and are not to be construed as real. Any resemblance to actual events, locations, organizations, or persons is entirely coincidental.

TESTING LIBERTY
Copyright © 2015 by Theresa Linden
http://theresalinden.webs.com
Print ISBN-13: 978-0-9968168-2-3
eBook ISBN: 978-0-9968168-3-0
First Edition Linden Publishing, November 7, 2015

Cover: Theresa Linden
Editor: Elizabeth Brenneman

DEDICATION

This book is dedicated to my sister who inspired me to become a writer.

ACKNOWLEDGMENTS

I wish to express my gratitude to the people who saw me through this book, to beta readers Carolyn Astfalk, Don Mulcare, Michelle Maitino, Holly Hilty, and Linda Eddy, and to Elizabeth Brenneman my editor. I wish to thank John Paul Wohlscheid for his contribution: creating the character Grenton. Above all, I want to acknowledge the love and support of my husband and boys who kept me going. This book would not be possible without them.

"Testing Liberty is an action-packed thrill ride that'll have you rooting for freedom, self-determination, and Liberty."
　　　　~**Carolyn Astfalk**, author of *Stay With Me*

CHAPTER 1

Four bleak walls surrounded me, mocking my failed attempt to live free. I, Liberty 554-062466-84 of Aldonia, was a child of the Regimen Custodia Terra.

A droning noise filled the corners of my mind, pushing out all other thought. Did it come from within my head? The sickly overhead light magnified the annoying quality of the sound. How long could I bear it?

Cold air penetrated my bones and made me shiver. I hugged my waist, rolled to the wall, and buried my face in the corner. Exhaustion overwhelmed me but I couldn't sleep. I hadn't slept more than two hours in a row since they brought me here. Was it daytime? Nighttime? How many days had passed?

The humming noise sounded louder here in the corner. It rang in my head.

I groaned and threw my hands over my ears. I had to think about something else before I lost my mind. A song. A poem.

"Ring around the rosy," I whispered, "a pocket full of posies."

I laughed and then shivered. Where had I heard that poem? Not a poem, a nursery rhyme. I learned it in the Maxwell Colony a month or so ago. It felt like years had passed since then. As pilgrims from Aldonia, Bot, Jessen and I had attended morning classes with the colony teens and followed them to their homes to see what their parents did. Bot hated the experience, considering it too juvenile for a man pushing thirty. I had just turned twenty. Jessen was a few years older. We'd had a good old time. I loved watching family members interact with one another and siblings play.

I envied the sense of belonging they probably took for granted.

Three little girls in ragged tunics held hands in my mind. They danced in a circle. A tiny hand reached out to me. "Come play with us, Liberty." I gave a warm smile but rejected the offer. I couldn't shake the feeling that I didn't belong.

Ring around the rosy, a pocket full of posies. Ashes, ashes, we all fall down. The girls fell to the ground giggling, arms and legs sprawling.

Something in the distance banged, and I sat bolt upright. It banged every few minutes, so it should no longer come as a shock, but my heart still jumped every time it sounded. It reminded me of the guard who'd brought my meals lately. The cell doors opened by remote. First, a low buzz sounded, then a lock clicked. The guard needed to manually open a second lock, a one-sided deadbolt that made no sound. This guard had the habit of flinging open the door and letting it slam against the wall. He always stepped into the room with a crooked grin, amused at having startled me.

The humming sound echoed in my head. If it were more like a white noise, maybe I could sleep. I put a hand to the cold wall and got to my feet. As I straightened up, a calming sensation swirled through me.

The presence within me, the one I had always simply thought of as *My Friend,* wanted to speak to me. Again. In fact, ever since I arrived at the Re-education Facility, he wouldn't leave me alone. He seemed to find pleasure in my imprisonment. His communications made no sense, gave no reason for hope, no plan for escape, and nothing to hold onto. However, with each message came a sensation that stirred my soul to its depths, making me feel loved and successful even as my body trembled from the cold, my head ached, and my empty stomach threatened to bring up more bile.

I was not successful. I had failed. In my selfish desire to save a friend, I put an entire community at risk. I brought destruction to the Maxwell Colony. And I lost the friend I had set out to save. Abby. Abby Rosier.

The Regimen never used her second name. They replaced it with numbers. But I would think of her by her full name. The Regimen had taken her smile, too. Replaced her joy with hopelessness.

When I had worked in the Senior Living Center, I once saw a picture of her smiling. I had even witnessed a hint of joy in her blue-green eyes when she reminisced about her childhood. Which wasn't often. With a flexi-phone on her wrist or a surveillance camera overhead, Abby would not speak of the past. I tried to tell her that the cameras only recorded images, not voices. But she thought they could read lips. Maybe they could. They were always watching, listening, waiting to catch a threat to society.

Ready to send an offender here.

The Re-education Facility was not as I had imagined. Over the years, I had met a person or two who had gone through Re-Ed. No one ever spoke of the experience, so I really had nothing to go on. Still, I imagined something less physically and mentally draining than this. I imagined being forced to listen to and memorize Regimen ideologies day and night. Maybe I hadn't entered that stage yet.

My Friend stirred my soul again, a flutter of butterfly wings against my heart.

I gave in and closed my eyes, leaning against the cold wall to attend him. A sky appeared in my mind, blue and crisp like an early fall day. Something in the distance moved, drawing nearer. I focused on it until I realized it was a black hawk soaring through the air. It did not fly in the usual carefree manner of a bird gliding on air currents, dipping and swooping. It flew straight, rigid. A better look revealed the truth.

My stomach turned to rock. The trembling in my body intensified. It wasn't a bird at all. It was a drone.

Things aren't always as they seem.

The distant banging sounded.

My eyes snapped open. I slid down to the mattress under my feet. I had seen the drone on my trip back to Aldonia. I thought it was a bird. Dedrick knew it was a drone, a drone searching for me, or at least searching for anyone who dared to cross the Boundary Fence and venture into the Fully-Protected Nature Preserves. Man, the enemy of the earth, had no right to be there.

The message continued. Four gray walls surrounded me, but I was not imprisoned. I was free. Free as a bird in the sky, gliding on air currents. Gliding, swaying, swooping, left and right, free and easy. The sensation of vertigo overcame me.

I took a deep breath.

The message ceased.

Trembling, I wrapped my arms around my waist and pulled my legs in. Goose bumps covered my skin. The flimsy gown I wore came only to my knees, and the temperature in my room had dropped again. I considered crawling under the thin mattress, but the hard floor was colder than the air.

The lessons on true freedom, which had begun in the Maxwell Colony, continued here. At Re-Ed. I understood now that inner freedom had more value than physical freedom. Inner freedom came from making right choices no matter the consequences or from accepting the consequences of bad choices. Inner freedom allowed one to have confidence in trials.

I wavered between courage and despair. Abby once used a phrase I found fascinating. It applied to me today. *I have been weighed in the balance and found wanting.*

These were not the lessons the re-education staff wanted to give me. These came from *My Friend.*

My official lessons at Re-Ed had yet to begin. I assumed the next phase of my re-education would include the History Lessons. I did not look forward to them. When first taken to my cell, I passed the open door of the Lesson Room. It resembled the 3D arcades at the mall, housing a moveable tread pad surrounded by wall-to-wall, cushioned flooring. I knew the history taught by the Regimen Custodia Terra. They taught it in Primary and Secondary, and in college for those who qualified for further education. We watched it in movie format. I have since learned that the Regimen's version of history was not the truth. I did not want to see it in 3D, to hear, smell, and feel the lessons on the brutality and destructiveness of the human race—man against man, man against earth—before the RCT took over.

The banging sounded again, nearly obscuring the buzz of the cell door. The door clicked.

I scrambled to my feet, my heels slipping on the mat.

The door flung open and slammed against the wall.

My heart leaped into my throat. I folded my arms over my chest and forced the misery from my expression. I wouldn't give the guard the satisfaction.

"Hey, there, Breeder." He sauntered into the room, one hand to his taser gun, the other holding a tray of food. He had a rough complexion, black holes for eyes, and a chin that resembled a large, dimpled potato.

"It's feeding time." Grinning, he set the tray on the floor and pushed it toward me with the toe of his shoe.

I didn't give the tray more than a glance—a hunk of bread and a steaming bowl of bean soup—but my stomach growled. "Seems like you forgot to bring my lunch. What is it, dinner time?" The scant meals brought to me each day came at irregular intervals, further confusing the passage of time. I imagined that was their goal.

"I told you already, it's *feeding* time." He snickered. "Nothing like the meals at the Breeder Facility, huh? You really blew it, getting yourself in here."

"How come you're the only one who brings my meals lately?" For the past two days, I had seen no other guards but him. Maybe the facility was short-staffed.

He swaggered closer, his eyes roving all over me. "Most girls can only dream of scoring the vocation of Breeder. You get everything you want in there, don't you?"

I tried not to shrink back, to show fear or weakness. He was a fool for moving so close to a resident. I doubted he approached the male residents like this. At the right time, I would use his stupidity against him.

I smirked. "What girl doesn't want her eggs harvested and then to carry a genetically-modified embryo for nine months?"

"That's how that works, huh?" His black eyes rolled upward. He rubbed his potato chin. "I had a different image going through my mind."

I scowled. He stood so close now that with a single step, I could try to take him. Then what? How many people worked in the Re-education Facility?

"What time is it?" I said. "Is it daytime? Night?"

"You don't have to worry about anyone wanting your eggs now." He took the last step to me and brushed the cold double probes of his taser against my abdomen.

I shivered and a sneer came to my face. I bit my lip to keep from spitting on him.

"We'll have you sterilized and placed in a factory job. You'll be making the drones that support our economy, working twelve-hour days. Doesn't that sound fun? Maybe some of your backwoods friends can work with you. If they're smart enough."

Red filled my vision, my breaths quickening. My *backwoods friends* were the Maxwell colonists that the Unity Troops had ripped from their homes. The adults were sent for re-education along with me.

"Did you really live out there in the Nature Preserves?" He touched me, ran his fingers down my arm and then grabbed my side. ". . . like an animal?"

My hands shot out and landed on his chest, forcing him back. I wasn't ready to make my move, though. I wished I hadn't done it. I had no plan. If I could escape this place, I would never do it alone. I had to save every colonist. They were here because of me.

He chuckled, grimaced, and then his hand flew to my face.

I backed into the wall and turned away as the impact stung my cheek.

"Later, breeder girl." He laughed as he left my cell. The door swung shut.

Several thoughts came to me at once.

First, mechanical things interested me, so I couldn't help but visualize the deadbolt. The latch and deadlock bolts slid over the strike lip, momentarily depressing, then sliding into place. The latch bolt needed to extend fully in order to secure the door. It also depended upon the deadlock bolt to function properly.

Second, I assumed the guards were not allowed to harass the residents, so he must've known no one was watching. Or else he didn't think the other facility employees would care if he violated the rules. Either way, it made me think.

I slid down to the mattress, sat cross-legged, and lifted an icy finger to the wall. A plan was building in my mind, components coming into place. Perhaps I could repair the damage I caused the colonists. I had to try.

I traced a line on the wall.

Images flashed in my mind, searing my heart, but I did nothing to stop them. As I ran my finger along the wall, up, down, around, I purposely dwelled on each face and figure, committing to memory each colonist the Unity Troopers had taken. The Chief of the Citizen Safety Station had forced me to watch their *nature reclamation* efforts over and over. I had watched as helicopters descended upon the Maxwell Colony, as colonists ran, as they surrendered, as they moved by gunpoint into the helicopters. I watched as Maxwell burned. The house of the Shenoys, my sponsor family. The common Dining Hall. Dedrick's home. All in flames and billowing black clouds of smoke.

My eyes grew heavy with tears. I traced a circle on the wall. Another line. Up, down, a circle. A stream of tears warmed then cooled my cheeks and chin, but I would not give in to grief. I had work to do. If I had seen all the colonists on the videos, if I had counted it right, the Regimen took twenty-nine of them that day. I whispered their names as I traced on the wall, aware that a surveillance camera hung high on the opposite wall. I didn't care. I needed to say them. Pronouncing the names of Dedrick's family proved the hardest, nearly impossible: Mr. and Mrs. Ryder; Dedrick's brother, Andrew; his sister Paula. I would not forget what I had done to them. Would Dedrick ever forgive me?

My Friend tried to beckon me, a prickling in my chest that I chose to ignore. I could not hear his words of comfort now. These people no longer lived free. Because of me. They'd taught me about love and about family. Their words rang true and deep. I wanted what they had.

The concept of *family* was foreign to Aldonians. We had facilities: the Breeder Facility where life begins, Primary where children go at age five, Secondary for teens, and then out into the world to make your contribution to society. Once a person retired, he transferred to the Senior Center, where I had worked. I loved the old folks there. Abby had felt like family. That was what had compelled me to rescue her.

Dr. Supero had told me of her death. He seemed pleased, whether at eliminating another drain on the Regimen or at my misery, I didn't know. My heart broke into a million shards of glass that day. I hadn't saved her. She'd died. And I brought misery to the people who had welcomed me into their lives.

I ran my finger down the wall and circled back. The camera above me would pick it up. I hoped the Mosheh watched. If they understood my message, I could help the colonists escape this place.

CHAPTER 2

Dr. Supero attempted to fix his gaze on the wall monitor before him. A newscaster blathered on about another endangered species and a hole in the ozone that scientists had yet to repair. Propaganda. He knew that now. Not that it bothered him. It assured citizens of the necessity of strict Regimen ways. It promoted compliance to rule and order. And as long as citizens made their contributions to society, he stood a better chance of securing the funds he needed for his pet projects.

A putrid odor wafted to his nose.

Dr. Supero wrinkled his nose and glanced at the man seated to his right.

Dirt smears on his pants, a week's worth of stubble, black fingernails . . . . He probably worked for Resource Recovery. Four molded plastic couches in the waiting room of the Citizen Safety Station and the filthy man had to sit next to him.

The man tore his eyes from the mindless game on his flexi-phone and raised his brows at Supero. "Got a problem?"

Unable to suppress feelings of disdain, Dr. Supero forced a pleasant smile. "*I do not.*" He returned his gaze to the wall monitor. Chief Varden should have allowed him to wait in the central surveillance room, as he had in the past. The Head Physician of the most advanced medical facility on the continent should not be corralled to the waiting room to sit with the common citizens.

"You look familiar." The odorous man stared.

"I am sure I do not." Not wanting to converse, Supero did not spare a glance. Perhaps the chief meant this as punishment. Varden had proven his own inefficiency in the search for one girl: Liberty. He would not have had success without Dr. Supero's help. Or without the vain boy—what was his name?—Sid. It must've driven the chief mad.

"No, I've seen you before." The foul-smelling man rubbed his scrubby chin. "I'm sure of it. It's the beard. What is that, a star on your chin?"

Supero's upper lip twitched. He threw a seething glare to the man. "I am sure I am not the only man you've seen with a goatee," he said, though he personally knew no other man with a star-shaped goatee. He had grown it in his younger years and now found it difficult to part with. It appealed to women almost as much as his pale violet eyes did.

"I got it. I've seen you on TV?" The man leaned forward and waved an arm, sending a burst of body odor Supero's way. "Some special about improving quality of life, changing the genes or whatever. That's some pretty weird stuff, huh? You can actually get in there and change the DNA?"

"Genetic engineering is not something new." Supero glanced past the man, at the computer screen on the far wall, the virtual receptionist. How long would Chief Varden keep him waiting?

"Well, it's not something you hear about often."

"Surely you jest. Was this a first for you, watching the news? You've been taught since Primary about the advantages our society enjoys due to scientific developments in human germline gene manipulation."

The man jerked back. Brows lifted over startled eyes. "Wow, so you are that doctor . . ."

The door next to the virtual receptionist slid open, commanding Dr. Supero's attention. A young woman stood in the doorway, her dark hair falling over one shoulder, and her figure making the bland gray Citizen Safety Station uniform attractive. He knew her. The girl had drawn his attention during those frustrating days he spent in the Central Surveillance Control Room.

Her sultry gaze locked onto him.

He stood.

She tilted her head to acknowledge him and then turned away, not watching him at all as he approached. Perhaps the scandalous behavior of his assistant and his ex-assistant had tainted her opinion of him. It was unfortunate. Both girls had barged in on him the same evening during official business at the Citizen Safety Station.

"Chief Varden will see you now." Her dark eyes flashed and one brow was raised, judging him.

"Very good." He walked beside her down a long, empty hallway and stopped at the closed door to the Central Surveillance Control Room.

She kept walking and spoke over her shoulder. "You can wait in here." She motioned toward the door to a conference room, her gesture ending at the ID implant reader. The door slid open.

"A conference room?" He strutted to her, sneering to show his displeasure. "Is there a reason I am not permitted in the surveillance room? You are aware that I have met with the chief there since I first visited CSS."

She shrugged and glanced at her nails. "Can I bring you some water?"

"I do not remember your name." He stepped closer, tilting his head to appear taller.

She locked her dark eyes on his but gave no answer.

"Is there an emergency situation, something the chief does not want me to know about?" Perhaps the chief had made a mistake. Something big?

A door across the hallway slid open.

"Dr. Supero," Chief Varden bellowed like a man with a need to prove his power. He strode toward Supero, a cocky grin on his strong-jawed, freckled face. "What brings the good doctor here? Another girl you want me to chase down? Liberty wasn't enough?" He extended a hand, the muscles in his forearm rippling.

Dr. Supero hesitated but then shook the chief's hand of stone, feeling a pinch from the strength of his grip. The two of them entered the conference room and the door slid shut. "What overwhelming challenges face the CSS that you have kept me in the waiting room?"

"You're lucky I let you wait at all. We're busy around here. Don't you have work to do at the hospital? Certainly Aldonia's Head Physician has something to do." Chief Varden glanced at his flexi-phone and scraped a chair out.

"I have more than enough to do." Dr. Supero seated himself across from Varden, rested his elbows on the table, and clasped his hands. "And yet, I find myself here, wondering about the efficiency of CSS."

Chief Varden laughed. "Your girl Liberty is in Re-Ed. Isn't that what you wanted? We got that for you. And a whole lot more." He leaned across the table, one eye narrowing to a slit. "Thirty-seven off-grids we found out there in the protected wilderness. What more can you want?"

Supero leaned back. He had found great satisfaction in watching the Unity Troops capture Liberty, in watching Chief Varden and the others interrogate her, and in questioning her himself. Perhaps his obsession over her resulted from misguided anger. She represented all that was wrong with the world, a cancer threatening to destroy the integrity established by the greatest minds. Liberty was a cancer. His cancer.

Dr. Supero drew in a sharp breath. Nonetheless, it pleased him to know she would no longer spread her poisonous ideology and that she would get the re-education she needed. But he needed something else now. "Have you given up the search, then? Do you honestly believe those thirty-seven were the only ones living out there?"

Chief Varden's eye twitched. His mouth curled up on one side. A grin or a sneer? "Leave us to our business and you stick to yours."

"I would, if I had confidence in the thoroughness of your methods."

Both eyes twitched. "Listen, doctor, we found your girl. If you've other business with CSS, make it known. Otherwise—"

The door opened and a dark haired, muscular young man stepped into the room. "Hey, uh . . ." He lifted his head, revealing tan skin and blue eyes that conveyed a rollercoaster of emotion. *Sid.* He sauntered to the table and rested his hands on a seatback, as if he had every right to barge in on a private conference. "One of your guys said you were in here. I need to talk to you." His gaze swiveled to Dr. Supero. "Oh, hey, doctor. What's up?"

"What is up?" Supero's eyes bugged, against his will. "I am having a private conversation with the chief. Who do you think you are that you barge in here without even knocking? And how, how did you even get in here?"

"What do you need, Sid?" Chief Varden shifted in his seat, turning his back on Dr. Supero.

"Yeah, you know, I've been waiting for you guys to, uh . . ." He stuffed his thumbs into the belt loops of his low-riding jeans, dropped his gaze, bit his bottom lip. A little boy waiting for his nanny to read his mind.

Supero's patience snapped. "Out with it. You interrupt my business, speak and be gone."

"Well, you know, Dr. Supero, they made a deal with me. I didn't help you find Liberty out of love for Mother Earth. The chief here made me a promise."

Chief Varden chuckled. "I guess that's true. Sorry, Sid, your girl's already in Re-Ed. Nothing I can do about it. Put in a Vocation Change Request with the RCT Vocational Department. Get a job out at Re-Ed." He chuckled again, harder.

Sid's jaw twitched. His thumbs slid from his belt loops, his hands clenching. "No, I ain't doing that, and I ain't going away. I want what's owed me. If it wasn't for my help, you wouldn't have her."

Dr. Supero and Chief Varden both laughed.

"You flatter yourself. We didn't need your help." Chief Varden pushed out his chair, went to the door, and slapped the control panel. The door slid open. "Find yourself another girl. Aldonia's full of them." He gave Sid the once-over. "Shouldn't be too hard for a guy with your build."

"Uh-uh, man. I don't want another girl." Sid stomped up to the chief, two men facing off in a wrestling match. He stood a few inches shorter, but the fire of his desire could easily bump him into the same weight division. "I want her. And you're gonna arrange it."

A smirk crept onto Chief Varden's chiseled face. He turned and left the room.

"I am not done here." Dr. Supero jumped up and dashed after him. "You do not even understand the reason for my visit!"

Chief Varden breezed into the main surveillance room. "That's all the time I have for you, doctor. Feel free to schedule an appointment." He rubbed a hand through his cropped blond hair and stood arms akimbo, his attention on the wall monitors.

Dr. Supero came up beside him and spoke through clenched teeth. "You are searching the Nature Preserves, I am sure. I need to know your progress. I have reason to believe more people are out there." He had personally examined every one of the off-grids. He'd found a thyroid condition, high triglycerides, and other trivial conditions that science had eradicated. But one man had scars from an open heart surgery. Who was the surgeon? How does a man gain that skill living in the wilderness with three dozen others? They admitted to growing their own food and devoting themselves to the necessities of life. None of them struck him as particularly intelligent. An ID implant had never pierced their virgin palms. How did these people live? There had to be more of them. There had to be a surgeon, maybe someone who once lived in Aldonia. He needed that surgeon.

"Give it up. We did an exhaustive search. We found everyone there is to find."

"I do not believe that." A sharp pain ripped through his head. His hand shot to the spot. He imagined he felt the tumor growing inside him and stretching its tentacles deep into his brain. He'd discovered its cancerous nature a year ago, before Liberty had escaped from Aldonia last fall. The Medical Care Evaluation Panel had denied the surgery he needed, despite his importance and immense contribution to society. Budget cuts, they claimed. So the destructive malignancy had had free reign within him for one entire year. He needed to find that physician.

"Dr. Supero, I've had enough of you." Chief Varden turned his icy gray eyes to Supero. "It was a mistake for me to allow you free access to this place. You don't belong here. Go back to your hospital, or your board meetings, or your women, or wherever you go when you're not here. Can't you see we're trying to work?"

The headache dulled but his face warmed. This man would be the death of him. "We found thirty-seven off-grids in the Fully-Protected Nature Preserves. Thirty-seven people who lived selfishly with no regard for their impact on the rest of the earth." His voice came out high and raspy, the voice of a madman, but he could not gain control. "If there are more, we risk setting into motion, again, the feral plague on the earth that the Regimen Custodia Terra has long since neutralized."

"Doctor Supero," Chief Varden spit out his name but then shut his mouth. He cut a glance to either side, clamped a hand to Dr. Supero's arm, and led him to a quiet corner. "Listen and don't ask questions. Our resources are limited. We need permission from higher authorities to do anything. But I agree, we need to keep searching. I want to widen our search with drone scans. But right now, we've got trouble at the Jensenville borders, and it's sucking up our resources."

"How does this concern CSS? Let the Unity Troops handle that. What are they for, otherwise?"

"The Unity Troops are useless without us." He stood taller, emphasizing the several-inch difference in their heights. "You people don't realize how important CSS is. But whenever anybody needs anything, they come to us."

Supero shook his head. Ordinarily, he would have a rude retort, but the headache now came in waves that made him wince. "Do what you can to establish priorities. Keep me informed." Supero turned to leave.

"I'm supposed to keep you informed, huh?" Chief Varden shouted and then laughed.

Supero didn't look back. It took concentration to walk without staggering. The headache would pass. His temper brought it on. It was not necessarily a symptom of the tumor. He would beat this thing.

Someone behind him spoke, saying words he could not decipher, probably Sid demanding his rights from Chief Varden.

Chief Varden replied in a low voice, "Aw, come on now, kid. Face reality."

CHAPTER 3

Dedrick Ryder replayed the video sent days ago from a Unity Troop's helicopter to Aldonia's Citizen Safety Station. They, the Mosheh, had intercepted it. He had avoided watching it or any other live feed since his initial viewing, keeping himself busy with safety measures and waiting for the Mosheh to call him into action. He hated waiting. Especially now.

He sat slouched in a cushioned office chair at the corner station of the Mosheh's Control Center. Indiscernible chatter and an electronic hum surrounded him. Darkness stretched out behind him. The light from overhead lamps did nothing to diminish the cavernous effect of the sprawling subterranean structure. Bluish images from the array of wall monitors flashed high in his visual field.

He stared without blinking at the image on the glassy monitor before him.

A figure emerged from the woods, a little stringy-haired girl in a pale dress. The image zoomed in on the nine-year-old. She raced across a field, running as if her life depended upon it. The helicopter descended, the gale from its rotors sending her hair and skirt flapping wildly. She shielded her eyes and looked up, directly at the camera it seemed. She shot a look of anger and courage.

Dedrick's heart twisted with guilt and sorrow.

Paula. His little sister was too brave for her own good. Why hadn't she followed the safety plan? When the alarm sounded in the Maxwell Colony, she should've ran for the Communications and Advanced Technology Cave. She shouldn't have worried about anyone else.

Dedrick shifted in the chair and folded his arms over his chest. He could feel Paula throw herself into his arms for a hug, practically knocking the air out of him, pressing her little body to his. Her arms around his neck. Her hair in his face. Her smooth cheek against his. She always smelled like grass and fresh air.

How was she handling life in Primary, away from Mom and Dad?

A woman in a blue dress and an apron dashed from the woods and onto the field. *Mom.* He could read her lips. She was calling Paula's name, frantic for her baby's safety. Dad came into the picture next, shouting and waving his arms. He glanced at the helicopter as it touched down. He kept motioning to someone in the woods on the other side of the field. Motioning, shouting, motioning. Until Andy stepped out armed with a rifle. The look on Andy's face: he didn't want to run. He wanted to fight.

Four Unity Troopers, weapons at the ready, disembarked from the helicopter.

Andy stood face to face with Dad for a moment. Dedrick could almost hear his father's plea. "Give me the gun, son. We can't fight them this way." Andy wilted as he relinquished the rifle. Dad tossed it aside and threw an arm around Andy, pulling him close. There they stood in a huddle— Mom, Dad, Andy, Paula—as the Unity Troopers surrounded them. Their last moment together.

Once the helicopter brought them to Aldonia, they had been separated. Dedrick had heard the command that day. Children to North Primary, teens to Secondary, adults to Re-Ed. Mom and Dad would not be permitted to see each other even though they lived in the same facility.

Andy may have found some satisfaction in being here in Aldonia even though he was captive. Dedrick knew how his brother's mind worked. Andy considered himself an adult. He wanted in on the action.

Dedrick peered up at the high, dark ceiling. He had never liked the Regimen, but now he hated them. Three stories up, above ground, stood the Regimen Custodia Terra's government offices and Aldonia's Primary Medical Facility. They had no idea that an opposing faction, the Mosheh, operated at the bottom of one of Aldonia's sealed off and long forgotten parking structures.

When would the Mosheh make their move?

Dedrick leaned over, the chair squeaking under him, and buried his head in his hands. Was this his fault?

"There you are."

The voice snapped Dedrick from his thoughts. He straightened up, wiping the water from his eyes before Miriam saw it. "Yeah, hey, what do you need?"

Miriam wore gray camouflage pants and a long-sleeved charcoal-gray shirt, a packed gun belt hanging low around her slim waist. She ran a finger through the white strands in her otherwise dark hair, then tucked her hair behind her ear. "Your sister Ann called in from the CAT Cave. She wants to speak with you." She didn't exactly smile, but something in her expression always conveyed a light mood, no matter the gravity of the situation. Maybe age did that to a person.

Dedrick shut off the video. It had moved on to scenes of houses burning in the Maxwell Colony, his house one of them. He couldn't think about that now. It was out of his hands. His older sister Ann was safe. He would think about that.

"What's she want? And where're you going?" He glanced at Miriam's gun belt.

"I'm checking tunnels on the far side of Aldonia, close to the Jensenville border. An explosion went off above ground. Need to make sure the tunnels are okay. Care to join me?" Miriam slapped him on the back and then looped an arm around his. She led him toward the opposite side of the island of workstations.

"No, I've been in the tunnels for days, securing access points and checking on false walls. Besides, I'm waiting for the Mosheh to make the rescue plan."

"That could be awhile."

He shook his head, impatience bringing a sneer to his face. "I don't see why. I gave them my plan. They need to move."

"What makes you think they'll let you help with the rescues? You've got at least one family member in each facility. I'd say you're a bit compromised."

They stopped at a workstation under the wall monitors. The kid at the workstation removed a big black headset and handed it to Dedrick. "No video. Just audio."

Dedrick nodded, watched the kid walk away, and then yanked the plug. He glanced at the overhead monitors. Several of them showed Maxwell colonists in their cells at the Re-education Facility. He forced himself not to view the images of his parents. His gaze caught Liberty. She sat in a dimly lit room, cross-legged on a bare mattress and running her finger down the wall.

His heart wrenched. He looked away. "Ann, you there?"

"I'm here, Dedrick. Please tell me you're doing something to rescue our family?"

He placed his palms on the desk and leaned over, bristling at her impatient, bossy attitude—not that he didn't expect it. That was her way in tough situations. It kept people moving. The Mosheh could use her.

"I'm doing what I can." He glanced over his shoulder and exchanged a look with Miriam. "I'm waiting."

Ann let out a frustrated groan. "Well, stop waiting. Get in there and rescue my little sister. You're always so quick to help when the Torva's in need."

"That's not fair," he said. The Torva lived liked nomads. So, of course, they found themselves in need. He couldn't simply turn a blind eye when he came across them.

"Look, Ann, this isn't my fault." He cringed, feeling like a liar. His gaze shot up to the monitors, to the live video feed of Liberty. She stood with her back to the camera now, her unkempt hair hanging loose around her shoulders.

15

"I'd go in *now* if I could," he said. It was true. He'd go alone. He'd risk his life. He'd do anything to save them.

"I know," she whispered. "I'm sorry. I can't stand to think of Paula in that ungodly place. I can only imagine what they're trying to teach her. And how the other kids are treating her. They're not exactly nice in those places."

"Paula's strong. She knows truth when she hears it. Don't worry. We'll have her out of there in no time."

"No time?" Miriam whispered, smirking.

He rolled his eyes and shrugged.

"So how're you doing? Hanging in there?" He couldn't imagine the fear and grief his sister must've felt watching the Regimen descend upon Maxwell, watching their home go up in flames and knowing that everyone in their family had been taken. Everyone but the two of them.

"We've scoured the area, salvaged the few things the flames spared." Her voice broke. "Things stored underground in basements and such. I think those troopers must've gone through the area. They didn't just burn. They plundered."

Dedrick had heard every command given to the troops. They were only to destroy. "Yeah, well, it gives us a chance to get back to basics, right? I mean, maybe we were getting too comfortable."

"Yeah, right." Someone else spoke. A man. "Is that supposed to make her feel better?" The voice sounded familiar. And loud.

"Bot?" Dedrick put a name and face to the voice. Mottled blue eyes, messy red hair, a man in need of a shave. He'd rescued Bot from Unity Troopers a few days before he rescued Liberty from the Breeder Facility.

Dedrick's gaze snapped to Liberty's image on the overhead monitor. She was still standing, tracing figures on the wall. She wore a dress. No, more like a patient gown that draped down to her knees. Every man and woman in Re-Ed wore the same thing. Still, had he ever seen her in a dress?

"Yeah, it's me," Bot said. "I wasn't trying to snoop on your private conversation, but Ann's standing right here. She could've used ear buds if she wanted privacy. No one gets that around here anymore. This CAT Cave is crowded. You got any idea when the transfer is supposed to take place?"

"Transfer?" Dedrick turned to Miriam for the answer.

Miriam nodded, eyes wide. She mouthed, "We have to talk."

"Yeah," Bot said. "The Rivergrove Colony sent an invite to all our displaced colonists."

"Rivergrove?" Dedrick said. "That journey would take two weeks at the very least, considering you're moving families."

"Yeah, so when do they get started?"

"I don't know. That's not my decision. I'm focused on rescues now."

"Well, while you're waiting on that, you need to check out this 3D game we developed. You know about the historical documents I uncovered, how that got me started on a dangerous path? According to the Regimen. I've found more to motivate me right here in Maxwell." He laughed. "You probably learned all about it in school, but it's new to me and it's foreign to everyone in Aldonia."

Dedrick shook his head. "This guy'll talk forever," he said to Miriam. "Made me wish for earplugs when I led him to Maxwell. The tunnels never seemed longer, the woods deeper. I couldn't wait to—"

"Are you listening?" Bot shouted. "This is important."

"Not to me, Bot." Dedrick leaned over the desk, speaking closer to the miniature microphone. "All I care about is rescuing our people." His gaze traveled up to the array of wall monitors. He meant to scan all the images of the colonists in their cells, but he stopped at Liberty. She still traced shapes, making invisible pictures on the wall. Had she lost her mind? No. Not her. They couldn't break her that easily. Besides, she was only in the second stage of the re-education program, wasn't she? She of all people should be able to handle it.

"That's cuz you're not seeing the big picture," Bot said.

"Forget it, Bot," Ann said. "Right now I want him to focus on saving our people. He can save the world tomorrow."

Bot's voice came softer over the speaker, as if he now stood at a distance from the phone. "I'm telling you, Ann, this game has the power to change the world."

"Right. Okay, Bot," Ann said. "Dedrick, please let me know when anything happens. I'm dying over here."

"I know, Ann, me too." He thumbed the control to disconnect the call. His gaze remained fixed on Liberty's image as he tried to decipher her invisible drawings.

She ran her finger over the wall, making a counter-clockwise circle. She lifted her finger and drew a line. Down, up, and a forward circle. Lift and tap. After she tapped the wall, she stepped back.

The realization of her motive hit him like a punch to his gut. He spun to face Miriam. "What is she doing?"

"Who?"

"Liberty. It looks like she's writing messages on the wall."

"She is. She's trying to communicate with us. The Mosheh knows already. If they can use her ideas, they will." Miriam slipped her arm around his and tugged.

"Come on. Before I head for the tunnels, I'll show you the plan for the exodus from Maxwell. I've got maps laid out on the crates."

The crates sat stacked against a far wall. A few yellow, low-pressure sodium lamps hung over them, emitting a soft luminous glow that drained the color from everything it reached.

Dedrick took a few steps but stopped at the end of the workstations next to a support beam with a mess of wires running up it. "Well, that's a dumb thing for her to do. The Citizen Safety Station might not have the brightest workers, but they'd figure that out. It'll make them wonder who she's trying to communicate with, might give them the idea that someone monitors their live feeds." He wasn't taking another step until Miriam understood the danger.

Miriam smiled. "Relax, Dedrick, they'll think she's crazy. She's writing verses from old nursery rhymes."

Something fluttered in his stomach. Liberty knew nursery rhymes by heart?

Dedrick shook his head, trying to stay focused. "How is that a message for us?"

"It's clever, really." She sat down at an empty workstation. "She must've learned a few traditional nursery rhymes from her days at Maxwell."

"I'm not following you. Show me the message."

Miriam brushed her fingers over the smooth control panel, bringing up several files and manipulating them until she found the one she wanted. A text file appeared on the monitor.

Dedrick leaned over her shoulder and read:

Ring around the rosy,
a pocketful of posies,
ashes, ashes, *take the power* rosy.

Handy Spanky, Jack-a-dandy,
Loves plum-cake and sugar-candy;
He bought some at a grocer's shop.
Hand out he came, hop-hop-hop. *Out he came.*

And the dish ran away with the spoon.
To the trees by the light of the moon.
And out he came, hop-hop-hop.

"Uh." He looked for the humor in Miriam's eyes but didn't find it. "I'm not getting it."

Miriam waved her hand over the control panel and pulled up another file, more rhymes—longer ones. "Didn't your mother read you nursery rhymes?" She brought Liberty's rhymes and the originals up, side by side. "Liberty changed a few words to give us her message."

"Which is?"

Miriam met his gaze. "Well, she replaced *we all fall down* with *take the power*, which we interpreted as *she wants us to take the power down*. Then she changed *and* to *hand* and added an extra *out he came*. What else could that mean?"

"She wants us to get an ID implant remover over there." Dedrick began to appreciate Liberty's method. "Probably wants it left somewhere outside."

"Right. Maybe in the trees," Miriam said, smiling. "*To the trees by the light of the moon.* They'd have to climb a barbed wire fence to reach the tree line. There's also a river back there. She probably thinks we could use that. I'm sure she expects us to come up with the rest, like how to get the colonists to safety before troops and drones arrive."

"Isn't our biggest problem getting into the facility? With Liberty on the inside—"

She laughed. "I know Liberty means well, and she wants to help, but do you see her taking down a guard or something?"

He straightened up. He needed to take this to the Mosheh. "No, but my father could. Liberty only needs to get the cell doors open. And with the power down . . ."

Miriam nodded, her expression showing she now agreed.

"Let's go see the Mosheh," Dedrick said. "It's time to make a move."

CHAPTER 4

A banging sound woke me, but I didn't want to open my eyes. Was it the distant sound that came every few minutes, or was it the door slamming open? Despite the cold and the aches in my muscles—the result of lying on a thin mattress—sleep felt good. I hadn't slept more than a few hours in a row since I got here.

A soft chuckle came to my ears.

I struggled to lift my heavy eyelids and the weight of sleep from my body.

"Time to get up, Breeder." Footsteps. The swish of fabric. Breathing. The guard stood somewhere nearby.

I forced my eyelids open and blinked at the light. Fuzzy gray shapes filled my vision, something near my eye.

My heart rate quickened. I swatted the air, hitting nothing.

At the same moment, something cold and hard smacked my thigh. "Get up, Breeder. If I have to reach down and drag you to your feet, you'll be sorry."

Energy returned to my limbs, slow and rough like an engine shuddering to life on an icy morning. I placed a palm on the mattress and pushed myself up. My head swirled from overtiredness or maybe dehydration. Cold air stole the scant warmth that had been mine in sleep. My vision returned.

The dull light illumined the four bare walls and the black-eyed guard at the foot of the mattress. He stood with his head tilted to one side, smirking down at me, a hand resting on the taser at his hip. A casual posture or a devious one?

I scooted away from him until my back hit the wall and sent a cold shiver through my body. "What time is it?"

"Time for you to get up." He leaned, reaching a meaty hand out for me.

"Okay!" I threw my hands up to block his touch. "I'm getting up."

He laughed, glanced at the overhead camera, and backed away.

Someone must have been watching us. I had the feeling this was not always the case, that the Re-education Facility did not have a reliable staff.

I climbed to my feet, my legs numb and cold, and adjusted the thin gown. "What, no food? Or do I eat in the dining room today?"

"The dining room, yeah." He laughed and yanked open the door. "Hold onto that thought. Maybe this'll be easier on you." He motioned for me to go first.

Barefoot and hugging myself, I stepped into the dark hallway. Closed doors with dark windows lined the walls on both sides. Prisoners in every cell. Colonists in most of them. Over the days, I had seen a few colonists being led to or from their rooms. Dedrick's father had the cell across the hallway and two doors down. His mother also had a cell in this hall, but the little window in my door did not allow me to see it.

Each time a guard took me from my cell, I studied everything. I now had a partial map of the facility in my mind. The hallway past the cellblocks led to a service door. This would be the least conspicuous door for our escape. The problem: microchip scanners at the entrances ensured that only authorized personnel could get through. The scanners would read our ID implants and signal security both here at the facility and at the Citizen Safety Station. They would dispatch Unity Troops immediately.

Possible solutions came to mind. A piece of foil should prevent a read, but we would still need an authorized person to open the service door. This we could achieve by force. The first guard to notice us would become our key.

A power outage might work better. I assumed the facility had a fail-safe system that would automatically unlock the cells in case of emergency. That may have been the reason for the second lock, the one-sided deadbolts. A guard would need to open them manually. But if I could jimmy the lock to my cell door, I could free the others. Then we'd only have the problem of opening the service door.

Once outside, I would have to get my bearings. I caught bits of information, eavesdropping on the staff's conversations. We would need to climb a barbwire fence, then run to the trees and maybe head to the river. I had no idea about the location of the Mosheh's secret entrances, but I hoped one was nearby. My plan went as far as getting the colonists out of the facility. The Mosheh would have to do the rest.

Taser in hand and keeping a distance, the guard directed me down the hallway. We neared intersecting hallways.

"Take a left," he said.

"Where are you taking me?" I had been down this hallway once before, the day of my arrival. A single room had caught my attention: the Lesson Room.

"You're moving on to the next stage of your re-education."

Acid rose in my throat. A cool sweat broke out on my skin. The History Lessons. They would start today.

"Keep walking," the guard said, keeping his distance.

I took one step, then another, my body turning to lead. No, I couldn't do this.

The urge to bolt seized me. Then a wave of peace overcame it, washing through me like a violent storm, a gentle dewfall, *My Friend* reminding me of his presence. My head swirled as it had when I first woke. I reached out to steady myself.

My fingertips skimmed the wall as the lights flickered.

The lights flickered again.

Then all went black.

The guard cursed. "Hey, what's going on?" A faint blue light appeared, issuing from the flexi-phone on his wrist, giving the outline of his potato chin and his mouth.

"I-I don't know." The tinny voice came from his flexi-phone. "Power's down. Back-up generator should kick on . . ."

Something made a thud.

The guard grunted and flew forward, causing a breeze that tickled my cheek. A shadowy figure emerged from nowhere and swooped down on the guard. More thuds, more grunting. Sounds of a fight I could not see.

I backed into the wall, stunned. Had the Mosheh come to rescue us?

A hand brushed then gripped my arm. "Come with me," a man said, his voice muffled. "We've got forty-five seconds." A beam of light appeared, cutting the darkness from his black-gloved hand to the floor, revealing the reason his voice sounded strange. He wore a dark helmet.

I ran with him, back the way I had come, keeping pace with him and following the beam of light. We came to the intersecting hallways and he slowed. He mumbled something, flashing the light in either direction, then we turned down the hall that led to the service door.

"Put this on." He stuffed a stiff fingerless glove into my hand. "Over your implant."

I didn't need the last instruction. I knew the glove had a layer of foil inside that would keep the scanner from reading my implant. I didn't know how he planned to open the door. Without power or a key, it would be impossible to—

The lights flickered on. Someone down one of the hallways shouted. Security? Other rescuers?

My rescuer stopped at the door and stuffed the flashlight into a pocket. Then he pulled something from his jacket and waved it over the scanner. The door clicked. He grabbed my wrist and slammed his shoulder to the door.

We burst out into fresh air and twilight from the setting or rising sun. The sight of daylight shocked me. I assumed it was nighttime because I had been sleeping, but it also seemed like the best time for a rescue.

His grip on my hand tightened. "Over there," he said, pointing.

Across a cracked driveway and a stretch of grass, a black 250 motorcycle sat among overgrown bushes. Its chrome reflected the sunlight.

We ran to it.

I kept my eyes to the ground, watching every step to avoid slicing my bare feet on loose gravel.

"What about the others?" I said, breathless. I looked up in time to see a black helmet sailing towards me.

"Let's go." He gripped the handlebars, swung a leg over the motorcycle, and put a boot to the kickstand.

I slid the helmet onto my head, its visor making the world dull and blurry. It fit snug and smelled of gasoline and sweat.

"Hurry and get on." He dipped his head. "You don't have shoes."

I grabbed his shoulders and climbed onto the bike. "What about the others?"

The moment I spoke, he twisted the throttle and the engine turned over. The rumbling of the exhaust drowned my words. I had barely planted my feet on the footrests when we took off.

CHAPTER 5

Dedrick stared at the closed door of the private meeting room as he and Miriam approached it. At least one senior member of the Mosheh was inside, maybe more. They could be having a conference call. It was probably about the rescues.

"What's the matter with you?" Amusement rang in Miriam's tone.

His body tensed. She held his arm and probably noticed. He ran a hand through his hair as an excuse to break their connection. "Nothing's the matter with me." He shouldn't let his thoughts go to the last time he was in that meeting room.

The elders hadn't spoken to him since, not officially. Individual members had offered condolences and assured him they'd do everything to help. Elder Lukman had been in the control center when Dedrick tossed around ideas with other members, formulating rescue scenarios. Dedrick still hadn't answered the Mosheh's original questions. They probably had more to say to him. There would be consequences for his actions.

"Is there a problem?" Miriam stood with a fist raised to the door, smirking at him.

"Huh? No, let's do it."

She knocked and opened the door, not waiting for the invitation to come in. He would never have done that. The elders made him feel like a teenager trying to prove himself. He never knew what they expected.

"Miriam. Dedrick." Elder Lukman sat the far end of the long table, alone. Live images of two other elders, Rayna and Dean, showed on the wall monitors. Elder Lukman smiled and motioned for them to join him at the table.

Maps and several files glowed on the tabletop. A 3D image of the Re-education Facility hung in the air before Elder Lukman. He tapped a control and it all vanished.

"Your name came up a moment before you knocked on the door," Elder Lukman said to Dedrick. His hair and beard glowed as white as Moses' after he had seen the face of God. His face was a roadmap of wrinkles. Wisdom exuded from his pores. Elder Lukman was a legend with the Mosheh, a founding father. Elder Lukman *was* the Mosheh.

Dedrick took the seat across from him. "Oh yeah, my name came up?" He wiped his sweaty palms on his jeans in case the elder wanted to shake hands.

He wanted to blurt out the ideas he got from Liberty's message but *no*. He should take it slow. The elders probably doubted his judgment now.

"Where are we with the rescue plans?" Dedrick said.

"We're working out the final details," Elder Lukman said.

"Good." Dedrick glanced at Miriam. Maybe she would bring up Liberty's plan.

Miriam had taken the chair next to him. She nodded at him and tucked a lock of gray hair behind her ear. "Yeah, that's good. It's hard waiting when people you love . . ." She pressed her lips together and gave her eyes to Elder Lukman. Did she think she offended Dedrick with the comment? Did Elder Lukman have someone in the facilities?

Elder Lukman appeared unfazed.

"So, Primary first?" Dedrick said. It only made sense to rescue the youngest ones first. The teens and adults would want it that way.

"No, no," Elder Lukman said. "To rescue from one facility before the others would likely alert the Regimen to our efforts, cause them to tighten security. We can't have that."

Dedrick shifted in his seat. He had expected to be involved in each rescue operation. "So we'll go in all three facilities at once?"

"That's the plan. We're organizing teams. Primary will be the easiest rescue, the Re-education Facility the toughest."

Miriam pushed up her sleeves. "We have easy access to a utility room in Primary. A night rescue would work best, less staff. One person could sneak in and out without notice."

Elder Lukman nodded. "Camilla and Alix are the Primary team."

Dedrick flinched. *Paula.* She would be expecting him to rescue her. He knew which tunnels connected to the Primary Residence. He knew how to unlock the hidden access door. Every night since her capture, he had gone through the rescue in his mind.

"We want our young women to handle this rescue." Elder Lukman seemed to read Dedrick's mind. "If anyone catches sight of them, they won't seem out of place."

Dedrick knew the girls. Alix was Aldonian, pretty with pale skin and short, jet-black hair. She had a dark attitude but a kind heart. Camilla came from the

Maxwell Colony. Dedrick grew up with her. She had a tan that didn't fade in the winter and brown hair always worn in a ponytail. Talkative, a history buff, and good with languages, including sign, Camilla would seem out of place if she opened her mouth.

"Women work at Primary. Mostly," Miriam said, the hint of a grin on her face.

"Yeah, so?" He glared. He could get in and out undetected. Didn't need a girl to do that.

She smiled. "So who's on the Secondary team? We don't have underground access there, do we?"

"No, but we have a solid plan. Half the colonists are scheduled to move to a Secondary Residence in Jensenville."

"What?" Dedrick glanced at the faces on the wall monitors before locking eyes with Elder Lukman. "Since when?" The Mosheh kept this from him. Why? Was his brother on the transfer list?

"Not to worry, Dedrick. I understand the stress you must be going through, but you need to trust our ways—"

"Your ways are taking too long." The words flew out before he could stop them. "We need to act now. My brother isn't one to sit idly by. He's probably got a plan going through his head right now."

"Yes, he does." Elder Dean spoke. He had been sitting motionless with his bald head tilted forward and his eyes closed. Now he peered through eyes that seemed to see into the depths of a person or a situation.

"What do you mean?" More they hadn't told him? They didn't trust him anymore.

"Your brother's been sneaking around the facility storage rooms and kitchen gathering items," Elder Dean said. "Seems to have made a few Aldonian friends. A few are even potential candidates."

"No more on that." Elder Rayna threw a glance to one side, her dark skin making the whites of her eyes flash. She and Elder Dean must've been at the same remote location. She faced forward again, peering at Dedrick through the screen. "Rescues at Secondary will not be as easy. As you know, Dedrick, we have never gone into that facility. We wait until our candidate comes out."

He knew well enough. They rescued on quiet streets and alleys. They had no underground access to Secondary, no secret way in.

"Our Secondary team is prepping," Elder Lukman said. "One of ours will drive the transport bus. We've cloned the signal, stolen the information from an official Regimen driver's chip. Polo and Rider will go inside to get the nine transfers."

Dedrick's jaw tightened. He wasn't on this team either.

He took a breath. They probably wanted him for the toughest rescue, the one at the Re-education Facility. Maybe they did have confidence in him. With two exceptions, he had followed the Mosheh's every rule. He had never once botched a rescue. He excelled at self-defense and could stay cool under pressure, make snap decisions if he had to. He knew the tunnel network inside and out, the routes that tunnel karts could access, the water-bogged routes, every single access point . . .

"Okay for the nine colonists being transferred," Miriam said, "but what about the others?"

"Polo will distract the staff. Rider will bring gloves that suppress the RFID transponders. He'll route the other colonists through a side door."

"When does this happen?" Dedrick said.

"Rescues can't be rushed," Elder Rayna said. "We're still developing the scapegoat."

Dedrick clenched his teeth and glanced at her image. He shouldn't feel hostility toward an elder. "So what's the plan for the Re-Ed Facility?" he asked Elder Lukman.

The question hung in the air for a moment.

"That rescue poses a greater challenge." Elder Lukman leaned back and let out a long sigh. "Security is high. Greater number of staff. The nearest access point is an alley by the north recycling center, too great of a hike."

"None of the rescues can take place until we get Intel on the surveillance cameras," Elder Dean said. "We need to find safe routes that avoid the Regimen's eye."

"What happened to our source?" Dedrick said. They used to receive a steady stream of Intel from a kid in one of the Environmental Stewardship Units. They could go about freely anywhere in Aldonia without getting caught on camera.

"Finley was our source," Elder Dean said, "until the day CSS interrogated him."

"CSS interrogated him?" Dedrick said.

"They interrogated everyone connected with Liberty." Elder Dean propped his forehead up with his hand. "Fortunately, Finley knows nothing about us. He works through a middleman. Worked. Past tense."

"We'll have to get him back," Dedrick said.

"We've tried," Elder Dean said. "He's scared."

"We could bribe him with a new game," Miriam said. "You know he's obsessed with 3D games, right? I bet he'd rise above his fear in order to be the first user of a new game."

Elder Dean lifted his head and narrowed one eye. "I hadn't considered that. Think it might work?"

"I do. We should at least try. And we've got just the game." Miriam nudged Dedrick. "Bot's game. It won't have the Regimen seal of approval, so that'll add to the appeal."

"So, what's my role?" Dedrick glanced from one elder to the other. "I'm on the Re-Ed team, right?" He almost preferred it, now that he thought about it. They were right, anyone could rescue from Primary. And the plan for Secondary seemed sound, possible.

"Dedrick." Elder Lukman straightened up, leaned over the table, and clasped his hands together. "We need you somewhere else."

"What?" Dedrick again glanced at each elder, his heart rate quickening. "Where else? No. I need to be part of the rescues."

"We have other critical jobs. The Maxwell colonists need escorted from the CAT cave to the Rivergrove Colony. The Torva haven't gone south yet and—"

Dedrick jumped up, his chair rolling back. "No." He slammed his palms on the table. "Get someone else. My family members are prisoners in Aldonia." He swung his arm in the general direction of the facilities. "I *will* be involved in these rescues. Maybe you think this is all my fault, and maybe it is." A pang of guilt wrung his heart. He needed to get control of himself, to sit down and shut up. "Maybe you don't trust me anymore. But you can. It's taken every bit of patience I have to keep from acting on my own, but I'm waiting on you. I have no idea why we're waiting, but I am waiting."

"No one blames you," Elder Lukman said, his expression calm and sincere.

"Dedrick, sit down." Miriam was by his side, grabbing his arm.

He bristled at her touch. He should sit down but he couldn't.

"We do not act in haste." Elder Rayna spoke in a harsh voice, like a woman too familiar with the results of acting on impulse. "Every action of the Mosheh has consequences. We've been weakened. You should know. You organized the sealing off of several tunnels, the destruction of access points. And you're aware CSS now suspects that someone outside created, or at least knew of, the operational pattern for their surveillance cameras. They've added features to protect from spyware."

She shook her head. "No, Dedrick, we must do nothing more to arouse the suspicion of the Regimen. We will act once we've provided a solid scapegoat, created a false trail, something that will satisfy the Regimen."

"Which is?" Dedrick said. He yielded to Miriam's physical redirection and took his seat.

Elder Lukman nodded, seeming pleased that Dedrick composed himself enough to sit. "We plan to make use of the tension that exists between Aldonia and Jensenville. Jensenville sends a good number of vocations to Aldonia, but they don't feel Aldonia returns in kind or degree. They don't have the workers they need. Strife over this and other issues grows daily. The transfers from Secondary are meant to appease Jensenville's Regimen. When we've rescued all the colonists, we want Aldonia's officials to blame Jensenville and turn their search in that direction."

It made sense. Totally made sense. "So we're waiting on surveillance Intel? And that's it?"

"We're still working on the plan for the Re-education Facility," Elder Lukman said. "Like I said, that will be no easy rescue."

Dedrick and Miriam exchanged a glance. It was time to tell them.

"What do you think of Liberty's messages?" Miriam said.

A smile flickered on Elder Rayna's lips. "She's a prisoner. What can she do?"

"She can help from the inside." Miriam sounded as irritated as he felt. "She has good ideas. She's resourceful."

Elder Rayna shook her head. "We will generate our own plan. If she tries anything prematurely, it will only increase security, at least around her. No, there is nothing she can do. And you, Dedrick, can't help either. We need you to lead the Maxwell colonists safely to their new home. We're forming a team and we need you to lead it. No one knows the forest from Maxwell to Rivergrove better than you."

"And you have a unique relationship with the Torva," Elder Lukman said. "They are an unruly group that few can deal with."

Dedrick shook his head. They no longer trusted him, probably thought his closeness to the situation would affect his judgments.

"Remember the promises you made when you joined the Mosheh," Elder Rayna said. "You promised obedience and to always put the directives of the Mosheh before your own interests."

"Trust us, Dedrick," Elder Lukman said. "We'll get your family to safety."

Dedrick stood, using self-control this time. "No, Elder Lukman. *I* need to bring my family to safety. The Mosheh needs to respect that. I want in on the rescues." Unsure of what he would say or do if opposed at this moment, he headed for the door.

He strode through the cavernous underground structure toward the busy control center. The cool air and indistinct chatter came as welcome relief from the intensity of temperature and emotion in the conference room.

Footfalls sounded behind him. Miriam came up and threaded her arm through his. "I didn't know you had a stubborn side."

"Yeah, well, when it comes to family . . . ." He stopped at an end workstation and stood hands on hips to release her hold. "They're the stubborn ones. I mean, I respect them and all, especially Elder Lukman, but man."

"Watch yourself, Dedrick." Her expression turned hard. She was a lifelong Mosheh and would someday become an elder herself. "Elder Lukman is one of the original Mosheh."

"I know." He glanced at the nearest kid in the control center, a short boy with glasses and a headset. Wade?

"Think of our history," she said. "The original colonists escaped before the Regimen finished the Boundary Fence. But there were others in Aldonia who longed for truth, goodness, and freedom, who would never find fulfillment in the lies and control of the Regimen. Elder Lukman had a heart for them. He was younger than you are now when he helped organize the first team that went back. Living in secret, watching over Aldonia, rescuing people who didn't fit in. Daily risking his life."

"Look, I know. I meant no disrespect." Elder Lukman developed the training program that Dedrick had gone through, that all who wanted to serve as Mosheh went through. He admired the man's talent. Other founding members developed ways to spy on the Regimen. Meanwhile, the Regimen turned FEMA camps into re-education facilities and developed ways to break people and force them into compliance. He respected every one of the Mosheh. Even Elder Rayna. She had reasons for her attitude. Probably.

"Hey, anyway . . ." He smiled, attempting to lighten her mood. "That was smart bringing up Bot's game. Think he's really got something?"

Miriam gazed at something behind him. A strange look flashed in her eyes. She pushed past him. "What's going on?"

Dedrick turned. Several monitors on the wall had gone black. The boy at the nearest control station, the kid with the glasses—Wade?—jerked his head up then down, his hands flying from one control to another.

Someone shouted, "Did we lose the live feeds?"

"Feeds to what?" Dedrick moved in, scanning the array of wall monitors. He glimpsed video from Primary, Secondary, and external locations, but no images from the Re-education Facility.

"Re-Ed," Wade said. He yanked the headset off and shouted, "Power's down at the facility."

People dashed from one station to another. Three dozen people talked over each other.

"Their lights have been dimming all week."

"What's their energy source?"

"Water and solar. It's been cloudy all week, but they've got hydroelectric power for backup."

"Liberty's gonna think this is us," Dedrick said to Miriam. "She's gonna break out."

"If she can." Miriam motioned for a petite woman to give up her workstation.

The woman stood back and chewed on her bottom lip, her brows drawing together. She was new to the Mosheh, Clara, an older volunteer from the Rivergrove Colony. Intelligence showed in her eyes, but her face showed uncertainty.

Miriam took Clara's chair.

Dedrick leaned over the desk. "What type of locks do they have on cell doors? Do we have access to that info? Think she can pick one? Has this ever happened before, a total blackout? What's their procedure for that?"

"Give me a second." Miriam pulled up one file after another, flipped through video feeds, and opened Regimen security channels.

"Power's back on," someone shouted.

Dedrick jerked his face to the overhead monitors. None showed black this time. He glimpsed one colonist in a cell, then another. His mother sat on a thin mattress, her arms wrapped around her waist. His father stood in a different cell, his eyes on the camera. Dedrick glanced from face to face, counting colonists. All sixteen were there in their cells. Liberty's cell was empty.

She did it. She got out.

He felt a surge of pride and then panic. This could only mean trouble. She was counting on the Mosheh.

He pushed Miriam's hand from the control panel and toggled camera views. "We need to see the halls. Liberty's escaped her cell."

"What?" Miriam looked then set to work designating different video feeds to various monitors. "She's not in the cellblock hallways. Where could she be?"

"Hey, look!" Wade shouted, pointing.

The video showed the exterior of the building. Two figures raced down a sidewalk. One wore a helmet. The other wore the patient gown.

Dedrick's heart stopped. He staggered back. Liberty? Who was breaking her out?

He snatched the wireless earpiece from his belt, stuffed it into his ear, and grabbed Miriam's shoulder. "Miriam, call me when you get more, like where they're headed."

She jumped up. "Oh no you don't." She glanced in the direction of the conference room, probably thinking how the Mosheh would disapprove of this course of action. "You're coming with me to check out tunnels."

"What?" She wasn't going to stop him. No one was. If she wouldn't keep him updated, he'd have someone else do it. He glanced at the boy with the glasses. "Hey, Wade."

Wade looked. "It's Walt."

"Keep us posted, Clara," Miriam said to the woman whose station she had commandeered.

Clara nodded, her mouth becoming a thin line of determination. She swung into her seat.

"We're on our way to check out the tunnels on the far side of Aldonia," Miriam said. "There was an above ground explosion earlier today."

"Gotcha." Clara said. "I'll let you know which way they go."

"Oh, you're gonna . . ." Dedrick said. Miriam was going to help him find Liberty. "We're checking tunnels."

"Yup." Miriam looped her arm through Dedrick's and they took off together.

CHAPTER 6

The vocation of Breeder is one of the most crucial vocations in our society. The process of selecting candidates must be approached with diligence. Once a girl is determined to have a superior genetic makeup, the process has only begun. Other factors must be given careful consideration. These factors include the candidate's intellect, physical abilities, health, appearance, mental state, ideology, and social history.

One must not ignore or underrate the ideology and social history of a candidate. A Breeder with a healthy ideology and social expression brings a positive influence to all others in the facility. Likewise, a Breeder who clings to a poisonous ideology and whose history indicates dangerous social contacts can damage the attitude of others and jeopardize the mission of the Breeder Facility. Therefore, the appropriate evaluation panels must observe and thoroughly interview each candidate before selecting a girl for the vocation of Breeder.

Dr. Supero stroked his goatee as he re-read the instructions he had dictated for the *New Guidelines for Breeder Selection*. Increased rigor in the evaluation process should prevent the mistakes of the past. He would not allow another *Liberty* to slip into the facility. The methods of the Regimen Custodia Terra maintained balance in the world. One girl would not undo them.

Liberty's escape from the Breeder Facility probably spared them inestimable damage. Perhaps they should have thanked rather than pursued her.

He directed his gaze to the monitors above his desk. One showed children at computer stations in the Primary Residence. Another showed teens at work in Secondary. The third showed a man, one of the newly acquired patients, hunched over in a cell at the Re-education Facility. Liberty belonged there. Perhaps she would develop a healthier outlook.

How many others remained off the grid out there in the restricted Nature Preserves? They lived like primates, ignorant of scientific and technological advancements, unaware of global environmentalism. Reckless. Human-centered. As if humans had greater value than any other life form on earth. If everyone lived like them, the earth would see a complete ecological collapse.

Dr. Supero's upper lip twitched. Chief Varden should not have diverted resources away from the search of the Nature Preserves. Higher Regimen officials would not approve of his lackadaisical attitude toward protecting the environment. They would not likely approve his decision to prioritize intercity issues. The protection of the earth came first. Perhaps he should inform someone of the chief's decisions.

A grin had snuck onto his face. Perhaps he would.

He tapped the control of the flexi-phone on his wrist to summon his new assistant. His skin crawled in anticipation of hearing his office door slide open, in anticipation of seeing the twig of a boy clip into the room. He despised his new assistant. The board had denied him the privilege of selecting his own assistant this time. Perhaps they blamed him for the incidents with his past two assistants, as if he could've predicted that both girls would develop an overpowering desire for him. Who was to say the boy would not?

The door slid open.

Dr. Supero swiveled his chair and looked the boy over from head to toe.

Muse had the long limbs of an ornamental tree and a wardrobe of clothing that emphasized them. Today he wore striped skinny pants and a long-sleeved pullover. Tufts of over-processed black hair stood on end like the fur of a startled cat. Rings in his ears and nose drew attention to his face and maroon eyes that gazed too long on any one object.

"You wanted me, Doctor?" Muse said, grinning and throwing a glance at his feet.

"No, but I need to speak with the Regional Secretary of the Department of the Environment."

"The who?" Muse squinted. The boy had little experience, came straight from Vocational School to work for Aldonia's Head Physician. He pulled a tablet from a back pocket and tapped the screen.

"Pull up the Directory of Regimen Officials," Supero said, rolling his eyes. "The Regional Secretary of . . ." *No.* He did not like that woman, that sea urchin with spiky orange hair and an unflinching gaze. At the last financial meeting, she'd sat across from him, contesting his every suggestion and pushing her own inane projects.

"Perhaps one of the Environment and Sustainability Officials," he mumbled to himself. They thrived on sending overzealous inspectors to businesses and factories. Should they not investigate our own Citizen Safety Station?

"Environmental official and what?" Muse thumbed the screen of his tablet.

"No, not them." Dr. Supero sighed. They always claimed they were understaffed. "They take too long. I need action now." Perhaps he would give Chief Varden a chance.

Muse peered up at him, his mouth hanging open. "So uh . . . who did you want to talk to? I didn't get what you first said. Regional Secretary something."

"Did you really graduate at the top of your class?"

"What? Yeah, of course."

"Pathetic." He gave a dismissive wave of his hand. "You may go."

Muse pinched his bottom lip. "I'm new, you know. Not really sure what you called me in here for."

"You are dismissed." He turned his back on the boy and tapped the control panel.

The patient index appeared on the desk's glassy surface. He selected one of the new patients, Michael 911-000000-27, the man with the scar down the middle of his chest. His holographic image appeared. Tests and exams proved he had received open-heart surgery.

Yes, somewhere out there in the Fully-Protected Nature Preserves lived a skilled surgeon. The earth mother alone knew how many off-grids remained out there.

Dr. Supero shoved his fingers through his hair, slowing as he brushed the lump of the tumor. Headaches troubled him with greater frequency and intensity. His memory failed him too often, in little things, nothing anyone would notice. Had anyone noticed? Perhaps his personality would change without his knowledge. What symptoms would assail him next? Slurred speech? Blurred vision? Fainting?

He cursed the Medical Care Evaluation Panel and slammed a fist to the desktop. The rotating hologram quivered.

They were wrong to deny the procedure to someone of his caliber. Granted, a society need not waste resources on expensive medical care for any Joe Resource Recovery worker from off the street. Still. They ought to weigh the intellect and value of the individual. After all, not everyone affords the same benefit to the earth. His research helped to create healthier, stronger people. Who could possibly replace him?

Names, faces, articles came to mind. The latest medical journal had a full eight-page report written by a doctor from Jensenville. Her research produced breakthroughs in thought-activated communication. And there was that doctor on the other side of the continent with his developments in molecular biology.

Regardless! He had only a primary brain tumor, one with well-defined borders. Cancerous, true, but a neurosurgeon should have no problem removing it completely, given the proper equipment and technology.

More images flashed in his mind: a slideshow of wild animals, tracts of wasteland, and largely uncultivated regions. What equipment and technology could a neurosurgeon in the wild possibly have?

Perhaps Michael and his doctor had snuck into Aldonia for the heart surgery. Where could the doctor have studied? Perhaps he came from Aldonia or Jensenville. Was there an actual neurosurgeon living in the wild? A cardiovascular surgeon would not necessarily make a good brain surgeon.

Why wouldn't the new citizens talk? Fear kept their lips tight. Maybe now, nearly three weeks after their capture, they would be relaxed enough to share their secrets. Perhaps they have discovered that life in Aldonia is not as terrible as they had imagined. The children anyway. Certainly the adults would need more time. But the children . . .

Dr. Supero tapped controls on his desktop to contact the psychiatrists' office. A person with a high voice answered.

"This is Dr. Supero. I need to speak with Dr. Kaden about our newest citizens."

"One moment, please."

"Dr. Kaden is unavailable." A different woman spoke, her familiar voice a balmy breeze. "This is Sage. Can I help you?"

Supero inhaled. Images flashed through his mind, sensations through his body. Silk. Sweat. Skin. Their relationship had ended too abruptly. "This is Supero." He cringed at the smooth sound of his own voice. He should've used his title. This was not a social call.

"Supero?" She laughed. An outburst of mirth.

He bristled.

"Dr. Supero, I thought I recognized your voice. How can I help you?"

"I need to speak with Dr. Kaden concerning our newly-acquired citizens."

"Would you like to schedule an appointment?"

"No, I would not. I require an update now."

"Oh. Now. Well, I suppose I can help you."

"Very good." He turned his gaze to the monitors. "I am watching the three children in Primary. One of the little boys is sitting, pouting on his bed, refusing to join the others in the computer lab, it appears."

"Yes, that's probably Simon. He's the stubborn one."

"And the other two, how are they adjusting?"

"Well, the girl, Paula, still cries at night, but I'd say she's adjusting better than the boys. Making friends, anyway. Pleasant with the teachers. The boys stick together and treat everyone else like the enemy."

36

"What about their counseling sessions? Do they speak about the community they came from out there in the woods?"

"The boys don't speak much. They answer with shrugs and headshakes mostly. Paula talks about her family and her quaint religious beliefs. Like the other new citizens, she is strong-willed."

Supero sneered. None of them seemed open to reason in the initial interviews. "They cling to their invisible God but haven't the slightest concern for the earth. I am certain Paula is spreading her poisonous ideas to the other children, confusing their impressionable minds. She is another Liberty. She belongs in Re-Ed."

Sage laughed but then spoke with a scolding tone. "She's a little girl. Children don't go to re-education. She simply needs to learn how the modern world works. She's been sheltered from that. It'll take time to help her realize the mistakes of her parents' ideology."

"Do not refer to them as parents. The word insinuates they have a unique relationship with her, or that they have some authority over her. She needs to understand that the Regimen is the only authority over her now. She is free of the radical influence of others."

"She still refers to them as Mommy and Daddy in counseling. We can't change that."

"Perhaps she would benefit from a period of isolation that does not end until she rids dangerous words from her vocabulary."

"Isolation?" Sage laughed. "It's a good thing you don't work with children."

"Perhaps they need someone like me." An idea occurred to him. He jerked forward, his mind formulating a plan. "I require an appointment after all."

"With Dr. Kaden?"

"No. I want to speak with the children. One at a time." Maybe he could get them to talk by threatening them with isolation or re-education. Surely, one of the children would give him the information he needed.

CHAPTER 7

I knew of nowhere in Aldonia that had a deeper stretch of grass-covered land or more trees than the area surrounding the gated Re-education Facility. Unity Troopers had first brought me to the facility in the black of night, in a car with tinted windows. I had seen nothing.

Today, as we made our escape, I studied everything.

The two-story, sprawling building was similar in size and blandness to my Secondary Residence. It stood in the middle of an unkempt yard, three small outbuildings at odd distances around it. High, razor barbed wire fencing surrounded the entire facility. We wouldn't have been able to climb it. Grassy fields and thick clusters of trees painted orange and lime green grew on the other side of the fence.

I assumed guards watched the main entry points. We made our exit through a half-open gate, leaving the gate banging behind us. We saw no one as we escaped.

I didn't recognize the route we took, but I had never been on this side of Aldonia. Hundreds of wind turbines decorated the hilly landscape, a garden of ugly three-petaled flowers barely moving on this windless day. A solar farm stretched out on one horizon, its panels turning like plants to the sun. Even through the shaded visor of my helmet, the glare blinded me, forcing me to look away.

The cool air bit my bare legs, making the ride feel endless. Nevertheless, the road soon brought us to familiar sights and sounds, to towering apartments and office buildings of steel, concrete, and composite, to an occasional shout and the hum of mopeds. After passing a recycling plant, we took the less crowded streets and alleys, heading one way and then another as if finding our way through a maze. I assumed my rescuer meant to avoid surveillance. I hoped he was successful.

Had the other colonists been rescued too? Of course they had. The Mosheh would not rescue one over the others. I couldn't imagine how they could send one rescuer for each colonist. They had their ways, though. They were not new to this.

We neared the end of a residential street, failing sunlight winking between older, five-story apartments on our left. The motorcycle slowed, whined, and shifted into a lower gear. We turned down a long driveway and rode to the back of a gray building. The ride stopped.

I slipped my arms from around my rescuer's waist and straightened up. I had found a degree of warmth pressed up against his back, but now cold air surrounded and shuddered through me. The discomfort I experienced at the facility did not compare to riding half naked and barefoot on a motorcycle on a forty-degree day.

Gripping his shoulder, I climbed off the bike. My feet had long since gone numb and felt useless. I hoped they would not fail me. I hoped they would at least get me inside.

Where had he taken me? Where were the others?

I scraped the helmet from my head, welcoming a breath of fresh air and more light. We stood at the backside of an old barn with a steep roof and dingy gray siding. Neighboring buildings rose up beside and behind us. The barn was out of place in this neighborhood of three- and five-story apartment buildings, a waste of space, a relic of the past.

Weeds pushed through cracks in the cement. A few scraggily bushes grew in a nearby strip of dirt.

My rescuer maneuvered the motorcycle into the midst of the bushes, hiding it from view. Still wearing the helmet, he turned to me.

I was trembling, feeling stupid in the patient gown and stepping in place, my attempt to resurrect my feet.

"Sorry, I didn't think about shoes. You're probably frozen." He stepped toward me, turning up his gloved hands. "Need me to carry you?"

I tried to make out his face through the shaded visor but couldn't. Did I know him? The voice, muffled by the helmet, sounded familiar. Dedrick? No, he would've rescued his parents first.

"No, I'm fine." My teeth chattered. I hated feeling helpless. I had imagined myself playing a key part in rescuing the colonists, and here I couldn't even handle the cold.

He nodded, my reflection bouncing on his visor. Then he shoved a hand into his jacket pocket and went to the back door of the barn. "It'll be warmer in here."

As the door cracked open, a loud mechanical hum greeted us.

"Where are we?" I stepped through the doorway and onto cold grated flooring. The smell of old machinery lingered in the warm air.

The lights went on as he shouted, "It's an old pump station. No one comes out here. It's safe."

Fluorescent lights hung from a high ceiling over a row of huge blue pipes. The pipes, a meter in diameter, curved up from somewhere under the grated flooring and stretched across the room, ending in a wall. They had big crank wheels on each end, vertical split case pumps in the middle, and hoses connected at various points.

I followed my rescuer, studying him as we crossed an open area and headed toward a single door on the far wall. He wore a black jacket and faded jeans with a black cord crisscrossing down one leg. He had a dense, muscular build and a rolling walk, his body moving a bit from side to side. Whoever he was, he was not Dedrick. My instincts had told me this already. Dedrick would have given me his jacket.

Who was he?

He stopped at the door, tried the knob, and reached into his jacket pocket.

"Where are the others?" The hum drowned out my voice. Perhaps this place had access to the Mosheh's underground network and I'd see them all soon.

He turned his visor to me as he unlocked the door. "It'll be quieter in here."

We stepped into a modified motor control center. Bulky, out dated computers and instrument panels lined one wall, a refrigerator, sink and microwave the other. This room had a tiled floor that was warm to my thawing feet and a row of fluorescent lights, only one of which worked.

My rescuer closed the door behind me, reducing the noise of the machines to a soft hum.

Still cold and trembling, I rubbed my arms and scanned the room for supplies or at least a blanket. Two canvas bags sat on the countertop by the sink. There was a box on the floor.

A sound made me turn.

The swish of his helmet coming off, the soft thud as he set it on something. He stood by a little table next to a dark, open doorway. Then he turned to face me.

My breath caught in my throat and I stepped back. Dread and anger overcame me.

"Liberty," he said, his voice no longer muffled by the helmet but soft and laced with emotion.

40

A shudder ran through me. I couldn't believe I stood here barefoot, scantily clothed, and completely vulnerable before the man who had pursued me since we first met three years ago. Sid.

My reaction made his expression wilt. His eyelids grew heavy, his lips pouty. Then his gaze dropped to my legs.

I became aware that goose bumps covered them. They were probably purple. The thin patient gown, the goose bumps on my limbs, his eyes focused on me . . .

My mind flashed to the first of the physicals I had undergone before they selected me for the vocation of Breeder. I stood in a conference room before ten adults. Mostly men. My holographic image hung over their table, spinning slowly. Files with my name and information I didn't understand glowed on the glassy desktop. "Your name is Liberty," one of them said. "That's an interesting name." One whispered something to another. "Perhaps you are unaware, but you have a superior genetic makeup," another one said. "You may have a role to play in helping us create a stronger, healthier generation. Does that appeal to you?"

"I thought we were already stronger and healthier," I said, fighting a scowl. They told us this repeatedly in Secondary. Thanks to the Regimen Custodia Terra and advancements in science and technology, we had become a superior society with fewer health problems and greater care for the earth.

Some of them chuckled. Others sneered. "Well, there is always room for improvement, don't you agree?"

~ ~ ~

"You're cold," Sid said.

"How did you . . .? How is it possible . . .?" I closed my mouth. My head shook, partly from the cold but more from shock.

"Sorry about that ride. I didn't want cameras picking us up, had to follow a certain route." He took a step closer.

Dreading his touch, I stepped back.

"I didn't think about what you'd be wearing."

"How did you pull this off?" I found the strength to complete my question.

"I got some clothes for you." He pointed over his shoulder to the open door next to the table. "There's a shower. Should work. And a bed if you're tired. I imagine it's rough in Re-Ed." He gave me a lingering look then shifted his gaze to some point behind me. He moved past me and opened the refrigerator.

"I can't understand how you did this. How did you do it?" I shook with anger, my body like an engine in need of a tune-up or a loose part about to break free and hit the floor. I should go find the clothes he offered.

He stood casually with his weight on one leg, an arm resting on the open refrigerator door. "I bet you're hungry. I brought food. I'll heat something up." He acted as if we were roommates and I had just come home from work.

I was an engine about to blow a rod. Why wouldn't he answer me?

I needed to calm myself. Maybe he was working with the Mosheh. He didn't seem like the type they would trust, but . . .

"Who are you working with?" The trembling made me stutter. My body forced me to swivel around and dart into the room for the clothes.

I hit the light switch and left the door open, desperate for an answer.

"Why do I have to be working with someone?" He spoke louder than necessary.

The bedroom reminded me of my Regimen-assigned apartment. A bunk bed with only a lower mattress sat against one wall and a scraped-up shelving unit against another, leaving barely enough room to move between them. Another door came off the foot of the bed, but I only cared about the pile of folded blankets next to a canvas bag on the bed.

"You couldn't have done this on your own!" I shouted as I crawled onto the bare mattress. Sitting cross-legged, I unfolded a blanket, anxious for warmth.

"Oh, yeah? Why's that?" Something clanked while he spoke.

"There's too much security." The blanket, coarse and black, had a gray image of a tree and a worn logo in the center. I wrapped it around my shoulders and opened the canvas bag. Clothes.

"I have connections." Something banged, and he cursed Mother Earth.

I dumped the clothes onto the bed. A black miniskirt, black stockings, slim black pants, ankle boots, and three formfitting tops. I huffed in disgust. He had to know this was not my style. Ever since Secondary, I preferred to wear loose clothes that didn't draw attention. The girls there had given me a hard time once they discovered I had been selected for the coveted vocation of Breeder.

"I don't see what's so special about you." The girl had looked me over, her gaze lingering on my chest.

"It has nothing to do with my body," I told her. "It's my genetic makeup." I tried to walk past her. Three other girls blocked my way.

The first girl made a face. "I still don't get what's so special about you. We were all made the same way. Doctors chose the best stock for every one of us."

"Look, I don't know. I'd trade vocations with you if I could. I don't want to be a breeder."

The girls let out a collective gasp.

"She's just saying that."

"She thinks she's better than us."

~ ~ ~

More clanking came from the other room. Sid cussed again. "Can't you be satisfied? You're out of there. Why do you care how I did it?"

"What about the others?" I rubbed my frozen feet and my yellow, lifeless toes. The room was equally lifeless. A single exposed bulb hung from the ceiling. Its weak light revealed dingy cement walls, dirt in the corners, and dust on the shelves. A black bag sat on a top shelf.

I stuffed my feet into the tights, wrestled them up my legs, and went to see what was in the black bag.

Dark jeans, t-shirts, and long-sleeved shirts. His clothes. They should fit me fine.

I grabbed black jeans and a pine-green, long-sleeved hooded pullover from the bag and the ankle boots from the bed. For privacy, I dressed by the foot of the bed, by the dark doorway that probably opened to a bathroom. Would I have to wear the fingerless glove forever? Sid would have no way to remove the radio frequency ID implant in my hand.

The jeans and shirt fit loosely, the way I liked it. The boots fit perfectly. How did he know my shoe size? Maybe Tatum, my ex-roommate, and her boyfriend Finley were involved in this. Finley worked with the Environmental Stewardship Units. He always boasted he could avoid surveillance.

Still cold, I wrapped the blanket around my shoulders and left the room.

The microwave glowed and hummed. A can opener, metal spoon, and open can sat on the countertop under the microwave. Sid lay stretched out on the floor, his head and shoulders in the cabinet under the sink, one leg jerking as his arms moved. He sat up and cracked his head on something. Hand to his head, he got up and gave me the once-over. "Didn't you see the canvas bag?"

"Yeah, I saw it." I squatted and peered under the sink. "What's the problem here?"

He squatted beside me. "You think the water'd be working, you know, this being a water pump station and all."

I straightened up. He probably needed to open a valve. I could've done it, but I went to the table instead.

"Sid, we need to talk." I slid a chair out, brushed dust from the wooden seat and folded my arms.

He went to the fridge. "You should rest. Eat something and lay down. We can talk tomorrow." He came to the table with a bottle of reddish liquid and two cups. "Thirsty?"

"What is it?" Suspicion rang in my tone and probably showed in my eyes.

His upper lip curled on one side. He nudged a chair out with his foot and sat down. "Ain't you never seen juice before?" He filled the cups and slid one across the table to me.

I watched him take a gulp, then brought the cup to my mouth. The drink was fruity but lukewarm. Either the refrigerator didn't work properly or he had recently put the juice in to chill. "Did you spike this with anything?"

He huffed and leaned back, draping an arm over the chair back. "Everything I do, I do it for your good. I'm not gonna hurt you."

That convinced me he had put something in the drink, maybe a drug to relax me. I set the cup down. "I get that you don't want to tell me *how* you pulled this off, so tell me *why*. Why did you rescue me?"

He turned away, the pouty look returning. "Why do you think?" He faced me. The blue of his irises rolled like storm clouds. "I care about you. I'd do anything for you."

"What about the others? Do you know they locked up sixteen others, same day as me? They didn't do anything wrong. They don't belong in there."

"Sorry, girl, but I don't care about them." He lifted the cup to his lips, threw his head back, and gulped the rest of his drink.

"Well, I do." I gritted my teeth to keep from saying more. How could I accept freedom while they remained prisoners? Their imprisonment was my fault. "Besides, what makes you think the Regimen won't find us here? They see everything." I glanced around the room, trying to find a surveillance camera. One could be hidden in the control panels or computers.

Sid smirked. "Don't worry, girl. We're safe here for a day or two. Then I have other plans." He locked eyes with me. His jaw twitched. "I'm gonna take care of you. You don't have to worry."

Plans? What plans? I didn't ask. I considered the message of *My Friend*. Things aren't always as they seem. The drone was a bird. My rescue brought me to a new prison. *My Friend* would have me feel free. This did not make sense.

CHAPTER 8

The tunnel stretched on forever, endless brick walls arching overhead. The beam from Dedrick's flashlight bounced off the pale mortar between the bricks, giving the impression the tunnel closed in around them.

Dedrick found himself stooping a bit and straightened up.

"This tunnel's long," Miriam said and flashed a smile. Her holster, and whatever else she had dangling from her belt, swished against her coat as she walked.

"Yeah, I remember it being shorter."

They strode with long steps, finding it difficult to run at the gradual incline. Their footfalls on the dry concrete as they walked in sync reminded him of Unity Troopers on patrol. Something clanked in the distance, echoing off the walls of a wider tunnel up ahead. He couldn't wait to get to the next tunnel. A tunnel kart awaited them there. They'd make better time once they reached it.

"Can I ask you a question?" Miriam said.

"Yeah?"

"What'd the Mosheh say when you first returned from Maxwell?"

He knew she had sensed his discomfort when they stood at the door to the meeting room. "Ah, I'm sure you can guess. They weren't happy with me."

"What'd you tell them?"

He glanced to read her expression. She always seemed to know more than she let on. "I pointed out that we had work to do, told them they could grill me later."

He had never sweated more in his life. A cool sweat broke out on his chest even now as he thought about it . . . .

He had recently parted with Liberty. She should've been halfway to her destination. Safe. On her way to contact her friend Abby. The plan would work. It had to. She just couldn't dally. She knew the importance of timing. She'd make it to the underground access point.

Four of the Mosheh sat around the long table in the meeting room, Elders Lukman, Matilda, Rayna, and Jakov. Elder Dean and three others watched via videoconference, their images seeming to stare at him from the wall monitors. Elders Rayna and Jakov glared through unforgiving eyes. Elder Dean rested his forehead on his hand, eyes down, lifting his head only once. Elders Matilda and Lukman did the questioning, neither one breaking composure.

"What emergency provoked you to organize this rescue?"

"What reason justifies planning a rescue independent of the Mosheh?"

"Did you think it wise to give us such short notice?"

"Certainly you are aware of the precautions we typically take."

With each wasted second, Dedrick's heartbeat quickened, a bomb about to explode. He had run most of the way here, but sitting under the disapproving glare of the elders did something to a guy's confidence. "Look, interrogate me later. Right now, we need to secure specific tunnels and destroy a few underground access points. We've been careless. And the Regimen is sniffing around."

The elders had listened to him. They sent him to the control center. He worked continuously, sending Mosheh members here and there to seal off tunnels and destroy access points. He accomplished his goal. The Regimen found no trace of the Mosheh's secret structures, had no clue that the Mosheh existed.

But they found the Maxwell Colony. They found his family.

~ ~ ~

"You think that's why you're not part of the rescue teams?" Miriam said.

Dedrick returned to the present moment. "Don't you? They can't trust me."

The brick tunnel ended, opening to a wide crossing tunnel and a gust of dank air. The odor reminded him of jeans he once wore on a trying journey. They had gotten wet then dried while he slept on the ground.

Dedrick stepped around the corner to where he had left the tunnel kart. The Mosheh never bothered hiding things in this tunnel. It was part of the abandoned sewage system, and Aldonians had no clue it existed. He knew the tunnels better than he knew the lands between Aldonia and Maxwell. Some tunnels remained dry, others flooded. Some a kart could travel through but others a person had to walk. Aldonians used a good number of tunnels for sewage, pipes, network connections and such, but they had abandoned many others years ago. The Mosheh had created tunnels over the years, connecting key routes. Dedrick knew the quickest way to get from one point to another.

He jumped into the driver's seat and cranked the engine to life. This tunnel would take them to the center of Aldonia. Hopefully someone at the Mosheh Control Center would soon give them more to go on.

Miriam climbed into the passenger seat. "I think you're wrong. I think they trust you."

"I can't trust myself. Look at me. What am I doing going after her?" The tunnel kart spluttered as he accelerated, the sound echoing off the walls. A comforting gasoline aroma wafted to his nose.

"You're doing what needs to be done. You were ready and jumped into action."

"Without permission. And I have no plan." He never acted without a complete plan. Attention to detail came naturally to him. "And besides, my brother is on the verge of doing something crazy. I should be keeping an eye on him, ready to be there for him."

. . . Not going on a wild-goose chase to rescue Liberty, risking his privilege to serve as one of the Mosheh. The last thing he wanted was for his service to end in disgrace.

The Mosheh had shown leniency the first time he acted without permission. Liberty was only a candidate for rescue at that time. He had been watching her and a few others on video surveillance at a Mosheh Control Center. He had seen her walking into a trap. Sid's trap. He couldn't let that happen. She needed an immediate rescue. Fortunately, she was unconscious when he brought her in and so posed no threat to the Mosheh's secret existence.

"I hear you," Miriam said, laying a finger on her earphone. She glanced at Dedrick.

He turned on his earphone as a boy said, ". . . on a motorcycle but we're not sure it's them. We aren't tied in to all the CSS surveillance yet, but the rider seems able to avoid working cameras. We should've at least picked them up once or—"

"Where are they headed?" Dedrick said. The tunnel branched off up ahead and he needed to decide which way to go.

"East, right now. Where are you?"

"We're heading for the center of Aldonia," Miriam said.

"It's strange," the kid from the control center said. "CSS doesn't seem to be looking for them. I know we're not getting all their communications yet, but we did get one. Re-Ed contacted CSS once their power was restored, said everything was fine. No mention of an escape."

"They don't know she's missing?" Dedrick said to Miriam, incredulous.

She shrugged. "Maybe they think she's in another part of the facility for training or counseling. That could be good for us. We won't have to dodge Unity Troopers."

"No, something's up." He turned down a northeast tunnel. It led to the outskirts of Aldonia and, beyond that, the Jensenville border. The headlights swept over a pile of rubble in a crook of the road, the aftermath of his job closing an access point.

His stomach soured. For safety's sake, he had to do it, but he hated closing so many points. It limited their access to Aldonia's streets. Would it ruin his chances of saving Liberty today?

"Who do you think took her," Miriam said. "And why?"

He had his suspicions. "I just want to know where he's taking her."

"Could be anywhere."

"No, there're places Aldonians can go to avoid the Regimen's eye. He'll take her to one of those."

"I've heard rumors. Illegal hideouts where drones can't pick up their ID implant signals or flexi-phones."

"Yeah. They have a special material that blocks the RF signal. They put it in attics or along ceilings, I guess." Dedrick slowed the tunnel kart. They needed to take tunnels, now, that Aldonians could access. He should leave the kart and go on foot. But did they have time?

Miriam hopped off before he came to a stop. She sprinted to the tunnel wall, to a slab of cement framed with steel beams and studs.

He stopped the kart and jumped off to help. He took a wedge from his belt and popped five bolts from one side of the frame. Using the wedge again, he pulled the frame back.

She did the same on the other side. "I got it." Gripping the frame overhead and at her waist, she leaned into the wall and began to slide it open.

He jumped into the kart and drove through when the opening was wide enough.

Miriam scraped the false wall closed and pulled the latches that yank the stud and bolts back into place. She skipped to the opposite side and secured it, too. "Let's go," she said, swinging into the passenger-side seat. Her energy and abilities belied her age.

"We got them."

Dedrick's senses perked at the voice coming through his earphone. He stepped on the gas pedal and shouted, "Where?"

"Northeast residential neighborhood. We have an access point near the pump station at the end of a road. We've got the feed, off and on, to three surveillance cameras. We'll keep you posted when we see them again. Maybe we can find which house—"

"No, they're going to the pump station." Dedrick rounded a corner, turning onto a damp tunnel that smelled of sewage. "He won't risk anyone seeing him. Residential's too crowded."

"Up there. Look," Miriam shouted.

Darkness fell back to a pile of debris. Chunks of cement blocked the tunnel from floor to ceiling.

Dedrick screeched the tunnel kart to a halt and leaped out to assess the situation.

"Our tunnel's blocked, probably damaged from the riots near the Jensenville border," Miriam said, her hand to her earphone. "They've been toying with explosives. We need a new access point."

"No, we don't. I'll get through." Dedrick stepped onto a slab of cement near the bottom of the mound. Gravel slid under his boots. He grabbed onto higher chunks of cold cement, his gaze on the patch of black at the top of the mound.

CHAPTER 9

We had only just met, but Sid and I worked as a team. He picked off the opposition while I assembled bombs. I set the timers for five minutes, but the instant the bombs met extreme temperatures they would probably explode anyway.

"You done yet? I could use a little help here." Sid took two shots and leaped. He did a wild somersault before landing in a crouched position and shooting again. Three of our attackers fell. More climbed up on either side of the roof, the factory's security officers in dull black armor, a pack of dung beetles after us.

I attached one last wire and gathered all four bombs into the crook of one arm. "We're good to go." I drew my gun and fired random shots as I straightened up.

Our mission: to destroy the environmentally destructive factory so we could gain enough points to move to the next level.

Our plan: to climb the two central smokestacks and drop the bombs down them, attach the pulleys we had found earlier in the game to cables that ran from the chimney tops, and use the cable like a zip line to make our escape.

"Let's do it." Sid snatched two bombs and dashed for one of the smokestacks.

I covered him, picking off the nearest dung beetles. Then I bolted for the other smokestack. The bombs fit nicely into my vest, leaving my hands free to climb the ladder and shoot. Reaching the top, I dropped the bombs into the dark opening of the smokestack, slapped the pulley onto the cable, and let myself go. I would've loved to feel the rush of air and the stomach-dropping effect a person would ordinarily experience in a moment like this. But a 3D game can only do so much.

More than halfway down the cable, a bald eagle crossed my path. I snagged it to keep it safe—bonus points! Then the factory exploded behind me. The cable broke. I let the bird go, and I fell the rest of the way. I landed in a crouch, did a somersault, and popped up straight and tall. Numbers flashed on the TV screen, climbing higher and higher, points gained from our victory.

Tatum, Finley, and their other friends praised us. Sid howled and cussed with delight.

I whipped my 3D headset off and lifted my arms, wanting to slap hands for our victory.

Sid grabbed my waist and pulled me close. "We did it," he whispered in my ear. "Said you never played, but I knew you'd be good." He leaned in to kiss me.

I turned my head and his lips grazed my cheek. Then I planted my hands on his chest—firm and muscular—and shoved him back. "Watch it. I'm not your girlfriend."

"Not yet." He waved his brows.

It was then, almost three years ago, that I first noticed the emotional turbulence in his blue eyes. We had only met, but he wanted me with a strange intensity, an intensity that would only increase over the years.

~ ~ ~

A banging sound, followed by a string of cuss words, brought me back to the moment. Sid crawled out from under the sink and tossed a pipe wrench. "Still no water. I turned everything there is to turn."

I laughed. A black cloud lifted from my mind. The four gray walls of my cell in the Re-education Facility no longer mocked me. True, the other colonists remained prisoners, and I did not have complete freedom, but Sid alone stood in my way. Sid had orchestrated my escape from a high security facility, apparently without drawing the attention of the Citizen Safety Station, the Unity Troops, or anyone else, but he couldn't figure out how to turn on the water. I would have little problem escaping from him at the right moment. First, I wanted more information from him and a plan of my own.

Sid brushed his pant legs and stared at me. "Nice to see you smile."

My smile faded. I didn't want to give him false hope. I would never belong to him. But I felt sorry for him, so I spoke with a kind tone. "There's probably a valve out there." I pointed to the door to the main part of the pump station.

The door opened to the loud hum and scent of warm machinery. Pipes ran under the grated flooring, some of them angled toward the room from which we came. Other pipes ran along the ceiling and walls.

I spotted the valve that most likely controlled the flow of water to the kitchen unit, but I wasn't ready to mention it. I wanted to explore a little first. I might need a better understanding of my surroundings when it came time for me to leave Sid.

Sid made a sweeping glance up and around the place as if he didn't know what to look for. He stopped by a row of drums. One of the drums sat on a raised platform. A pipe with a huge handwheel connected the drum to other pipes.

"I don't see a valve," Sid shouted, his gaze still sweeping, skimming over at least a dozen valves of various shapes and sizes.

I chuckled and strolled toward the drums. A yellowed, smudged label showed the contents of the drum, a chemical with the strange name Norethcyproterone-lestradiol, a water-purifying or softening chemical, I imagined. A smudge made the date hard to read, but I thought I read 2018. Scientists had probably developed better, safer chemicals since then.

"So, Sid, tell me . . ." I wanted to sound friendly, but I had to shout over the hum of the machinery. I strolled past him, from the first drum to the last in the row. "How did you know about this place?"

"I just do."

His vague answer made steam escape from my ears, but I forced a pleasant smile. "If you expect me to trust you, you should trust me. Tell me how you rescued me. How did you get the power down at Re-Ed?"

He sauntered to me, his moody blue eyes taking me in from head to toe. "I told you, I'm gonna take care of you." He reached. Thinking he was going to touch me, I shrunk back. But he placed his hands on the big handwheel that controlled the valve to the drum of chemicals.

I grabbed his arm. "Don't do that."

"Why not?"

"Because you're going to dump some seriously old chemicals into the water supply. You don't want to do that." One would probably need to open other valves to actually reroute the water through the chemicals, but I didn't want to risk it.

"See those pipes?" I pointed to the visible pipes under the grating. "They go from the water pump to the computer room. The valve's right there." I pointed out a small shut-off valve like the ones in bathrooms and under kitchen sinks. It was low on the wall, near the door.

He strode to it, squatted and twisted it.

"So where do we go after this place? You said a day or two, right?" Hoping for an answer, I smiled again.

He hesitated, probably considering what he should or shouldn't say. "There's a secret community where we can stay and never be found."

My thoughts went to the communities in the woods. The Maxwell Colony was not the only one. Dedrick had once mentioned others. Could Sid possibly know about these other communities? I couldn't imagine the Mosheh trusting him. Could he have discovered them on his own? Without the Regimen knowing? It didn't seem possible. I had to know more.

"Somewhere in Aldonia?" I said. My smile no longer felt sincere. I hoped he didn't notice.

"Maybe. Maybe not."

"Where then? Outside the Fence of the Boundaries?"

He laughed. "Think I want to die? Electricity runs through those. I don't know how you did it. Did you really live out there? What did you eat?" He placed a hand on the doorknob to the computer room.

I did not want to return to that little room with him. His comments convinced me that he wasn't working with the Mosheh and that he probably planned to take me to some place in Jensenville. Maybe Jensenville had less surveillance than Aldonia.

"Sid, try to understand, I don't want you to take care of me."

"Yeah?" He smirked. Then he opened the door and gave a nod, directing me to go first. "Wish you were back in Re-Ed? Like it better there?"

"No, I don't like it there. But I shouldn't be free if the others aren't." I folded my arms to convey that I would not go back into the room.

A plan formed in my mind, a quick and careless plan. I could leave here and avoid surveillance by taking the same route he had taken through the neighborhood. Then I'd keep my face hidden and find a way to the mall. I believed the Mosheh had people and even an access point somewhere in the mall. Or maybe the Mosheh would see me on surveillance. Did I want to return to the Mosheh, the sole person free? The rest of the colonists still imprisoned? I couldn't rescue them myself. The Mosheh probably had a plan. Maybe I could help. Of course, if the Mosheh saw me on surveillance, the Regimen would also see me . . .

His hand slipped from the knob. He reached into a back pocket. "There's nothing you can do about the others. Try to relax. You act like it's your fault they're in there."

"Maybe it is."

"No one told them to live in the Nature Preserves. People aren't allowed out there. They brought it on themselves." He took slow steps toward me, hips swaying, one hand behind his back.

"They haven't done anything wrong." The hum of machines reverberated through my chest. My body trembled again.

"That place has you all messed up. You should be happy now, thanking me you're not locked up in there." He continued to approach, swinging his hand into view. He held a thin black sheath. He reached into it.

"What is that?" I stumbled back, the trembling increasing and my courage waning. He had worked in construction since he transitioned from Secondary, developing stamina and muscles, hard and strong. I hadn't eaten a good meal in days and had hardly slept. How could I fight off a man with strength like his? He did seem slow to reason and slow to react. I would have to use that to my advantage.

"I wanna help you," he said. "Why don't you let me?"

"No. This is not me. I can't do this." I turned and started to walk away, toward the exit. I knew he wouldn't simply let me go. What was I doing?

He grabbed me from behind, one hand tight around my arm.

I jerked free and twisted to face him. My gaze snapped to his other hand. The thin black case fell to the floor. He held a syringe.

"It's not like you can go back to your old apartment, your old job, your old life. You won't be able to buy food or go around in the open. Someone scans your implant and Unity Troops will be all over you."

I backed up, him keeping step with me. "A-a-and how will *you* get food?"

"I have connections. I got you outta there, didn't I?"

"What's in the syringe?" I kept backing up, hoping to stumble across something I could use as a weapon. I didn't like the idea of hurting him to get away, but I saw no other option.

"You need rest. You'll see things differently tomorrow."

"Tomorrow won't change the way I feel." My back smacked into something sharp, a lever sticking out from a pipe or the wall.

He stepped closer, so close that I had to look up to see his face. He brushed my arm with his free hand and then gripped it tight, bringing up the syringe. "Don't be scared of me. I'm not gonna hurt you. This'll calm you. You'll see."

"You said that before. Then you injected me with *Thrill*." I remembered the effect of that street drug. With the suddenness that only fear can produce, I leaned into him and thrust my knee into his groin.

He grunted and his grip on my arm lessened.

I cracked my elbow into his chin and darted past him. The exit stood a mere six meters away, but I doubted I could open the door halfway before he grabbed me. And even if I could, then what? He would follow me. My legs were my strength, but I couldn't outrun him in my present condition.

I needed the keys to the motorcycle, and I needed to incapacitate him.

"Leave on your own and the Regimen will have you." He approached, the syringe at his side. "You won't know how to avoid surveillance."

"I'd rather take my chances with the Regimen." With one eye on him, I walked the length of the large pipes and pumps. Fluorescent light reflected on the shiny blue paint. Motors hummed. No tool, no loose section of piping, nothing I could use for a weapon lay anywhere. Then I remembered Sid working under the sink. And the pipe wrench. That I could use.

I dashed for the computer room and grabbed the doorknob.

Heavy footfalls sounded on the metal grated flooring.

A hand gripped my arm.

"You don't mean that." He spoke low, his lips to my ear. "You want to be with me. You'll see."

I twisted the doorknob and yanked.

Sid slammed a shoulder against the door, making the knob slip from my grasp. Still holding my arm, he leaned against the door. With heavy eyelids and a pouty mouth, he appeared relaxed, casual as he spoke and repositioned the syringe in his hand. "You want free of them and their control. I want it, too. We can be free. We can hide."

"No, you can't keep me." My heart pounded violently.

He brought the needle to my arm. "I wish you understood me. You might not have needed this."

A chill shuddered through me. I twisted my arm and bumped the hand holding the needle but couldn't break free.

His grip tightened.

I dug my nails into the skin of his hand, then peeled back one of his fingers. I could not let him do this to me. Panic overtaking me, I slammed the heel of my left hand against his nose.

He grunted, his head jerked back, and the needle pricked my skin. Then it slipped and clanked on the grated flooring.

Stunned, I hesitated. Had he injected any of the drug?

Sid raised a hand to his nose but then lunged for me, shifting into high gear. Grimacing, cursing, he tried pinning my arms. "I'm done trying to reason with you."

I pried one of his arms from my waist only to find the other around me. I swung my elbow back, wanting to crack him in the ribs.

His arm threaded around one of my arms and then the other. He had me.

I struggled to no avail as he dragged me down.

My knees cracked the metal grating. Pain shot through my legs.

"Where'd that thing fall?" he mumbled. He locked my arms behind my back and then groped the floor for the syringe.

I peered at the floor on either side, hoping to see it first. Maybe I could kick it out of reach or get it to fall through the holes in the grating.

"Ah, got it," he said, sounding triumphant.

A wave of nausea hit me. I squirmed.

He tightened his hold and leaned over my shoulder, pressing his cheek to mine. "Girl, you're gonna see life a whole world differently when you wake up."

Something across the room banged. Was the door swinging open?

"Get your hands off her," a man shouted in a ragged voice. Hurried footsteps pounded the metal grating.

Sid cursed and shoved me forward, letting me go. He jumped up.

I threw my hands out, saving my face from hitting the floor. Then I lifted my head and twisted enough to see the intruder. My breath caught in my throat. *Dedrick.*

He wore blue jeans and a brown leather jacket. No cape. No mask. Nothing to keep CSS from identifying him should he get caught by surveillance. And for reasons I did not at once understand, he did not seem himself. With a snarl on his face and hands curling into fists, he strode toward us.

Sid met him in the middle of the room and swung.

Dedrick ducked, avoiding a shot to the head. He rammed his shoulder into Sid's chest.

Sid staggered back, the look of a drunkard passing his face. Then rage filled his eyes and he lunged. He threw a punch to Dedrick's face and another to his gut.

Dedrick blocked each attack but not with the refined movements I had come to associate with his fighting style. He kept little distance between them and edged closer and closer, forcing Sid to back up. Feet pounded the metal grating. Dedrick blocked and swung, blocked and kicked, fighting at an accelerated pace, like a man on the edge.

Sid took a hit to the face, to the ear, to the gut. He backed into the big pipes. Then he managed an upper cut to Dedrick's chin and climbed over the first horizontal pipe. He threw a desperate glance to either side, maybe looking for a weapon as I had done.

I did not pity him. The syringe lay in a crack between the wall and the flooring. I grabbed it and stood up.

Dedrick planted a hand on the pipe and hurdled over it to continue the fight. Before his feet hit the floor, Sid rammed his shoulder into him and Dedrick's head cracked against a vertical pipe. His body slackened. Sid's fist ripped across his jaw. Dedrick doubled over and fell from my view, hidden by a horizontal pipe.

Syringe in hand, I bolted for Sid.

Sid turned his head, glanced at me, and then did a double take, noticing the syringe.

Behind him, Dedrick straightened up, a black storm cloud rising. Sid noticed just as the lightning let loose, fists tearing through the air, connecting with his chin, then his gut. He grunted, his body jerking under the impact and his arms coming up as weak shields. He stumbled into the big pipe that now lay between us, flinging his arms over it to keep from falling to the floor.

I took my chance and plunged the needle into the only exposed skin I could see: Sid's neck. It took a fraction of a second to inject the contents.

Sid's face spun to me, his eyes wide. "You didn't."

"I did." I dropped the empty syringe. It clanked against the metal grating, slipped through, and clattered to the cement floor underneath.

Mouth hanging open, eyes revealing the gears turning slowly in his mind, Sid shook his head. He rubbed his neck and then climbed over the pipe, toward me.

I stepped back.

Sid staggered closer. He grinned and licked his lips. "Why you gotta be so hard?"

Dedrick sat on the horizontal pipe and swung his legs over it. "What was in the syringe?" He glanced from Sid to me.

I shrugged. "Something to relax me, I guess."

"That'll work. Now where do we put him?" He grabbed Sid by the arm and yanked.

Sid groaned but yielded to Dedrick's direction, his eyelids growing heavier, blinking slower by the second.

"In there." With a glance, I indicated the door to the computer room. Then I pulled Sid's arm over my shoulder and wrapped my arm around him. Sid had injected me with Thrill in the past. If that was his plan today, I knew what to expect. The drug had made me numb and weak. Everything seemed to move in slow motion. Then I lost consciousness. Fortunately, I had been given the antidote before I woke. I would not have wanted to know the sensory sensations kids used Thrill to achieve. Sid would have to experience the drug's effect alone.

"How'd you find us?" Sid slurred. Supported by Dedrick and me, he dragged his feet with lazy steps. "I'm sure no one followed us. There's no way you could-a found us."

"Yeah, well, here I am anyway." Dedrick's edge had melted.

"Not possible," Sid said, his voice nearly lost in the hum of the machines.

We guided Sid through the computer room and to the sleeping quarters.

"You have a jacket?" Dedrick glanced at me over Sid's head.

"No." I shrugged Sid's arm off my shoulders and angled him around to the bed.

Sid dropped with a thud onto the bed, his entire body turning loose and rubbery. "Don't leave me."

Dedrick slid a hand behind Sid's head. "Sorry, pal, we're gonna need your jacket." He peeled the jacket from one shoulder and then the other. "And your bike."

"No, man. They'll find you." Sid lay back and turned glazed eyes to the ceiling. His eyes blinked once and closed. His features smoothed, making him look as peaceful as a boy taking a nap in the summertime.

Dedrick dug the keys from the pocket and tossed the jacket to me. "Grab a helmet and let's go."

CHAPTER 10

A siren erupted.

Unity Troopers nearby. Another challenge added to this doomed rescue mission.

Dedrick tightened his grip on the handlebars and sped past an abandoned factory. Had the Regimen finally received word about Liberty's escape? Took them long enough.

He glanced to each side, looking for blue and orange lights to paint the dark faces of buildings. He did not know these streets well enough to outsmart the Regimen. Maybe they'd be better on foot, sneaking through shadows.

"Fulton, give me something," Dedrick shouted into his helmet.

"Uh, do I hear sirens?" Fulton's voice came through the earphone. He had replaced Clara as soon as Dedrick got above ground. Fulton was one of the Mosheh's best route planners. He had a supernatural ability to juggle knowledge of Mosheh access points, the Regimen's surveillance system, traffic patterns, and hiding places. On a rescue mission, he was the best. The sound of his voice, clear with an underlying note of humor, typically gave Dedrick confidence. Not today, not with the lack of Intel.

"Yeah, sirens," Dedrick said, "so give me direction."

"Okay, I see them now, Unity Troopers racing down McBay. Go straight."

Two motor scooters raced down the side street, coming toward Dedrick, blue and orange flashing lights behind them.

Adrenaline surged through him. He liked a good chase. When he could count on a good escape, that is. Dedrick stepped on it.

"No, no, no, I take that back," Fulton said. "Don't go straight."

Dedrick had gone half a block. Sirens blared. A car screeched. He and Liberty were a target riding straight down the road, easy pickings for the troopers.

"What then?" Dedrick shouted, easing off the throttle.

"We got video feed for a surveillance camera a block down, directly under a streetlamp. If those Unity Troops don't get you, CSS will catch you for sure."

"Copy that." Dedrick squeezed the breaks, breaking to the threshold of skidding.

Lights flashed in his side mirror. The motor scooters and the Unity Trooper's sleek black car sped past, racing down the intersecting road he had passed.

He exhaled. They weren't after Liberty. Yet.

A crossroad lay ahead, appearing striped under widely spaced solar-powered streetlamps. A right would point him in the direction of the mall. Left might be safer, more of a back road, dark and with minimal surveillance cameras. He could weave down neglected roads, taking the long way to the mall.

Dedrick stopped at the intersection, pulling close to the curb, and dropped his boots to the ground. Fortunately, they had been riding alone down this road, so he had no one on his tail. He could spare a moment to get a safer route. "Which way, Fulton?"

"Give me a minute."

Dedrick shook his head. Liberty probably had doubts about this rescue. About him. He showed up with no disguise, started punching without first asking questions. Rode like a man with no direction. He had turned left and right too many times, circled back once, and now he didn't move at all. She said nothing though. Maybe Sid had hit her with the needle, got some of that drug into her. No, she would've passed out like Sid had.

He cracked the visor on his helmet and spoke over his shoulder. "You alright back there?"

She nodded, her black helmet reflecting the white glow of a streetlamp.

Too bad the Mosheh access point near the pump station had sustained so much damage. They could've been travelling underground, safe from the Regimen's eye. At least he had made it through to rescue her from Sid.

Dedrick had dug his way through the rubble, bit-by-bit, tossing chunks of concrete and scooping aside sand and gravel to create an opening wide enough to crawl through, then losing the opening as the debris shifted. Unable to think of another way but refusing to give up, he'd kept at it, tossing and scooping. At one point, a new layer of sand and gravel rained down, blinding him, sticking in his hair, creeping into his jacket, his shirt. He could feel it even now on his sweaty back. Once on the other side of the rubble, he had a fifty-yard dash and a two-story climb up the steel rungs of a fixed ladder. He surfaced through a manhole and had only a short jog to the pump station.

"Okay, Dedrick," Fulton shouted, his voice filling Dedrick's helmet, "I think we got it. At the next intersection, take a right. Eight blocks later, you'll have to go south. I'll give you more in a bit."

"Copy that." Dedrick took off for the next intersection, glad to be moving again. He rounded the corner with ease. Liberty seemed experienced riding two-up on a motorcycle. She shifted her weight and leaned in the right directions. Their helmets never banged once. She didn't drop her feet from the pegs when he came to a stop, and she rested her hands on his hips. He wouldn't have minded a firmer grip. He liked knowing she was there and she was safe.

Maybe not safe. Unity Troops could be around the next corner. She was safe from Sid anyway.

Andy always hung on for dear life when they rode two-up. Of course, Dedrick didn't use as much caution with his brother. Andy had reason to believe they might take a spill now and then.

Dedrick grinned remembering a ride they took last spring. They followed a deer trail a mile from home. Cottonwood trees stood in a field on one side, letting loose their fluffy white seeds. Sunlight caught the shower and made it glitter like snowfall on a fine spring day. They raced through the snow showers toward the foot of a hill, planning to go around it. Got a little too close to a steep incline. Dedrick counter steered into the turn, leaning and making a hard left. He hadn't noticed the stretch of mud until too late. The dirt bike took control, deciding its own way to go, leaving him to hang on and hope for the best. Hope wasn't good enough. The back end of the bike slid, they lost momentum and took a spill. After catching their breath and laughing so hard they cried, they dragged the bike into a sunspot and decided to break for lunch.

Dedrick frowned, remembering their conversation. It troubled him more today than it had last spring.

"So what went wrong yesterday?" Andy had shoved a quarter of his sandwich into his mouth and chewed, cheek bulging.

"Nothing went wrong," Dedrick said. "Pilgrims are safe."

"Yeah, so what happened to your face?" Andy brushed the back of his fingers against his chin.

"Eh, nothing." Dedrick put a finger to his own chin, making the slightest contact with the sore and swollen skin. It must've looked bad. He'd cleaned up after the incident but hadn't checked himself in the mirror.

"Nothing?" Crumbs flew from Andy's mouth. He snickered, chewed, and swallowed. "You can tell Mom that but not me. I want details. Did it happen in Aldonia?"

"Na, it's not like you think, rescuing people. You got some romantic notion about it all. It's risky. Dangerous. And the danger doesn't only come from Aldonia."

"I know that. You mean the Torva. I'm not afraid of them. That what happened to you? One of them?"

"One of them?" He glared, insulted. His brother knew he could handle himself with several untrained Torva boys at once. "You know they don't wander alone."

"Okay, two of them?" He grinned, a look of challenge in his eyes.

Dedrick returned the grin. His body still ached from the beating he had taken. He and the four pilgrims had nearly reached the mining tunnel when the Torva surprised them. He usually detected their approach from birds flying up from trees, animals running, a branch cracking, a whisper, even a swish of clothes. The wind ripping through the branches must've hidden the signs. He hadn't had the chance to draw his gun before a Torva kid darted from the shadows and tackled him to the ground. The other one grabbed the girl. Dedrick wasn't about to let them take the girl he had just rescued from Aldonia.

In some ways, the Torva were no better than the Regimen. They had no qualms about stealing girls to be their brides, robbing them of the freedom to choose. But they weren't as bad in other respects. They valued family and human life.

"I'm not afraid of danger." Andy drained his thermos in one long gulp and wiped his chin with his forearm. "I want to help. When you gonna talk Dad into letting me join you and the Mosheh?"

A smile stretched across Dedrick's face. Andy was impatient, rash, and overestimated his own abilities. Despite all that, Dedrick admired his little brother's zeal to help others. "You're still in school, Andy. What's the rush? I was eighteen when I joined."

"Well, some guys join younger. This is my calling and I know it. Why should I have to wait?" He gazed off into the distance, pressed his lips together, then faced Dedrick again. He wasn't easily turned away from a goal. "George Washington was out surveying land at sixteen. Ben Franklin, he was an apprentice in his brother's print shop. He was twelve."

"One thing you've got to learn, Andy. Impatience puts others at risk." His own advice haunted him now.

~ ~ ~

Dedrick had counted eight blocks and now turned south. "Fulton, you there?" He hadn't heard a sound through his earphone since the last communication. "I turned south. Now what?"

No reply.

They passed one intersection, two. The mall rose up on the left, visible over streets of old single-story businesses and abandoned buildings, a sprawling, geometric structure with dingy solar panels sprouting from the roof. It was an ugly union between sterile architecture and green technology.

"Fulton, you there?" Dedrick tapped his helmet even though it wouldn't have any effect on his ear phone, if that was the problem.

"Dump the bike, Dedrick."

Dedrick exhaled, thankful to hear Fulton's voice. "I thought I'd lost you. What's the problem?" He backed off the throttle.

"Stop at the next alley. No way to avoid surveillance past that point. If CSS saw what we saw from the Re-Ed security camera, they'll be looking for two people on a motorcycle. So dump the bike, avoid eye contact with troopers, and blend in."

"Troopers? What troopers?"

"Unity Troopers spotted in the area. We'll have to terminate communication, too. Don't want anyone intercepting our call."

"Copy that." Dedrick turned the bike down an alley and stopped a few yards in. He should've looked down the alley first. This did not look like an ideal situation.

Flames leaped from a metal garbage can, throwing light on a gang of kids probably fresh out of Secondary. They sat on and stood around stacks of crates and a dumpster halfway down the alley. A girl danced on a crate, waving her arms and shaking her hips. Half a dozen kids stood leaning against the backs of shops. A smaller group, mostly guys, squatted over a box or something in the middle of the alley. One boy even sat on the closed lid of the dumpster. Every one of them stopped what they were doing and stared at Dedrick and Liberty.

Dedrick glanced at Liberty and nodded, indicating for her to get off the motorcycle. He didn't want trouble. They would ditch the bike and get to the mall.

Her grip on his hips tightened, and she leaned into him as she dismounted.

He dropped the kickstand, shut off the bike, and peeled off his helmet. Music played, an unfamiliar song with a good beat. The cool air refreshed his sweaty head though it reeked of spray paint and cigarettes. He put up the hood of his jacket and got off the bike.

"Here they come," Liberty said. She hugged her helmet and shook out her hair. Stringy locks cascaded over one shoulder.

"Well, let's not stick around." He glanced at her black jacket. Sid's jacket. Made of some kind of polyester eco-fabric, it would probably melt in the rain. "You don't have a hood."

She stuffed a hand in a pocket. "I've got shoes and a jacket. I'm fine." Her eyebrows climbed up her forehead as she spoke and her head bobbed to each side, a smug sort of look.

A grin forced its way to his face. He remembered that she had worn only a patient gown on her ride to the pump station. A cold experience, no doubt. "We need to hide our faces. We don't have shades."

"Oh." She glanced behind him, probably at the approaching kids. Gray moonlight showed a hint of her expression, a schoolgirl making a calculation in her head.

He didn't want to look at the kids, didn't want to invite trouble. They needed to get underground as quickly as possible. He couldn't shake the feeling that tonight he would be caught by the Regimen for the first time.

The thought sickened him. He had his family to rescue, his brother on the edge. He had taken off to rescue Liberty without thinking, without Mosheh approval. She needed immediate help though. He had no choice. Besides, it was done. Couldn't be undone. He would just have to make things right.

"Come on." He strode three steps before realizing she hadn't come with him.

Liberty had approached the kids in the alley, the five boys who had started over. She did the talking. They did the listening. And the leering. Foxes ready to attack. Maybe she didn't know how pretty she was or what a group of boys in an alley without surveillance cameras might do to her.

She swung an arm out and pointed at the motorcycle. The boys' twisted smiles faded as they turned their eyes from her to the bike. One of them nodded, reaching into a breast pocket. Another dashed back to the kids by the crates.

Dedrick strolled to Liberty's side and gave the four boys before her a threatening glare. "What's up?"

"Uh," one of them said, peering up through eyes surrounded by dark makeup. They all exchanged glances, grinning, two of them snickering. The tallest one had a nose like an opossum, long and thin. He held Liberty's helmet at his side. They were lost boys, created by a cold society, cared for by no one.

Liberty handed Dedrick a pair of black sunglasses and smiled. "These nice boys say they'll watch our motorcycle and lend us their sunglasses."

The fifth boy jogged from the gang at the crates back to Liberty, a pair of sunglasses in his hand. "You really gonna leave us the keys?"

Liberty smiled at Dedrick and lifted her brows.

He chuckled. It was a great idea. It might even keep the Unity Troopers off them. "Yeah, sure." He dug the keys from his pocket and slapped them into the boy's hand.

Dedrick felt Liberty's glance twice, but they jogged down dark streets without speaking until the mall came bouncing into full view. A trolley stopped on the drive that circled the mall, letting off a dozen people, adding to the pedestrians that migrated toward the mall. People strolled under beams of light that fell from glowing streetlamps, bright solar-powered LEDs.

Most people converged on the mall, wanting to blow personal entertainment credits before the credits expired. The Regimen thought relaxation, self-expression, and entertainment were important, so, twice a month, a person could watch one of the movies made on the western side of the continent, get something to wear other than Regimen-allotted clothes, buy a piece of jewelry, or fulfill a craving with candy. With permission, one could even save their credits for something big like a motor scooter. A person couldn't say the Regimen never gave them anything.

Not wanting to stick out, Dedrick stopped jogging and matched his pace to that of the others. They approached a group of chatty girls and walked on their heels. A girl in a short, patterned dress said something about purses. Another girl said she wanted blue hair. Or something like that. Maybe Dedrick heard her wrong.

A single Unity Trooper stood by the main door to the mall, his black armor shining like obsidian, his hand hovering by the weapon on his belt. His head swiveled from side to side as people funneled in through a glass entranceway. He might've been scanning retinas. There was only one trooper, though, so he probably wasn't actively searching for a particular person. They typically sent a stream of information back to their base, most of it mundane.

Liberty walked beside Dedrick, head down, hair in her face, sunglasses hiding her eyes. She glanced at him and then weaved through the group of girls, keeping one body or another between her and the trooper's line of sight. She had an innate ability to move with stealth.

He took a different path through the crowd, a route farther from the trooper.

"You people are slow," a boy behind Dedrick shouted. He bumped shoulders with Dedrick and put a hand on another man, trying to get through.

Impulse made Dedrick want to face him, but he would've had to look in the direction of the trooper. The trooper probably had his retina scan on the boy right now. Better to keep his head down.

"I'll meet you in the arcade," another kid shouted. He waited inside the glass doors. The self-confident look in his eyes and the hair hanging down to his shirt collar reminded Dedrick of Andy.

"No, you'll wait for me," the impatient boy said. The younger crowd often headed for the arcades. That could be a problem.

Dedrick stepped through the glass doorway with his head down, well aware that surveillance cameras, high on the walls, flanked the entrance. They would have to pass a few more cameras in the mall before they reached their destination. They couldn't risk getting caught. If the Regimen realized they came into the mall but hadn't left by ordinary means, they would investigate.

Liberty continued to walk with strangers at her sides a few yards ahead of him. They passed three boarded up shops, a shoe store, a candy shop, and a clothing store. The group of girls broke up, some turning into the clothing store.

Liberty stopped by a bench under a camera, a blind spot. She wouldn't know their destination. She meant to give him the lead.

Dedrick gave the slightest nod, indicating for her to follow. Unlike most of the Aldonians he had led to the colonies, he trusted she would pick up his signals. He walked under stationary cameras and paused under rotating ones, pretending to window shop until the camera turned away.

A surveillance camera hung above the arcade, pointing out at the common area. As he stepped under it, he cringed. He hated the foyer to the arcade.

Videos played on huge screens on black walls, advertisements of the latest 3D games, images flashing in rapid succession. Dark hallways came off each side of the foyer, leading to the game rooms. The floor trembled with the sound effects, the rumble of engines, deep synthesized voices, bombs exploding. Ultraviolet lights made geometric patterns in the carpet glow. It also illuminated the full, white hair of the man behind the metallic host station.

Dedrick's stomach dropped. The man at the station was not Rigby, the Mosheh's plant. Now what? He took a step back and turned away, bumping into Liberty.

"What's the problem?" she said. Colorful images flashed on her shades, reflections of the videos. This rescue probably had her worried from the start.

"There is no problem," he snapped, irritated at himself. "Remove the shades." He didn't want to see the doubt, the worry in her eyes, but they should take their shades off to avoid looking suspicious. The cameras wouldn't see them here. He removed his and hooked them onto his belt.

"I, uh, we don't have credits," he said, turning up a palm and glancing at her. Everyone paid in credits with a quick scan of one's ID implant.

Liberty removed her shades. Determination, not doubt, showed in her pale green eyes. "Maybe we can trade something," she said.

"May I help you?" The man at the station spoke with a surprisingly high voice. His wild, glowing hair made him appear younger at first glance, but his bloated face and wrinkled forehead aged him. He gripped the corners of the station and rocked back and forth, staring at them through indifferent eyes.

"Yeah." Dedrick approached. "I don't have the credits, but we . . ." A glance at Liberty. ". . . we're dying to play."

"No credits?" The corner of his mouth quivered as if he suppressed a laugh or had a nervous tic. His gaze slid to Liberty. "And you?" His gaze dropped, probably in search of a hand to scan.

She shook her head and kept her hands in her pockets. She wore a fingerless glove on her right hand and undoubtedly meant to keep it hidden.

The man smirked. "What do you expect me to do? Let you pay with your looks?" His gaze had swiveled to Dedrick as he spoke. "Or do you have something else in mind?" He cocked a brow.

Irritation ruffled the hair on Dedrick's neck, but he tried not to show it. He opened his jacket. "I thought maybe a trade." His hand went to the flashlight at his hip. He wrestled it from his belt and stared at it. It was a good one, small but powerful. They would need it. He should trade something else. His Leatherman tool, his pocketknife? He couldn't give up the pocket knife. His father had etched his name into it and given it to him when he was a boy.

"What do I want with a flashlight?" The man reached behind the station and brought out a flashlight of his own, a big, ugly one. He held it under his chin and turned it on, shining the beam on his face, making strange shadows above his eyes and nose. The tips of his spiky bangs looked whitish violet. He gave a silly grin and shut the flashlight off. Then he leaned over the station and peered at Dedrick's belt.

"I like that." He pointed.

Dedrick wrapped his fingers around the pocketknife. "Yeah?" He gulped. An image popped into his mind. His father. Eyebrows drawn together in a look of concentration. The hint of a grin as he whipped the knife across a field and stuck it in a dead tree trunk.

Still, what choice did he have? It was only a knife. He could give it up. "Okay." He slid it from its holder and offered it to the man.

"What is that?" His lips curled on both sides, making wrinkles pop out all over his face. "A knife? I don't want that. I want the belt." He pointed. "What's it made of?"

"Uh, leather."

The man stuck out his upturned hand. "I'll take it. What game would you like to play?"

Dedrick and Liberty exchanged a glance. Success.

Dedrick shoved the knife in a pocket of his jeans, popped holders and items from his belt, unbuckled, and stripped the belt from his waist.

"Wonderful," the man said, turning the belt over in his hands. He brought it to his nose and sniffed it. "Every room is full at the moment. You can wait out there." Eyes still on the belt, he pointed at the common area, to a bench that sat in full view of a surveillance camera.

"Yeah, thanks." Dedrick put his hand on Liberty's back and guided her to one of the dark hallways that led to the game rooms. They could wait just inside it and avoid surveillance and the gaze of everyone walking through the mall.

"Hey! Excuse me. You two," the man shouted from the station. "You can't wait there. You have to wait in the common area. There's a bench." He pointed, his arm fully extended.

"No, uh, we need to talk. We won't be trouble." Dedrick grabbed Liberty's upper arm and backed her to the wall with a bang. He misjudged the distance. His gaze snapped to hers. "Sorry."

She pressed her lips together, laughter in her eyes.

The strangeness of the situation and fear over what he intended to do kept him from smiling back. He lessened his grip on her arm but didn't let go. Instead, he rested his other arm on the wall by her head and leaned closer. She wouldn't be able to hear the wild drumbeat in his chest. She wouldn't interpret it to mean that he liked her. He only wanted the man to think they had a reason to want privacy. She would know that.

"What are we doing here?" Liberty whispered.

A wave of heat washed over him, carrying the scent of his sweat and deodorant to his nose, probably to her nose. *We're pretending to have a reason to stand here, other than to avoid surveillance,* he almost said, but then he realized what she probably meant. He leaned closer still and whispered in her ear, "There's a way down in one of the rooms."

She turned her face, her lips all but touching his. "What if he doesn't give us that room?" She lifted her eyes, black orbs in the shadows surrounded by the hint of pale irises.

He found his hand sliding down her arm, his gaze dropping to her mouth, his lips burning. He shouldn't feel this way about her. The situation probably stirred these feelings. Helplessness. Fear. Desperation. Standing so close to her. He'd never known a girl so pretty.

He leaned, dispelling the breath of space between them.

Something in the foyer moved.

His gaze darted to the station. The man was gone. Some kid's gaming time had probably expired. It would be their turn next, but he didn't want just any room.

Dedrick grabbed Liberty's hand and dashed down the dark hallway. Around the corner, little purple lights edged the floor. He ran to a door marked Room 15 and opened it.

Two boys his brother's age, both wearing 3D visors and gloves, stood in the middle of the room. One crouched and aimed a controller gun at images on the wall. The other dodged, probably avoiding an imaginary projectile.

"Hey," Dedrick shouted, "Room 5 has the new game. Come check it out."

The boys turned in unison.

He nodded. "Come and see." He left the door open and took off for Room 12. A girl played alone. She turned at once when he called. He gave the same message.

"What new game?" The girl removed her visor, revealing a wary look.

"The illegal one," Dedrick said and gave her a sly grin. Gamers in Aldonia always wanted the newest. Illegal ones were even better. "Nothing like it. Come check it out." He glanced to either side.

Liberty stood at the door to the next room. She cracked it open and told them about the new game. She sure picked things up fast.

The girl from Room 12 pushed passed Dedrick. "Room 5?" she said.

"Yup." He watched her sprint down the dark hallway.

Two boys emerged from the room by Liberty. She flattened herself against the wall to let them pass.

"In here." Dedrick gave a nod to indicate Room 12.

Blurry, moving images of a jungle scene filled one wall of the otherwise dark room. Thick pads, dull and worn in places, covered the floor up to the two circular treads in the center.

Dedrick lifted one of the pads on the far side of the room, revealing an access panel in the floor. "We'll have to hurry. That girl will—"

Liberty had her hand on the latch of the access panel before he even realized she had come to his side. She flipped the latch and yanked open the panel as if she had done this before.

"You first," Dedrick said.

Without hesitation, she swung her legs into the dark hole and jumped down. Her feet landed with a metallic clang on a rung of the ladder. The rest of her steps made no sound. She descended, disappearing into the darkness.

He put a foot to the ladder and followed, thumping down the rungs, stopping halfway. He swung the access door shut. It clicked. The pad would slide back into its original position. The girl would return to her game, irritated at Dedrick's lie but with no clue as to his motive. They were safe now.

CHAPTER 11

I stepped off the rung ladder and onto a hard cement floor. Weak, pulsing light outlined the edges of the access door and Dedrick's silhouette as he climbed down after me. It revealed wires running along rafters and the hint of a distant cement-block wall but little else.

The access door clicked shut, making the darkness complete. The thrill of the motorcycle ride and of avoiding surveillance in the mall vanished. Wariness and foreboding replaced it.

I was five years old again. My first night after transitioning from the Breeder Facility to Primary. Darkness and the immense size of the room prevented me from seeing the walls or the bedroom doors. I made out shapes of beds and bodies and more beds. The room had no end. I was small and alone. Trembling, I pulled the blanket over my head and immersed myself in *My Friend*. *Do not be afraid*, he said without words, *I am with you*.

The rungs made a metallic sound with each of Dedrick's steps. The slightest breeze touched me before he landed with a thud. He probably jumped, skipping the last few rungs.

A soft electrical humming sound came from nearby. Otherwise, we stood in silence.

I peered into the dark, straining to make out something other than the gray swirls of blindness. I expected Dedrick to give us some light. Then I remembered his flashlight. I had stuffed it into my pocket.

As the beam cut through the dark, Dedrick lifted his head and looked at me. He stood at the foot of the ladder, one hand on his back pocket. He patted his jacket, and then stuck a hand in one pocket and pulled something out. A Swiss army knife?

He put the knife away and squinted at me. "Hey, that's mine."

"The flashlight?"

"How'd you get it?"

"Seriously?" I had taken it from him when the arcade man asked for his belt. Dedrick had seemed a bit flustered, as if the request was a shot at his dignity.

I turned in a circle, sweeping the beam up and down. Cement block walls surrounded us, making the room twice as big as the game room above. Pipes ran along one wall. The electrical wires in the rafters were neatly tie-wrapped here and there. The wires ran to big electrical cabinets on the wall and to a hallway that came off the corner of this room.

I started toward the hallway.

Dedrick stepped in my path, blocking me. His jaw twitched, agitation or annoyance flickering across his face. The beam of the flashlight emphasized the blond streaks in his tousled dark hair. He had dyed his hair months ago as part of his disguise before he rescued me from the Breeder Facility. Now, half grown out, it made him look Aldonian. But Dedrick was Mosheh all the way.

"I need that." His fingers brushed mine as he took the flashlight. He went to one of the electrical cabinets and opened it. Wires ran to circuit breakers, switches, knobs, and displays.

"What're you doing?" I rubbed my hand. The impression of his touch lingered.

"Seriously?" He imitated the tone of voice I had used when he asked me about the flashlight. Squatting, he reached inside the cabinet to its floor. Something banged and slid. The cabinet trembled. Another banging and sliding sound. The cabinet tipped slightly. He seemed to be adjusting the feet. "I'm getting us out of here."

"What's down the hallway?"

"Nothing. Other areas under the arcade, under the mall." He straightened up and faced me, the flashlight hanging at his side. He opened his mouth and dropped his gaze. Was he trying to decide whether to tell me something? How to tell me?

My lips burned. As I pressed them together, a single thought flooded my mind. Dedrick had almost kissed me. His lips had brushed mine, making the slightest connection, a breeze on a petal. Then he had turned away. He probably thought he should kiss me, to make our cover believable, but couldn't get himself to do it. I didn't blame him. Thick smoke billowed between us, houses burning in Maxwell.

"Hold this." He shoved the flashlight into my hand and turned to the cabinet. Gripping the top and the side, he slid the cabinet down the wall. A curtain drawing back.

I aimed the beam at the wall behind the cabinet. A wooden panel the size of a small door came into view.

Dedrick flicked a latch at the top and another at the bottom. The panel swung open, inviting us to more darkness, more unknown. Dedrick stepped through.

I followed, shining the flashlight up, down, and all around, trying to make sense of the new surroundings. The floor sloped down a bit on this side of the wall. Cool air kissed my cheeks. Pipes ran along the ceiling. Thick support beams rose up every few meters, cement block walls in the distance.

Dedrick grunted. He had moved the electrical cabinet back into place. Now he squatted and leaned through a panel in the back of it, switching the rollers back to stationary feet, I assumed. Straightening up, he swung the little wooden door shut and latched it. Then his gaze went to the flashlight in my hand.

I offered it to him, avoiding contact this time. "Now what?"

"We got a long, strange route ahead of us." He walked as he spoke, keeping to the cement wall. "You up to it?"

"Do I have a choice?" I said it in fun, wanting to lighten the heavy mood that grew in me. The Regimen would not find us underground. Sid would not find me. We were safe. But my stomach tightened at the thought of our destination.

At the end of tunnels and darkness, I would have to stand in the light. I would have to face the Mosheh and the consequences of my actions. Smoke swirled in the recesses of my mind, around every thought, homes burning in Maxwell.

Dedrick flashed the light at me. "Do you need a rest?"

"Nah, not me. Let's go." I would not rest for a long time.

We strode through this open area of support beams and darkness, walking what felt like the length of the mall. My thighs ached at first but soon warmed, remembering the workout they used to get daily. We reached a cement block wall and turned, following it a short ways. Then Dedrick stopped. He shined the light on me and walked into the wall, disappearing and taking all but a sliver of light with him.

I knew it was only an optical illusion, but my heartbeat raced. Not wanting to be left alone, I dashed to the sliver of light.

The cement wall actually ended and another began. The second wall set back a bit, overlapped by the first. It made me think builders had started at opposite ends, meaning to make a single wall but misaligning them. Three meters in, light showed through a narrow opening in the hidden wall.

"Are you with me?" Dedrick's voice came from the narrow opening. He stood sideways a few meters down, his back to a cement wall, his face to an old rock wall and the flashlight aimed at my waist. Darkness swallowed up the walls beyond him. How far did they stretch?

"We'll have to walk sideways," he said, twisting a bit as if to prove it.

"For how long?"

He shrugged. "It's not bad." He transferred the flashlight, sliding it along his abdomen to his leading hand and shedding light on our narrow path.

Taking a deep breath, I went in shoulder first. My jacket scraped the gritty cement wall, brushing debris to the ground. A heavy odor of dirt and decay hung in the stagnant air. Maybe it came from the dark mold that grew between cracks on the rock wall.

I scanned the wall above me. Something web-like dangled above my eyes. My face and neck itched. I shuddered and let out an involuntary gasp.

Dedrick, shuffling onward, glanced back. "You aren't claustrophobic, are you?" His smile took me back to the Maxwell Colony. We stood side by side, skipping rocks in the river.

"What if I was?"

"I'd make you go first."

My next step brought me too close, and my arm bumped his. He had stopped without me realizing it. The teasing look on his face stirred up feelings inside me, feelings I shouldn't have had for him. I turned my eyes to the wall.

"You do look tired. You gonna be okay?"

"I'll have to be. Can't fall asleep in here."

His question, the tight space, and the stagnant air made my eyelids heavy. I sidestepped along after him, cleaning debris and webs from the wall. Shoes shuffling on the cement, jackets brushing the rough wall. Every sound, every breath close and warm. I longed for a bed, my bed in the Shenoy's house, the house of my sponsor family in the Maxwell Colony. I could hear the soft tinkle of the wind chime and picture it glittering under moonlight outside my bedroom window.

Our path sloped downward, going deeper and deeper into the earth. Dedrick moved with simple rhythm, stepping easily to the side. Nothing bothered him.

I wanted to scream. How long could I do this?

I took a deep breath and closed my eyes. We were crabs shuffling through endless underground tunnels in the sand, safe from predators. Unknown to all.

My first week at Primary, I had uncurled my fingers from the blanket and rolled out of bed, dropping onto the smooth, cold floor. The whispers, sniffles, and giggles of the other girls had long since ceased. A single girl breathed heavily, creating a lulling sound. I crawled under my bed. Wooden slats hung above me.

They brushed against my hair and nightgown as I moved. Heart pounding, barely breathing, I crept from under my bed to the next bed, bed after bed until I reached the door. I awoke late in the afternoon, curled up between boxes in the utility room. My stomach growled. I had to pee. I opened the door to the utility room. Two nannies stood in the kitchen, their eyes on me. "Who's this girl?" one nanny said. "I don't know. You'd better get her dressed." No one knew I'd been missing. No one cared.

The light dimmed. Dedrick inhaled then slipped around a corner. Our narrow path between walls had ended. He let out a groan, a sound of long-awaited release.

I reached the end of our crab tunnel and stepped out into a small, dark room.

Dedrick jumped in place a few times and shook out his arms like a runner preparing to race. Then he bent over and brushed his hair with frantic movements that didn't fit his typically controlled demeanor. "I hate it between walls. Feel like I've got things crawling all over me."

I laughed, brushing myself, too. I had never really appreciated having enough room to stretch.

The flashlight lay on the floor, its beam making a big triangle on the damp cement and casting a dim light on a brick wall. The room was odd shaped, an uneven quadrilateral. Not counting the crack we crawled from, tunnels came off three of the walls.

Dedrick finally stood still. He took a deep breath, wiped his face, smoothed his hair, then snatched the flashlight from the floor. "Okay, we're halfway home." He shined the beam on me. "Ready?"

I nodded but his question made me think. Ready for what? To move on or to face the Mosheh?

We walked side by side through a brick tunnel that curved up over our heads. Dedrick held the flashlight casually at his side, lifting it now and then to peer ahead. How many tunnels ran under Aldonia? Did Dedrick know them all?

"So the Mosheh has no access point near that pump station?" I blurted out the question in my mind, but I probably should've kept it to myself. I didn't want him to think I doubted him. In the past, he had told me repeatedly that I could trust him.

He huffed. "Access points had to be closed. Regimen was looking, *is* looking." His voice rose. "We've lost our surveillance informer. Got troubles hacking into CSS video feeds. Everything's messed up." He gritted his teeth and shook his head. He probably had more to say. He probably saw his parents, his sister and his brother, every time he looked at me. Would he ever forgive me?

My heart dropped. "I'm sorry. I didn't know." I had only been thinking about the colonists who were now prisoners. I hadn't considered the effect on the operations of the Mosheh. I hadn't even considered what the others in Maxwell would do. Would they rebuild? Would they move?

"Things are different now." He spoke in a calm, controlled tone. "We have to make do."

"Thanks for rescuing me," I said.

He glanced. A few beats later, eyes to the path, he said, "So why'd you go with him?"

"Him? Sid?"

"Yeah, Sid. I seem to remember him attacking you in an alley." Another glance. A strange look in his eyes. "And what do you think he had in that syringe?"

"Well, it's not like I knew it was him. He wore a helmet. I thought he was . . ."

"Thought he was who? Me?" Dedrick swung the beam toward me and glared through narrowed eyes, his mouth hanging open. I had offended him.

"No. I knew it wasn't you, but I thought it was someone with the Mosheh. I thought we were all being rescued."

In my mind, I answered his earlier question: I was not ready. I, the sole person responsible for the ruin of Maxwell, could not face the Mosheh as the sole person rescued from Re-Ed.

Dedrick strode a few more paces, tension in his steps. "So how'd he do it? How'd he get in?"

"I don't know. I was on my way to History Lessons when the power went out. Next thing I know, he's there beating up the guard. Then he led me to a service door and used something, not his implant; he ran it by the scanner to open the door."

"Someone had to have helped him."

"Yeah. I asked but he wouldn't say."

A pause and then, "What was the rest of his plan? He couldn't have kept you there." His head turned, his eyes swiveling to me with a look that said he wasn't sure he should've asked.

"He said there was some place we could go, some place we could live without the Regimen knowing. I don't know where he meant. He couldn't know about the colonies, could he?"

"No." The answer came without pause. "There are places within Aldonia, Jensenville, too. I've heard of them. You wouldn't want to live there. There are different reasons for wanting to live free of the Regimen, not all of them admirable."

"I'm glad the Mosheh sent you for me."

"Uhh . . ." He glanced, wincing.

"What about the others? I hate to think of them still in there."

"Yeah, we'll get them."

"Do you have the colony children? I saw them on video. I saw Paula." My throat constricted, making my voice a whisper. I had to force each word out. "They made me watch as the helicopters . . ." I swallowed back an unexpected rush of grief. "Tell me you have them."

Dedrick bit his lip and shook his head. He met my gaze. "No, we don't have them. Paula's in North Primary, and so are two of our boys. We've got more in Secondary."

"Why?" My voice came out high and tight. I saw Paula clutching a blanket in my old bed and then hiding in the utility room, alone and afraid. "What are you waiting for?"

He sneered, staring straight ahead. "We're working on it. I told you, we're at a disadvantage now. We can't move about like we used to."

"Tell me the plan. I want to help." He had lengthened his stride, making me have to jog between steps to keep up.

He shot a cold look. "You can't help."

"I have to help. I never intended to leave Re-Ed alone."

"Mosheh's not gonna let you help. You need to recuperate."

"I don't need to recuperate. I need to help. They're in custody because of me."

He grabbed my wrist and stopped walking, jerking me to a stop. A vein in his neck throbbed. "No." His lips wrapped around the word, conveying a sense of finality. "You will not be helping. We know what they do to you in Re-Ed. We watch the live feeds. You need to rest. You're in no condition to help anyone."

"I just need to eat and get a little rest. I'm fine."

A smile flickered on his face. He shook his head, avoiding my gaze. "I know you think this is all your fault; you feel this need to make up for it. But it's not your fault and there's nothing you can do."

I wrestled my wrist from his grip. They had taught me in the Maxwell Colony that to be truly free one must accept the consequences of his actions. I made a selfish choice and it had led to the destruction of Maxwell. I would submit myself to whatever punishment, whatever trial the Mosheh saw fit. I would lay down my life to save these people.

"You don't know me," I said.

CHAPTER 12

Miriam leaned into a waist-high, wooden crate long enough to be her casket. The yellowish light from the low-pressure sodium lamps on the wall gave her a ghostly appearance. A camouflage backpack lay at her feet. She dropped half a dozen dehydrated meals to the cement floor and continued rifling through packages that crinkled and rattled at her touch.

Dedrick stood resting a shoulder against a stack of crates. He couldn't get himself to sit since their arrival at the Mosheh's Control Center. Miriam had greeted them and then led Liberty, alone, to the private meeting room. The elders had told him to wait.

"What do you think's taking so long?" he said, wiping the back of his neck. The cool air and lack of movement had made his skin clammy. His head and a few other places ached from his brawl with Sid. Nothing too bad, but he could've avoided the pain if he hadn't been so sloppy.

Miriam, still bent over the crate, glanced at the TekBand on her wrist and then at him. She continued digging through the crate as she spoke. "Hasn't been that long. I'm sure they want to learn everything they can from her days in Re-Ed. Every bit can help."

"I guess." Dedrick took a swig of water. Miriam had tossed him a bottle as soon as they had come over to the crates to wait. Would Elder Lukman have offered Liberty anything? She would need it more than Dedrick would. When was the last time she'd had a good long drink?

"Liberty told me she wanted to help with the rescues," he said. "Can you believe it?"

"Sure. Why not?"

"Really? You think that's a good idea? She just came from Re-Ed. They mess with your mind in there. She hardly slept, hardly ate." He found himself scraping at the label on his water bottle and glaring at the far side of the area, at the steel-gray, windowless door to the meeting room. The room was designed for privacy, making it one of the few places in the underground network with a low ceiling and soundproof walls.

He set the water bottle down and pressed his palms against the edge of the crate through which Miriam dug. "You don't think they'd consider it, do you? Letting her help?"

A smile flickered on Miriam's lips. She held a first-aid kit in one hand and neatened a stack of medical packets with the other. Miriam never did anything halfway. She straightened up and met his gaze, all amusement gone from her expression. "Liberty's got firsthand, inside information. She should help. I wouldn't worry about it. She's tough. We'll get her a good meal and a bed. She'll be fine." She dropped the first-aid kit and two more packages onto the pile on the floor.

"Next thing you know, she'll be wanting to join us, wanting to make a commitment."

"So? She wouldn't be the first *rescue* to want to rescue others."

He shook his head. He couldn't put his thoughts into words, but it wouldn't be right. Liberty didn't belong with the Mosheh. She should get as far from Aldonia as possible.

Miriam grabbed the lid to the crate. Dedrick came around to help.

"You don't want her to join because your commitment here is almost up. What do you have, a few more months? Then what? You want to settle down, don't you? Start your own family?"

His cheeks warmed as he helped scrape the wooden lid onto the crate. "I don't know what you're saying." Yeah, he'd told her that before. He enjoyed serving, rescuing people. But he had never intended to make a career out of it. Yeah, he wanted a wife. He wanted children. He wanted to live free, far away from Aldonia or any other Regimen-controlled city.

Miriam laughed and pulled herself up to sit on the closed crate. She patted the lid, inviting him to sit beside her.

He shook his head. The elders would finish with Liberty and want to speak with him soon. He didn't want to sit.

"Dedrick, I'm saying she means something to you. You don't want to return to the colonies without her."

He stared at her, his mouth hanging open. "I . . . no . . . . Of course she means something to me. Every Aldonian I rescue means something to me." His burning cheeks had probably turned flaming red which, hopefully, the ugly light from the sodium lamps would conceal. "I get to know them, and I-I don't forget them. I can tell you every one of their names, every person I rescued for the past three and a half years. Yeah, she's important to me."

A smile showed in her eyes. "I don't doubt that you care about them all, but are you going to deny it's different with her?"

"Uh, yeah. I see myself marrying a colony girl."

"Oh, someone I know?"

"No, I-I don't have a girl picked out. I'm just saying. When I marry, I'm marrying a colony girl. They know all about the family life I want, the values I want to pass to my children. They know hard work—"

"Okay, Dedrick, stop." Miriam scooted off the crate and squatted by the pile of supplies. She shoved dehydrated meals into the backpack. "I never realized you were prejudiced."

"What? That makes me prejudiced? To want certain virtues in my wife?"

"We don't rescue just any Aldonian. If a person doesn't display a hardworking, virtuous character, they aren't a candidate for rescue. They wouldn't want colony life." She stuffed the last of the items into the backpack and yanked the zipper as she stood up. "But then you know that. I've seen you watching her, months before her rescue."

"Her? Liberty?" His senses heightened, giving him the impression that the kids at the island of workstations had stopped their incessant chatter and now stared at them. It was ridiculous, of course. They were too far, and the cavernous area magnified the hum of the computers and distorted voices anyway.

Miriam smirked. "Yes, Liberty. We've all noticed."

"I, uh . . ." He glanced over his shoulder and made a quick scan of the distant workstations. The overhead lights made the area glow, emphasizing the darkness stretching out around it. Most kids sat or stood alone at stations. A group of three huddled together. No one looked his way. "Miriam, I watch every candidate. It's my job. I have to know a person so I can plan the best time, the best place, the best method of extraction." With a sarcastic edge, he added, "But then you know that."

She smiled. "Yeah, I know that." Using two hands, she hoisted the backpack onto the crate. "I need to get in there." She pointed to a crate at the bottom of a stack of new crates.

He grabbed one end of the top crate and helped her lower it, the rough wood cutting into his calloused hand. They stacked it on another crate.

"What's in it?" he said.

"Weapons." She pried the bottom crate open with a crowbar and let the crowbar fall to the floor with a clang. She lifted a layer of foam and tossed it behind the crate. Various sized packages tied with thick twine filled the box.

"Do you ever wish we didn't take the vow to avoid personal relationships?" she said, her eyes in the crate.

He glanced at her. Twice. "No. Don't you think it makes sense? Can't have a guy focused on one person." He forced the next words out. "I-I know how it looks, my behavior lately. You think I've got it bad for Liberty. I don't. I only want to do the right thing, not shirk a responsibility. Can I really be expected to hold back when I know I can help someone?"

Miriam unwrapped a six-inch, black flashlight and studied the end of it. She turned it for him to see. "It's a taser gun, er, taser flashlight." Two metal prongs stuck out of the LED end. "You blind your opponent so you can get close enough to zap him."

"Yeah, cool." He threw another glance at the meeting room door but forced himself not to check the time on his TekBand.

"I wish Matthias and I could've worked together."

Dedrick's gaze snapped to Miriam. His heart skipped a beat. She had never mentioned Matthias to him before. Rumor had it, she hadn't spoken of him since his death.

A slight smile lingered on her face, a distant look in her eyes as she spoke. "We were on the same team for a long time, until we realized . . ." She dropped her gaze. ". . . we were in love. If I had remained on his team, we could've protected each other. Four Unity Troopers came from one side, two from another. Matthias told the rest of the team to take the kid they were trying to rescue and run. Then he drew the Unity Troopers' attention." She lifted her gaze to Dedrick and gave him a sad smile. "He hadn't known about the single Trooper who came up behind him, or he would've gotten away. If I had been there—" Grief flashed across her face.

The look overwhelmed him. He grabbed her arm and leaned toward her until their foreheads touched. "Yeah," he whispered, her grief rippling through him.

Miriam sucked in a breath and laced her fingers through his, peeling his hand from her arm. "I know it's hard for you, Dedrick, having your family in those places, maybe feeling a bit responsible for it all, but hang in there. Keep your head together. We'll get them out." She squeezed his hand and gave him a determined look. "The elders have a plan. You and me, we only have to focus on the right thing to do in the present moment."

Too choked up to speak, he nodded. She was right. He did feel guilty. He should've talked Liberty out of her impulsive decision to return to Aldonia for Abby. But everything about Liberty that night—her tone, posture, expression—showed her steely determination. He couldn't have stopped her, and he couldn't let her go alone. She would've failed, probably would've killed herself at the electric Boundary Fence. He knew the Mosheh wouldn't be pleased with the spontaneous request for assistance. Every fiber of his being warned him it wouldn't work out. He should've listened to the inner voice.

Miriam turned her head and squinted.

A group of four stood outside the open door to the meeting room: Elder Lukman, Elder Rayna, Camilla—the girl from Maxwell who they had assigned to the Primary rescue—and Liberty. The light behind them made their faces impossible to read, but Camilla's voice carried. Her tone of voice and posture, hands on hips and chin jutting out, took Dedrick back to his teenage years in the Maxwell Colony to when Camilla's mother wouldn't let her join the other teens on a midnight hike.

Elder Rayna put up a hand, a sudden movement that made Camilla stop talking. The elders distinguished themselves with tunics of homespun linen. Elder Rayna's had a pattern around the neckline and hung to her ankles. Elder Lukman's tunic came to his knees, half covering his denim jeans. Elder Lukman caught sight of Miriam and Dedrick and raised his hand, motioning them over like Moses summoning his people.

Miriam dropped the taser flashlight back into the crate and grabbed Dedrick by the arm.

"I guess it's my turn," Dedrick said, a hard pit growing in his stomach.

The four by the meeting room continued to talk among themselves. Liberty hadn't appeared to notice Dedrick and Miriam's approach. She faced Elder Rayna.

"You don't have anything to worry about," Miriam said to Dedrick as they strode toward the group. "We're all on the same team here."

"I haven't been playing by the rules," he said.

"There's not always time for that." Miriam flashed a smile. "You need a special instinct to know when to break them."

Liberty crossed her arms over her waist, seeming out of her element. She glanced but didn't make eye contact with Dedrick. Their last words in the tunnels had been harsh. He'd made it clear he didn't want her helping with the rescues. She'd said he didn't know her. They'd walked the rest of the way, tunnel after tunnel, in silence. She must've told the elders she wanted to help. What answer had they given her?

"Why don't you take Liberty to get something to eat?" Elder Lukman said to Camilla. "I bet she'd love that potato soup I smelled when I passed the dining hall."

Elder Lukman had a way of making everything sound classy. The *dining hall* was a long area sectioned off with partial, makeshift walls and netting for a ceiling to catch debris. Lanterns hung from the ceiling. Thick candles sat on the tables. The strongest light came from the kitchen, over a counter that separated the two *rooms*. Two crews of four worked back there, one in the morning, the other in the afternoon. They did their best with whatever they received. Some days were better than others.

"Fine," Camilla said. Her head turned from Elder Lukman to Liberty, her ponytail swinging. "Then I'll show you where you can sleep."

Liberty's gaze skimmed Dedrick and went to Miriam.

Camilla looked too, her frown turning into an open smile when she saw them. "Hi, Dedrick! Miriam, you ready for your journey? I asked to go with you." Her smile faded and her voice went flat. "But they told me to take care of Liberty."

"Where're you going?" Dedrick said to Miriam, but Miriam spoke over him.

"Don't worry about me," Miriam said to Camilla. "Two guys from Maxwell are going to meet me. They've started out already."

Camilla grabbed Miriam's hand. "Good, cause I—"

"Camilla, take care of Liberty," Elder Rayna said. "She needs some rest." The light from the open doorway of the meeting room shone on her ebony skin, revealing her stern expression. Her eyes turned to Dedrick. "We'd like to speak with you."

Liberty was walking away, but at Elder Rayna's last words, her gaze clicked to his. He couldn't interpret the look. Pity? A warning?

Elders Rayna and Lukman shuffled into the meeting room, mumbling to each other.

Miriam gave Dedrick a farewell smile and took a few steps backward. He had assumed she was preparing for something, over by the crates. His selfish thoughts had kept him from asking.

"Wait," he said, "where're you going?"

"Someone's got to escort the Maxwell colonists to the Rivergrove Colony. Might as well be me."

He opened his mouth to reply.

"Dedrick!" Elder Rayna beckoned from the meeting room. "We need you in here."

~ ~ ~

Dedrick stood behind the chair that Elder Lukman indicated for him to take. Miriam was going to escort the colonists, the job the elders wanted him to have.

Knowing that he didn't want the job, she had probably volunteered. A twinge of guilt stabbed him. Should he be the one to go? The colonists were in good hands with her anyway. She knew the land as well as he did.

Elder Rayna closed the door, cutting off the outside hums and chatter. Her shoes made a soft padding sound as she came to the table. The slightest noise drew attention: the rollers of the chair as she pulled it out, the squeak as she sat. The thumping of Dedrick's heart.

Elder Lukman waved his hand over a flat control panel on the glassy surface of the table. He tapped a control a few times, probably referencing some information. No wall monitors came on, so it would only be the three of them.

Liberty would've provided any information needed to assist with the rescue efforts. What reason could they have to speak with Dedrick except to rebuke him?

Dedrick cleared his throat, deciding to speak first. "Look, I know you guys work hard to keep everyone safe. And some missions take longer than I'd like, but . . ." He grabbed the back of the chair and dug his fingers into the coarse fabric. "You want to talk to me about my impatience and how I-I've been irresponsible lately. I took off without permission and I—"

"Dedrick." Elder Lukman's low voice reverberated through Dedrick's chest.

Dedrick shut his mouth and swallowed.

"Have a seat." Elder Lukman made a nod.

"Yes, sir." Dedrick rolled out the chair and seated himself. "I don't want you to give up on me. I'm here to serve and I . . ." He forced himself to shut up.

Elder Lukman put a fist to his mouth and cleared his throat. Loudly. "Don't get all worked up now, Dedrick. We didn't call you in here to chastise you. We understand why you took off after Liberty today."

The defensive statements weaving through Dedrick's mind froze in place. "You . . . do?"

"Miriam filled us in, once she returned," Elder Rayna said, lifting a thin black brow. "She told us you know an emergency when you see one. And we shouldn't expect you to wait in every situation."

"She . . . did?"

"I'm not saying we approve of our members freewheeling." Elder Lukman's stern tone softened. "But perhaps we would be wise to rely more on the abilities and instincts of our people. Next time, however . . ." His tone hardened. He waved a finger in the air. "Next time you sense a need for urgency, speak with me first. I was sitting right here." He jabbed the tabletop with his index finger. "You could've stuck your head into the meeting room."

"Yes, sir. I . . . You're right." Dedrick nodded, shook his head, and then moved it erratically. "Won't happen again."

"Good." Elder Lukman leaned forward and clasped his hands on the table. "There's something we need you to do right now."

"Sure, name it," Dedrick said, feeling a sense of relief and a debt of gratitude to Miriam.

"We need to get a message to your brother. He's up to something, trying to organize an escape, we believe. We want you to convince him to wait, to give us two days."

"Two days?" Dedrick needed to hear it again. He'd stepped into the meeting room expecting to face a firing squad. This was almost too much to believe.

"In two days we will have all our people free." The confidence in Elder Lukman's voice left no room for doubt.

Dedrick glanced from one elder to the other. Elder Rayna nodded, assurance in her dark round eyes.

"That's great. What do I need to do?" He wouldn't be able to simply call his brother with the message. The kids in Secondary didn't have flexi-phones or any other way to communicate with the outside world. They often went on field trips, though, and outsiders could visit the residence for various reasons.

"You'll need to go out after curfew, after the city goes dark." Elder Lukman tapped another control on the table and a wall monitor came on. All eyes turned to it at the same time. "You won't go alone."

"Hey, Dedrick. Haven't worked with you in a while." Bolcan's image appeared on the screen, a golden-eyed lion with a mane of dark-blond hair that hung down to his shoulders. His thick build and cautious behavior belied his strength and ability. He'd been known to take down half a dozen men at once.

"Bolcan," Dedrick said in greeting. He would never forget sparring with Bolcan, nor the speed and power behind his punches.

Bolcan smiled, one side of his mouth curling up, his eyes remaining hard. Bolcan had grown up in Aldonia but never accepted their ways, probably due to stubbornness rather than virtue. He'd also spent more time in Re-Ed than any other rescue had. Re-Ed did something to a person that couldn't be undone, but that wasn't Bolcan's fault.

"So, I'll be working with him?" Dedrick turned to Elder Lukman. He bit back a complaint. In two days the colonists would be free.

CHAPTER 13

Dark clouds rolled over a vast stretch of cracked land. Shadows moved and deepened. A figure appeared, an emaciated man in robes of purple and gold. An erratic wind blew, making his robes flap and twist around his angular body. He reached into a bulging sack that hung from his shoulder and withdrew a handful of tares. The corner of his mouth curled up and his inky eyes narrowed. He flung the tares. The wind carried them away. He threw another handful and another, the wind taking them to every corner of the land. Torrents of black rain let loose from the clouds. In an instant, the tares took root and weeds sprung up at the man's feet. The man grew taller. As the weeds spread out in every direction, racing each other, fighting each other to cover the land, the man grew and grew. His job complete, he curled up on a bed of weeds and rested.

While he slept, another figure appeared in the field of weeds, a man in sandals and a long white tunic, the enemy of the first man. He too carried a sack over his shoulder. Appearing undisturbed by the wind and rain, he reached into the sack and brought out a handful of tiny yellow wheat seeds. He tossed them onto every bare patch of soil he could find. Would the seeds take root? Would they survive amidst the weeds? They had to. They just had to.

I sucked in a breath of air, snapped open my eyes, and flung back the covers. Sweat covered me. Perhaps the heat accounted for the strange dream. Where was I?

Blue light from a cylindrical LED lantern illuminated a patchwork wall of corrugated metal, wood panels, and thick sheets of plastic. Metal beams tied it all together. It reminded me of one of the quilts in my sponsor family's home back in Maxwell. Pictures, jars, and decorations sat on the beams. I saw names and dates everywhere—scratched into the wood, etched into the metal—names of past Mosheh members, I assumed.

I sat up, peering at the bed above me and listening for sounds of life. Distant voices came from the other side of the wall. Nothing nearby. Curtains hung between the bunk beds. I peeked behind the nearest one and found an empty, perfectly made bed.

Camilla had shown me here, to the girls' sleeping quarters, last night after I ate. She had also shown me the showers, but nothing else. I had questions for her but she'd left me alone. I guess I had fallen asleep before the other girls came to bed, and I must've slept right through their wakeup.

I slept hard last night, harder than I'd ever slept in my life. At the Re-Ed Facility, the incessant humming sound, the constant lights, and the sporadic banging noises had kept me awake. Here I had heard voices, distant conversations, but it took me back to the home of my sponsor family where voices traveled up the stairs at night. It even reminded me of my apartment in Aldonia where the thin walls had allowed me to hear the quiet sounds of the neighboring apartments.

I stood and stretched, feeling rested and ready, anxious to get the day started. I grabbed the clothing and towel Camilla had laid out for me and pushed aside the curtain in the doorway. After meeting with the elders last night, I had gained a new sense of purpose.

~ ~ ~

Walking alone, I passed the dining hall on my way to the ramp that led down to the Mosheh Control Center. The cool air on my wet hair refreshed me. It also rid me of the bad taste my dream had left in my mind.

My stomach growled. I wanted more of the potato soup they had given me in the dining hall last night. Camilla had not eaten with me. She had sat slumped and frowning, turning away from me whenever someone came by. As soon as I reached the bottom of the bowl, she stood up. "You're probably tired. Come on." I wanted more soup, but my stomach would've probably cramped from eating too much too soon after having had so little for so long. I had my suspicions as to why Camilla didn't like me and why she didn't want anyone to see her with me. I hoped it wouldn't affect her directive to help me.

I strode along a patchwork wall that darkness swallowed up farther ahead. A single lantern illuminated a distant door. It was a real wooden door, not a curtain. Everything on this level, above the control center, seemed thrown together with scraps, sheets of metal, wood, and other materials that most likely came from abandoned buildings in Aldonia. Aldonians often scavenged through such places. Why not the Mosheh?

I reached the ramp and started down, scanning the place with new eyes. The meeting room was off to my left, its gray door open and the doorway dark. The control center, an island of computer stations in a black sea, glowed with monitors and overhead lights. A dozen people, kids mostly, sat or stood at stations. A group of five stood around the nearest station. Their voices, hurried and excited, carried to me. "Nice work." "We'll see how it turns out." "You're a regular artist."

If Camilla wasn't among them, maybe they would know where I could find her.

Someone in the group laughed. Three of the kids dispersed, and a guy who had been hunched over the station straightened up. *Dedrick.* He turned and his eyes caught me, his smile fading.

My chest tingled, and my hand went to the sore spot on my palm. I brushed my finger along the tiny slit left by the implant remover. Miriam had removed my ID implant yesterday before she even said *hello.* It must've posed a risk to the underground community. She'd given me a bandage and said, "It takes no time to heal," then hugged me. The removal process was nothing compared to when Dedrick had removed my original implant with a scalpel and a defibrillator.

"You okay?" Dedrick's gaze dropped to my hands.

"Yeah, I'm good." I tucked my hands into the back pockets of my pants.

The kid sitting at the station, a tall, dark-skinned boy in a baseball cap, gave me a nod and turned to the monitor.

I didn't want Dedrick to think I came for him, so I blurted out, "Hey, either of you seen Camilla?" Feeling compelled to avoid eye contact with Dedrick, my gaze went to the image on the dark-skinned boy's monitor. It showed a picture, a painting maybe, of two boys on a tilted motorcycle.

"Not today," the boy at the station said, glancing from me to Dedrick.

I sensed that Dedrick stared at me. For some reason, he made me nervous. In the tunnels, he had told me I shouldn't feel guilty about the Maxwell colonists, but a part of me still expected him to confront me.

I glanced at his face, then his hands.

He stood with his hands at his sides. They were dirty, his fingers covered with purple and black speckles.

I forced myself to meet his gaze. "So have you seen her?"

"Who?" He gave a little headshake, his thoughts obviously somewhere else. Maybe he was embarrassed to be seen with me, too.

"Camilla."

He made a cursory glance to one side, his cheeks turning pink, and then locked his gaze on the monitor. "No, I haven't seen her."

I looked at the monitor again, too. The dark-skinned boy had zoomed out on the image, revealing it to be graffiti painted on the side of a tall gray building. Sunbeams and snowflakes showered down on the boys. The tilt of the motorcycle made it look ready to crash. At the bottom of the picture were big purple and black words. *Impatience puts others at risk.*

My hair bristled, chilling my head. The words struck me as a personal condemnation. My impatience put too many lives at risk. My impatience might prevent my admittance to the Mosheh. "You're a strong girl with many virtues," Elder Rayna had told me last night, "but you have no control over your impulses when you think you are doing good." I wanted to convince her and all the elders that I had changed or that I recognized my fault and could change.

"Like it?" the dark-skinned boy said, grinning at me. He looked like a boy with a good sense of humor, someone who could put a person at ease. "It's Dedrick's handiwork."

Dedrick's blush deepened. He folded his arms over his chest. "Not all mine. Bolcan helped, probably did most of it."

"Well, it's your design," the boy said.

"This is Fulton," Dedrick said to me. "He helps from the inside when I'm on a rescue."

Fulton extended a hand. "I know who you are. You're Liberty."

"Yeah." I shook his hand. His grip renewed the soreness in my palm, but I tried not to show it.

We all looked at the monitor again. Fulton zoomed out more. Dedrick and Bolcan had painted graffiti on a forty-story-high building, the tallest one in Aldonia.

"That's the Regimen building," I said, hardly believing it.

"Yeah," Dedrick said, "we needed it to be somewhere noticeable."

"You spray painted the Regimen building? When did you do that?"

"Last night."

"Why?" It occurred to me that I didn't really know Dedrick, that I had only known one side of him. Dedrick followed the rules. He cared about people and would do anything to save anyone. I never imagined him capable of defacing property, not even Regimen property.

"My brother, Andy, is not known for his patience." He gave me a sideways glance. Was he telling me I should understand because I knew Andy or because I was impatient? "We think he's working on a plan to bust out of Secondary. He'll take all our colonists and probably half the Aldonians with him. Regimen will be all over that."

"So it's a message for Andy. How's he going to see it?" Secondary kids went on fieldtrips, visiting factories, offices, and shops. Our instructors didn't mean to suggest we had options. We didn't. They would determine the best place for each of us. They only wanted us to realize that everyone played a part in working for the good of the whole society. If one person did not cooperate, everyone suffered.

"We're hoping it makes the news," Fulton said. The image on his monitor flipped to the news channel. We watched the news three times a day in Secondary.

Dedrick bit his bottom lip, looking like he had something to say to me. "You sleep okay?" he finally said.

I shrugged and then nodded.

He stepped closer and turned his back on Fulton. Fulton put a headset on and tapped the control panel on his desk.

"How'd it go with the elders?" Dedrick said, keeping his voice low.

The experience had felt so personal that I couldn't come up with a quick answer. "It wasn't what I expected."

"Yeah, that's how my meeting went. Totally not what I expected."

I did not intend to tell him more. He didn't want me to join the Mosheh, so he wouldn't have liked the direction in which our conversation had turned. "You want to work with us?" Elder Rayna had hesitated between words as if my request had come as a surprise.

"I do. I know this is my fault, the colonists in captivity, the destruction of Maxwell." I trembled as I spoke to them, feeling scrutinized and judged.

"Now wait a moment there, Liberty." Elder Lukman stroked his white beard then dropped his hand to the table, extending it in my direction. "You cannot blame yourself. The Regimen made a few discoveries concerning our methods. You are not responsible for that."

"If I hadn't tried to come back that night—"

Elder Lukman's hand went up, silencing me.

Elder Rayna spoke. "Therein lies the problem with your admittance to our group. You lack patience. You don't follow the proper channels. Without discipline and obedience among our members, we would fail."

Excuses came to mind. I had tried to follow the proper channels. I had begged Dedrick to speak with the Mosheh days in advance. Had he? I wouldn't use excuses though. Everything she said was true. I lacked patience. I wanted them to accept me now so I could help rescue the others. One day in a Regimen facility was one day too many for the colonists.

"Camilla gave you those clothes?" Dedrick's gaze skimmed me.

I wore gray workout pants and a thin jacket over a white tank top. "I'm supposed to train today."

A grimace flashed on his face. "Train, huh? You asked to join the Mosheh? To make a commitment?"

"You don't have to worry. Yet. They didn't give me an answer. They just asked Camilla to teach me a few things."

Dedrick averted his gaze and shook his head. "You should've gone out with Miriam to the colonies."

"She went last night, didn't she?" I understood that one ought to be willing to sacrifice to accomplish something, but I couldn't imagine going anywhere last night. I was so tired I doubted my body would've cooperated.

"Yeah, last night." He took a deep breath, his chest rising. A strange look passed through his brown eyes. Uncertainty? Distrust?

"There's someone I want to take you to see," he said.

"Who?" Did he know someone he thought could dissuade me?

"It's a surprise." He smiled.

His expression reminded me of skipping rocks in a stream and strolling under shade trees to see goats on a farm in Maxwell. It made me want to go with him now. I could pretend that Maxwell still stood and that his family still lived there, safe. I could pretend that Dedrick had no underlying feelings of resentment toward me.

"I can't go now. Camilla's expecting me." I couldn't pretend. I had to prove myself to the elders and to *My Friend*. I had to make myself strong and capable, ready for anything.

"Yeah, okay. I'll take you to the training rooms." Dedrick led the way to the ramp I had come down. "They're on the same level as the sleeping quarters. She didn't show them to you?"

"Uh, no. I didn't get much of a tour. I gather Camilla doesn't talk much."

"Camilla?" He glanced with eyebrows knitted together. "It's hard to get her to stop talking."

"Well, then I guess she doesn't like me."

He opened his mouth but then closed it and faced the ramp. We walked in semi-darkness along the patchwork wall, heading toward the single lantern and the wooden door.

He put a hand to the doorknob. "Keep in mind, you asked for this." He yanked open the door.

A girl lunged across the room, grunting and jabbing the air with a black staff. She reached one end of the room, planted the staff, and twisted, high kicking the air. Then she straightened up, brought the staff chest high, and stood panting.

"Hey, Alix," Dedrick said, stepping inside the room.

She dropped the staff and peeled the 3D helmet from her head. Short, jet-black hair fell in layers around her pale, angular face. She turned her eyes of gold and black, flame and coal, to me. Alix was Aldonian. "I thought you changed your mind."

Dedrick shifted, moving so his shoulder nearly blocked my view of her. "Where's Camilla?"

I stepped farther into the room. Mats covered the floor and walls, except for a sunken shelving unit in one corner. The shelves held a flat control panel, a miniature monitor, several 3D helmets, and a bunch of other accessories.

Alix's eyes followed me. "Camilla had something to do."

"Isn't she supposed to train Liberty?" he said.

Alix grinned, her eyes snapping to Dedrick. "We traded jobs."

Dedrick's jaw twitched. "Maybe she should wait." He looked at me. "You eat?"

"I'm not hungry." My stomach growled, but I didn't care. Was he trying to excuse me from training with Alix?

"She might not want to eat, until after." Alix put a toe to the staff and it flipped up into her hand.

"I'll eat later."

Alix turned her flaming eyes to me and gave me a crooked grin. Something about her reminded me of my dream. "Then let's get started."

CHAPTER 14

Dr. Supero strode alongside Sage through a long hallway in the Primary Residence. Light streamed through windows in the classroom doors and shone on the smooth concrete flooring. A mishmash of odors wafted to his nose: stale air, old computer equipment, sweat, and the hint of urine. Somewhere amidst all those odors came a sultry perfume.

His gaze slid to Sage, to her hips that swayed with each step. He missed having her for his assistant, not that she was efficient. She certainly was not. She was a distraction. Did she have someone new? A woman with her curves and powers of seduction . . . Of course she did.

Sage stared at the notepad in her hand, her dark eye makeup glittering. "Paula was apprehended with a woman and a man who DNA tests confirm are her biological parents. They're in Re-education. There was also a teenage boy. His name is Andrew. Tests confirm he's her brother. Of course, he's in Secondary."

"Yes, I am well aware." Dr. Supero fixed his eyes on the glass door at the end of the hallway. "Her entire biological family is in custody."

"As far as we know." Sage brushed her finger along the screen, searching records. "She is not very informative in counseling sessions, but she's spoken with the other children about missing her family. She also talks about the food they ate and about canning, chores, God. It's all on video if you would like to see it."

"I have seen it already."

"I must say. . ." She swung her arm down and held the notepad at her side. "I find her very interesting. It's hard to imagine how her life must've been."

"There's nothing to imagine." He sneered. "You've studied primates. These people have simply chosen to regress. They have rejected human progress, evolution."

"I suppose."

"You suppose?" He stopped at the door and spun to face her. She couldn't be serious. Did the notion of living in the wild appeal to her?

Sage pushed open the glass door using a hip and one hand. Sunlight turned her copper hair to flames and revealed hairline wrinkles around her eyes and shiny red lips. "Well, there she is." She gestured to indicate the little girl sitting alone at a patio table.

"Very good." Supero allowed himself another second to soak in Sage's beauty and then turned to the stringy-haired girl. "Hello, there."

Chin down, the girl peered up through eyes the color of mud.

Dr. Supero scanned the grounds, smiling to appear friendly as he sat opposite the girl. Children played nearby, swinging, fighting, climbing on a green and brown fort . . . One little girl attempted to slice the rubber surface of the playground with a stick. Two nannies leaned against the facility wall, talking to each other, their eyes not on the children. No one looked over here at the furniture on the cement patio. Still. This did not seem like the ideal location for an interrogation.

He faced the girl, leaned forward, and smiled. "I am Dr. Supero. I hope you do not mind speaking with me for a few minutes."

She looked at her hands and shrugged.

"Perhaps you remember me from the physical examination when you first came to Aldonia."

She wrapped her arms around her waist. Still no eye contact.

He shouldn't have brought up the examination. It had not been a pleasant experience for her.

"I remember you." He strove to convey gentleness and concern. "Your name is Paula."

She said nothing.

He had little experience speaking with children. What tricks could he use to make her speak? Perhaps flattery. "I have heard many good things about you since you've entered Primary." He leaned back, assuming a more relaxed posture. "The nannies report that you have been very helpful with chores, especially in the garden."

She gave no indication that she had even heard him.

Perhaps a different tactic. The nannies and teachers were not permitted to mention her family or the others who lived out there. Only counselors could bring it up. "I imagine you learned much about growing your own food out there from your parents."

Her head lifted. She glanced but then lowered her head again. A chip in the ice.

He grinned. "I would like to understand how life was out there. Would you be willing to answer my questions?"

She made another glance in his direction.

He leaned forward, rested his forearms on his thighs, and spoke in a low voice. "I believe we do things much differently here on this side of the fence. Perhaps we could compare."

Her gaze lifted to his. She stared through big black pupils surrounded by dirty little irises. "Why does your beard look like that? It looks like a flower."

"My beard?" He smoothed his goatee. "A flower? No, no, it is not a—" An idea came to him. He clasped his hands on the table and leaned closer to her. "I will answer your question, but then you must answer one of mine. My beard, it is called a goatee and it is trimmed in the shape of a star. It is *not* a flower."

"Why? Why is it like that?"

"Why? I . . ." How to explain to a child? "Have you ever sat on a rooftop at night, after curfew when the city lights are off? Er, well, not city lights for you."

"I've watched the stars at night. Me and my brothers—" She gasped, her hand flying to her mouth, her eyes popping open. Two fried eggs, shiny whites around strange brown yolks.

So . . . Andrew, the teen in Secondary, was not her only brother. Supero smiled, trying to appear disarming. "You understand me, then. You know what it is like to gaze upon luminous stars in a sky of black velvet. A person cannot look down to see a star. You must look up. A single star is full of energy, magnetism, power. The human race has always stood in awe of stars. They became the source of myths, representations of deities."

"What does that mean?"

"A deity is a god. I understand that you believe in a god. Perhaps your god came from one of those stars."

"So your beard is shaped like a star because it reminds you of God?"

"No. *You* believe in God. *I* do not. I believe in power. But it is my turn now. I answered your question, so you must answer mine." He had her now. He needed to choose his questions wisely, not waste words. "I know there were more in your community than the few we have in custody. I would like you to tell me about your physicians, your doctors."

"Doctors?"

"Yes. Who did you go to when you were sick?"

"My mommy," she whispered, her eyes dropping pitifully.

"Yes, but what about a broken arm or something worse?"

"We take care of each other. Dedrick once had a broken—" Her eyes popped. She gasped and covered her mouth.

Dr. Supero had sucked in a breath at the name, too. Did she refer to the same Dedrick that had been with Liberty? This was her brother?

He forced a pleasant smile. He needed more. "Dedrick had a broken *what?*"

She wrapped her arms around her waist. Her gaze snapped to her lap. "Nothing."

"It's okay. We already know about your brother Dedrick. He's being helped, too." The lie would motivate her to speak.

Her gaze crept back to his. Her pink face turned white. "Helped?"

"Sure. He's in our Re-education Facility. Would you like me to give him a message? I will do that for you." He had the upper hand now. She would tell him everything he wanted to know. "But you must first answer my question. I need to know about your doctors." At some point, he had stopped smiling and his voice had turned hard.

She shrunk back. "I'm not telling you anything. I don't want you to talk to Dedrick." She jumped to her feet and shouted in a shrill voice, "Leave him alone. Why can't you all just leave us alone? I want to go home." She took a step, ready to dash away.

Dr. Supero grabbed her by the arms, catching strands of hair in his grip. He forced her to face him. "You have no home to go to," he spit. "It's all been burned to ash."

Anger and disbelief showed in her teary, mud-puddle eyes. "That's not true."

"It is true. This is your home now, little girl. The sooner you talk, the sooner you will heal and find your place in society."

She twisted and jerked, trying to free herself. "Let me go!"

He tightened his grip and pulled her closer. "Answer me first. Who are your doctors?"

She leaned toward him, her head dipping down. Was she going to whisper the answer?

Teeth sunk into Supero's upper arm, daggers stinging through his sleeve. Dr. Supero released his hold and shoved her.

She took off running.

He stood up, rubbing his arm. Her bite had not punctured the sleeve, but his skin would probably bruise.

Paula raced to the two nannies that stood leaning against the wall. One of them stooped to listen to her. The little animal belonged in Re-education along with her parents. Dedrick was her brother, huh?

Dr. Supero grinned. He would find a way to use that.

He strode to the glass door. As he reached for the door handle, his flexi-phone buzzed. A call from Sid.

He tapped the phone to answer it and opened the door. "What is it you want? Be quick. I am busy." He stepped out of the sun and into the shady hallway and stale air.

"She's gone." This was not the smooth voice of the kid Supero knew. The voice dripped with desperation, a disturbing sound in the quiet facility. "I want you to help me get her back."

"*She* who?" Dr. Supero took a few steps and then stopped, his gaze wandering to the window of the nearest classroom door. Kids sat hunched over computer tables.

He knew whom Sid meant. He did not want to hear her name, but he needed to hear it.

"Who?" he shouted into his flexi-phone.

The kids in the classroom looked up.

"Liberty," Sid said. "Chief Varden helped me. He arranged things, you know, so I could have her for a while. I took her to this water pump station. But she's gone now. That kid took her."

"What. Kid?" He knew the answer even before he asked. Dedrick rescued Liberty. Liberty was no longer in Re-Ed. She was on the streets. Free.

White gnats swirled in his vision. Red flashed. Dr. Supero slammed his fists against the wall. A jolt of pain. "No!" he shrieked. This could not be happening. They'd had her in custody.

Doors creaked open. Faces appeared. Figures emerged from classrooms. Voices. Questions.

Dr. Supero could not make sense of them. He could barely hear them over the shrill voice that rattled obscenities through his raw throat.

A door flung open and banged a wall, the result of a swift kick. Did he do that? His fist went through a window, the sting giving him a shred of comfort. The harsh voice continued to shriek. A deafening sound.

Other voices filled the air, and then hands gripped his wrists and yanked his arms behind his back.

CHAPTER 15

Alix began my training with few words. "Let's see what you got," she said, pacing like a wild animal, her eyes locked on me.

I tried to pinpoint the reason she reminded me of my dream. As the emaciated man sowed weeds, I had felt cold and sickened at the presence of evil. I wanted to have hope when the second man appeared, but the evil had spread so far and the weeds had grown so thick. It seemed hopeless.

Without warning, Alix slipped her foot behind my calf and shoved.

I landed on my backside and lay there for a second. Then I pushed myself up on my elbows. "What was that? I thought you were going to train me."

My Friend fluttered in the back of my mind, calming my temper. His presence had become constant since I arrived at the Mosheh's Control Center. Aside from the dream, which may or may not have been from him, I had no distinct message from him. I simply had the assurance of his presence and a gentle prompting to make myself ready.

Alix reached down and yanked me to my feet. The gold of her eyes intensified. "The first thing you need to learn: stay alert." She paced again, her hands on her hips, her eyes on the mat. "The Mosheh does not seek to hurt, only to save and to remain hidden." She spun toward me, her leg flying out. An attack!

I jumped back, avoiding the impact and gaining a degree of confidence in my abilities.

She was still moving, sinewy limbs slicing the air, a figure in my peripheral vision.

My hair bristled.

She was directly behind me, and her arm slid around my neck.

My hands shot to her arm, a limb of muscle and tendons. I couldn't pry it away. It was Sid's attack all over again. I considered cracking my head into hers.

"The Mosheh seek to avoid contact with the Regimen," she said over my shoulder. "But you'll need to learn to defend yourself." She released me and shoved me forward.

I faced her and assumed a fighter's stance, feet spread and fists ready. "So teach me."

She laughed with an unfriendly glint in her eyes. Then she turned away and sauntered to the shelves. "Here." She tossed me a 3D helmet. "We'll begin with basic self-defense moves."

The helmet fit snug. A bluish world surrounded me, an ocean along one horizon, palm trees on the other, sand at my feet. Sounds of wind and seagulls tickled my ears, then footfalls.

Alix stepped into view, manipulating controls on her wristband. She looked like a video game character, her features cleaner but more dramatic than in real life. Her hair stood up artistically on one side. Her eyes glowed. She wore camouflage clothes, high boots, and an empty gun belt.

Two figures appeared and faced each other, one a blonde woman, the other a Unity Trooper in uniform. They stood with their feet shoulder-width apart and their hands at their sides.

"Do what the girl does," Alix said, facing me and taking the same stance as the Unity Trooper.

The Trooper grabbed the woman's wrist and yanked. The woman staggered forward a few steps but then stopped. She bent her arm, brought her elbow low and leaned in, breaking the Trooper's grip. Then she took off.

"So I'm the girl and you're the—"

Alix grabbed my wrist, her grip tight.

Instinct made me want to pull away, but I did as the 3D woman had done and leaned in, bending and twisting my arm. I broke Alix's grip with ease. Then I took a few steps back and laughed. It was easy.

"That's when the Unity Trooper draws his taser gun," Alix said, putting a hand to her belt and imitating the movement of drawing a gun. She pretended to shoot me in the face. "We'll cover that later."

The 3D woman reappeared in front of the Unity Trooper for the next demonstration. The self-defense lessons went on for an hour, move after move without break. Then we removed the 3D helmets and Alix tested me on every move. I remembered them all without exception.

After the last test, she put her hands on her hips and glared at me, her lips twisting to the side. "Good," she said and turned away. "We'll move on to weapons and then some more aggressive fighting moves." She leaned over the control panel on the shelving unit. A target appeared above her, on the wall.

I came up beside her and watched her tap out commands. "Did Camilla really have something she had to do?"

Alix's eyes swiveled to me and then back to the monitor. She tapped the controls a few more times and rummaged through different game accessories. She handed me a controller shaped like a pistol, took one for herself, and walked to the far side of the mat.

I followed. "I get the feeling she doesn't like me."

Alix gripped the pistol with both hands and stood with her feet shoulder-width apart. She extended her arms toward a target on the far wall and fired. A red dot appeared on the target, directly in the center. She lowered the pistol and looked at me. "Are you here to train?"

I sighed and assumed a shooting posture. I aimed and shot. A red dot appeared on the edge of the target.

"Again," she said. "Focus on the sight, keep the sight on the target, and don't lock your knees."

For hours, she taught me methods of self-defense, marksmanship, and fighting. I had shed my jacket, and sweat drenched my tank top, turning it from white to gray. I landed on the mat over a dozen times. Everything from my chin to my shin ached. Bruises would color my skin tomorrow. Alix's mean glare had scorched my mind so that I couldn't close my eyes without seeing coal ringed with flames. Her cold attitude irritated but challenged me.

Hours later, we took a break. She gave me water and a tasteless nutrition bar. Then she left me alone. Twenty minutes later, she returned and we were back on the mat. She tested my self-defense moves again and then led me through strategy games. These took place in a 3D version of Aldonia, in an area familiar to me.

"You really know the streets and alleys," she said as she shut off the games. "That'll help." It didn't feel like a compliment so much as an observation.

"Thanks." I sat cross-legged on the mat, not wanting to get up. Not wanting to move. I could picture myself sprawling out right here and falling asleep. It probably wasn't bedtime, but my stomach told me it was past dinnertime, and my body demanded a long rest.

Alix gathered the 3D helmets, bands, and controllers we had used. She arranged them on the shelves, taking more care than I would've expected from her given her rough behavior with me and with everything we used during training. When she finished, she turned around, folded her arms, and stared at me.

"Camilla's from Maxwell," she said. "Her house is ashes, and her family's moving away."

My heart wrenched. I understood Camilla's attitude toward me. She, and the other Maxwell colonists, blamed me for what had happened. I should've expected that. It didn't explain Alix's attitude. Her eyes identified her as Aldonian.

"You can't expect everyone to like you, even if the elders allow you to join us."

"You're not from Maxwell. What's your problem with me?"

She smirked. "The Mosheh's been compromised. Maybe I blame you."

Maybe they all blamed me, Aldonian and colonists alike. I would have to live with that. I would not give up my mission.

Alix extended a hand to me. "Come on. Get yourself something to eat. I need to get out of here."

I grabbed her hand and let her yank me to my feet. "Where're you going?"

"Your old stomping grounds." She grinned. "Breeder Facility."

"Those were never my stomping grounds. I was there for a day." I knew, even as I spoke, that she already knew that.

She opened the door and backed into it, letting me go first. "There's a kid in there whose been snooping around. His name is Dash. He cleans the labs. Last week he uncovered a secret."

"What secret? And why does that make him a candidate for rescue?" I stood under the sole lantern in this area. Light traveled up the ramp to the lower level, but it didn't reach us here. Other lights pierced the darkness farther away, in the direction of the dining hall. Savory aromas filled the air. My stomach growled.

"It doesn't. It just makes it his time for rescue." She headed toward the dining hall. "The breeders are told that one girl's fertilized eggs are frozen and implanted in someone else, years later. But it's not true. They only say that so a girl won't feel possessive of the baby she carries, her baby." She paused and looked at me. "But Dash, he discovered the truth, and he shared that secret with one of the breeders. In a few days, every breeder is going to know. And in a few more days, he'll be in Re-Ed. If not for us."

She stopped at the opening to the dining hall and pulled an old-fashioned cell phone from a pocket of her pants. "One day of training is nothing. I'll see you tomorrow."

"Thanks," I said to her back. She was halfway to the ramp, on her way to the control center.

I filled up on beans and rice, sitting alone in the dining hall, and then decided to go lie down. Camilla or someone had left a bag of toiletries on my bed. I took them and washed up, then headed back to the sleeping quarters.

Strings of tiny lights hung from the top edge of the sleeping quarters, setting them apart from other mishmashed structures. Between the boys' and girls' quarters sat an arrangement of furniture: a worn couch, two armchairs, a wooden chair, and little tables with lamps.

Hurried footsteps sounded behind me.

I glanced over my shoulder as a girl flew past me. "Clara," she shouted, whipping back the curtain to the girls' quarters. "We need you on surveillance. Come now!"

Clara, a thirty-something petite woman with a red bob, burst through the doorway. The two of them dashed past me, creating a breeze.

Their urgency transferred to me, a surge of fuel to an idling engine. I tossed the toiletries onto an armchair and took off after them.

By the time I reached the top of the ramp, the two girls had cleared it. I stared for a moment at the commotion below. The girls ran to a station under the array of wall monitors, the younger girl talking nonstop to the older one. A few other kids sat at stations, every one of them enwrapped in their work, talking to someone through a headset or manipulating control panels. One kid bolted from one side of the station to the other. Dedrick and Elder Lukman stood together talking.

I headed for them, taking long strides. Something was going down, something unexpected. If it had to do with the colonists, I wanted in. I wanted to help. So what if I had received only one day of training?

The images on the overhead monitors flipped from scene to scene, pausing a few seconds on each. It was dark, after curfew. How could the kids watching the monitors see anything? What were they looking for?

"I need to go up there." Dedrick's voice rose above the chatter.

My attention snapped to him and the white-haired elder.

Elder Lukman mumbled a reply, his head shaking. I heard only the words "swarming with Unity Troopers."

Dedrick stood with his legs apart. He rolled forward on the balls of his feet while forming and releasing a fist. "They've obviously got our surveillance Intel. We'll stay in the dark if someone doesn't go up there." He turned away, ran a hand through his hair, then faced the elder again. "You know I can do this. Let me find out where they are."

Elder Lukman dropped his gaze and shook his head again. He looked at Dedrick and flung a hand in the air. "Fine. So go!"

Dedrick took two steps backward. "I might know where they're headed."

"Go find our kids," Elder Lukman said.

Dedrick turned and bolted, smacking into me. "Oh, shoot, sorry." He grabbed my arms as if to keep me from falling, or to keep his own balance.

"What's going on?" I said. "Where're you going?"

He gave a headshake, not meeting my gaze. "He did it, Andy, he broke out. I gotta find him, see what I can do." He tried to walk around me, but I kept pace with him.

"Alone? You're going alone?"

"I'm the only rescuer available. We weren't expecting this."

"Let me go with you." I grabbed his arm and stopped him from walking.

His gaze traveled in the direction of Elder Lukman. "I don't think that's a good idea. I'm just going to scout anyway. Maybe you can help here." He glanced at me and jogged away, heading for one of the dark tunnels.

I wanted to go. My legs nearly propelled me forward, after him. This was it, and now was the time. Camilla and Alix had gone on a rescue at the Breeder Facility. There was no one else to go with him. Dedrick shouldn't go alone.

Dedrick disappeared down the dark tunnel.

Tearing my gaze from the shadows, I scanned the control center. As busy as everyone was, no one noticed me. I could go with him and no one would care.

Then again, the Mosheh had been saving people for years. They didn't need me. I needed to trust them. If I ever hoped to join them officially, I needed patience. I needed to accept that I might have no part in rescuing the Maxwell colonists.

My eyes had strayed back to the dark tunnel. I found myself rubbing the sore spot on my palm, the healing skin. Dedrick shouldn't go alone. I wasn't Mosheh yet. I didn't have to follow their rules. I knew the streets of Aldonia. I could help.

My hands had tightened into fists. I screamed in my mind. I could not take off without permission. And with only one day of training, I knew they would never let me—

"Liberty."

I spun to face the man who called my name and sucked in a breath of air. I hadn't heard Elder Lukman approach.

"Take this." He grabbed my hand and secured a bulky watch around my wrist. "This button here . . ." He pressed a button on the side of the analog clock face. ". . . will allow you to communicate with me. Keep me informed. And keep Dedrick out of trouble. He's one of our best, but I'm worried his judgment might be affected by, well, you better go."

"You're letting me go with him?"

"Go on now." He took a step back and swept both hands at me. "Might need to run to catch up."

I ran.

CHAPTER 16

Pulsing light crept through Dr. Supero's eyelids. Pain rushed to his head. He breathed and pushed himself up.

"What happened here?" he said, rubbing his head with a sore hand that didn't want to uncurl.

He sat alone in his office on the suede loveseat in the darkest corner. The monitors over his desk flipped through random images and files, providing a bluish light that throbbed with the rhythm of his headache. The light fell on a messy stack of little boxes on the glossy desktop. His favorite abstract painting leaned against the wall, the frame damaged.

A muddled memory came to mind. He had grabbed his desk chair and whipped it against the wall. A few other things went flying, too.

Dr. Supero took a deep breath and looked at his hand. It hurt to open it. Pink knuckles, a cut on his thumb, scratches and dried blood on his forearm . . . As long as he didn't have any glass in the cuts, he'd be fine. He shouldn't have punched the window. Or the wall.

Security guards had escorted him from the Primary Residence, reporting the incident as they marched outside. He sat on the curb, waiting to see what would happen next. People gawked at him as they passed. "Chief Varden says to let him go," one guard said to the others. "What? Are you kidding me?" "That's what he said. Give him a warning and let him go."

The marble-top coffee table sat askew. Dr. Supero pushed it with a foot and stood up. He grabbed an armchair to steady himself as he checked the time on his flexi-phone. Had he really slept until five? He also had six messages. He didn't remember hearing his phone ring. He tapped controls to see who left the messages. Sid, Sid, Sid . . . all of them Sid.

He sighed and returned the call as he stumbled to his desk.

"Hey, man, where you been?" Sid's voice came through the flexi-phone. "How come you don't answer my calls?"

"What do you think I am doing?" Dr. Supero tapped a control on his desk to turn on the overhead track lights. He squinted at the burst of light then set them to low. Another tap and he switched the monitors off.

"Well, you cut me off this morning, but I wasn't done talking."

"Yes, I know what I did." Dr. Supero picked up one of the boxes from his desk. It held bandages. Behind the boxes lay the remains of his coffee mug, broken pieces placed inside the biggest piece. "So you want help finding Liberty, do you?"

"Yeah, that's right."

Dr. Supero grabbed bandages and a packet of antibacterial ointment and headed for the bathroom. "I cannot believe Chief Varden let you take her from Re-Ed. I cannot even imagine how you accomplished that."

"Yeah, I'll give you the details later. Varden don't know she got away from me yet. Least I don't think so. And I don't want him to know. I just want her back."

Dr. Supero unfastened his flexi-phone and set it with the bandages on the granite sink top. He glimpsed at his image in the mirror, at ashen skin and puffy eyes. "If we are not going to use the Citizen Safety Station, how do you intend to find her?"

"I think I know where they went, same place I was planning to take her."

"You took her to a water pump station." He cranked the faucet on and plunged his hands into the sink, the water stinging the cuts.

"No, I know," Sid said. "That's where the chief told me to take her. That was the plan. But I had a plan of my own, somewhere else for us to go. I'm not giving her back."

Dr. Supero laughed while wincing at the pain the soap caused his wounds. Sid planned to betray Chief Varden. "Where are you?"

"What?"

He shut the faucet off and took a towel to his hands and arms. "Tell me where you are and I will pick you up. You said you know where she is. Give me a few minutes. We will go and get her."

Sid gave the address of his apartment building and said he'd wait outside. Dr. Supero tended his wounds and returned to his desk. He pulled up two pictures and displayed them on the monitors over his desk: one of Dedrick, the other of Paula.

If Liberty would not give him the information he needed, he would get it from Dedrick. He could use threats. Dedrick would not want to see his little sister suffer.

The office door slid open.

Dr. Supero shut the monitors off and swiveled his chair around. It creaked and tilted.

Muse stepped into the room, running a hand through his frizzy black hair. He wore a loose maroon shirt that matched his eyes and jeans so tight they revealed the entire shape of his kneecaps.

"Um, excuse me, Doctor." He toyed with the gold loop that curled into his nostril. "You okay?"

Dr. Supero stood up, glaring. Had he no privacy? "I am fine."

Muse's Adam's apple bobbed inside his long neck. "Okay. I-I tried cleaning up after . . ." He pressed his lips together and made a goofy, lipless smile. "You know, after you trashed the place. And I rescheduled your appointments for the day, but there's someone here." He flung a lanky arm out and pointed at the door.

"I do not permit unscheduled appointments."

Muse opened his mouth to reply, but a woman pushed past him, a tall woman with spiky orange hair. The Regional Secretary of the Department of the Environment. The sea urchin who irritated him at every council meeting by pushing her agenda over his.

"Hello, Dr. Supero," she said, extending a hand . . . or rather, a sea urchin tube foot. "We missed you at the last couple of council meetings." She glanced around the room.

"Yes, I am sure you did." He shook her hand, wincing as she squeezed his fresh wounds. "What brings you to my door?"

"May I sit down?" She raised her penciled brows and then headed for the seating arrangement in the back corner of the room.

He followed, irritation propelling him along. "I am a busy man. Perhaps you should've called first. I am not always in my office."

"So I hear." She seated herself on the loveseat and smoothed her shiny coffee-brown pants while staring at the skewed coffee table. "The council is concerned about you."

"Oh?" He approached the coffee table, shoved it into place with his foot, and peered down his nose at her.

"We received word of the unfortunate incident at the Primary Residence this morning."

He flinched and stepped back. The report had already reached the Aldonia City Council?

"We held an emergency meeting this afternoon. A member of council suggested that your health issue may have been to blame."

"My health issue?" He regretted his question. He did not want her to be specific. He did not want to hear her say—

"Your brain tumor." Her expression brightened as she said it. "We are all aware of the variety of symptoms such a condition can cause. Your altered mental state at the facility—"

"What is the reason for your visit?"

She blinked. "The council has decided that a vocation change is in order."

"A vocation change?"

"The duties and responsibilities you face as Head Physician are quite extensive. We feel you would benefit from a less stressful job. As it turns out, Aldonia's RCT University is in need of someone to head up their Department of Genetics, so we have decided—"

"The council is recommending that Aldonia's Head Physician transfer to the University?" His chest tightened. Strength drained from his limbs. "Do you not know the work I do? The contributions I have made over the years? And who are you to tell me this?"

"Who am I?" Her brows lifted. "I suppose you haven't heard. You missed the elections at the last council meeting."

Dr. Supero's eyes threatened to burst from his head. He staggered back. "No."

She stood and extended her hand as if she thought he would want to shake it in congratulations. "I was elected President of Aldonia's City Council. I won by a narrow margin."

"No." Head shaking, he glanced at her outstretched hand.

"Yes." She withdrew her hand.

"Let me guess . . ." He sneered. The woman already had too much power and influence. "Are you also on the Medical Evaluation Panel?"

She chuckled and swaggered to the door. "Of course not."

"Wait! When does this vocation change take effect?"

"Effective immediately." She stopped at the door. The door slid open.

Muse stood on the other side, gawking. He cleared his throat and turned away. He must have been listening. Could he hear through the door?

"You have a new residence on campus and two days to vacate the Head Physician's residence. And, until further notice, you are forbidden from visiting the Primary and Secondary Facilities." She smiled, venom seeping from her spines. "We wish you the best."

Muse turned around and sauntered into the room, watching the sea urchin over his shoulder. The door slid shut. He locked his maroon eyes onto Dr. Supero. "Need me to get you a box?"

"No."

"Do you need, uh, like a doctor?"

"I *am* a doctor. You may go. I do not need you at all."

CHAPTER 17

Why hadn't Andy waited? Didn't he get the message? Of course he got the message. He was impatient, thought this was his calling, overestimated his abilities . . .

Dedrick clipped his flashlight to his belt and slid into the seat of the tunnel kart. He flipped the headlights on as he turned the ignition key. He got a clicking sound instead of the rattle of the engine. He tried again. It figured the only kart available was the one with the messed up starter. Last time he had to whack the starter with a hammer to get the thing going.

He hopped out of the kart and flung open the storage box in the back. The top layer held folded capes and various glasses. He stuffed a cape and night vision glasses into his jacket pockets. He should've grabbed a trench coat before setting out. The Citizen Safety Station had designed an algorithm to look for the mottled pattern on their capes in all the surveillance footage. Maybe he could wear the cape wrong side out. The solid black would work better at night anyway.

Dedrick dug through the tools, looking for a hammer. He didn't have time for this. Unity Troopers and drones were probably swarming Aldonia. How could Andy and the others possibly get to a safe place without detection? What would the Regimen do once they caught them?

He found the hammer.

"Dedrick, wait." A girl's voice echoed in the tunnel.

Dedrick peered. A girl emerged from the darkness, her gray workout pants and white jacket growing in visibility as she jogged closer. Liberty?

He rolled his eyes and huffed. Did she plan to go with him? Maybe she only had a message for him. He grabbed the hammer, stomped to the front of the kart, and whacked the starter. Mechanically-inclined members of the Mosheh had designed the tunnel karts ten years ago using the frames of golf carts and workhorse tractors, and creating simple engines that ran on natural gas. They were easy to fix, but they broke down a lot.

Liberty appeared beside him, blocking his path to the driver's side. "I'm glad I caught you." Her gaze snapped to the engine. "Got a problem?"

He stepped around her, slid halfway into the seat, and turned the ignition key. Click.

"How's the battery?" she said.

"The battery's not the problem," he said, avoiding eye contact.

"Oh, it's the starter?" She skimmed past him and went to the storage box.

He nodded, irritation yielding to admiration. He still didn't want her along. Too many risks. One day of training was nothing. She wasn't ready. "What're you doing here?"

She zipped to the engine, a screwdriver in hand. "Go ahead and start it." She touched the screwdriver to the posts on the relay, bypassing the starter solenoid. That was going to be his next move.

He turned the key and the engine rattled to life.

She tossed the screwdriver into the storage box and slid in beside him, as if she expected he'd take her along. Had she considered the response the elders would have to her impulsive decision?

He stared for a moment, debating whether to warn her or not. He didn't like the idea of her joining the Mosheh anyway. "They're not gonna like you going with me. It'll ruin your chances of joining the Mosheh, if that's really what you want to do."

"Elder Lukman told me to go," she said.

His mouth fell open. "Really?"

She nodded. "What's the plan?"

He grunted and stepped on the gas pedal. The kart lurched forward. The headlights cast a dim beam on the gritty concrete floor and brick walls. The breeze cooled his burning cheeks.

Two beats later, he forced himself to answer her. "I need to get above ground so I can spot them."

"Think they'll try to come here?"

"Here? They don't know where we are. The colony kids know we exist, but that's it. The Aldonians—"

"Aldonians? You mean Aldonians escaped too?"

"Uh, yeah." He slowed a bit, cranked the steering wheel, and whipped around a sharp corner. Liberty's hand flew to the dashboard. "Nearly two dozen kids escaped, eighteen of them ours. Guess they all worked together. Colonists wouldn't have a clue where to go, but the Aldonians—" *Of course!* He tapped his earphone. "Fulton, you there?"

"Yeah, Dedrick, we got nothing." Fulton's voice came through the earpiece. "These kids are in the holes and corners. I think you're right about them snagging our surveillance Intel."

"Somehow their guy got to Finley before our guy did," Dedrick said.

Liberty's head turned at Finley's name.

"Listen," Dedrick said to Fulton, "I need you to get the names of the Aldonians in the group, see which of them have connections with outsiders. They couldn't have done this without outside help."

"Copy that. I'm on it."

A pile of rubble lay ahead in the tunnel, chunks of cement from the ceiling. They'd have to fix that someday soon and check on the integrity of this tunnel. They needed this route to reach key locations in the underground network.

Dedrick weaved to avoid hitting the pile, bringing the passenger side close to the wall.

Liberty leaned in. "What'd you say about Finley? What's he got to do with this?"

"With the escape? Nothing. Finley works for the Environmental Stewardship Units and repairs things in the city, things like surveillance cameras."

"Yeah." Her tone said she wanted more of an explanation. Of course she already knew Finley's vocation. He was her ex-roommate's boyfriend.

They neared the brick wall that separated the Mosheh tunnels from the ones Aldonians could access. Dedrick stopped the vehicle and jumped out. He flipped the locks on one side of the hidden door, one high and one low.

"Finley used to give us Intel on the surveillance cameras," he said, the tunnel amplifying his voice. "Told us which ones were down."

Liberty stood by the other end of the hidden door, watching. She must've gotten out to help. She found the other two locks and flipped them. "Finley works with you guys?"

"Not quite. He goes through a middleman. Finley's just a kid trying to get his hands on anything concerning 3D games. He's like an addict." He never could understand Aldonians' obsession over video games. He hated the intense feelings they generated in him and the effect they had on his personality.

"Wow, I never knew," she said.

"Somehow Andy got his hands on that Intel. They've got outside help."

Dedrick grabbed a horizontal steel bar in the middle of the moveable wall and yanked the wall onto the track that allowed it to slide sideways. Then he threw his weight into the job and slid the wall aside. The stench of sewage wafted through the dank air. Dim lights showed in the distance, down the tunnel that now stretched out before them.

The engine of the tunnel kart revved. Liberty sat in the driver's seat, ready to roll through the opening. Apparently, once she knew what to do, she acted without hesitation. That could work in her favor. Or against her.

Dedrick motioned for her to drive through and then dragged the wall back into place. Liberty relinquished the driver's seat, sliding over without his asking. He took the wheel and drove on. The tunnels grew damper and narrower. They would soon have to abandon the kart and walk.

Fulton's call came through. "We got something, Dedrick. One of the girls, an Aldonian named Wren, makes contact with a delivery guy by the name of Kelsey almost every time he comes to the residence. We reviewed footage of Kelsey. Found him on streets near a closed-off area, the old city center. You know where that is?"

"Yeah. Good work." Dedrick stepped on the brake pedal as he approached intersecting tunnels.

"Where're we headed?" Liberty said.

"Old city center. I told you there are places Aldonians can go without the Regimen knowing, remember?"

"Yeah, like where Sid wanted to take me."

"Right. Well, we're headed for one of those places. Kids on the street call them Gray Zones. They're abandoned buildings or neighborhoods the Regimen has no use for. They're usually fenced off, but nothing kids can't get through. Occasionally a drone will fly by, but there's no surveillance in Gray Zones. Unless Unity Troopers are searching the area."

CHAPTER 18

Dedrick climbed the metal ladder, his boots clanking on the rungs and Liberty clanking along behind him. It felt good to stretch after stooping to walk through the last tunnel. He stopped near the top of the ladder, close to the manhole cover, and tapped his earphone.

"Hey, Fulton, brief me on the location of Unity Troopers. How many are in the area?"

"Doesn't look good," Fulton said. "They're everywhere. They swarmed Secondary and fanned out from there, searching on foot, bike, and car. Even got drones searching. Don't know how those kids are doing it. Nobody knows where they are."

"We're at the access point, an old manhole on 2nd Street, corner of Main. How many troopers are we gonna see?"

"Give me a second. I'll get a count."

Dedrick handed Liberty his taser flashlight. He had given her a cape and night-vision glasses before they abandoned the tunnel kart. She wore the cape black side out, the way he did. The glasses hung from the neckline of her white tank top. They would need the night vision since the area had no streetlights. Bonus feature: the glasses would prevent Unity Troopers from getting a retina scan.

Liberty shined the light overhead on the metal and cement manhole cover.

"Not entirely sure but . . ." Fulton's voice came through Dedrick's earpiece. "Three cars drove in there a few minutes ago. Two troopers are on foot. We're working on intercepting the audio and video. Should have the GPS on the cars soon."

He couldn't wait. He needed to get above ground now. Dedrick fished night-vision glasses from his pocket and put them on, making everything a greenish hue.

With an arm draped over a rung, Liberty drew her glasses from the neckline of her shirt.

"You wait down here," he said, his command stopping her from donning the glasses. "I'm gonna check things out."

"No." She slid the glasses over her eyes. "I'm staying with you."

"Did you bring a weapon?" He knew she hadn't. He only asked so she would realize she wasn't prepared for this.

"No."

"You ever been to the old city center? Know your way around it?"

"No."

"Unity Troopers are crawling all over, probably even drones."

She gave a single nod, then gripped the sides of the ladder and placed a foot on a higher rung. "I'm ready."

Dedrick sighed, releasing his frustration, and reached up to the manhole cover. He was putting Liberty at risk again. She should've gone with Miriam. She'd be safe in the forest, probably sleeping under the stars right now.

Using his head and hands, he pushed the cold cement cover up enough to get a peek. Rain poured down. Blue and orange lights flashed at the nearest intersection. No sirens announced the vehicle.

He dropped the cover back into place. A drone might have caught the movement, but the troopers in the car most likely scanned the buildings.

"Well?" Liberty stared up at him, the glasses giving her bug eyes.

"Waiting for a car to pass. I told you troopers are everywhere. I'd prefer you remain here."

"I'm going with you."

After waiting a few seconds, he heaved the cover up and scraped it to the side. Rain beat on his head as he climbed out. Weeds poking through cracks in the crumbling pavement brushed him. The taillights of the Regimen vehicle reflected on the broken ground, shrinking as the car rolled away. Orange and blue lights pulsed on the remains of a building in the distance. Searchlights cut through the dark sky, lighting up raindrops.

Liberty climbed from the manhole and glanced around.

"That way," Dedrick said, indicating the direction with a nod. "Find cover."

She took off, the black cape flapping around her. She headed for a boarded up two-story commercial row of buildings.

Straddling the manhole, he scraped the cover over the hole and kicked it into place, then bolted after Liberty. As he reached the remains of a sidewalk, glass and gravel crunched under his boots. Weeds skimmed his shins.

"In here," Liberty said. A board hung askew over a wide window. Her face appeared through the darkness inside the shop. Then it disappeared.

He pushed the board aside a few inches.

The slightest movement overhead, silent as a ghost, made him freeze. He dared not look, but he knew what he would see. A drone hovered over the buildings, directly above him. Had it detected their movements?

Dedrick held his breath. Rainwater rolled down his face, into his eyes and mouth. His heartbeat sounded in his ears. He could feel the thumping of his heart against his ribs, his blood coursing through his veins, the hair on his neck standing on end.

It would take a single step for him to disappear inside the building, but drones detected movement. He would have to wait until it moved on. Did it still hover above him? Would he know when it had gone? Drones moved without sound.

A beam of light ripped through the darkness, so close he could reach out and touch it. It swung left and right, moving closer. The drone had detected him.

Dedrick lunged into the building, forcing himself through the narrow opening between the window frame and board. Rough edges scraped his cheek and shoulder.

"We've been detected!" he shouted.

Liberty spun around, the beam of the flashlight swinging to him. She crunched over debris, coming from the far side of the shop. Broken shelving units and a metal cabinet lay on the floor, items too damaged to interest scavengers.

He took two long strides to get to her, then snatched the flashlight and shined it on the walls. They needed a way out. "Drone spotted us. It'll signal the troopers. Sometimes these buildings connect. We need to get moving before—"

A siren erupted. Blue lights pulsed through the opening between the board and window frame. A car screeched.

Dedrick considered blocking the window with the metal cabinet, but it wouldn't hold the Unity Troopers back for more than two seconds.

"Over here," Liberty said. She stood in the corner of the room, yanking a tall sheet of plywood from the wall.

Joining her, he grabbed an end of the plywood. It creaked back, inch by inch. The nails sunk through the old veneers and popped from the wall.

"Think it's a way out?" Liberty said.

The plywood came free except for the lower corner. It opened to a dark doorway.

"Probably connects rooms." Dedrick pushed Liberty through the doorway and followed, debris sliding under his feet.

A voice called out, amplified through a speaker. "These grounds are off-limits. We have the building surrounded. Turn yourselves in."

A crack then a crash sounded inside the shop, a Unity Trooper busting through the half-boarded window.

Dedrick slipped behind the plywood and dragged it shut. The trooper would discover the doorway in no time. He shined the flashlight from one end of the room to the other. They stood in a narrow stairwell between shops. Liberty pressed her shoulder to a door on the opposite wall, her hand on the knob.

"Up there." He motioned with the flashlight, indicating the open staircase.

A voice and crashing sounds came from the shop they had left. The amplified voice continued to bellow outside, the words unclear from here.

"We'll be trapped." She bounded up the stairs even as she protested.

"Apartments stretch across the second story, I think." He climbed up after her, trying to keep his footfalls quiet.

Liberty reached a door at the top of the stairs and tried the knob. "It's locked."

Dedrick's hand went to the lock pick on his belt, but he hadn't the time. He pushed her aside and rammed his shoulder against the door, once, twice. It yielded to the impact. He stumbled through the doorway and fell to one knee. A heavy odor of animal urine and excrement assailed him.

Liberty scrambled past him and half-skipped, half-ran down the dark hallway.

He stood up and slammed the door shut. He needed something to block it.

Banging sounds came from below, then the sound of something crashing, probably the plywood blocking the entrance to the stairwell.

"Here!" Liberty called from a room off the hallway.

A few doors hung open and mottled gray light showed in the doorways. Liberty dragged a thick slab of wood down the hall. He grabbed one end. They carried it to the door they had come through. She dropped her end, and he wedged the slab under the doorknob.

"Now what?" she said.

They jogged side by side down the hall, their feet falling in unison.

Boots pounded on the stairs. It sounded like one man.

"Now we get out of here," Dedrick said. His gaze caught the glint of a knob that hung from the ceiling, probably an attic door. He leaped and yanked the knob. The door creaked open, revealing a folded wooden ladder. He tugged the top layer and the whole thing slid down, dust and debris with it.

Liberty skidded to a stop and looked back, her dark hair fanning out. "Up there?"

"No." Dedrick grabbed her arm and ran with her, leaping over rags, smashed boxes, and piles of garbage to the door at the end of the hallway. He didn't bother explaining the attic ladder was a diversion. She probably guessed that already.

Nearing the end of the hallway, he released her arm and kicked into high gear. He turned his shoulder to the door an instant before impact, and bam! The door flew open. A sharp pain ran down his arm.

Liberty closed the door behind them and darted to one side of the room, no doubt looking for something to block the door. An old armchair sat in the corner, its cushions ripped and disintegrated. She grabbed it.

He dashed to the window on the back wall. An old cracked blind covered it, duct taped at the top but loose on the bottom. He ripped it off and peered outside. Nothing but the nearest raindrops caught the light of his flashlight, appearing green through his night vision glasses. The window's locks didn't budge, so he planted his hands on the top and bottom of the frame and forced the window up. Raindrops sprinkled his face.

Footfalls sounded overhead, a trooper in the attic. Doors banged open in the hall. More than one trooper searched the building.

Liberty came to his side and stuck her head out the window, peering below. "We have to jump?"

"Yeah." He snapped the flashlight to his belt.

She grabbed his shoulder and hoisted herself up. Gripping the window frame on either side, she sat hunched in the open window, her back to the outside world. She slid the dark glasses from her face.

Darkness prevented him from seeing her expression. He imagined the look her eyes held, one of a girl steeling herself to do something she had never done before, something dangerous.

"I can't do this," she whispered. Her feet banged the wall and she tottered.

The sound of her voice, the thought of her falling, and a deep feeling he couldn't explain struck a chord in him. His hands flew out. He latched onto her arms before he even considered touching her. The desire to keep her safe swelled to a force over which he had no control. He hated himself for letting her come along.

The banging and stomping sounds in the hallway grew louder.

He lessened his grip on her and breathed, regaining self-control. "You'll be okay. Swing one leg out and face the building." He kept his voice calm, wanting her to relax. "You can hold onto the window frame and be halfway down. Bend your knees before you land."

She swung one leg out and glanced at him.

"You can do it," he said, wishing there were another way. More Unity Troopers had probably been routed to the old city center. Would they meet them on the ground? How would they avoid capture?

Someone banged on the door.

Liberty gasped. She gripped the frame, eased her other leg out, and let her body swing down.

Dedrick leaned out the window and grabbed her wrists to keep her from slipping too soon. "Ready?"

"Okay."

She didn't scream or squeal as he half expected her to. He hadn't even heard her land. He heard only the rain on the window and the trooper banging at the door. Something splintered, maybe the chair.

Dedrick climbed out the window and dropped down. He landed with bent knees and fell into a roll. Wet weeds surrounded him, probably cushioned the fall.

"Liberty?" Crawling on his knees, he reached into the darkness around him. "Liberty?"

She groaned.

His mind reeled. Was she hurt? He snatched the flashlight from his belt and whipped the beam in the direction of her groan.

Liberty lay on her back a few yards away, the remains of a couch under her legs. His thoughts snapped to the night they had sneaked back into Aldonia. They had run across a pitted field and she'd twisted her ankle.

He flung himself toward her. "You okay? What hurts?"

"Get that light out of my eyes." She pushed the hand that held the flashlight. "Shut it off. Look!" She twisted around and dove behind the couch.

Trusting her instincts, he shut off the flashlight and did the same.

A Unity Trooper advanced around the corner of the building, a gorilla in bulky black armor. The beam from his helmet swept the area, making the shadows of tall weeds slither like snakes.

Liberty and Dedrick ducked at the same time. The couch and the weeds should cover them. They stood a chance as long as a drone didn't pass by.

"You there!" The voice came from above. A trooper leaned out the window, the light from his helmet falling on them. "Put your hands in the air and stand up slowly."

Dedrick shoved his hand into his cape and wrestled his pistol from its holster. He disengaged the safety and pulled back the slide. He'd have to aim well. A bullet wouldn't penetrate a trooper's chest armor.

The Unity Trooper on the ground bolted toward them, the beam of light from his helmet bouncing, a gun of some sort in his hand.

"Stay down," Dedrick commanded Liberty, shifting to shield her with his body. He squinted into the light.

The trooper on the ground leveled his gun.

Dedrick snapped into position, planting his forearms on the couch back, and squeezing the trigger.

The trooper's body jerked. The gun fell from his hand, landing a short distance away. He collapsed to the ground in slow motion, then twisted to one side, reaching for his leg or the gun.

Dedrick jumped up and sprinted, yanking back the slide on his pistol.

A shot rang out, probably from the window.

The trooper flung himself forward and clawed the ground, reaching for the gun. He latched onto it, then swung it around and leveled it.

Another shot rang out.

Dedrick closed in and punted, kicking the gun from the trooper's hand and sending it sailing. He leaped onto the man on the ground, wrapped his arms around his armored torso, and rolled, making a shield of the trooper's body.

Two shots rang at roughly the same time, sounding like an echo. Pain seared Dedrick's shoulder. He found himself thrown hard against the ground. The pistol slipped from his hand. A fist ripped across his face.

Another shot. The body beside Dedrick jerked.

Liberty was saying something, but he couldn't see her. He saw nothing but swirling black velvet and lime-green raindrops.

"Are you okay? Where're you hit?" Liberty hovered over him. She peeled the goggles from his eyes. A motionless beam of light fell across her face, illuminating her eyelashes and loose strands of her hair. Her pale green irises glowed like mist in a forest, like foam on the sea.

His gaze drifted to the window from which they had jumped. He could see it over her shoulder. The room glowed with a warm yellow light, clear and peaceful. Raindrops outside the window glowed too, a miniature meteor shower. He could picture his mother sitting on the couch listening to Paula read about Pocahontas. He had expected to see the silhouette of a trooper, a gun in his hands, his sights set on them.

"Get up!" Liberty shrieked, tugging his arm. "We have to run!" She grabbed the front of his shirt and tugged until he was sitting.

Dedrick dragged in a deep breath of cool air and shook his head. His wits returned to him, bringing clarity. The rain had lessened. A trooper lay on his back moaning, the beam from his helmet light shining on them. Liberty crouched beside him, her brows creased with worry. She handed him his pistol.

Dedrick holstered it and forced himself to stand, wincing.

"Are you shot?" she said, her eyes roving over him.

"I'm okay." His shoulder throbbed with pain, but he could move his arm. He'd probably been grazed. He wouldn't waste time checking it out. The other troopers would find them if they didn't move. He forced himself to the corner of the building, Liberty keeping step with him.

Four black Regimen vehicles sat on the street, all at odd angles. Their lights flashed on the surrounding weeds, bushes, and broken pavement, creating a kaleidoscope of color. The cars looked empty.

"Where do you think the hideout is?" Liberty whispered.

"Over there." Dedrick peered through the rain and darkness, searching for a glimpse of the old courthouse at the very end of the street. Did he have his bearings straight? "Let's run for it while they're searching for us over here."

Liberty glanced both ways, peered up at the sky, and grabbed his hand. They took off together, running over broken pavement and through knee-high weeds. Halfway down the street, the courthouse came into view, a hulking three-story shadow that dominated the block.

Liberty ripped her hand from his and gasped.

Hot white light pierced the darkness, dazzling Dedrick. He shielded his eyes and squinted in the direction of the source. Two balls of light, headlights from a parked vehicle. The car sat between them and their destination. No sirens. No flashing lights. It was not a Unity Trooper vehicle.

Liberty had gone ahead of him, running for the cover of unkempt bushes that grew in front of a crumbling building.

He drew his pistol and ran after her. They would need to throw off their pursuers.

"Stop! Wait!" a man called.

Angling himself to protect his shoulder wound, Dedrick pushed through floppy wet branches. Water splashed his face and ran down his neck. A thicker branch yielded unwillingly but snapped back, striking his shoulder and renewing the pain.

He grunted and slammed his back against the brick wall of the building. Nothing more than a few sprinkles of rain reached them in the tight space between the wall and the bushes. But it was no hiding place.

"That was Sid," Liberty said, panting.

"You sure?" Dedrick peered through branches.

A siren flipped on and then off. Searchlights weaved through the darkness in the direction of the crumbling building and the car. A voice sounded over the speaker. "These grounds are off limits. Step out of the vehicle with your hands up."

"You cannot be serious," the man near the car shouted back. He said something in a quieter voice, sounding irritated. He probably spoke to Sid.

"Step away from the vehicle," came the voice through the speaker.

"I am Dr. Supero," the man shouted, stepping into the street. He stopped halfway, hands shoulder high, a beam of light illuminating him. Two troopers stood behind the open doors of their vehicles, their guns trained on him.

"Dr. Supero?" Liberty whispered, bumping Dedrick to get a view through the bush. "What's he doing here?"

"Lower your weapons, you fools. I have been working with Chief Varden at CSS for months now. Contact him if you do not believe me. And explain to me why eight troopers are searching this rubble."

The troopers made no response.

"There are two dozen runaways from Secondary. Do you honestly think they are here?" He brought his hands together, waist high.

The troopers' guns clicked. "Put your hands up."

"I am calling Chief Varden. If you shoot me, you will pay."

"What is he doing?" Liberty pushed branches and rocked from side to side, trying to improve her view.

"Beats me." Dedrick tugged her back. "Let's get moving before the attention turns to us again." They could creep to the corner of the building, remaining hidden behind bushes. Then they could sprint across the street.

Dedrick motioned for Liberty to follow his lead.

She glanced but then continued peering at the spectacle. Supero said something about teens being spotted near Jensenville, and about the incompetency of Unity Troops searching one fruitless area, and about the two he spotted being too old, a waste of time.

"Does he mean us?" Liberty said to Dedrick.

"Sounds like it. Come on." He grabbed her hand and tugged.

"Your chief wants you at the Jensenville border," Dr. Supero shouted, his tone terse. "Waste no more time. We need to find those teens. Get to the border!" A few seconds later, a car door slammed.

"Did he get back in his car?" Dedrick asked Liberty, pushing branches aside to see for himself.

"Seems like he's helping us," Liberty said.

The thought made Dedrick pause. It could work to their advantage, having the Regimen think the teens escaped to Jensenville. He tapped his earphone. "Fulton, we need a diversion. Think you can cause some trouble at the Jensenville border?"

"Can I?" Fulton laughed. Dedrick pictured him hunching over his workstation, his fingers tapping controls, his mind already wrapped around an idea. "Yeah, sure. My pleasure."

Dedrick grabbed Liberty's hand and tugged. "We need to get somewhere safe. They might not listen to Dr. Supero."

"Look," Liberty said, wriggling her hand free and leaning into a bush.

Three troopers emerged from the two-story row of buildings across the street. Two more came out from behind the buildings. They all got into cars. The blue and orange lights went dark and headlights came on. The doctor turned his car around and drove off, in the lead.

"They're leaving." Liberty looked at Dedrick.

"Good, we need to go, too." He motioned for her to follow. They wouldn't have to worry about getting spotted unless drones flew overhead.

They kept to the cover of the bushes, picking their way over piles of bricks and splintered window frames along the crumbling building. The rain had lessened to a sprinkle. Dedrick risked the flashlight as they moved into the street. Weeds and grasses had turned the pavement to gravel, nature reclaiming the land.

The old courthouse rose up before them, a four-story sandstone building of eroded columns and decorative lintels with triangular pediments over the highest windows, bars and boards over the lowest ones. Bare trees with twisting limbs grew in the grass between the courthouse and the street. It had probably once been a sight to see.

Dedrick swept the beam of his flashlight over the lower windows. Something glinted. He snapped the beam to the spot, a boarded up window missing a slat of wood. The glass in the dark opening glinted again. He headed for it.

"We're going in through a window?" Liberty said.

"I doubt the doors will open to us."

"They probably have a secret entrance."

"Yeah, but we don't have time to find it."

They reached the window with the missing slat, a narrow, waist-high opening. He counted twelve slats from top to bottom. They'd only need to remove the lower ones.

Earthy odors of dirt and grass permeated the air. The rain roared in his ears. It fell harder now, pelting the hood of his cape and snaking in through the neckline of his jacket. Raindrops like icy fingers traced patterns on his chest, searching for his bones.

He wedged the flashlight in the branches of a bare tree, directing the beam to the window. Then, standing with one boot in a tangle of weeds and the other in a dirty puddle, he gripped a slat and pried it off the window. He found a double hung window behind the boards, its glass broken on one side, shards clinging to the frame.

Liberty pushed in beside Dedrick, bumping his shoulder wound and renewing the pain that the cold had numbed. She gripped the next slat. They worked together, prying slat after slat, some taking no effort at all, others requiring force. Soon they had all the lower slats removed and enough of an opening to get inside.

Liberty squatted, looking like she might dive through the broken window into the darkness and unknown.

"Wait." Dedrick snatched the flashlight from the branches where he had wedged it and gave it to her. "You'll cut yourself on that glass." He peeled his cape off and wrapped it around his hand and forearm. Using enough force to break the glass shards, he thrust his arm inside. Glass tinkled to the floor. He grabbed the window frame and lifted the lower sash.

She ducked under the rising sash. Her feet landed on the floor before he got the window up.

The window clicked in place and then shifted. He dove through without waiting to see if it would stay. It crashed down behind him, glass shattering in its wake.

"I guess we're not looking to surprise anyone," Liberty said, smiling and shining the beam of light on him.

He shrugged and stuck out a hand for the flashlight. "I'm sure they're on high alert anyway, what with all the commotion outside."

In one corner of the room sat an old desk with dark holes for drawers. Garbage took up another corner, a pile of drywall slabs, old picture frames, and ceiling panels. A strange blanket hung over a doorway.

Dedrick drew nearer, studying it. It looked like a weave of milky white plastic strips and thick threads made from multicolored wrappers.

"Think this is the place?" Liberty stood in a corner he hadn't investigated next to a rolled up sleeping bag.

"Probably. Let's look around." He pushed aside the curtain of recycled materials and swung the beam of his flashlight into the darkness beyond.

The flashlight was ripped from him. Hands clamped onto his arms. A blur of faces and limbs appeared, bodies moving erratically like bats swooping for prey. Then darkness.

CHAPTER 19

The ugly curtain of recycled materials swallowed Dedrick whole, leaving me in darkness. I wanted to believe he was playing around. But Dedrick didn't play around, not on this side of Aldonia's Boundary Fence.

He grunted. Once. Twice. Feet shuffled on the other side of the curtain. Fists and bodies collided with soft thuds.

My eyes couldn't open any wider, and still, I saw nothing. I couldn't move. I dared not call his name. His attackers would find me. I wasn't ready for this.

I reached for the curtain, a movement so slow in the dark it almost didn't seem to happen. I gripped the weave of plastic and foil. The prickly material did not move like fabric, flowing and graceful. It moved as whole.

Orange faces and bodies, all in motion, appeared. Faces turned to me. Hands tightened around my wrists. I sailed forward, into the mix. Someone grabbed me from behind, twisting my arms behind my back.

The self-defense methods Alix taught me remained locked in my brain. I couldn't breathe.

Dedrick took a step and twisted, his chest angling down, his leg swinging out, two blades on a windmill. His foot struck a kid in the neck and knocked him to the ground.

Three more boys moved in, fists at the ready.

Dedrick froze for a split second, poised with one leg bent before him and the other stretched out behind. Then he sprang into action, his arms like whips, deflecting attacks and counterattacking, striking one boy with the heel of his hand, another with his fist, a third with the point of his elbow.

I couldn't look away from the fight, the silhouettes clashing in the amber glow from distant lanterns.

Dedrick's movements, fluid and instinctive, contrasted the crude and untrained movements of his adversaries. One by one, they fell or staggered back. Then they jumped in for more, their fury making them careless.

A boy swept into my space, blocking my view. He gestured, jerking his hand up and in my face. "You're not welcome here." A trace of light fell over his eyes, gold and black like Alix's.

I pretended Alix stood behind me, locking my arms. I knew what to do. I flung myself back, hurling my weight onto the body behind me.

My captor's grip broke and we crashed to the floor.

I scrambled to my feet, a surge of adrenaline driving me into the fight. I picked the nearest target and swung. The side of my palm struck a boy's neck. He stumbled back. A girl rushed towards me. I squatted and swept my leg out, meaning to strike her shin.

She leaped, avoiding my attack. Then she brought the side of her hand to my neck.

A shock wave ran down my neck and back. I stumbled into arms that tightened around me.

The kid with Alix's eyes slid into view, shaking his head at me and smirking. He brandished a blade.

Shadowy figures with faces and arms of orange surrounded Dedrick and a boy. Dedrick hopped like a boxer in a ring. The kid swung. Dedrick jumped back. The boy held something that glinted in the light. A knife.

"We're not here to fight." Dedrick said, peeling his jacket off.

I gasped and fell back into the cold chest of the kid who held me captive.

A diagonal tear and a long, dark spot marred the sleeve of Dedrick's white shirt. His arm, orange in the light, looked streaked with mud. It was blood. The Unity Trooper's bullet had found its target.

Dedrick's shadowy opponent lunged, swinging the knife.

Dedrick blocked the attack with the jacket. The knife clattered to the ground. Arms and fists flew and collided at a frantic tempo until Dedrick gained the edge. His attacker sailed to the floor, landing on his side and sliding two meters.

The spectators spoke and moved at once, falling upon Dedrick like a rainstorm without warning and blocking my view.

"You're done," a girl shouted. The other kids backed off, forming a circle that included my captor and me. The girl held a handgun. She motioned for Dedrick to drop down.

Dedrick raised his hands and got down on his knees.

"We're not here for trouble," he said. A single lantern and a staircase with a metal railing rose up some distance behind him, creating a background of black and amber stripes.

A short, lanky boy stepped forward and stooped over Dedrick's jacket. "He's got a gun." He drew it from an inner pocket and waved it in the air.

"Which I could've used on you but didn't," Dedrick said, his face to the boy he had fought. The kid stood near the staircase, hugging his ribs.

"I told you we're not here for trouble." Dedrick faced random kids as he spoke. "I'm looking for my . . . for our . . . We're looking for friends."

"He's got another gun." The lanky kid pulled a smaller gun from Dedrick's jacket. The size and shape resembled the ID implant remover Miriam had used on me.

"That's not a gun," Dedrick said. I could picture him showing impatience with an eye roll.

"Check his belt," the girl said. Was she in charge? She wasn't any taller, didn't appear any older than the others. "Check her, too." She turned to me.

My captor released me.

The kid with Alix's eyes closed his knife with a flick of the wrist. He grinned at me, a leering look common to Aldonian boys his age, and gave me the once over. Then he flipped my cape from my shoulders and eased my jacket open. "Yeow," he said, his eyes on my chest, reminding me why I usually wore loose-fitting clothing.

Dedrick's face snapped to me, the shadows revealing nothing of his expression. He dropped the band from his wrist into the outstretched hand of the lanky boy.

"Where's your flexi-phone?" the golden-eyed kid said to me.

"I don't have one." I removed the bulky watch Elder Lukman had given me. In all the chaos, I had forgotten to check in with him.

"Everyone has one. But you can't have them here. They read your implant and send your location to the Regimen."

"I don't have an implant."

Several kids snickered.

"We don't need those," Dedrick said.

The lanky kid dangled a dark, fingerless glove in Dedrick's face. Everyone here wore a glove on one hand.

"She's not lying." Dedrick faced the girl in charge. "We don't have implants. If you have a reader, check us out for yourselves."

"Get up," the girl said, motioning with the handgun. She stood with a hand on her hip and dropped the gun to her side.

As Dedrick stood, the lanky boy tossed him his jacket. Dedrick glanced at me as he eased his bleeding arm into the jacket.

128

Did he see the worry on my face?

"Move." The boy behind me spoke over my shoulder, his stale breath making me turn away. He nudged me forward.

The group moved toward the stairs, kids mumbling to one another and throwing glances at Dedrick and me. Were we their first unexpected guests?

"To the Judgment Step," the girl in charge said, leading the pack.

The boy behind me grabbed my arm, squeezing too hard. Kids pushed ahead of us, then ahead of Dedrick and the boys flanking him. Feet pounded the marble steps that rose up in the middle of this open area. Voices grew loud, echoing. Excitement filled the air, electricity zipping from one kid to another.

I studied my surroundings.

Dark doorways, one or two with actual doors, lined the walls on either side of the staircase. Hallways extended beyond the reach of the light. We passed an elevator at the foot of the staircase. Its open doors showed the bottom half of the cab. Scraps of yellow caution tape lay scattered about near doors and railings.

"Up you go." My guide shoved me toward the stairs.

I stumbled and cracked my shin on the edge of a worn marble step.

Dedrick, several steps ahead, stopped. He yanked his arm from one of his guides and looked at me. His gaze shifted to my guide, a threat in his eyes.

Once I continued climbing, Dedrick allowed his guide to lead him.

They made us stop on the second step from the first landing. Names, numbers, and words had been scratched into the step from one end to the other. The word *guilty* jumped out at me.

"Turn around," Dedrick's guide said. He and six other boys stood on the main level, a few of them leaning on railings. Another lantern, amber LED lights in a milky plastic container, hung above them.

Dedrick and I turned around, our hands bumping. I had a strange urge to grab his hand, but I didn't want him to know that I was afraid.

The girl in charge stood on the landing above us, resting her arms on the railing. I had imagined her younger and uglier, hardened and grim, but the amber light revealed a woman in her thirties with dark blonde hair that accentuated almond-shaped eyes and thin lips, features too elegant for a crime boss. More kids sat or stood around her, mumbling to one another.

The group quieted and the kids stepped aside.

A man with cropped hair and a long, gray coat sauntered forward and stood beside the woman. They exchanged a glance. Then he gazed down at us, tilting his chin upward as if to show his superiority.

His coat . . . I had to study it. He wore the gray wool coat of a higher Regimen official.

Panic flickered through my chest. Then I studied him.

A single button held the coat closed over his bare chest. Frayed jeans, unlaced work boots, a stubbly jaw . . . No, he was not a Regimen official. He had probably stolen the coat. My gaze snapped to his hands. He had only one.

"I'm told you have no implants," he said.

I found myself rubbing the scar on my palm. "I had mine removed."

He lifted his handless arm, shoving the sleeve up to reveal a pale stub. "So did I." We had been warned that an implant would release a destructive chemical if a person tried to remove it. I had never seen the result until now.

"There's a safe way." Dedrick slapped his jacket pocket as if he had forgotten that he'd been stripped of weapons and gadgets.

"What's your business?" the man said.

"My name is Dedrick." Mud streaked his boots, his wet hair stuck up in tufts, and he kept squeezing the wrist of his wounded arm, but his voice conveyed strength and honesty. "We're looking for our friends. We think they're here, probably arrived shortly before we did."

The man rested his hand and his stump on the railing. He leaned forward. "How old are you, Dedrick?"

"I'm twenty-two."

"How old are your friends?"

"Fifteen to eighteen. They're from Secondary."

"And you know them . . ." He shook his head slowly. ". . . how?"

"I told you, they're friends. I grew up with them."

Snickers and whispers filled the air. I understood the problem they had believing us. Kids grew up with kids their own age. Secondary kids didn't know any adults except those who came to the facility. Even if Dedrick had gone to Secondary, his youngest friend would be nineteen. If the colonists were here, they must've just arrived and had little time to explain where they originally came from.

"How do I know you aren't a Regimen spy?"

Dedrick exhaled and shook his head, casting a sideways glance to me.

"We're looking for Andy," I said, unexpected emotion in my voice, "John, Kevin, Catherine, Cyril, Julie . . ." I gave every one of the eighteen colonist's names. I had memorized them in Re-Ed. Their faces hovered in my mind. I would not rest until they came to safety.

The man straightened as I spoke. He exchanged a glance with the woman. She nodded.

CHAPTER 20

The windshield wipers thumped to the beat of Dr. Supero's headache. He drove with his right hand and massaged his head with the left.

Sid cussed and slammed his palms against the dashboard for the fifth time. His voice came out higher and more ragged, his strikes more powerful each time. One hand had the protection of a strange, fingerless glove.

"You will stop or you will get out of my car," Dr. Supero said. Not that he cared. He would probably have to return the car anyway. Funny the sea urchin hadn't mentioned it when she informed him of his change of vocation and residence. She'd seemed so thorough.

Dr. Supero turned down a quiet street, heading back to his apartment. He shut off the wipers and let raindrops gather on the windshield. His headache made him grimace every few seconds. He needed to take something for the pain. Headaches had never lasted this long before.

Sid slumped back and slammed his head against the headrest. "I don't know why you're doing this, man. We had her. I'm telling you that was her."

"I, too, have eyes."

"So what the earth, man? She won't stay there now. She saw us. She'll stay someplace else."

"Is there someplace else?"

Sid looked but gave no answer.

The view of the road blurred, the windshield showing raindrops on top of raindrops. He flipped the wipers back on. "If we had run after her, we would have alerted CSS. They would have her right now. Not us. Not you. Be thankful they are busy with those Secondary kids. I doubt they know about her yet."

A rock had settled in Dr. Supero's stomach. He couldn't believe the teens from the Nature Preserves had all escaped. Had someone helped them? It couldn't have been Dedrick and Liberty. Who else cared?

Dr. Supero and Sid had been on their way to the old city center when they learned about the escape. Unity Troopers crawled along the streets. Sid panicked, thinking they were after him. "They know, man. I'm screwed." He grabbed handfuls of his own hair and yanked.

"You do not know that," Dr. Supero had said.

He called Chief Varden. "Why is every UT and CSS vehicle on the road? I cannot even drive down the street."

"You're not gonna like it," Chief Varden had said, his voice thundering through the phone. "Half of Secondary has escaped."

"You cannot mean that." Dr. Supero had slammed on the brakes, making the car hydroplane a few meters.

"Yup, I mean it. Well, maybe not half but every one of the wild kids and a good number of Aldonians. We got twenty-four teens on the loose."

"Why does this not surprise me?"

~ ~ ~

The thumping of the windshield wipers grew unbearably loud. Supero shut them off again. He had only two more roads to take. He could drive blindfolded from here.

"So what's our plan, man?" Sid said. "Are we gonna wait? You sent them all to the Jensenville border to get rid of them, right? Then we're gonna circle back."

Dr. Supero sighed. "I am going home. I have had a long day."

Sid dragged his gloveless palm down his mouth and neck, then shook his head. "Let me out then. I'm going back alone."

"You will draw the attention of CSS. They will be watching that area. If CSS has no idea about the community of miscreants that you say live there, Liberty and Dedrick will feel safe with them. We will return another day."

"Another day?" Sid said in the whiny voice of a child.

"Liberty heard every word I said. We just did her a favor. She knows we are not trying to get her caught. Perhaps she will trust us. And as long as she still has friends in custody, she's not leaving Aldonia."

"How long are we waiting?"

"I'll talk to Chief Varden tomorrow. I'll see if they have eyes on the old city center. If they don't, we'll pay them a visit." The rest of his plan, he kept to himself. Once Chief Varden caught the teens, Dr. Supero could question them. The sea urchin forbade him from visiting Primary and Secondary, but she said nothing about the Citizen Safety Station.

"You got a headache, man?" Sid said. "You're always rubbing your head."

CHAPTER 21

Our guides led us up the next flight of stairs. Cracked marble slabs and damaged wrought iron railing littered the floor. This floor also had dark doorways, few actual doors, and strips of caution tape everywhere. Trim molding ran diagonally up the wall, showing where a narrow flight of steps had once climbed to the highest level of the building.

At our guides' direction, we followed the others into a storage room. Buckets, cans, and various scraps lay on the floor. A rope ladder dangled from an opening in the stained ceiling. Voices and laughter traveled down to us. One kid after another climbed, some of them like squirrels racing up a tree, until Dedrick and I stood alone with the two guides.

Dedrick stared at me and then climbed up first. I laughed to myself though his chivalry touched me. He probably couldn't decide if it would be safer to let me go first or last.

I took off my cape and climbed up after Dedrick, the ladder swaying with each step. At the top, I hoisted myself through the crude opening and onto scuffed hardwood flooring. I stopped.

Kids huddled nearby, colony kids, their hands and arms connecting them in a display of affection unfamiliar to Aldonians. Dedrick stood in the middle of the group, his arms around his brother's shoulders, his face in his brother's hair. Then he pressed his forehead to Andy's and spoke to him, words I could only imagine.

Emotion welled up in my chest, threatening to bring tears to my eyes. I wanted what they had. I backed into a support beam and averted my gaze.

Guys and girls sat around upside-down crates, talking or playing old-fashioned card games. A few teenage Aldonians stood watching the colonists. They might have been the other Secondary teens. The man in the Regimen jacket leaned against a wall, talking to the thirty-something woman and another kid. The kid walked off, mumbling to himself. He passed by me, glaring, and then walked through a doorway behind me. A sound like the flutter of wings came from the room.

The attic had a wide area down the middle and several rooms off the sides, all with doors or makeshift curtains.

A tall, muscular figure with a shock of silver hair popped out of one room and disappeared into another. The person, a woman in a black tank top and low riding cargo pants, reappeared in the doorway and locked her eyes on me. It was Silver.

My jaw clenched. Two memories popped into my mind at once. First memory: I struggled against her. She held my arms while Sid injected me with the street drug Thrill.

Second memory: I needed her help. Unity Trooper closed in on Dedrick and me. Silver stood between us and the only place where we could hide. She stepped aside and sacrificed herself to the Unity Troopers, getting arrested to save us.

Silver nodded, indicating for me to come to her. She leaned a shoulder against the doorframe and looked me over as I approached, taking me in from head to toe, the way a guy does.

I wanted to zip my jacket but didn't.

"I thought all that commotion was for the runaways." She smirked. "Now I'm not so sure."

I stopped by the opposite side of the doorframe, debating whether or not to go inside the room for a private conversation. I never understood why she had sacrificed herself to save us. "What are you doing here?"

Her eyes narrowed, her heavy eyelids almost hiding her silvery irises. She glanced over her shoulder into the room. "Do you know where you are?"

I made a few random glances at my surroundings. "Sure. Attic of an old courthouse."

She pivoted on her shoulder and sauntered into the room. "You, girl, are in Aldonia's finest black market." She flung an arm out, her muscles rippling, and turned in a circle.

Lanterns hung in the corners of the room, revealing rows of boxes and crates. Containers filled the room, all of them closed, most of them secured with heavy padlocks.

"You're here on the right day but the wrong hours. You missed all the action." Silver kicked a box, sending it crashing into a gray toolbox that resembled my old one. "And I freaking wish I would've left earlier. I don't like staying the night. Makes the Regimen suspicious when you miss roll call."

"You never know when they do roll call," I said. The Citizen Safety Station checked at random hours. Their computer was designed to send a message to every citizen's flexi-phone. The phone read a person's implant and reported the location. Missing roll call meant a person's flexi-phone wasn't close enough to read their implant.

"*You* never know. But I do." She raised an eyebrow. It disappeared for an instant behind wild bangs of pewter hair.

My attention returned to the gray toolbox. "That looks like my toolbox."

"Yeah, it is."

"Where's the other one?" Irritation crept into my tone. I had two toolboxes, both of which I left in her care before I entered the Breeder Facility. She had promised to return them to me, not that I believed her.

"Once I heard you escaped, I never figured you'd come back. Why did you come back? You were on the other side of the electric Boundary Fence, weren't you? How'd you get out?" She moved closer, her voice lowering. "What's out there?"

I didn't like craning my neck to look up at her, so I turned away, pretending to scan the boxes and crates. "Tell me something. Why did you cover for us at the bomb shelter? You could've ratted us out and gotten a reward. They reward that, you know?"

"Oh, I know." She sat on a low crate and pulled a thin, metal case from a pocket. "They locked me away for a while, cuz of the guns." The case held cigarettes. She took one and offered it to me.

I shook my head and moved to where I could see Dedrick through the doorway. He and Andy stood alone. Dedrick shook his head, turned away, and then turned back. Andy raised his hands as he spoke, a defensive gesture. Dedrick's hand flew out, a finger pointing at the other colonists. His voice rose, but I didn't catch what he said.

"You got out of Aldonia." Silver sat with legs straight out, leaning her elbows on a taller crate behind her. Smoke seeped from her nostrils. "That's no small feat. I thought maybe if I helped you, you'd tell me how you did it. You'd owe me one."

She took a long drag off the cigarette, staring at me with an unfocused gaze. She exhaled the smoke through her nose, a smile creeping onto her face. "The Regimen sees me as the community physical instructor, the one who provides therapy to citizens in need, gets them back on their feet and productive again." She glanced at the cigarette or maybe at her nails. "But I see myself as a trader. That's where I make my profit. If I knew how to come and go from Aldonia, how to get through the Boundary Fence without electrocution, I could sell that information."

I shook my head. I wanted to think Silver had a good side and that she helped us because she thought it was the right thing to do. But she had only done it to gain something.

"Sorry," I said. "I don't know what to tell you."

"Oh, no problem." She took another hit off the cigarette. "I did my own research. Took me awhile, but I found the answer to my own question."

"Wh-what do you mean?"

She sat forward, grinning. "I mean I found a way out."

"You . . . what?" I stared, dumbfounded. She couldn't mean what she said.

She laughed. "I haven't decided how to market it yet, how to sell it. Because I can't see why someone would want to live out there. It'd be a risk, leaving and coming back. It'd be a struggle to survive out in the Nature Preserves, what with all the wild animals and no commissary." She chuckled. "Unless you know something I don't."

"What do you mean you found a way out?" I stepped toward her, wanting to drag her to her feet and shake the answer from her, a feeling I'd never act on given our difference in size and strength.

She laughed again and stood up, towering over me. "You liked being the only one who knew a way out, huh?" She blew smoke off to the side and grabbed a strand of my hair. "Regimen discovered your way out, didn't they?" She rubbed my hair between her fingers and thumb. "Can't use it anymore? Tell me what's out there, and I'll tell you my way out."

"There's nothing out there." I flipped my hair back behind my shoulder, breaking her hold on it.

"So where did *they* come from?" She nodded at the open door.

Two groups of colonists sat on the floor, a few of them resting on each other's shoulders. Others stood talking to Aldonians. Dedrick paced alone, his hand to his ear. He was probably speaking with the Mosheh, arranging our departure. Someone had returned his belt to him and probably his gun and ID implant remover.

"They wear the clothes, but it's obvious they're not from around here," Silver said.

"It doesn't matter where they came from. They wanted out of Secondary and they're out." I walked to the door.

She grabbed my arm, stopping me. "How will they live? They won't be able to use their implants to get things. They're runaways. So where are they going?" Her silver irises shifted from side to side as she studied my eyes.

I pressed my lips together, not sure what to tell her.

"They can't stay here. Not permanently. This is Guy's place. And Angel's."

I gathered Guy was the man in the Regimen coat and Angel was the girl in charge of the security detail that met us when we broke in.

"No one else lives here permanently. We all have to go home now and then." She gave a crooked grin. "Where they gonna call home?"

My breath caught. Silver found a way through the Boundary Fence. Would she try to follow us when we returned to the Mosheh?

CHAPTER 22

Dedrick stood with Guy, Angel, and two young men. Angel spoke to the young men, pointing and gesturing as if giving them a list of things to do. Dedrick said something to Guy. Guy nodded. The young men took off as I approached the group.

The other three looked at me.

"We need to talk," I said to Dedrick, half whispering.

He lowered his head and whispered back, "Yeah, I know." He clutched the elbow of his wounded arm. His eyelids flickered, pain or severe irritation showing from under them.

"Is there anyone who can treat your arm?" I said.

"Let's not worry about that now," Dedrick replied. "Unity Troopers are stationed to this area for the next several hours. We need to remain hidden and get some rest."

"I'd like to know how you know that," Guy said. "Who are you talking to?" He tapped his ear, no doubt indicating Dedrick's earphone.

"Friends," Dedrick said.

"An enemy of the Regimen?" The corner of Guy's mouth curled up.

"You could say that," Dedrick said.

"I'd like to meet them."

"That's not possible. They work in secret."

Guy snickered and exchanged a glance with Angel. "So do we. Maybe we could help each other."

"I suspect we have a different set of goals, a different view of freedom." Dedrick paused. "I'm as close as you'll get to meeting them." A hint of finality rang in his tone. "If ever I can help you out, I will. I appreciate that you've opened your door to my brother and my friends."

"Your brother?" Guy's eyes held a questioning look. Aldonians did not understand the word the way colonists did. To us it had a general meaning. He must've gathered that Dedrick meant it in a more personal way.

138

Angel stepped forward, her eyes on Dedrick. "What's wrong with your arm?" She reached into a pocket of her vest and drew out a set of keys.

Guy grinned. "Angel here; she's our doctor. She can fix you up."

Dedrick shook his head and glanced, or rather glared, at me. "It's only a scrape."

Angel handed the keys to me. "There's a storage room over there." She pointed to a door some distance behind us. "You'll find bandages, medical supplies." She turned her back to us and faced Guy, who now leaned against the wall. She whispered something to him. He slid his hand around her waist.

"Thanks," I said.

"Leave it neat," she said without a glance.

~ ~ ~

I swung the door open and an overhead light flickered on. Unlike the weak amber glow from the homemade lanterns throughout the building, white light reached every corner. Boxes and supplies filled shelves in neat rows on three sides of the room. An old office desk with a metal top sat in the middle with barely enough room to get around it.

Dedrick darted to the shelves on one side of the room and grabbed one item after another.

The shelves I scanned held bottles and jars of various medicines and, on the lower shelves, canned goods.

He turned around with a pump, spray bottle, tube, roll of tape, and two little boxes. They tumbled out of his arms and onto the desk. "I got this," he said. "I'll just be a minute."

"You're going to tend your own shoulder wound?" I grinned and picked up the spray bottle. It held some kind of saline solution.

"Yeah." He took the bottle from me.

I snatched it back. "No, you're not. Take off the jacket and have a seat." I patted the metal desktop.

He held my gaze, his mouth hanging open as if he wanted to say something. Then he gave an eye roll, exhaled through his mouth, and eased the jacket off.

While he scooted onto the desk, I pumped hand sanitizer into one hand. The orange scent of the solution filled the air as I rubbed my hands together in my best effort to clean them.

"I need to tell you something," I said, glancing at the ripped, blood-red sleeve of his white shirt. Goosebumps came out on my arms.

"Yeah, me, too." He sat slouched with his hands on his thighs and his legs swinging ever so slightly. His eyes were glazed, most likely from the pain.

139

"Okay, you first," I said. The sanitizer left my hands feeling cool and dry. I opened the boxes and laid out gauze packets. Then I stepped close to him, imagining I could feel heat between us. I stuck my thumbs under either side of his bloody sleeve.

He jerked his arm from me, crossing it over his chest. His face reddened. "Really, I don't need any help." He stared in the direction of the closed door. "I'm capable of treating my own wound."

"Don't be silly." I grabbed his forearm, pulled his arm back into position, and eased the sleeve up over his shoulder. Then I stifled a gasp. I understood why he didn't want to bother with his wound.

He stared at the door, his jaw twitching. He didn't want me to see this. Dedrick had a dark brown tattoo or scar on his shoulder, a spiky letter "S" with thorns and strands coming off at various points.

I focused on the wound. It was a good distance below the scar, a seeping oval gash the length of Silver's cigarette. I ripped open a gauze packet.

"What did you want to tell me?" he said, staring at the door.

I took a breath, relieved to have something to say. I had almost forgotten to tell him. "Silver . . ." I sprayed saline solution on the wound and under it where the blood had dripped, trying my hardest to ignore his wincing. "She questioned me about the colonists, where they came from, where they're going."

His head turned, his gaze cutting to me. "What?"

I dabbed the wound and my stomach twisted. Blood had never bothered me, but I had never cleaned a wound this size before. "Silver said she found a way out of Aldonia through the Boundary Fence."

His eyebrows drew together, a crease forming between them.

"I'm worried she might follow us."

"Uh, yeah, that'd be bad." He glanced at his shoulder and then at me. I could see the deep brown of his eyes in my peripheral vision. "We'll have to do something about that."

Hesitant to make intimate contact, I touched and held his arm, supporting it so I could clean up the blood with fresh gauze. Bloodstains curved around his bicep and ran almost to his elbow. Tiny golden hairs popped up as I freed them from dried blood. The wound glistened with fresh blood but didn't drip. I glanced and found his eyes still on me, his blush gone.

"What did you want to tell me?" I said.

He shook his head, grunted, then glared at the door while he spoke. "It's Andy. He wants to stay here."

"Stay here? You mean here at the courthouse or here in Aldonia?" I squeezed antibacterial ointment onto a gauze pad.

"Yeah, both. And not just him, over half of them."

"Why?" I dabbed the wound, applying the ointment.

"I don't know. He's not thinking straight. He thinks they can make a difference, thinks he can change Aldonia." He huffed.

"Make a difference, how? The Regimen controls everything."

"I don't know. He doesn't make sense. Ask him." He pulled his arm from me and grabbed a sterile gauze pack. I guessed I wasn't working fast enough. "Yeah, maybe you can talk to him. We have to stick around for a few hours anyway." He ripped the pack open.

I snatched it from him before he touched the gauze with his dirty hands. The gauze only covered half the wound, so I opened another.

A rapping sounded on the door and then it creaked open. The golden-eyed kid stood in the doorway. He looked different under the white light. Cleaner. Less crude. "We got a situation," he said.

Dedrick scooted forward.

Holding first aid tape in one hand and the gauze on his wound with the other, I blocked Dedrick with my body. "Wait, I'm not done."

"What's the situation?" Dedrick said. "You're Juno, right?"

"Yeah, that's me." Juno waved his brows at me. "We got a Unity Trooper stopping by for a visit."

"What?" Dedrick and I said together.

"Nothing to worry about. Just warning you to stay quiet." Juno backed up, swinging the door shut.

I smoothed a fourth strip of tape to the edge of the gauze pad, completing the dressing of his wound.

Dedrick jumped up and caught the door before it shut. "Why is this nothing to worry about?"

"You'll see."

CHAPTER 23

We sat in a long room that Angel called a bedroom, the two dozen teens, Silver, seven of the kids who had greeted us with their fists when we first arrived, a group I had not seen before, Dedrick, and I. Boards covered the windows. Boards covered every window, we were told, except for those in the lookout rooms. They couldn't risk a drone picking up light or movement. I figured we had come in through a lookout room. It explained the missing slat.

Hammocks hung from low makeshift frames along the inner wall. They had made the hammocks from rope and plastic bags, braiding the bags and then weaving them together. Makeshift dressers, desk drawers in a clumsy frame, stood against the two shorter walls. Black mats lined the wall under the boarded-up windows. They were the kind used in 3D arcades, only these had patches and duct tape on the edges.

I sat on the mat nearest the door. The colony girls and one Aldonian girl also reclined on the mats. Two colony boys went for the hammocks, seeming to fall asleep the second they stretched out. It was late. If my head hit the mat, I would probably do the same. Other boys sat on the floor gathered around a lantern, the glow turning their faces orange. They spoke in hushed voices.

Angel permitted two lanterns. She carried them into the room herself and placed one at each end. "Might as well get some rest," she said. "Don't worry about the trooper downstairs. He'll be leaving soon." She also had kids bring us a plastic crate of snacks, a water cooler, and ceramic mugs with strange logos on them.

Andy took charge of distributing snacks. He gave me a pack of peanuts. An Aldonian from Primary—I heard someone call him Saxon—filled mugs with water and directed other teens to distribute and collect them. We only had ten, so we had to share.

Dedrick paced from one end of the room to the open doorway, checking things on his belt. Maybe he wasn't sure they had returned everything to him. I wished someone would offer him a clean shirt. I hated looking at the bloodstained sleeve even though I knew his arm was fine.

Stifled laughter came from outside the room.

Dedrick stopped and squinted through the open doorway. "What're they doing?" he said.

A boy stood outside the door. He pivoted to face Dedrick. It was Juno. His tawny eyes caught the amber light of the lantern as they swiveled from Dedrick to me and back to Dedrick. "We keep rats. We release them on special occasions." He smirked.

"You release them?" Dedrick said.

"Sure. Nothing says abandoned building better than a swarm of rats clicking along the old marble floor."

Dedrick cracked a smile. "Nice. So how do you get them down there?"

"Ah, you know, we got it all rigged up." Juno folded his arms and shrugged. "We keep them in cages in the vents and elevator shaft. Then we use ropes and pulleys to open the cages and vents. We got crows, too. We'll send them out if we have to. Only they're harder to collect."

"Crows?" Dedrick sounded impressed.

Sudden, unrestrained laughter filled the air.

"What happened?" Dedrick darted from the room.

"Trooper's gone!" Guy shouted, though I couldn't see him from where I sat. "Time to relax."

Hoots and calls came from the Aldonians outside the room and even those in the room. Guy and Angel embraced. They kissed. It started as something little, a celebration of the moment, but now they groped each other, kissing hungrily.

I looked away, hoping this wasn't the only *bedroom*.

Dedrick and Juno strolled into the room together, talking. They sat with the other boys around the lantern nearest me. My gaze traveled to the group around the farther lantern. One of the men wore a long black robe and had a dark beard. He gestured wildly as he spoke. He reminded me of the two priests I had seen in the Maxwell Colony. I couldn't imagine why a priest would live in or visit this place, a black market. The kids near him hung on every word, making me wonder what he said.

"Naw, I don't think so, Andy." Dedrick's voice caught my attention.

Andy stood over him with a guitar. "Aw, come on. Do you know Aldonians don't learn to play instruments? They don't even get to watch live performances?"

Andy spoke the truth. Toddlers who displayed an innate musical ability were sent to a city on the west side of the continent. All our songs came from there. They had a specific institute for developing the children's talent and for studying genes involved in musical abilities. They didn't waste resources by teaching more than rudimentary music to the rest of us.

Andy sat beside Dedrick and shoved the guitar into his hands. Dedrick looked the instrument over, plucked a few strings, and handed it back. "Well, I can't play it sitting on the floor."

"Somebody get this man a chair," Andy shouted, jumping up.

Within a matter of minutes, a stool appeared and twice as many people filled the room, all eyes on Dedrick and Andy. Andy sat on the plastic crate our snacks came in. He had a smaller guitar, one that reflected the light of the lanterns that now filled the room. He plucked strings and turned the knobs on the end of the neck. "Getting it in tune," he said. Dedrick tuned the larger guitar, which had a dull finish and a deeper sound. The brothers mumbled back and forth to each other.

I sat between two Aldonians, a sixteen-year-old blonde named Wren and golden-eyed Juno. The colony girls squeezed together on the next two mats, giggling and talking. Guy and Angel strolled into the mix last. They crossed the room and climbed onto the dressers.

"You'll have to tell me sometime," I said to Wren, "how you guys busted out of Secondary and got all the way here undetected."

Wren leaned back on her arms, bringing her heart-shaped face closer to mine. I sat cross-legged, farther back on the mat. She smiled at me. "It helps when you have outside connections. I'm friends with a delivery guy who deals here."

"Do you know Guy and Angel?" My gaze had drifted to them. Guy sat cross-legged and held Angel's hand. Angel's legs hung down and swung over the faces of drawers. She whispered to him, making him smile.

Wren shrugged, the ends of her blonde bob curling up on her shoulder. "I know Guy's story. I know this is his place and that he started the whole operation."

"So what's his story?"

"You're wondering about his hand?"

I shrugged. I was wondering about all of it. How does a man live in Aldonia without the Regimen finding them? How long had he been here?

She sat up and scooted to sit even with me. "He ran away from Secondary when he was seventeen, over ten years ago. He couldn't risk search drones reading his ID implant, so he dug it out with a knife."

I made a face. My hand shot to my palm. I remembered Dedrick slicing the implant from my hand.

"The poison they warn you about, that's real. It started spreading through his hand. The pain's real, too. He was almost delirious, but he dragged himself to the hospital and waited in hiding for a shift change. He saw a girl come out. It was Angel. She didn't know him yet. He threatened her with the knife, made her get him into the hospital and help him. She didn't know what to do, but she knew the poison was spreading. So she amputated. Then she sent him away with fresh bandages and pain killers and stuff."

"Why didn't she get caught? CSS sees everything."

"She reported the incident right away. What could she do, he had a knife. She said she didn't know where he went, but she lied. Angel followed him. He hid in a boarded up shop in a strip mall near the hospital. It was all he could do to get there. She went to him every day, felt sorry for him, I guess, treated his amputation and brought him food. She got good at finding streets without surveillance cameras."

"How'd the courthouse ever become his home?"

"Once he healed enough and got his strength back, he started thinking of how he could live without the Regimen's aid. At first, he stole things. Then he realized people were willing to trade, so he made himself the middleman. Eventually, he discovered this area. It's fenced off. No surveillance. Most of the buildings are crap, unlivable, but the courthouse—"

The strum of guitars in unison made us, and everyone else, quiet down. Dedrick and Andy repeated the same notes and chords a few times and then Dedrick opened his mouth and sang.

"There's a tire swing in the backyard of the house my father built . . ." He watched Andy while he sang and strummed the guitar. Each of them tapped the beat with one foot.

Dedrick's voice, strong and raw, came from somewhere deep inside him. It carried to the surface emotions I never imagined him having, secrets almost too personal to share. Yet here he was, pouring them out.

My heart wrenched with a fleeting desire. It wanted the impossible, the unreasonable. It wanted to claim him.

I closed my eyes and tried to think of something else. The words of the song painted pictures in my mind. I could see the boy in his backyard, wasting time on the tire swing. He had a fence to mend and vegetables to gather from the garden. His mother was in the kitchen and *the smell of apple pie was on the wind.*

The viewpoint in my mind zoomed out, and I saw the house his father built. People, families, lived in their own little houses. They weren't crammed together as individuals into apartment complexes, forced to room with strangers. They weren't separated from society as children, living in group homes, raised by the government. What happened to the old farmhouses?

Andy joined Dedrick now. They sang in harmony, "Living in America where the milk and honey flow by the sweat of my brow and the crops I grow . . ."

Their song weaved a thread through us all. Soon, almost everyone was clapping or moving to the beat. When the chorus came around, we joined in, singing something close to what Dedrick and Andy sang. By the time the song ended, I had tears in my eyes and a smile on my face. I wanted more. Everyone wanted more.

Dedrick glanced at a few faces and then looked to Andy. They mumbled to each other, picked a few notes and began strumming, their hands and fingers running up and down the necks of their guitars. "When I met you . . . my life felt new . . . and it would never be the same . . . You turned my head . . . you stole my heart . . . you brought me to my knees . . ."

They sang about a man who loved a woman so much he would wait for her. They sang about a love that we knew little of, a love that waited, sacrificed, and lasted, a love with roots and branches. The Aldonians saw love as something quick and physical, satisfaction now, more like a game than life.

Again, my gaze found Guy and Angel. His arm was around her. She rested her head on his shoulder. They'd been together for years, living through unbelievable dangers. Perhaps they knew love with roots and branches.

The next song was slow and, at first, only Andy strummed the chords. They sang together, slow and in harmony. "My country 'tis of thee, once home of liberty, of thee I sing."

Dedrick's gaze connected with mine.

Heat rushed to my face, but I didn't look away. The sound of his voice, the expression on his face as he sang, transfixed me. I wanted to memorize the words, the sound, and every impression.

"Land where my fathers died, land of the Pilgrim's pride, from every mountain side, let freedom ring."

I couldn't grasp the full meaning of the words. I learned about Pilgrims in History, how they came to this continent and wiped out the natives, how they had no regard for the earth. But this song reflected them differently, favorably.

"My native country, thee, once land of noble free, thy name I love. I love thy rocks and rills, thy woods and templed hills. My heart with rapture fills like that above."

Dedrick and Andy faced each other now. Their voices, manly and sorrowful, put an ache in me that I didn't understand. I had lost something. Or maybe I never had it.

". . . Let mortal tongues awake. Let all that breathe partake. Let rocks their silence break, the sound prolong."

Their voices grew stronger and more intense as they sang, "Our father's God to Thee, Author of liberty, to Thee we sing. Lord set our land aright with freedom's holy light. Restore us with Thy might, Great God, our King!"

Dedrick stopped strumming before Andy did. He stood up. Whether we wanted more or not, he was done.

Applause started on the far side of the room and swelled to a deafening pitch. If the trooper were still wandering the lower levels, he'd have heard it. Kids stood, said a few words to Andy and Dedrick, shook hands, slapped shoulders, and shuffled from the room. Angel directed kids to take the extra lanterns.

Darkness and hushed voices returned to the room. Colony and Aldonian girls stretched out on the mats. Boys lay in hammocks. Dedrick, Andy, the Maxwell Colony hunters, and four Aldonian teens from Secondary sat around one of the two remaining lanterns.

Sleep called to me, but I wanted to know the plan before I lay down. I got up and joined the circle of boys. Dedrick gave me a cold look as I sat down, but I didn't think it had to do with me.

Andy was talking, glancing from face to face and gesturing with his hand. ". . . which is why we need to bring that back. Freedom for all."

"You're naive, Andy," Dedrick said. "You know a few Aldonians. You don't know them all."

"They've been lied to. These kids are here . . ." Andy swept his hand out, indicating the Aldonians in the group. ". . . because they recognize the truth. They've been lied to all their lives. They have a right to live free."

"Andy, they've been lied to in so many ways. Where do you start? Faith? History? Family? The hard truths? And who's going to teach them?"

"We are." He indicated the entire group with a glance. A few boys grunted in assent. "We'll plant the seed."

A shock wave hit me. I sucked in a breath of air. My dream! This had to do with my dream. *Tell them,* I thought *My Friend* said.

"You're worried we're going to fight," Andy said.

Dedrick smirked. "You'll have to fight. The Regimen will hunt you down. If you leave with me, you'll be safe. If you stay, you'll get caught. Your enemy is fully armored and has every technology on its side. They'll overpower you. You'll be sent to Re-Ed or worse."

"It's not about fighting or getting people out of Aldonia. I know that's how you, how the Mosheh sees it. And we'll do both if we have to. But we're not looking to leave. We're making a commitment to change Aldonia."

"Tell them," *My Friend* said again, the clarity of the message leaving no room for doubt. I didn't want to tell them. I didn't want to get between brothers, to say something that would put me on the side opposite Dedrick.

"I hate to disappoint you," Dedrick said, "but you'll find that the majority of Aldonians don't want change. They agree with the philosophies. They're content to have the Regimen run their lives as long as they don't have to do any real work and can still get their entertainment credits."

Dark clouds rolled over a vast stretch of cracked land. Shadows moved and deepened. A figure appeared . . . "Andy's right," I said, speaking too loudly, my voice as out of place as ice in a fire.

Dedrick's eyes, black in the dim light, snapped to me. The others turned to me, too, a few looking like they just realized I sat among them.

"I had this dream. I don't know exactly what it means. I thought it had to do with me alone, but now I'm not sure. Something you said . . ." I looked at Andy.

"Tell us," Andy said, pushing long bangs off his forehead. He had eyes and hair like Dedrick's, brown and earthy.

So I told them about the dream, about the dark clouds and the cracked land, about the evil man that sowed the weeds, and about the other man who sowed the wheat. "It felt imperative," I said, my voice cracking, "that the wheat take root in the field of weeds."

"You dream," Dedrick said, his face like stone. "You are not an Interpreter of Dreams." He made it sound like a job title, a specific vocation.

"But she dreams," Rick said, awe in his tone. I had seen him here and there during my days at Maxwell, but I remembered him from the videos of the destruction of Maxwell that they made me watch. He was the hunter who hesitated to lower his gun on the Unity Troopers that came for them.

"Are any of you an Interpreter?" Dedrick glared at every boy in turn. They each shook their head. Two colony boys whispered to each other.

Dedrick stood, fixing his gaze on the lantern. "Let's get some rest. We'll leave in a few hours. Whoever wants to can come with me. I'll be removing implants before we go."

The group broke up, everyone finding a place to lie down. The hammocks filled up and two boys stretched out on the floor. I stood up last.

Dedrick raised his eyes to me, peering at me over the lantern. He hadn't moved a muscle since standing. "Well, that was helpful."

"I-I'm sorry." I hated the wedge between us though I put it there myself. Wanting to speak privately, I forced myself to move closer. "What will you do with the Aldonian teens who want to go with you?"

"Are there any?"

"I don't know. But if there are . . ."

He shook his head and turned away, finding a place on the floor. I supposed he would have to get the approval of the elders. He probably hadn't thought to ask them.

I returned to my mat, the one nearest the door, and lay down. Wren lay with an arm over her eyes, breathing through her mouth. I tried laying on one side and then the other. Having no pillow, I couldn't get comfortable. The words of one of the songs played in my mind. "I'll wait for you forever." The image of Dedrick's cold stare pushed the words out. He hated that I sided with his brother. I admired Andy's strength of conviction and his willingness to sacrifice comfort and security for the sake of the Aldonians. Dedrick had the same strength, made the same sacrifices. He used the threat of the Regimen as his argument, but he only wanted Andy safe.

"Room for one more?"

I spun to face the owner of the voice.

Juno flopped down and stretched out beside me on the mat. He lay facing me, his head propped up on one hand, a grin on his face and his eyes half closed.

"You can't sleep here," I said, pushing myself up on my elbow. "Girls only on the mats."

He leaned toward me. "You want to get high? We've got every imaginable drug here."

I scrunched my face to show my disgust. "No, I don't. So go away."

He sighed. "Nope. I'm not going anywhere. I always sleep here when I stay."

"Not tonight you don't."

He laid his head back on the mat and closed his eyes. "Tonight I do. Relax. Maybe you'll even like it."

His leg jerked. Someone had kicked his foot.

I looked up.

Dedrick towered over him. He stood with his thumb in a front pocket of his jeans, clutching his jacket in his other hand. "I'm sleeping there. Beat it."

Juno snickered, threw nervous glances from me to Dedrick, and got up. "Whatever, man." I expected him to find a place on the floor, but he left the room.

Dedrick sat down. He handed me his jacket. "Makes for a nice pillow." He lay down and rolled onto his side, facing away from me.

CHAPTER 24

A beeping sound pulled Dedrick from a dream.

He breathed. A pleasant scent teased him. He inhaled again, drawing in as much air as his lungs could hold and savoring the scent. He pictured honey, an old wooden chest, and sunbeams bursting through the canopy deep in the woods. He breathed again, his head getting light. The scent stirred every cell of his being, made him hungry and warm and alive.

The beeping sounded again.

His breath caught. He held it. Something wasn't right. Where was he?

He lay cuddled up against something warm . . . Some*one*?

His eyes snapped open. His nose was buried in Liberty's hair, his arm draped over her waist.

"Shoot!" He flung himself back and rolled onto the floor.

Someone laughed.

Dedrick stumbled, trying to get to his feet. He dashed for the door, tapping his earphone to answer the Mosheh's call. Then he looked back.

Andy sat on a hammock in the darkness, holding his gut and laughing his head off.

~ ~ ~

"Yeah, do it," Guy said, his voice tight and eyes wet. "She can't use it anyway."

"Okay, but it's gonna hurt a little." Dedrick took Angel's calloused hand and turned it palm up.

"I can handle it," Angel said.

Dedrick had completed the task of removing implants from the Maxwell colonists and the Aldonian teens. Whether they remained in Aldonia or not, they'd never be able to use them. If they tried to, the Regimen would find them in a heartbeat, their last free heartbeat. The other Aldonians did not want their ID implants removed. They worked jobs and bought food at the commissary. They wanted their entertainment credits. Most of them had taken off as soon as Angel gave the *all clear*.

Dedrick squeezed the trigger of the implant remover. It worked by sending a focused beam of electricity to disable the anti-tamper feature, then sucking the implant out of a person's hand and into a cartridge. The cartridge was made of a material that blocked the most powerful implant readers. He'd had to dump the cartridge once already. Angel had given him a small metal box in which to store the implants. He'd have them destroyed when he returned to the Mosheh.

Angel winced but didn't moan or cry out like all the others had.

Guy winced, too, just watching. He bit his lip.

"Put a bandage on it for a day," Dedrick said to him. "She's good to go."

"Thank you," he whispered. A tear rolled down his cheek.

"Get a grip, man," Dedrick said, slapping Guy on the shoulder. "You're ruining my image of you as a soulless Aldonian."

"You lump us all together, give us a single judgment?" Guy tilted his head back and stared down his nose, the way he had when Liberty and Dedrick stood on the judgment step.

"Naw, I can't honestly do that, can I?"

"No, you cannot." Guy shook Dedrick's left hand and patted Dedrick's arm with his stump. "I still want to meet your people."

"I'll let them know." Dedrick handed the implant remover to Guy. He decided to give it to him in case they should need it in the future. He'd get another one from the Mosheh, no problem.

"This way," Angel said, lantern in hand. She started down the rope ladder. Had she even grabbed a bandage?

Dedrick climbed after her and followed her through dark corridors and down the two flights of stairs they had first come up. Their footfalls echoed. They approached a corner room. Voices came from inside, Andy's voice. Andy laughed. Was he talking to Liberty?

Dedrick's cheeks burned. He hadn't gotten more than a glimpse of Liberty since he woke. Did she know he had his arm around her last night? He'd have to apologize.

Angel breezed through the doorway and into the room.

Dedrick followed, a moldy stench hitting him.

Big gray pipes ran along the ceiling and down to an ancient furnace like the arms of a freakish monster. Two water heaters with a mess of their own pipes stood on the opposite side of the room. A group of kids hung out by a heavy metal door.

"Hey, bro," Andy said, a quirky grin on his face. He stood next to Liberty and three colony girls. Seemed like they all stopped talking at once. Every one of them had a strange expression. Maybe Dedrick was paranoid.

"Okay," Dedrick said, "so what's the final number? How many are coming with me?" Dedrick did a quick head-count. All of the colonists were in the room.

Andy's grin faded. He breathed in and exhaled through his mouth. "Um."

"Just spit it out," Dedrick said. "I no longer care. I'll do my best to explain your choice to Mom and Dad. Once I get them out of Re-Ed, that is. Of course, they'll know exactly what's in store for you should you get caught."

"Knock it off." Andy frowned.

"Seven colonists are going with us," Liberty said, looking directly into his eyes, "and two Aldonians."

Dedrick nodded but found it hard holding her gaze. He faced Andy. "So most of them are staying with you, huh, Andy?"

"We'll be all right," Andy said. "Guy said we can stay here. There's a priest that stays here, too. Did you see him?"

"No. . . . Yeah, I guess I saw him."

"I took that as a sign. This is what I'm called to do."

"A priest has to go after the sheep, regardless of how far they stray. That's his job. You, Andy, are no priest."

The colony girls giggled. Liberty tilted her head and glanced from face to face. She hadn't lived in the Maxwell Colony long enough to understand the priests.

Dedrick grabbed Andy's sleeve and dragged him farther down the wall to where the water heaters stood. "I hope you haven't blabbed too much about the Mosheh already. You need to keep quiet about us. Not everyone can be trusted. Don't use our name. Don't mention where we hide. Don't talk about our methods. And, I don't know how you got it, but we need our Intel back from Finley."

"Uh, we might need it, too. We'll have to share."

"How's that gonna work? I just told you to keep quiet about us."

"Hey." Angel stepped into their huddle. "If you need to travel in the dark, you'd better get going. It's nearing dawn."

"Yeah, okay." Dedrick scanned the faces of the others in the room. They all stared at him. They all counted on him. He'd never moved so many people through Aldonia at once.

Angel walked to the door.

"So, if you change your mind, or you need me," he said to Andy, "you can get a message to me, right?"

"Yeah, sure. I'll paint some graffiti on the side of a Regimen building." Andy smiled.

Dedrick debated internally whether to hug Andy or not. He didn't want Andy thinking he condoned his behavior. His heart won out, and he pulled Andy to his chest. Then he mussed his hair and turned away.

Angel stood by the door, her hands on her hips and eyes on him. "So this comes out the back of the building. There's a retaining wall built around old air conditioner units. It's dark. Don't walk into them. There're no surveillance cameras to worry about, so you can take any streets you want. We tell our visitors to head north. There's a hole under the fence. It's easy enough to get through."

Dedrick nodded and yanked open the door. A gust of soggy air rushed in, relief from the moldy air inside. Water dripped from several unseen points outside, splashing in unseen puddles.

"Thanks for helping us," Liberty said, taking Angel's hand.

Angel gave a controlled smile, not looking at all like the woman who held a gun on him yesterday. Dedrick's mother gave the same smile whenever he left for a rescue mission. "Stay safe, Dedrick," she would say, "I want to see you soon." Then she'd hug him with the strength of a bear.

Dedrick's heart wrenched. He had come here to rescue his little brother. He was leaving without him.

He forced himself through the doorway. Darkness and uncertainty surrounded him, stretching on forever. The rain had stopped. Thick blackberry clouds hung in the sky, hiding the moon and stars and the shadowy forms of his surroundings. He groped for the flashlight on his belt.

The beam from the flashlight fell on the end of a chest-high air conditioner unit. It crossed the direct path to the gateway in the retaining wall. A mangled spider's web clung to the corner of it. A person could run right into the unit in the dark. Too bad they didn't have more flashlights.

He stepped to the corner of the air-conditioner unit and directed the beam to the gateway in the retaining wall.

The *rescues*, as he would think of them now, filed out: five girls and two boys from the Maxwell Colony—their families would be glad to see them—and two Aldonians. They all wore the same style of clothes, slim pants and pale jackets made from bamboo and hemp eco fabrics. The talking and whispering lessened with each rescue that crossed the threshold. They followed the beam from his flashlight, shuffling out beyond the wall.

Liberty came last, a bounce in her step. "Hey, I need to tell you something." She wore night vision glasses and the cape, black side out. Probably a good idea. He had no idea what had become of his cape.

"Silver's gone," she said, sliding the glasses up onto her head. "She left early this morning." She fidgeted with something under her cape.

"Yeah, I figured. I'm hoping she thinks we'll head north like Angel told us to do."

Liberty pulled something out from under her cape and handed it to him.

"My cape?" He unfolded it, shook it out, and flung it over his shoulders.

"They look like glow sticks." She glanced at the rescues. "But there's no reason we shouldn't wear them."

He tried not to smile. He needed to stay focused.

"So we're not heading north, the way Angel suggested?" she said.

He shook his head. "We will for one block." He glanced at the open doorway. Angel leaned against the doorjamb, a curvy silhouette against a dim background. "The fence is easy enough to climb. We can come out anywhere we want."

"Okay." She pushed the cape off her wrist and looked at her TekBand—Elder Lukman's TekBand, that is. "I'll bring up the rear." She pressed buttons and the clock face lit up. "I know how to contact Elder Lukman. How do I communicate with you?" She kept her chin down and glanced up through her lashes, a look that appealed to him.

"Dedrick?"

"Um, yeah." He pressed buttons on his TekBand, making a call to the phone on hers.

Her TekBand buzzed. A button lit up. She gave a childlike smile and pressed the button.

"You need the earpiece." He pointed to where it set in the wristband. "Press the button that just lit up and you'll call the last person you spoke with. Me."

She installed the earpiece, smiling at him and batting her eyes. "Okay, let's go."

Liberty's smile rendered him senseless. It took him a good two seconds to recover. This wasn't a game. She had no reason to smile.

"Yeah, let's go." Dedrick counted the nine rescues and led the way.

They crossed a street and cut down a narrow alley. Garbage and debris lay scattered between the buildings. Dedrick walked backwards every few feet, shining the light for the others to see. Most of the rescues tripped anyway, the colonists grunting and saying "Ouch," the Aldonians cussing.

Once through the narrow alley, Dedrick turned left onto a longer alley that ran behind rows of decaying buildings. This alley had less garbage but more puddles, wide puddles they couldn't get around.

It didn't matter which streets or alleys they took through the old city center as long as they arrived at the southeast corner. Fulton had given him a route to the nearest Mosheh access point, one inside a Warehouse Zone. They needed to get there before sunrise. The warehouses got busy in the early mornings.

Dedrick splashed through the middle of a puddle.

"It's seeping through my shoes," one of the girls said.

Another turn had them headed in the right direction. A half-mile jog through weeds heavy with rainwater brought them to the southwest corner of the old city center. And the fence. Everyone stood in a row, staring at the six-foot-tall chain-link fence and the two rows of sagging barbed wire on top.

On the other side of the fence, land overrun with weeds stretched out to a smooth street of offices and apartment buildings. Hints of royal blue colored the scalloped edges of clouds along the horizon. They had less than a two-mile trek to the Warehouse Zone. How much time did they have before dawn?

"We have to climb that?" said Catherine, a fourteen-year-old colony girl, maybe the youngest of the rescues. She stood with slumped shoulders and folded arms. A cool breeze sent her stringy blonde hair flapping into her face.

"Just do what I do." Dedrick got a running start and leaped. He latched onto the top bar with both hands and stuck a foot to the fence. Pulling himself up with his arms, he ran farther up the fence. Then he grabbed the top of a barbed wire support to steady himself and climbed high enough to clear the barbed wire.

He swung a leg over, turned around, and stuck a foot in the chain links on the opposite side. He latched onto the top bar again and dropped to the ground. Nothing to it.

Julie, another colony girl who was maybe a year older than Catherine, bumped Catherine's shoulder and made a nervous giggle. "Wow, I don't see myself doing that."

"Is that barbed wire on the top?" Catherine said, peering up through round eyes. The wind had left a strand of hair in her face.

Liberty bit her lip and squeezed in between the girls, grabbing each of them by a shoulder. "We can do it. It might be a little tricky, but we can do it, right?"

"Um," Catherine and Julie said together. The three of them gazed at the fence. Julie covered her mouth with both hands and snorted. She had a reputation for hysterical fits of laughter.

John and Caleb, both sixteen-year-old colony boys, raced each other to the fence. Caleb leaped first. The boys grunted and the fence rattled under their feet as they climbed. They were up and over, thudding to the ground in a matter of seconds.

"Good," Dedrick said, slapping Caleb's hand. "Not too bad, right?"

The fence rattled. An Aldonian girl climbed, picking her steps.

What if the girls didn't have the strength to clear the barbed wire? Dedrick dashed, leaped, and beat the girl to the top. He ripped the cape from his shoulders, folded it with one hand, and draped it over the rusty barbed wire.

She reached the top and swung a leg over.

Dedrick yanked the barbed wires down. Age had made them sag, so it took no effort to lower them to the top bar of the fence.

One by one, the girls climbed over until only Catherine, Julie, and Liberty remained. Julie sat on the wet ground, laughing or crying into her hands. Catherine and Liberty whispered back and forth.

Dedrick shifted, trying to find a more comfortable position on his perch on the fence. He shook out one hand to alleviate the numbness. His fingers had permanent indents from the chain links. The royal blue that had edged the lowest clouds now filled half the sky. They still had two miles to go.

"Uh, girls," he said, "we need to get moving."

"Let's give it a try," Liberty said, leading Catherine by the elbow. "Come on, Julie, we can do this."

And she did, Liberty that is. She let the girls step on her clasped hands, then she heaved them up as high as she could. She cheered them all the way to the top where Dedrick offered his shoulder and used his arm to guide them over. John and Caleb stood below, waiting to catch them. No one fell.

Liberty climbed up and over last, taking her time as if the job made her nervous, too.

"You could've climbed that and jumped over in seconds," Dedrick said. They walked together through the field of weeds that grew between the fence and the paved road. He picked a few wide leaves from the weeds he passed, thinking he might need them in the future.

Liberty shrugged. "Maybe."

"Those girls might not be the fence climbing sort," Dedrick said, "but they're strong in their own way. Do you know how they got caught?"

"No."

"When the siren went off in Maxwell, they helped get the children from the schoolhouse to the safety of the CAT cave. One boy was missing. They went to find him. Didn't give up until they did. Unfortunately Unity Troopers found him, too."

~ ~ ~

They split into two groups in case anyone should see them. A group of five or six would draw less attention and arouse less speculation than a group of eleven.

Dedrick had Liberty take her group, the two Aldonian girls and the two colony boys, through a residential area. If anyone noticed them, he or she might assume they were first-shift workers getting an early start. Liberty's route was also more direct. They should arrive at the warehouses first. He instructed her to wait in the line of trees that separated the apartments from the Warehouse Zone.

Five colony girls jogged behind Dedrick, whispering and occasionally giggling. He caught a word every now and then. "My feet hurt." "I thought he said two miles." "Why do you think he did that to his hair?"

Dedrick and his group took the longer, less direct route down alleys behind businesses and shops. They would look out of place if anyone noticed them. Kids partied in certain alleys at night. An occasional kid traveled through them to get to or from work. The shop employees brought garbage out in the evening, but the alleys typically remained dead.

Swiveling beams of light illuminated an intersection a block away. A car, probably a Unity Trooper making rounds, would cross their path in a few seconds. They needed to hide.

Dedrick stopped jogging and turned around. The girls had fallen behind, but they neared a dumpster and a stack of crates he had passed. He sprinted to them.

"Back here. Quick." He pointed to the dumpster and then spun his hand, encouraging them to hurry.

The girls squeezed into the tight space between the wall and the dumpster. He dragged a crate over and squatted behind it next to Catherine. The dark of night had lifted, bringing shades of indigo to their surroundings. If anyone looked, they'd see him, maybe see her.

"What's the matter?" Catherine whispered, her eyes round.

"Nothing." The odor of wet metal and spoiled tomatoes came from the dumpster. He breathed through his mouth. "We're just going to wait here for a minute."

"We're taking a break," Julie said, "behind a dumpster?" She tried to suppress a giggle but it scraped out through her nose anyways. She was not the girl to take on a covert operation, which is why he took her instead of sending her with Liberty.

"I thought we were almost there," a girl whispered.

"Yeah, he said two miles," another girl whispered.

"We *are* almost there," Dedrick said, feeling defensive. "Warehouses are at the end of this alley. If we all moved a little faster—" He swallowed the rest of his reply and softened his tone. "You guys are doing great. And once we get underground, we'll be safe."

"Hey, man, whatcha doing back there?"

Dedrick's gaze clicked to the alley. Two girls gasped. Julie laughed. Or rather, she guffawed.

A man sauntered toward them. He wore a business suit, not the government-issued kind, but the kind a guy had to spend credits on. A cigarette dangled from his mouth.

Dedrick stood up and glanced down the alley. He didn't see light from the headlights. Didn't see a car. The Unity Trooper had probably passed.

Dedrick faced the approaching man.

"How many of them you got back there?" The man moved his head from side to side, peering. Smoke curled up from his cigarette, carrying a sweet grassy odor.

"None of your business." Dedrick shifted to block his view. His phone buzzed. Was it Liberty or the Mosheh?

Julie snorted and then cracked up.

Dedrick rolled his eyes and huffed. Why now? First, the waste of time at the fence. Now this.

One of the girls whispered harshly, probably telling Julie to quiet down. The laughter sounded muffled for a second, and then she let loose.

The man smiled. "You know it's morning, right?" He motioned with the hand that held the cigarette. "What's she on? I'd like to get me some of that."

Dedrick's mouth fell open. The man thought she was high. Maybe he thought they were all high. He could play along. "You say it's morning, huh?" He grinned and tried loosening his posture, standing with a slouch.

The business suit laughed. "Better get them girls home. I'm sure they have jobs to get to."

"Yeah, thanks."

The man strolled back the way he came.

Dedrick exhaled and tapped his earpiece. "Yeah, what's up?"

"We're here," Liberty said. "Where are you?"

~ ~ ~

A sliver of hot pink in the dark sky showed through gaps between buildings, a warning of the storm to come.

High fences surrounded Regimen Warehouse Zones, enclosing rows of storage units and warehouses. A code opened a sliding gate, the only way in or out. Fulton had given Dedrick the code this morning.

Dedrick, wearing his hood over his eyes, waited for the gate to slide open. No click. No little green light over the keypad. The fence didn't budge.

He scanned the empty streets and tried the code again, tapping the keypad with his closed pocketknife. He didn't want to leave fingerprints. As far as he knew, the Citizen Safety Station had nothing on him. He'd like to keep it that way.

The light on the keypad flashed red. The gate remained cold and immobile.

How many times could he try the code before a signal went out to CSS?

Something high in his peripheral vision caught his attention. He peered up at the surveillance camera mounted to a warehouse unit inside the fence. Fulton had told him it was down.

The light flashed on. The camera moved.

Dedrick wheeled around and ripped to the corner of the fence, out of camera range. Heart racing, he tapped his earpiece to connect to Fulton. "Hey, buddy, code's not working, camera is. You trying to get us caught?"

"What?" Liberty said. "What's going on?" A tap to his earpiece connected him to the last person with whom he spoke. *Duh.* He had spoken with her last, not Fulton.

Dedrick strode a few paces farther from the camera's range and took a deep breath. "The code Fulton gave me is not working."

"What do we do now? What's the backup plan?"

"Let me contact Fulton, see if he has a working code."

"We could climb the fence. We've all done if before." The girls with Liberty whined, making complaints he couldn't make out through the earpiece.

"Are you kidding me?" He glanced at the top of the fence. A black bird stood on a post. "This one's twice as high as the last one."

"Well, you could do it. Or me."

"Yeah, then what?" He needed to call Fulton, not waste time with her.

"Hot wire that jeep over there and open the gate. The gate opens automatically from the inside, doesn't it, when someone in a vehicle goes to leave?"

Dedrick lowered his gaze. Sure enough, a jeep sat inside the fence, outside the range of the surveillance camera and near the storage unit they wanted. "Then what? Park it in the gateway until you ten run through? They got surveillance here, you know. CSS will pick that up instantly. Unity Troopers will scour the area. They'll tear it up until they find out where we've gone. Puts our whole operation in jeopardy."

"So take the surveillance camera out."

He huffed. Did she ever give up? "I gotta talk to Fulton." He ended the call and pressed buttons on his TekBand to reach Fulton.

"Dedrick, been trying to call you. That surveillance camera's up."

"Yeah, I noticed." Dedrick sprinted for the fence and leaped. Chain links rattled at the impact of his hands and feet. He hung a good distance above the ground. Keeping momentum, he climbed like a cat seeking refuge in a tree. "And you gave me a bad code."

"Yeah, we're working on that. They must be tightening their security everywhere, changing codes and fixing surveillance. Meanwhile, you got a leaf shooter?"

"Got it. I'm on my way."

Dedrick's biceps complained as he heaved all his weight onto his arms and swung his legs over the top of the fence. At least he didn't have barbed wire to contend with. He climbed halfway down, inside the warehouse area now, and jumped.

He checked his belt to make sure he had the leaf shooter.

Leaf shooters had no range. They were kids' toys but, long ago, the Mosheh had found a use for them. They designed an adhesive from natural substances, one that would degrade within ten minutes. With a leaf, a dab of adhesive, and a shooter, they could blind a surveillance camera without raising suspicion.

Dedrick found himself jogging toward the jeep, a boxy, dull gray, get-the-job-done vehicle. It sat high on its five-spoke, eighteen-inch wheels. A simple shade top covered it, bungeed to the roll cage. Water beaded on the hard plastic interior. Tools and food wrappers littered the floor in the back.

He peered through the fence to where Liberty and the rescues waited in the trees. He couldn't see them, but they could probably see him. He'd better get moving before the streets got busy. The Mosheh access point was in a storage unit visible from the road.

From the top corner of the taller storage units, a surveillance camera swiveled from side to side, watching the gate. Dedrick jogged around the entire strip of storage units to come up behind it. He snatched the compact grappling hook from his belt and deployed the hooks. Still running, he whipped the grappling hook to the roof of the units. It hit metal and scraped until it reached the trim.

Dedrick tugged. It felt secure enough, so he climbed with his boots to the grooved steel door of a unit. Reaching the top, he heaved himself up and walked crouched across the ribbed roof.

The pink sun had inched higher in the sky, painting more clouds. He had to move faster.

He drew the leaf shooter from his belt, dug a leaf from a pocket, and squeezed adhesive onto the leaf.

His earphone buzzed. He tapped it. "What's up?"

"Trucks are coming." Liberty panted, sounding out of breath. "Two minutes, they'll be here." Something rattled . . . almost sounded like a chain-link fence.

"You'll be safe in the trees." He stretched out prone and aimed the shooter, waiting for the camera to turn enough for him to do the job. Cool water seeped into his clothing from the pools between the steel ribs of the roof.

"Have you got the surveillance down?" She grunted.

"In another two seconds I do." He narrowed one eye and adjusted his aim.

"Good, I've got an idea."

"What?" He jerked his face to the side. She gave no reply, probably ended the call. "Liberty!"

The camera swiveled toward him.

Dedrick took the shot and slammed his cheek to the cold steel roof. If he missed, the camera might pick him up. What did Liberty mean she had an idea? She was as impulsive as Andy. Neither of them had patience or knew how to keep themselves safe. He was stupid to leave in her in charge of a group of rescues. Elder Lukman was stupid to have sent her along.

He risked a peek. The camera turned away, the leaf sticking to its lens. Yeah, he was awesome.

He scooted back to his grappling hook, folded it, tossed it to the ground, and jumped down. He tapped a button on his TekBand to call Liberty, then wound the rope around the grappling hook.

She didn't answer.

Jogging around the strip of storage units towards the gate, he called Fulton.

"Hey, Dedrick, we got nothing. You're gonna have to come up with Plan B."

"Plan B? Thanks, I knew I could count on—"

Two glowing white eyes approached the gate, a delivery truck drawing near, another behind it.

Dedrick skidded to a stop and wheeled around. Unsure as to which way the trucks would turn, he made a decision to head for the jeep. He could hide behind it.

Around the corner and halfway down the row, he skidded to another stop and stared, dumbfounded. What happened to the jeep? Either someone had taken it, or he'd lost his direction.

He raced to the end of the strip of storage units and peeked around the corner. The two delivery trucks rumbled through the gateway and turned left. The gate moved, beginning to close. The jeep came from nowhere, its lights dark, and squeezed through at the last second. It turned right.

"Liberty," Dedrick mumbled, his blood boiling. He took off after the jeep.

She parked it in its original spot, near the storage unit they needed. Kids started spilling out. Other than a grunt or two, no one made a sound. How had she fit ten bodies into a jeep?

Liberty jogged toward him and peeled off her night vision glasses. "Now what?"

"Uh, yeah." He turned away from her and dug the key from a pants pocket, a dozen angry thoughts rolling around his head. She could've been caught. He unlocked the storage unit. She could've gotten them all caught. The door lifted with no effort. She needed to think before taking action.

The rescues rushed into the storage unit, filling the empty spaces between stacks of boxes. Liberty squeezed in last, having nowhere else to stand but beside him.

As he lowered the door, a black shadow swallowed up the magenta light of dawn. Scents pervaded the tiny space—sweat and fresh morning air—encircling him and bringing to mind honey, an old wooden chest, and sunbeams stealing through a canopy of leaves.

He was sending Liberty down the chute first.

CHAPTER 25

"Hold on." Dedrick tapped one of the vertical bars of the strange chair in which I now sat. He had set the flashlight on the floor, and its beam inverted all the shadows on his face and set fire to the blond streaks in his hair. He appeared sinister. Untrustworthy.

Something clicked, loud and in my ear. I gripped cold metal bars and took a breath. Every muscle in my body tensed.

The chair dropped.

My stomach abandoned me. I swooshed down, freefalling into darkness, a cool breeze whipping my hair, my body tingling.

I had experienced three types of Mosheh access points: manholes with ordinary ladders, chutes disguised as other things—a crematory in my case—and hydraulic chairs. The chair was my favorite. I imagined myself on one of the amusement park rides of the past, from back when people indulged in a number of reckless pursuits. Many of them died, we were told, but they risked it anyway. They didn't value life the way we did now. Not even their own.

My ride slowed at the last split second and ended with a hissing sound and a thud.

Darkness surrounded me.

I fumbled with the buckle, trying to unlatch it. Dedrick had nine others and himself to send down. He had seemed worried about the noise he would make setting up and operating the chair.

"Everybody back up, squeeze together," he had said, shining the flashlight in faces. He listened at the closed door to the storage unit for half a minute and then set to work. He shoved stacks of boxes aside, flung open a floor panel, and reached into a dark hole under the floor. Within seconds, he had hoisted the hydraulic chair up and into position.

He had adjusted a few levers, then his eyes clicked to me. "You're first."

The buckle finally yielded. I had wasted too many seconds. I shrugged the shoulder harnesses off and blinked at the darkness. Where was the floor? *Don't worry, just jump.* I couldn't get myself to do it.

I pressed a button that made the face of my watch light up, a turquoise glow that had no reach. I had to do it. I had to leap into darkness. It felt like a test.

"Why are you doing this to me?" I said to *My Friend*.

I took a breath and leaped from the seat. My feet hit ground, giving me instant relief. A part of me thought I would keep falling or that I'd land on a slimy creature, something out of fiction. It was strange what a person's mind came up with when faced with the unknown.

Dedrick had shown us the big red button we needed to press to send the chair back up. I waved the watch near the side of the chair, using the turquoise bubble of light to search for it, my heartbeats counting off every second I wasted. Dull metal bars ran vertically and framed the chair. The button looked gray under the light.

I smacked the button and stepped back.

The chair hummed and whooshed up the chute, causing a breeze that gave me goose bumps. A second later, I stood gaping at the darkness and decided to explore my surroundings. Dedrick would send the teens down one by one. We couldn't all huddle around the chair.

I turned and reached out into nothingness. While my vision proved useless, my other senses kicked into overdrive. The air, cool on my neck and cheeks, smelled of stagnant puddles and roots in rich dirt. Far above me, the chairlift hissed and squeaked. It banged. No sounds came from nearby, no sounds from the underground. I continued to wave my hands before me, finding more nothingness.

Behind and above, something creaked. Then someone hooted, a boy, either John or Caleb, someone enjoying the ride as much as I had.

I spun to face the chairlift terminal.

There came a hydraulic hissing sound and a sweet, oily-scented breeze.

"Woohoo, that was unreal!"

I recognized Caleb's voice. I could hear him fumbling with the buckle.

"Liberty?"

"I'm here." I pressed the button on the watch. The light had shut off on its own after a few seconds. Now faint turquoise light showed a nondescript face and moving arms.

"Where's your flashlight?" Caleb made shuffling noises, then slid out of the seat and drew near.

"This is all I have." I moved my wrist toward the side of the chair, trying to find the return button. I smacked it. "Stand back."

We both took two steps back.

165

"Where are we?" he said.

"A tunnel, one of many. We're safe now."

He shuffled away from me. "Dedrick said you'd have a flashlight."

"Why didn't he send Catherine or Julie first?" Before Dedrick sent me down, I suggested he send them next so they wouldn't have time to develop immobilizing fear. If it reached that point, I couldn't imagine Dedrick convincing them.

"I dunno. He tried to. I guess they weren't ready." Caleb had moved several meters away. "Found the wall."

The creaking sound came again, followed by a hiss, a click, and a sweet oil-scented breeze.

A girl giggled. "Wow, I never want to do that again."

"Julie, is that you?" I said.

"It's us, me and Catherine. Dedrick let us go together." More giggles and whispers, something about the buckle, and then, "Oh, I got it."

"Here, let me help you." I turned on the turquoise nightlight. Grabbing arms I could barely see, I yanked Julie and then Catherine from the chair, each of them squealing in turn.

"Stand back." I smacked the return button and led them to Caleb. He leaned against the wall.

The rest came down one by one. Everyone asked about my flashlight, wondering why I didn't have it on. The darkness didn't bother anyone for long. They huddled together, mumbling and giggling like Primary kids who stayed awake long after the nannies put them to bed.

Several minutes passed after the last person came down.

"Isn't that everyone?" one of the girls said. "Aren't we all here?"

Someone was counting, probably tapping everyone in the dark.

"Dedrick's still up there," John said. "What do you think's keeping him?"

"I hope something didn't go wrong," Julie said.

Finally the creaking sound came, then the whoosh and breeze. Dedrick descended with a beam of light that fell on the walls and us. He hopped out of the seat and darted around to the back of it. He swung the beam of light to me and back to his business with the chair. "Liberty, why isn't your flashlight on?"

"I don't have a flashlight." I felt stupid. I hadn't really explored the watch. I gathered, now, that it had a flashlight on it.

He straightened up and came to me. "Hold this." He shoved his flashlight into my hand and lifted my other arm with a gentle touch. "Voila!" He flicked something on the front edge of the watch and a beam of light burst forth.

The kids moaned.

"She had that all along."

"Can you believe it?"

"Here we've been standing in the dark."

I scanned our surroundings. We stood in a cozy alcove with a high ceiling and a stone floor. Thick wooden beams supported dirt walls and crisscrossed the ceiling. A tunnel ran in either direction off the wall opposite the chair. The chair now sat enclosed in something that resembled an old-fashioned telephone booth.

I shined the light on Dedrick. "What took you so long? Everything okay?"

"Yeah, sure. I had to secure things. And I got a call." He walked past me toward the others. "Liberty's going to lead you through the tunnels. We have a community not far from here." His flashlight's beam landed on John. "John, you're with me."

John's brows, thick like black caterpillars, drew together.

"Where're you going?" I said, coming up beside him.

Dedrick grabbed my hand, brought it up waist high, and pressed controls on the watch. "Elder Lukman said we need to get the children from Primary. We need to go now."

"Now? Why?"

"In two hours, they're increasing security."

"I should go with you. I don't know these tunnels. I can't lead these guys anywhere."

"Sure you can. Here's a map." He was still holding my hand and staring at my watch. The hands and numbers of the old-fashioned clock face no longer showed. A map made of glowing white lines as thin as a strand of hair replaced it. "We're here." He pointed. "You need to go here. Now there's a tricky area—"

"No." I yanked my hand from his and tried to unfasten the watch. I couldn't get the buckle undone. "Let someone else lead. Let John lead. I'm going with you to Primary."

I needed to get the children. This was my mission, my redemption. I thought I had proved myself, getting the teens through the gate to the Warehouse Zone and not getting caught. Dedrick must've seen things differently. Maybe he didn't like that I came up with an idea and that it worked. He wanted to be in charge.

"No." Dedrick walked away. John met him in the middle of the alcove.

I went after him and jumped in between them. "Why not? I know the layout of that Primary Residence better than either of you. John doesn't know it at all. Do you, John?" I spun to face him.

John shrugged, his eyes wide under his caterpillar brows. "I-I, well, I . . . . No, I don't know anything about this place, Aldonia, I mean. It's all so strange. I just want to get home."

A pang of guilt struck me. He wouldn't be going home. His home no longer existed. Had no one told him? Did any of the Maxwell colonists know the extent of the damage? Maybe he knew but couldn't accept it.

"You have to do what I say," Dedrick said to him, stepping around and angling away from me.

"Okay," John said, bobbing his head and upper body. His naturally pouty lower lip made him appear younger. And scared. He glanced over his shoulder at the other teens. They were whispering, one of them giggling, none of them paying attention.

"Look, Dedrick," I shouted, "I know you're against me."

Dedrick, still with his back to me, froze. Everyone shut up. All eyes snapped to me. Dedrick turned around, pivoting on one foot. His Adam's apple bobbed. A guilty look flashed across his face.

"I know you don't want me joining the Mosheh," I said. "You don't think I've got what it takes to be one of you, and maybe I don't, but I can do this. I used to live there. I know when the nannies wake up and what they do next." My arm flew out, an uncontrolled gesture. "I know we have less than an hour before they wake up the kids."

Dedrick took a step toward me.

"I know how they feel about their job, how it's just something they have to do, and I know how they would respond to seeing strangers like us in the residence."

He came closer still. Everyone stared.

My voice came out higher than usual. I couldn't stop talking. "Even if one of the nannies sees us, I know how to put them at ease, eliminate suspicion. If one of the kids sees us . . ." My voice cracked.

Dedrick took my hand and pulled it to himself. "Okay," he whispered, "you're with me." He turned my hand palm up and unfastened the watch.

"John, you can lead the others." He slipped the watch from my wrist and tossed it to John. "One of the Mosheh is on his way, a kid named Bolcan. He'll meet you halfway or so."

"Okay."

"Put the TekBand on your wrist." Dedrick went over the functions of the TekBand with John. "Be careful with it. It belongs to Elder Lukman."

"Elder Lukman?" John spoke with awe in his tone.

"You know him?"

"Heard of him. Are we going to meet him?"

"Probably."

Each of the teens thanked Dedrick and told us goodbye. They turned and strolled, talking and giggling, down the tunnel. We turned the other way, without words and immediately breaking into a jog.

~ ~ ~

Dedrick jogged with his back straight and face forward, his arms relaxed and swinging with his strides. He reminded me of a Greek warrior.

In Primary, I learned about the Olympic Games and the destructive mentality resulting from them. They began in Ancient Greece and continued down through the years until the world governments united under the Regimen Custodia Terra. The Regimen encouraged exercise for health reasons, but they frowned upon competition. It gave a person a false sense of superiority, they said, and made others feel inadequate. We all had a proper place in society, the way all living things had their place in the world. No person, no species, should claim superiority.

The beam from Dedrick's flashlight bounced to the rhythm of our footfalls. The cool air against my sweat made my skin clammy.

I liked pretending I was an athlete. Athletes trained for and competed in different events. The foot racing interested me the most. I enjoyed walking, running, needing to suck air deep into my lungs, feeling the strain in my muscles. I couldn't fight like Dedrick. I didn't know the tunnels like he did. I couldn't even operate Elder Lukman's fancy watch, or TekBand, or whatever. But I could run.

A mile or so through the tunnels, Dedrick slowed to a brisk walking pace, the beam from his flashlight steadying. Every step brought us closer to rescuing the children. We needed to get them out before the nannies woke up.

I matched his pace, a hint of irritation seeping into my mood. "I hope you aren't walking on my account. I can keep going."

"What?" He breathed through his mouth. "No, I'm sure you can. I've seen you in action." He smiled. "We're over halfway there. We don't want to be catching our breath when we sneak into Primary. Might wake the wrong kid."

"Oh, yeah." He was right. Some kids awoke from the slightest noise. My first year in Primary, I never wanted to use the bathroom during the night. Whenever someone got out of bed or made a loud noise, this redheaded girl used to sit bolt upright. Her eyes popped open, two round moons in the night, but she never spoke or even looked around. A minute later, she'd lay back down. I'd hide under my blankets.

"Hey . . ." Dedrick said, glancing. He transferred the flashlight to his other hand and rubbed his wounded arm around the elbow. His mouth opened and seemed to wrap around a word, but nothing came out.

"Yeah?" I suspected he wanted to criticize my decision to climb the fence and hotwire the jeep. Maybe he wanted to use my impulsive action to show me how unworthy I was of becoming a Mosheh. Or maybe he wanted to talk about my dream, how I used it to defend Andy's decision to stay in Aldonia.

"I-I wanted to apologize."

I gave him a blank stare, then I realized what he meant. This had nothing to do with me. I exhaled. "Apologize to Andy?"

He gave a little headshake, his eyes narrowing. "What? No. Why would I apologize to him?"

"I don't know. You said you wanted to apologize."

"Not to him. I'm talking to you." He increased the length of his stride, the flashlight beam bouncing erratically.

"Me?"

He stared ahead, mouth shut, jaw twitching. Two seconds later he said, "I, uh, woke up too close to you, had my arm around you. I don't remember doing it, but . . ."

I smiled, touched by his simplicity. That was all? "I remember. It was about an hour before we got up."

He did a double take. "You were awake?"

"I had a nightmare." It was the same one with the weeds and the wheat, but I wasn't about to tell him that. "I woke up startled, might have said something out loud or moaned or something. You threw your arm over me."

"Why didn't you throw it back? Push me away?"

"I was going to. At first I thought the arm belonged to Juno, like he was making a move." I smiled. He didn't. "Then I realized it was you."

"You should've shoved me away."

"You were asleep." While I knew there could never be anything between us, his touch had comforted me. "You made me feel safe. I slept well that last hour."

He stared, his eyelids fluttering.

I looked away. My answer bothered him for some reason. Was he testing me? Would a colony girl have let a guy do that? Probably not.

~ ~ ~

For the next twenty minutes, we alternated between jogging and walking. We took tunnels so narrow that we had to go single file. Pipes ran along the walls and low ceiling of the last tunnel. We had to stoop. As we neared the access point, Dedrick went over the rescue plan.

Excitement raced through my veins. This was happening. It was really happening. The teens were free from Secondary. The children would soon be free. I was helping. After this, we would only have the adults in Re-Ed to rescue.

Dedrick finally stopped. He shined the light high and low, left and right on a meter-square panel waist-high in the wall. He put his ear to the panel for a moment.

"Okay, this is it," he said. He took a tool from his belt and removed finger-sized bolts from the panel. Then he lowered the panel to the floor, exposing an opening big enough to crawl through.

I went first, climbing in on my hands and knees. A deep sink stood in my way inside the opening, making it awkward to maneuver. I grabbed onto it and pulled myself up, then shuffled farther into the room. Dedrick crawled in after me.

A citrusy detergent scent hit me at once, taking me back to my childhood. I was standing in the utility room of my old Primary Residence. Mops and brooms hung in a corner. Shelves of canned vegetables and dry goods lined the walls. A line of dim light showed under the door. Little had changed since I'd hid under the shelf so many years ago. I imagined I could feel the cold vinyl flooring against my bare legs.

Dedrick held the doorknob and pressed his ear to the door. Two seconds later, he shut off the flashlight and eased it open. A yellow nightlight glowed in the big sterile kitchen. Tired off-white cupboards hung over dark countertops. The island countertop had crumbs on one side and streaks in the middle. One of the girls had cleaned it in haste, not caring about the results.

We crept through the kitchen to a dark hallway with two doors, both ajar. One led to the dining room, the other to the bedroom. Dedrick glanced at me, gave a nod, and pushed open the door to the bedroom.

I followed, stepping across the threshold, mealworms crawling in my stomach.

Track lights ran along the edges of the ceiling, creating a soft glow that revealed rows and rows of bunk beds. A green dot on the farthest wall indicated the bathroom. A red dot hung over another door, the door to the nannies' room. The two night shift nannies did laundry for half the shift and slept in cots for the other half. They were supposed to take turns so that one girl was always awake, but I never knew them to do it that way.

Dedrick's head slowly turned from one side to the other, as if seeing the place for the first time. He had probably never rescued a child from Aldonia before.

I touched his hand and pointed to the girls' side of the room. He would want to find Paula. I would get the boys. They slept on the opposite side of the room, though nothing separated the boys from the girls.

Faint smells of urine and bleach lingered in the air. Snoring and heavy breathing came from different points in the room, sounds that always soothed me.

I glanced at one boy and then another, scanning for Simon and Zachary. Their images hovered in my mind. Their images came from the video of the children when the Unity Troopers had caught them; their eyes had been filled with fear and anger. I saw only closed eyes now on faces that were peaceful and sweet.

Dedrick crept through the room as if he thought he might not recognize Paula and skip over his own sister.

A boy on a top bunk mumbled, moaned, and said, "Shut up," his voice so weak I almost didn't recognize the words.

I passed his bed, staring at him, amazed to find my eyes level with his face. The bunk beds used to seem so tall to me. The room had seemed larger, too.

The boy gasped. His eyes popped open.

I froze and put a finger to my lips, signaling him to stay quiet. If he shouted, we'd be caught.

"What you doing?" he said sleepily.

"I'm looking for Simon," I whispered, smiling and taking a risk. "He needs to go to the bathroom. Do you know which bed is his?" I hoped the boy wouldn't think this through. If Simon needed the bathroom, he would be up.

The boy pointed to a top bunk in the next row.

"Thanks." I smiled again. I probably shouldn't have. Nannies did not smile when they had to help a kid at night. "Better get to sleep now." I repeated the words the nannies repeated when I lived in Primary. "A good night's sleep makes you more productive."

He lay down and rolled over.

I tiptoed to Simon's bed. Simon lay with his arms wrapped around his waist, as if hugging himself. I stuck my hand through the railing and shoved his shoulder.

He groaned and muttered something.

"Get up," I whispered, shoving harder.

His eyes popped open and his gaze snapped to mine. "Who are you?"

"I'm Liberty." I didn't expect him to recognize me or my name. I did not remember him from my time in Maxwell. He was one of many children. I only recognized him from the video at CSS. "It's time to go."

"Go where?"

"Back to your family."

Simon pushed himself up, staring at me with doubt in his eyes. The look morphed into one of hope. "Really?"

I nodded, fighting back a tear. "Let's get Zachary."

He scrambled from the bed like a kid not wanting to lose something he barely had a grasp on. He ran three beds down, his bare feet squeaking on the floor, and grabbed the boy in the lower bunk. "Get up, Zachary, it's time. Get up."

Zachary's hands shot out and latched onto Simon's arms. They both turned wide eyes to me.

I motioned for them to follow. They did, each of them grabbing one of my hands. We ran together and met up with Dedrick in an aisle between beds.

He carried Paula. She clung to him with her bony arms around his neck and her head on his shoulder. Her stringy brown hair fell over her nightshirt.

Tears streaked his cheeks. He glanced back. Half a dozen girls sat up in their beds, all looking at us.

Dedrick nodded to the boys and then dashed into the hallway.

"Who are you? What are you doing with them?"

We all skidded to a stop.

A young woman with dark circles under her eyes stood in the kitchen on the opposite side of the island counter. A nanny. She slammed a glass down.

Dedrick set Paula down and swung an arm out in one smooth motion. He held a small container level with the woman's face. A mist came from it.

"I'm calling . . ." She lifted a hand from the countertop, a weak movement with no follow-through. Her eyes rolled up and her head tilted back.

Dedrick darted around the island and caught her before she slumped to the floor. He shifted her torso to one arm and scooped her legs up with the other. Then he carried her like a baby. "Get them out of here," he said to me, nodding toward the door to the utility room.

Before I could move, a low buzzing sound came from the front of the residence.

My heart stopped. I knew the sound. Someone was at the door, probably the security Dedrick had mentioned.

"Go!" Dedrick carried the limp body of the nanny down the hallway.

I opened the door to the utility room and ushered Paula and the boys inside.

"Where's Dedrick going?" Paula said, straining to peer back through the door.

"He'll be right back." I closed the door and led Simon and Zachary to the back of the dark room, to the hole behind the deep sink. I needed to go first to help them through, but I worried Paula wouldn't come without Dedrick.

"Paula, come here," I whispered.

"I can't see," she whined. "Where's Dedrick?"

I wished I still had Elder Lukman's TekBand. I could use the flashlight. "He'll be here in a—"

The door flung open. Dedrick slipped into the room and closed the door behind him. "We have seconds." He shined the beam of his flashlight at the hole in the wall.

I climbed down into the safety of the tunnel and reached for whichever child would come to me first. Simon fell into my arms. I set him on the ground and turned back to find Zachary climbing down on his own. Paula came next. She weighed next to nothing.

Voices came from the other side of the utility room door.

Dedrick jumped into the tunnel, dropped the flashlight, and whipped the panel over the opening. The flashlight rolled across the tunnel floor. With a shoulder to the panel, he withdrew a bolt from the front pocket of his jeans and shoved it back in place.

"What did you do to Nanny?" Paula said, standing with arms folded and stepping from foot to foot. Goose bumps covered her arms. She wore only a long, thin nightshirt.

I took off my cape and wrapped it around her shoulders. Then I snatched up the flashlight.

Dedrick stuffed another bolt in place and turned it by hand. "Huh? Oh, she'll be okay." He glanced at me. "I shoved a kid over and put her in the nearest bed. She won't remember the last few minutes."

"Where are we?" Zachary stood with arms folded, his hands in tight fists.

I took off my jacket and offered it to Zachary, holding it so he could easily stick an arm in an armhole. I wished I wore more than a white tank top underneath. The tunnels were cold. But I couldn't stand here and watch the boys shiver. If I had something more, I would offer it to little Simon.

Dedrick tightened the last screw and turned around. His gaze dropped to the flashlight in my hand—I think. Anyway, he blinked and his mouth fell open. His hand shot up to the clasp on his cape. He tossed the cape to Simon and shrugged off his leather jacket.

"We've got a bit of a journey, kids," he said. He snatched the flashlight from me and forced his jacket into my hand. "But you're safe. You're never going back to that place."

CHAPTER 26

The sound of their footfalls obscured the other tunnel noises.

Dedrick carried Paula piggyback. Her head rested against his neck, her arms around his shoulders. She smelled clean, too clean, sanitized. He wished she smelled like herself, like grass and fresh air.

He never wanted to step foot in the Primary Residence again. Voices and faces haunted him.

"Where're you going?" the girl in the next bed had whispered. Dedrick had just scooped Paula up into his arms.

"Is that your brother?" another girl had whispered. She peered down from a top bunk. Long bangs hung in her eyes, moving as she blinked.

One girl, two, three sat up. "Can I come, too?"

More voices and more faces spiraled through his mind. "Can you be my brother?" "I wanna go with you."

Each set of round eyes, each whispery voice had sent a dagger through his soul. He hated leaving the other girls behind, the boys, too, for that matter. He had pictured himself ushering them all to the utility room, to the tunnel entrance. The idea was silly. The nannies would've caught them.

If he didn't get control of himself, he'd lose all rational thought. They had Paula, Simon and Zachary. That was the goal. Mission accomplished.

"I can't feel my feet." Simon's whispery voice echoed off tunnel walls. He marched at a steady pace, his bare feet stomping out a rhythm on the cold cement floor.

"Here, stop for a minute." Liberty released Simon's hand and squatted.

Zachary wheeled around and shined the flashlight on her. Before they set off, Dedrick had given him *flashlight duty*. Zachary had accepted it the way any nine-year-old boy on an escape mission would, with a grim nod and a gleam of responsibility in his eyes.

Dedrick lowered Paula to the ground. He could use a break. His arms ached from carrying her for so long, especially his wounded arm, and he had been trying to identify a distant noise. Their loud footfalls and breathing made it hard to hear.

"Are we there yet?" Paula whined.

"Shh." Dedrick motioned for her to stop talking and crept a few yards farther down the tunnel. He strained to identify the sound. It reminded him of a neighbor in Maxwell, Mr. Williams, who liked to repair engines at the break of dawn.

The rumbling sound jumped up in amplitude. Now Dedrick recognized it. A tunnel kart approached. Elder Lukman must have sent someone to get them.

Liberty had untied her shoes. She leaned against the brick wall and wrestled a shoe off. Then she stuck a thumb in her sock and peeled it down over her heel.

Dedrick stared. His mind froze for a second. Something fluttered in his chest. She was going to give Simon her socks. If she wasn't Aldonian . . .

"Don't bother," he said. "Ride's on the way."

Liberty looked up.

Dedrick turned as the tunnel kart rounded a corner and came into view. A large, longhaired figure sat at the wheel. Bolcan.

Dedrick blinked and wished he were seeing things. Something must have gone wrong.

The tunnel kart squeaked to a stop and the engine rattled. Bolcan hopped out. "Hey, Rick-man, long time no see." He strutted toward them, his gaze sweeping the area and lingering on Liberty.

Dedrick stepped to the side, blocking Bolcan's view of Liberty and the children. "What happened? Didn't you find the teens?"

One side of Bolcan's mouth curled up, a lion ready to toy with his prey. "A lot less of them than I expected."

Dedrick cringed. He didn't want to explain Andy's situation. "I'm sure Elder Lukman told you the count. They didn't all want to come."

"Your brother orchestrated their escape, huh? Went through with it, even after all our hard work."

~ ~ ~

The night they painted graffiti on the Regimen building, Bolcan had balanced on the edge of a dumpster lid, his makeshift ladder. A flashlight had rested at an angle in an aluminum can, shedding light on a section of a pale brick wall. Bolcan's arm moved from side to side, slow, precise movements. He added touches to the work with a few jerks of his hand. The picture Dedrick had envisioned formed as if by magic.

Bolcan hopped off the dumpster lid, sending it crashing to the ground and the crate under it sliding. It was a minor miracle that the contraption had supported Bolcan's well-muscled body in the first place.

"How's your part coming along?" Bolcan came up behind Dedrick.

"You tell me," Dedrick said, his focus on his work. Bolcan had told him to paint the text. He didn't want to mess up another letter *s*.

"Impatience puts others at . . . risk?" he said, reading the message and guessing the last word correctly. "You would know."

"Meaning?" Dedrick straightened, shaking the paint can and forcing himself to look Bolcan in the eyes. The unnaturally vivid color annoyed him, but not as much as the cocky attitude they conveyed.

Bolcan laughed and stooped over the duffle bag of paint cans, his mane of hair falling forward. "That girl you took off after without the consent of the elders, what's so special about her?"

He hated Bolcan's love of gossip, his need to accuse and blame. He was so Aldonian. "She was in danger. You'd have done the same."

"I don't know." He peered at Dedrick over his shoulder and shook a can, the mixing ball rattling. "Isn't she responsible for this whole mess?"

~ ~ ~

"Andy has his reasons," Dedrick said, glaring. "Why aren't you with the teens? Did you leave them to find their own way back?"

Bolcan's grin stretched across his face. He walked around Dedrick. "Alix came with me. She's with them." In a louder voice, he said, "Hey, kids, ever ride on a tunnel kart?"

Zachary and Simon shook their heads, peering up at Bolcan through suspicious eyes. Paula said, "No," and pulled Liberty's cape tighter around her shoulders.

The beam from the kart's headlights caught the pale green of Liberty's eyes. She stared at Bolcan, looked him over as if assessing him. Maybe she liked golden-haired heavyweights.

Bolcan stared back with a look Dedrick couldn't decipher. Attraction? Recognition? No, they shouldn't know each other. They grew up in different Secondary facilities and lived on opposite sides of Aldonia.

Dedrick returned to Paula and tapped her chin to get her attention. "You're gonna go with them. I'll catch up." He hated to leave her, but the six of them wouldn't fit in the vehicle.

"No." Paula flung herself at Dedrick and wrapped her arms around his waist.

Dedrick's heart did a funny loop. He stroked Paula's hair. "There's nothing to worry about. You're safe now. I'll catch up to—"

"No, Dedrick," Bolcan said. "You're gonna drive. I'll walk. I wanted to get some exercise anyway." He smirked and waved his brows.

"Come on." Liberty grabbed Simon's hand and led him to the kart. She hefted him up, seating him on the back, and then rubbed his feet. Zachary joined them, climbing up without assistance.

"Thanks, man," Dedrick said. The boys could ride on the back, and Liberty could hold Paula on her lap.

Bolcan's gaze slid to Liberty and back to Dedrick. He gave Dedrick a knowing look. Maybe he hoped to impress Liberty with his act of chivalry. Or maybe he was making an insinuation.

Dedrick gave him a disapproving sneer.

~ ~ ~

Less than fifteen minutes later, they drove down the last tunnel on their route, a narrow one that amplified the rumbling of the kart. Whoever took the kart next would have to drive it in reverse to get out of the tunnel. Dedrick would probably get told about it, but he didn't want the children to have to walk with bare feet any more than necessary.

He stopped the kart near the low, metal door at the end of the tunnel.

"We're here," he said, hopping off.

The boys jumped off the back. Paula climbed from Liberty's lap.

"I've been here before," Liberty said, staring at the big dial on the door.

"Yeah, you have. The night you left Aldonia." Dedrick had led Liberty, Bot, and Jessen to the Maxwell Colony so they could begin their new lives. She should've stayed at Maxwell, but a part of her would be glad she didn't once she saw who now lived in this community.

He spun the dial one way and then another. It was like a big combination lock. The lock clicked, and he swung the heavy door open.

A hulk of a man stood inside the doorway, a machine gun gripped in one hand, a mug in the other. Warm light, savory scents, and voices came from behind him. They had reached Gardenhall.

"Hey, Maco," Dedrick said, stepping toward him.

Maco grunted. He took a sip from the mug and spilled coffee on his beard. "You got the merchandise?" He glared and wiped his beard with the back of his hand. Then his gaze dipped to the dried bloodstain on Dedrick's sleeve, and the hard attitude melted. "Dedrick, are you—"

"Get out of the way, Maco," Dedrick said. "You're gonna scare the children."

Paula giggled. The boys whispered.

Maco grumbled and shuffled back a few steps. "Welcome, friends," he boomed, raising the mug. "You now stand in Gardenhall, one of our oldest underground communities."

Liberty and the kids inched over the threshold, holding hands, their eyes turning in every direction.

Gardenhall had high ceilings, a cold cement floor, and dark expanses, similar to every underground place, whether residential or official Mosheh. But it also had throw rugs, women in rocking chairs, tables of old men, and rows of picnic tables. Medical teams worked in shifts here, too, in an area sectioned off with curtains. The beeping of the equipment only rose above the laughter and chatter in the silent hours of the night.

"The children are here!" a woman shouted.

Two middle-aged women scurried from the open kitchen area. Another walked over from the picnic tables where the teens sat eating. Three more came out of nowhere.

"I bet you're hungry."

"Oh, your cold little feet."

"You need clothes."

"I have some nice warm moccasins, might be a little big."

"Do you like grits?"

"We've got maple syrup."

Simon and Zachary yielded to the doting, getting swallowed up into the circle of women. Paula tightened her grip on Dedrick's hand.

A part of him didn't want to let go either. He'd just gotten her back. He couldn't fathom a minute without her, but there wasn't any danger. "Go on, Paula. I'll be right here at one of the tables."

She stared at him, still clinging to his hand.

"I promise." He smiled, pried her hand from his, and shoved her toward the group.

"I'll go help," Liberty said, taking a step.

Dedrick's hand shot out. He grabbed the sleeve of her jacket—his jacket actually. "No you won't. There's someone you need to see."

"Who?" She scanned the area, her gaze lingering on arrangements of furniture and on tables of early-rising old folks. Her gaze locked onto someone and she sucked in a breath of air.

"It. Can't be," she whispered, the color draining from her face.

"It is. It's your friend Abby. Go talk to her. She asks about you all the time."

Liberty studied his eyes. Her hands trembled at her sides. "But she . . . died. Dr. Supero told me."

Dedrick envisioned himself touching her hand, rubbing her arm. He wanted to comfort and reassure her, but the gesture would seem too intimate. "Dr. Supero wouldn't know. Abby took that pill you gave her. Made her appear dead." He stuffed his hands under his armpits. "You saved her."

Liberty brought a trembling hand up and covered her mouth. Her eyes glistened. She took two steps toward Abby and then ran. Abby had been carrying a mug to a circular table. She set the mug down a split second before Liberty threw her arms around her.

The sight stripped the shield from Dedrick's heart. He knew the love Liberty felt at this moment. Throat tightening, he turned away and sought out Paula.

The women had taken the kids to the supply room, an area sectioned off with canvas walls. There they would find clothes and shoes. Movement showed through the doorway. Paula would be with him soon. He should sit down and wait, try not to appear so anxious.

"Dedrick." Liberty had started back to him. She stopped, motioned for him to come, then returned to Abby at the circular table.

The two were rapt in conversation when he got there. Their hands sat on the table, close but not touching. Abby was saying something about medicine. They turned to him at the same time.

"Miss Rosier," Dedrick said, pulling out a chair.

Abby's turquoise eyes lit up. Her frown lines lessoned and crow's feet deepened. She looked like a woman unaccustomed to smiling. "The young men and women here are so polite. I vaguely remember people calling my mother and father Mr. and Mrs. Rosier. Of course, that all stopped once I left home for the boarding school." She peered at Dedrick. "Have I seen you around? You look familiar." She tugged at a strand of her hair, probably referring to the blond that still hadn't grown out of his.

He really should get it cut. It made him look Aldonian. Colonists didn't typically mess with their hair color. "Yeah, I've seen you in passing. I come through here on days I do tunnel repairs. Nobody makes a better meal than the cooks at Gardenhall." He smiled.

"Dedrick!" Paula ran up behind him and threw her arms around his shoulders. She wore a long shift and moccasins and carried a black t-shirt.

He scooted his chair back to let her climb onto his lap. "Told you I'd be here."

"The lady wanted me to give this to you." Paula handed him the t-shirt.

A woman followed Paula to the table. She set down a tray and distributed steaming bowls of grits to them.

"This is Paula," Liberty said to Abby, "Dedrick's sister."

"His sister," Abby said, a distant look in her eyes. "My parents wanted more children. They wanted me to have a brother or sister."

"It's hard for me to believe that you had parents," Liberty said, "a family."

"Oh, yes. There were many families when I was a little girl; they were growing smaller and fewer though. No one had babies anymore. Some gave up their girls. Before boarding school became mandatory, they used to offer scholarships to young ladies. The girls who won would have to go away, but they received the best education." She chuckled. "At least that's what they told us. My father and our neighbors used to talk. They never believed those things, said the government put something in the water to keep women from having children."

Liberty's eyes popped. She looked at Dedrick. "In the water?"

Dedrick shrugged. He hadn't heard about it.

"Did you see the drums of chemicals at the water pump station?"

"No, I was kind of occupied." He flashed back to the moment Sid had slugged him on the chin. His jaw tightened. What was Sid doing now? Still trying to find Liberty? It was strange that he and the doctor hadn't pursued them.

"Do you think it's true?" Liberty said to Dedrick. "Would the government have put chemicals in the water?"

"I don't know. They did something to bring the population down. Less than a hundred years ago, over six billion people lived on the earth."

"What?" Liberty turned white. The circles under her eyes said she needed sleep. "That's not possible. The earth can only sustain three or four hundred million people."

Dedrick shook his head, irritation putting a grimace on his face. "That's what they tell you. That's not true. Six billion people could fit in the state of Texas, each with twelve hundred square feet."

"Texas? Where's that?"

He huffed. The Regimen taught crap for history and renamed everything on the globe. "Well, they don't call it that now. There're two Regimen cities out there, Devall and Livingston. I guess nature reclaimed the rest of Texas, except for our communities."

Paula dropped her spoon into her half-empty bowl of grits and pushed the bowl away. She shifted on Dedrick's lap, peering into the distance. "Is that Andy?"

Dedrick's gaze snapped to the table of teens even though he knew he wouldn't see Andy among them. Zachary darted around the table, chasing Simon. One of the girls reached for Zachary and shouted something, laughing.

Dedrick rubbed Paula's arm and laced his fingers through hers. He hated having to tell her. "No, Andy's not here. But he's not in Secondary anymore. He's okay."

"Why isn't he here? Those kids are from our colony. Wasn't he with them?"

"Uh, yeah, but . . . Andy's doing something. He didn't want to come." His blood simmered thinking about it. Andy's decision to stay frustrated and angered him.

Paula twisted around and hugged Dedrick, pressing her cheek to his chest. "Mom and Dad aren't here either, are they?"

"No." He stroked her hair. "We'll get them." He needed to focus on that rescue mission without thinking about Mom and Dad sleeping on thin mattresses in those hospital gowns, deprived of sleep and food, and brainwashed in their weakened state.

Maybe this would be the last rescue for him. The objective of the Mosheh had once drawn him. It was an irresistible call. But now it seemed pointless. He rescued a man here, a woman there, a handful from the thousands of Aldonians. Few cared about anything or anyone outside themselves. Drug, crime and suicide rates climbed. Were there even ten righteous in the entire city? And even among those they did rescue, something of Aldonia remained in every Aldonian.

Once he rescued Mom and Dad, he'd take the family and find a community far from a Regimen city. He'd find a colony girl and settle down, raise sons and daughters who would learn to recognize, live, and sacrifice for truth and goodness.

"What are you thinking about?" Paula said, gazing up at him.

"Oh, nothing. Just anxious to see Mom and Dad."

"Me, too. I missed you so much." She squeezed him around the waist. "That place made me have nightmares."

"Have you been sick?" he said, stroking her hair. He'd only known Paula to have nightmares with a fever. Her shrieks and tears unsettled him to the core.

"No, but I have nightmares. Then I wake up and forget where I am. I keep thinking you'll come and hold me like you used to. But you don't come."

Dedrick glanced up, hoping Liberty hadn't heard. She'd be reminded of early morning and his arm around her.

Their eyes met. The hint of a smile flickered on her lips. Yeah, she heard. She turned to Abby and said something, pretending she hadn't.

Simon raced to their table, laughing. He ran away, drawing Dedrick's attention to an approaching figure.

A girl with short, dark hair and a confident walk emerged from the shadows on the far side of the room. It was Alix, and her eyes were on Dedrick. She must've had a message.

"Simon looks like he needs help. Why don't you go play with him?" Dedrick said, coaxing Paula off his lap. She hesitated but then dashed off to join the fun.

Alix stopped a few yards away, propped a hand on one hip, and nodded for Dedrick to come to her. *Aldonian.*

Dedrick got up and strolled to her. "What's up?"

"Bot from the CAT cave wants to see you."

"He wants to *see* me?" He smirked. "He's a little far for that."

She cocked her head and flashed a smile. "You can see him in the game room. He's got a 3D game to show you. It's pretty cool."

"Yeah, okay. He's been wanting to show me. I guess now's a good time." He twisted around. "Hey, Liberty." He nodded her over the way Alix had nodded to him. Maybe he shouldn't have called her. What was he thinking? 3D games messed with him, made him act like an idiot. Did he really want Liberty to witness his weakness?

Liberty raised her brows. "What?" she said, mouthing the word without getting up.

"Come here," he said, shouting and unintentionally sounding bossy.

She got up, her eyes narrowing to slits. Maybe she'd say *no.*

He should say something else, ask her to keep an eye on Paula or something. He should not invite her to the game room. His emotional state was wreaking havoc on his rational mind.

Liberty stopped two feet away, her eyes on Alix. "Training?"

"Oh?" Alix smirked, a strange glint in her eyes. "You're ready for more? Now?"

Dedrick angled his body to block their view of each other. He sensed they didn't get along. "No, it's just Bot," he said to Liberty. "He wants to show me something he's been working on, a 3D game. Interested?"

"You want her along?" Alix said.

"Why not?" Dedrick said.

"No, actually, I'm tired." Liberty rubbed the back of her neck and peered up at him.

Dedrick's thoughts floundered. *Pale green eyes peering through thick lashes. My arm around her. The scent of her hair.* She said *no!*

184

"I, uh, we'll pass the sleeping capsules. I'll show you where they are. I'm sure Bot won't keep us long."

She shrugged, her bottom lip sticking out in a sulky way. "Okay."

"Okay," he repeated, mindlessly. He should drop her at the capsules and see Bot on his own.

Alix led the way. Dedrick and Liberty followed, walking side by side.

"What're sleeping capsules?" Liberty said.

"Huh? Oh, it's a Japanese thing. A bunch of units, just big enough to sleep in, all stacked on top of each other. I guess they were gonna use them over here, in America, but they changed their mind. We use them when we're passing through."

"We?"

"The Mosheh."

"What's Japanese mean?" Liberty said.

He chuckled. "You need some old-fashioned geography lessons."

Alix stopped at the open door to the game room, one of the few rooms in Gardenhall with an actual door. She folded her arms and leaned against the doorframe. She waited until Liberty entered the room then said, "You got a sister with the Maxwell colonists, don't you?"

"Yeah, Ann."

"Then you might want to know that the Mosheh lost contact with Miriam."

"What? When?" His heart skipped a beat. *Not more trouble.* Miriam was leading the Maxwell colonists to a new colony. Ann was among them. He shot a glance at the control center, a group of workstations and four monitors, a smaller version of the main control center. He wouldn't be able to do anything the kids at the stations couldn't do.

"Might not mean anything," Alix said. "They're working to re-establish contact."

"Yeah, but it might mean danger," Dedrick said. "They had to cross through Torva stomping grounds."

CHAPTER 27

Dr. Supero poured vanilla soymilk into a mug of steaming coffee. His headache from last night had subsided but a fog lingered in his brain. The caffeine should help. Maybe a couple of pain relievers. Just in case.

Knowing the exact location of the painkillers, he reached into an overhead cupboard, into semi-darkness, and grabbed the bottle. It sat a bit off to the side, not in the exact location in which he had left it. As he withdrew the bottle, it slipped from his grasp and tumbled to the bar counter. Little pills scattered everywhere, red raindrops tapping the black marble countertop and tile floor.

Dr. Supero glared over the counter at the boy who slept on his leather couch, a sweaty body in ripped jeans and t-shirt on a sophisticated piece of handcrafted furniture. Sid had gotten into his medicine.

Orange and olive light colored the boy's skin, rolled along the walls, and reflected on the polished wood end tables, fluctuating like the ebb and flow of ocean waves. Dr. Supero preferred shades of yellow or red, depending upon his mood and emotional energy, but he never left the chromatherapy lights on overnight. Sid had been playing with them. Orange probably fit Sid's mood, his unrequited desire.

Dr. Supero popped four pills into his mouth and washed them down with coffee. His throat burned as the hot beverage rushed down it. He considered a chaser of water, but his favorite cup sat on the coffee table. Along with three dirty plates. Sid's shoes lay at odd angles, one upside down in the middle of the living room floor. The kid was a slob. Dr. Supero hated to imagine what his own apartment looked like.

If his headache hadn't incapacitated him, he would've driven Sid home last night or made him walk. Driving through the gate, parking between the lines, and walking to the elevator had felt like an accomplishment. Once he made it to his apartment, he had no choice but to down a handful of painkillers and collapse in his bed, leaving Sid free to do as he pleased.

Dr. Supero took a sip of coffee and whipped the empty pill bottle at Sid's head, hitting his target. "Get up. Do you not have a job to get to?"

Sid worked with a construction team, going wherever the Regimen sent them. A committee evaluated requests from businesses, offices, and the Environmental Stewardship Units, then ordinary citizens distributed work assignments to the construction teams. In general, construction workers never rushed a job. They rarely finished on time. And they ended up returning to a job three or four times to get it done right. Lazy bunch of—

"What the earth?" Sid sat up, squinting and rubbing his head. "You throw something at me?"

"I am getting ready to leave, and I don't want you here."

Sid grabbed the half-empty glass from the table and downed its amber contents. "You going to CSS?"

"Yes, we discussed this last night. I will see if they are watching the old city center. If they aren't, we can go in and find the object of your desire."

"I just wanna find Liberty." He stood up and stretched, biceps bulging, back cracking, skin showing. "She's not gonna be there. I'm gonna lose her for good."

He sauntered over and leaned his forearms on the countertop, his gaze snapping to the scattered pills. He flicked an outlier into the heaviest concentration of them, bumping two like marbles. "Man, this stuff blows your mind. I took some last night."

"I hope you did not take it with alcohol?"

"Being a doctor has its benefits, huh?" Sid flexed his hand and toyed with the finger holes of his fingerless glove.

"Every vocation has its benefits." Dr. Supero sipped the hot coffee. "I am sure even yours."

Sid licked his bottom lip and bit it, a taunting look coming to his eyes. "Can't get you everything though, can it? I saw what you been researching." He nodded over his shoulder at the dining room table.

Supero's upper lip twitched. He did his computer work there, using the shiny surface for the interactive monitor. He rarely closed his files. What did the boy glean from what he saw? Nothing. He wasn't too bright.

"You read that stuff while you eat?" Sid smirked.

"Some of us wish to do our part to make the world a better place. We do not limit our work to four out of eight working hours like others do."

Sid laughed. "You mean me? I don't work that many hours a day. I like to pace myself."

"Where is your job today? I will drop you off." He took a last swig of coffee, dumped the rest in the sink, and came around the counter. He'd left his shoes in the bedroom.

"No, I'm gonna wait here."

Dr. Supero stopped and spun to face Sid. "No, you are not."

"I'd go with you, but I don't want the chief asking me about Liberty. He can't know I don't have her." His hand shot out and latched onto Supero's arm. Blue storm clouds rolled in his eyes. "And you can't say nothing about that hiding place."

Dr. Supero jerked his arm free. "Do not touch me." He turned to his bedroom and ran a hand through his hair, but he did not allow himself to fondle the lump of the tumor.

"I know why you do that."

Supero stopped at the bedroom door but did not look back. "Do what?"

"Always touching your head on that side." Sid came up behind him and spoke over his shoulder. "At first I thought you had migraines, but now I know what you got. You got a brain tumor, don't you, Doc? A cancerous one." He leaned against the wall by the doorframe, his tan face and mocking eyes now in Supero's view. "Does it hurt?"

"My health is none of your business." He imagined he could feel the blood rushing to his head, feeding the tumor, making it pulse.

"They gonna operate soon? Shouldn't put a thing like that off. A person can die from that, huh?" A grin flickered on his lips.

The throbbing of the tumor increased. "Get your shoes. It's time you go." He strode into his room and stuffed his feet into the black leather shoes that he'd removed last night without unlacing.

"You make the recommendations to the Medical Evaluation Panel, don't you?" Sid leaned against the doorframe and stuck his thumbs in his belt loops.

Supero lifted his chin. "Get your shoes."

"Did they reject you?"

Dr. Supero locked his gaze on the front door and pushed past Sid. "Odd how an adult can remind me of a Secondary boy. I knew boys like you. I hated them." He kept his thoughts from turning to the unpleasant memories of what they did to him.

~ ~ ~

"You will get your hands off me." Dr. Supero twisted his arm, peeled his cheek off the wall, and thrust his weight back into the security guard who wanted his wrist.

"You can't just barge in there; I don't care who you are," the second guard said. He drew the taser gun from his belt.

"The reader doesn't verify your claim," the first guard said. "It says you work at the University."

"Hey, is that the good doctor?" Chief Varden's voice boomed in the hallway. He strutted toward them.

The security guards struck offensive poses.

"He refuses to wait in the waiting room," the taser guard said, training his weapon on Dr. Supero.

Dr. Supero brushed off his shirt and threw his shoulders back. Unwilling to wait with the others in the waiting room, he'd slipped through the door with the last person who gained admittance. Security guards had appeared immediately.

"I do not have half the day to waste at CSS," he said.

Chief Varden waved the guards away. "I got him. We don't want the good doctor having a meltdown here like he did at Primary."

Dr. Supero gritted his teeth so hard his jaw popped.

The guards snickered.

Chief Varden laughed. He wrapped a beefy arm around Dr. Supero's shoulders and led him down the hall. "Maybe it's your fault the kids ran away. You scared them."

"The Secondary teens?"

"The Primary kids. Isn't that why you're here? I'm the one who told them to let you off with a warning yesterday. You here to thank me?" Chief Varden stopped at a door to a conference room and waved his hand over the reader. The door slid open. Chief Varden motioned for Dr. Supero to enter first.

"What Primary kids?" Dr. Supero stepped into the room but did not sit down. Why had he been limited to conference rooms? He wanted access to the surveillance room.

"The new kiddos. All three of them. What're their names?" Chief Varden tapped the screen of his flexi-phone. "Yeah, Simon, Zachary, and Paula, the girl you were questioning. I heard you made her cry. Shame on you, doctor. Anyway, they're gone." He chuckled. "You know we don't interrogate minors like that. You're a real fireball."

"They're gone? When did this happen?"

"Sometime last night." Chief Varden pulled out a chair and sat on the table, planting a foot on the chair. "They wouldn't have been so lucky if they waited. We had plans to double security in the morning."

"Certainly your surveillance cameras picked up something."

"No. And we've got cameras all over the exterior of that property. We saw nothing. We're still conducting interviews, but only one kid so far admits to seeing anything. A boy says a nanny took them to the bathroom and never came back."

"How does this happen? Certainly you have found the teens?" If, perchance, they caught Liberty and Dedrick, they would send the two to Re-Ed. Maybe they would send the teens there as well. If he could not interview them at CSS, he could do so at Re-Ed.

"Nope. We don't have them."

"But there were so many, two dozen, you said. They cannot simply vanish."

"We'll find them. We have reason to believe they're in Jensenville."

"Do you believe they are responsible for the kidnapping at Primary?"

"Doesn't seem likely. But the same people may have arranged both the kidnappings and the escape." He stood up and propped his hands on his hips. "Don't worry. We'll take care of it. I'm sure you have responsibilities of your own, what with your new job out at the university."

Dr. Supero grimaced. Did everyone know?

Chief Varden jabbed a thumb in the direction of the door. "Meeting's over." He waved a hand over the implant reader and the door slid open.

"Wait." Dr. Supero lunged forward. He had not gained the information he needed. "Tell me something about your search. Have you sent troops into Jensenville? Or are you still wasting resources at the old city center? Why not use surveillance cameras on that dead end and put your people somewhere productive."

"Are you kidding? We don't have surveillance in places like that. What's there to watch? Those places need leveled. If ESU had the resources, they'd be nothing but gravel and weeds. In the meantime, we keep people out with fences. And I know a few losers slip by, but we're not interested in scavengers."

Dr. Supero found himself grinning. He and Sid would have no problem going there unnoticed.

Chief Varden stood in the doorway, his thick back preventing the door from sliding shut. "We're done with that place. We searched every building. No one lives there. And as for Jensenville, we have a lot of red tape to cut through in order to take our investigation over there."

"You searched every building?" Dr. Supero whispered, feeling his chances of finding help slip away. Sid was wrong. A secret community of miscreants did not live in the old city center. The troopers would've found them. "Why do you think they are in Jensenville?"

"What, with their high suicide rates and the way they lose babies? Failure to thrive or some such. They want those new people. They need 'em. Yeah, I'm pretty sure that's where our teens and children are. But I need you outta here. I got work to do."

Dr. Supero cruised through the doorway. He needed a change of plans.

CHAPTER 28

"Hold still." Alix squatted before me, attaching motion sensor pads to my ankles. She had already given me gloves and attached pads to my wrists, elbows, and knees. Now she tilted her face to me and glared. I had a nanny in Primary who used to give the same look. She hated kids.

I guess I had been bouncing on my toes. Bubbles of joy clouded my mind. Abby was alive. She looked good. She smiled. I couldn't remember ever seeing her smile like this before. She always seemed so sad. I hated the way the Regimen treated the elderly, sending them all to live in facilities and limiting their healthcare. Now Abby was free. I rescued her. I wanted to rescue others.

I became distinctly aware of *My Friend's* presence. I don't know why I felt he controlled things. Maybe it was a childish notion, but I found myself saying to him in my heart, *Please, oh please, let me join the Mosheh.*

Alix straightened up, bringing her flaming eyes in line with mine. "Put the helmet on and hold still while I run your calibration." She strode to the control panel in the corner of the game room.

I pulled the odd little helmet onto my head. It had a built-in headset and a special visor. Black, crisscrossing strips formed the top. I bounced twice, shook out my arms, took a deep breath, and then stood still with my arms at my sides and my feet shoulder-width apart.

Dedrick chuckled. He leaned against the wall, his thumbs in his belt loops, his eyes on me. He'd changed out of his bloodstained white shirt and into a black t-shirt that blended in with the dark room and made him little more than arms and a face.

"I thought you didn't like playing 3D games," I said to Dedrick.

"I . . . told you that?"

"Yes."

"Did I tell you why?" He folded his arms across his chest and shifted his position on the wall.

"Okay, your turn." Alix came up to Dedrick with a helmet, gloves, and a handful of sensor pads. She led him across the mat, out of view, talking in the flirtatious way of a Secondary girl. With me, she always had an edge to her voice.

The game room was similar to the training room, with mats on the floor, a big tread area, and sunken shelves on one wall. A grid of black lines covered the gray walls and ceiling, only visible when light hit them at a certain angle. Muted purplish light shined on the lower parts of the walls. Otherwise, the room was dark.

A green point of light appeared on the ceiling, illuminating the grid around it. It glided along the ceiling until it hovered directly above me. Several beams of light shot from it and fell on me like a glowing green shower. More beams shot out from the walls, crisscrossing with the first lines. They moved up and down my body.

Alix said something to Dedrick and laughed. He laughed, too.

I turned my head, caught a glimpse of her squatting at his feet, and turned back.

A low alarm sounded. The wall and ceiling sucked up the green lights.

"Wow, I told you to hold still," Alix said.

They both looked at me. Dedrick did a double take, the hint of a smile coming to his face.

Heat rose to my cheeks. "Sorry. I guess I moved."

"Worried I'll steal your boyfriend?" Alix grinned. "He's too old for me." She strutted over to me, looking back at him. "What are you, twenty-two?"

"Yeah," he said. "That's not old."

Alix placed a hand on either side of my helmet and turned my head face forward. "You have to hold still. The computer needs to acquire your measurements and calibrate it to your avatar."

"He's not my boyfriend," I said, feeling stupid.

Her eyes snapped to mine, gleaming with ridicule. "Just hold still."

The green beams of light sprouted again. Alix whispered and laughed to Dedrick. Dedrick mumbled a reply.

I held still as a statue. It didn't matter what they said. I was tired. I would see what Bot wanted to show us and then crawl into one of those capsules. They looked comfortable enough for me. Maybe I'd dream, or maybe I'd gain understanding about the message of my last dream.

I saw the weeds as my own faults and inabilities, the wheat seed as my potential. In order for the seed to take root, I needed to better myself physically, mentally, spiritually. Perhaps the man who sowed the seed was *My Friend.* I needed to improve my skill at listening to him.

My dream had meant something to Andy, too. He and the other boys who remained in Aldonia wanted to plant the seeds of truth. They hoped it would take root with the Aldonians. What had Dedrick meant when he asked if anyone was an Interpreter? I would have to ask someone about that.

Something beeped. The green beams shrunk and vanished. A man appeared. He wore a dark cape over a buttoned jacket, high boots, and baggy pants that gathered at the knees. Red tufts of hair stuck out from a broad-brimmed hat. His eyes, mottled blue and larger than life, magnified their natural intensity, but this was definitely Bot's avatar.

"Hey, Liberty. Good to see you." He spread his arms and peered down at his outfit. His eyebrows arched when he spoke. "Like it?"

I laughed. "Sure, it fits your personality."

"Like yours?"

I just realized my avatar wore a dark blue skirt that came down to her ankles. The gloves allowed me to actually feel the coarse material. Totally weird.

"Hey, you look nice in a dress." Dedrick came up beside me, fully calibrated to his avatar. He wore a black jacket over a white shirt with a fancy collar and short pants similar to Bot's. He had dark spiky hair with blond tips and big brown eyes, an exaggeration of his features.

"Glad you guys could come," Bot said. "I've been dying to show this to you."

"I'm glad you found something in Maxwell to keep you happy." I remembered how dissatisfied he seemed with the lack of conveniences.

"Yeah, can't say I like living in hiding, but . . . . This game we created is going to change the world."

"Bot's gonna change the world," Dedrick said, his large brown eyes still on me and my dress. His stylized little mouth held the hint of a grin. The helmet and sensors probably read physical responses like heart rate, facial expressions, and temperature to create the appropriate expression on the avatar.

"I'm serious," Bot said. "It's going to give kids an understanding of who we are and the people we came from. It'll be a wakeup call." His attention went to a handheld controller. He tapped it and ran a finger in a circle on the screen. "I'm setting you two up as husband and wife."

"What?" Dedrick and I said together.

My stomach flipped. When I had learned about marriage from the Maxwell colonists, it appealed to me in ways too deep to understand. But I did not want to pretend to be someone's wife—Dedrick's wife—in this game.

"You're stronger that way. It ups your courage and determination and all that, gains you more points." Bot nodded, still messing with the controller. "So does building a house, which you won't be able to do in this level. And also having a baby, which you can do anytime." He looked from Dedrick to me and grinned.

"Whoa," Dedrick said, stepping toward him with raised hands, "wait a minute, Bot. Maybe you'd better tell me about this game before we agree to play."

Bot laughed. "Don't worry. Your colony brothers wouldn't let me add certain features to the game." He slapped Dedrick on the shoulder, an action which Bot probably felt through his glove but I doubted Dedrick would feel. "It's Maxwell approved. All you do is kiss, a quick peck on the lips, and a little while later, a baby shows up. Doesn't work every time. Might have to try it more than once."

Dedrick's gaze slid to me.

I shook my head and tried to convey *no* with my eyes.

"Having kids eats up your resources," Bot said, pacing across the mat and tracing his finger along the screen of the controller, "but your strength, courage, determination, virtue, all that goes up."

"Sounds about right," Dedrick said, still staring at me. Maybe he couldn't get over seeing me in a dress. He sure wasn't thinking about kissing me.

"Keep track if you want." Bot pointed to something over my head.

Translucent glowing numbers and abbreviations hovered above each of us, things like STR 250, CRG 190, PWR 310, VRT 200. We each had different numbers next to the letters. It was the same with other role-playing games. Each character had different strengths and weaknesses.

"Jobs are easier to come by for married men," Bot said. "Stuff like that."

"So what's the goal of the game?" I said.

A clear sky appeared overhead, weathered wooden planks under our feet, and an ocean on the horizon. A seagull cried and a breeze blew in my ears. A huge merchant ship materialized before us, a relic of the seventeenth-century, complete with towering square-rigged masts, a long beak-like bow, and a lifelike crew. People surrounded us. Some stood talking in groups, their voices carrying to us. Others lugged crates toward the ship. A boy ran past me.

"The game begins here," Bot said. "We've named this part *The Ancient Beginnings of the New World Adventure*. It's a wild ride. You've got huge waves crashing against the deck. Things get damaged." He chuckled. "Like the ship's support timber. That's a good one. Passengers need to help repair it using supplies they brought along or things they find onboard. Then we got Captain Christopher Jones and the crew. If your character was a crew member, you'd use ancient instruments and procedures to make sure we reach our destination."

"Wow," Dedrick said, gazing at the ship and running a hand through his hair, "a page out of history. This the Mayflower?"

"Sure is," Bot said. "You'll be living on the gun deck, crammed in with a bunch of other smelly people, about a hundred-thirty total, including officers and crew. There'll be a clash of personalities to contend with, not to mention the weather."

"Sounds fun," I said, smirking. I wondered what my avatar looked like to them. Maybe I'd find a mirror in the game.

"You can thank me that I'm not putting you on the Speedwell. That one springs a few leaks before the journey begins." Bot motioned to a man who stood near us. The man lifted a crate and prepared to follow us.

"So we're pilgrims?" Dedrick took my hand.

I pulled away. "What're you doing?"

"You're my wife." The slant of his avatar brows showed that he took offense at my rejection.

"Yeah," Bot said. "You're pilgrims and I'm a ruffian of sorts, a merchant really. We'll be heading for the New World." He waved his brows. "That's where the game gets going, takes you through history at a rapid pace. So you need to survive this level."

"Can't we skip levels?" I could see this lasting all day. "I mean, you wrote the game, right? I'm kind of tired. Maybe you can take us to a few pivotal moments."

Bot frowned. "Well . . . I wanted you to experience it. But I guess that would take too long, huh?" He tapped the handheld controller and glanced at Dedrick. "You kiss her yet?"

Dedrick gave a boyish smile. His gaze slid to me. "Want to?"

I broke into a sweat and wanted to whip the helmet off. "No. We're not really playing. We're only checking out the game, right?" I couldn't believe he asked me that, him being Mosheh and all. Maybe he was toying with me.

Dedrick shrugged.

The scenery morphed, the ocean turning into three and four-story, boxy buildings with neat rows of tall windows. An evening sky stretched out overhead. More buildings appeared behind us, a dirt street underfoot. People strolled by, most at a casual pace.

"So you spend a few levels just trying to survive," Bot said, strolling along, "build a house, plant food, get along with the natives and whatnot. We got a couple wars and a lot of exploring in those early levels. Then we jump forward a hundred or so years, and we have the British flexing its muscle by imposing taxes and putting soldiers in your homes."

"The British?" My clothing had changed into a full, off-white skirt with a blue jacket and a dark cape. I also wore some sort of flimsy hat. It was all much fancier than the first outfit.

"You can think of them as the Regimen of the past, only without the technology." Bot turned down a street. "For these levels you need to identify your friends and your foes. You'll have to sneak around to deliver messages and plan events. Ever hear of the Boston Tea Party?"

"No," I said.

"Of course," Dedrick said. His clothing had changed, too. He wore a long brown jacket, a blue vest, and a different hat. Like his last outfit, his pants gathered at the knees, but these were tighter.

Bot glanced over his shoulder then crossed the street towards a shop. "You have to be careful in this level. Never know who your friends are." He squatted by a small pane window and motioned for us to join him.

Voices and a banging sound came from inside. The banging stopped and started repeatedly.

A milky film covered several panes, but I found one clear enough to peer through.

A man with black hands and a dirty apron stood by a strange wooden contraption on the far side of the room, pounding on a flat surface with a long-handled tool. He stopped pounding and the voices became clear.

"They must understand our concern," a man said, his tone level. He sat with eight other men at a table cluttered with papers, glasses, candles, and two bottles. "We have never forsaken our British Privileges."

"It is a violation of our rights as Englishmen." This man spoke with anger. He sat with his back to the window, bobbing his balding head as he spoke.

A second man strolled to the wooden contraption on the far side of the room. He placed a sheet of paper onto the surface the black-handed man had been pounding. The black-handed man slid the tabletop into the contraption. The other man reached overhead and turned a huge screw. I gathered it was a press of sorts.

"It annihilates our Charter Right to govern and tax ourselves," a man with a low voice said. His hair was tied at the neck with a black ribbon. All the men wore similar clothes, short pants and white shirts with low shoulders and loose sleeves. A few wore jackets like Dedrick's.

"They wish to keep us from growing strong. Why do you think they tax our lawyers and college students?"

"They want us to remember who is in control. A man cannot buy a deck of cards without paying a shilling to Parliament."

The man with black hands slid the tabletop back and peeled a sheet of paper from the wooden press. He handed it to the other man, who then hung it beside a row of papers on an overhead line.

"They want to tax every one of these." The speaker pointed to the papers on the line. Several lines of papers ran across the ceiling.

"You mean, they want to tax the pages of your pamphlet that condemns their new tax law?"

The men broke out in laughter.

"I get it," Dedrick said. He squatted between Bot and me. "It's 1765 and they're protesting the Stamp Act. So these must be the Sons of Liberty." They both looked at me, grinning.

"No," Bot said. "Not yet. They will be. Right now they're the Loyal Nine."

A man scraped his chair back and lifted a finger. "It is our indispensable duty to defeat the designs of those who enslave us and our posterity."

"Here, here!" the men shouted.

"In addition to pamphlets and secret meetings, we need public displays of opposition."

"Here, here!" Two men pounded their fists on the table. Others stamped their feet. One of them lifted his drink.

"I say we hang the guilty parties from a tree," the balding man said.

They all laughed. "Andrew Oliver, the stamp distributer," said one of them. "Hang him from the elm tree at the crossing of Essex and Orange Streets."

The man who stood to speak jerked his face to the window. "Who goes there?"

Dedrick and I dove out of view. Bot laughed and flattened himself against the wall. He brought the handheld controller up and tapped it. "You gotta be careful. You can make friends with either side, but you've got to prove yourself. This level is full of spying and secret missions." He strolled down the street and squatted at a part of the street that had faded. Was he picking something up? "But now I'll take you to . . ." He turned and tossed a rifle to Dedrick and another to me. "Lexington."

The crack of a gunshot rang out.

My breath caught in my throat. My eyes adjusted to the new surroundings.

The sun crested low hills on the horizon. A single tree and a few boxy buildings rose up a good distance away from us. People gathered in the shadows of the buildings. Dedrick, Bot, and I stood side by side in a field with a line of about seventy others. An array of men in red coats and white trousers stood in formation, their rifles leveled at us.

"Disperse! Return to your homes!" someone shouted. Commands I could not make out came from every direction. More shots sounded.

Dedrick slapped my arm. We turned and bolted. A low wall of stones stretched across the field. We, and several others, dove over it.

Dedrick slammed his back against the wall and sat with his knees up, wrestling with a leather pouch that hung from his shoulder—something new for this level. He stuck the rifle between his knees, muzzle up, and poured black powder from a horn into a small cone.

A cacophony of gunshots, shouts, and heavy footfalls filled the air. The Redcoats shouted something that sounded like *Huzzah!*

"What're you doing?" Groping my outfit, I found a similar pouch and horn. I yanked them off over my head and dumped the contents of the pouch onto the ground. Dedrick seemed to recognize the odd contents, but I did not.

"I'm fighting back." Dedrick poured the powder into the muzzle, thumped the rifle on the ground with one hand, stuck a strip of fabric into his mouth with the other, then dug through his leather pouch.

I followed his lead, pouring the black powder from my horn into a small cone and then into the muzzle of my rifle.

He dumped his leather pouch onto the ground and picked up a small metal ball. He stuffed that, along with the material he had been sucking on, into the muzzle of the rifle. Moving like a machine, he sliced the material with a knife I didn't realize he had, shoved the ball down the barrel with a tool, and rammed a long rod in after.

He fidgeted with something on the mechanism above the trigger and poured a bit more powder. Then his gaze snapped to me.

I had been watching carefully, wanting to imitate the process with my rifle.

"You shouldn't be here." He pulled the hammer back with his thumb, squeezed the trigger, and lowered the hammer.

"Oh, really?" I made eye contact so I could glare at him. Then I stuffed the end of the fabric I had found in my pouch into my mouth. It had no taste or feel, and I felt stupid, but Dedrick had done it, so it must've been necessary. I intended to fire this rifle.

Dedrick got up on one knee and whipped his rifle into position, propping it on the wall. "See any other women here?" He cocked the hammer and fired. A puff of smoke shot up from the rifle into his face, the sharp odor of gunpowder with it.

I didn't understand how a 3D game could create smells, but I didn't have time to analyze it. I tried to do exactly what he had done, stuffing the material and the ball into the barrel of the rifle.

He dropped back down beside me and grabbed the horn with the black powder.

After cocking my rifle the way he had, I wheeled around and got onto one knee to shoot. Smoke rose up all over the battlefield. Dark figures lumbered across my view. Some seemed to be using their rifles like spears, thrusting them at the colonists. I set my sights on a distant, red-clad figure.

Then I threw Dedrick another wicked glare. "You think I can't fight because I'm Aldonian or because I'm a girl?"

"Neither." He was already ramming the rod down the muzzle of his rifle. He glanced up, maybe at his overhead point display.

I took my shot, getting a puff of smoke in my face and the odor of gunpowder.

"Well, you've got some reason for not wanting me to join the Mosheh." I slid back down, dropping hard onto my hind end, the sharp pain telling me I landed on the tread rather than the mat. I snatched one of the horns of black powder. It amazed me that a computer-generated item felt so real in my hand.

Dedrick pivoted on a knee, getting into shooting position. "Joining the Mosheh is not a game. We train for months. We risk everything. We do what we're told." He took his eyes off his target and looked at me. "We make a four year commitment, a commitment you don't break without good reason."

"You don't think I can keep a promise?" I stuffed the tasteless fabric into my mouth and picked up a ball.

Dedrick stared for half a second, the guns and voices seeming to cease for the moment. Then he turned and took his shot.

I stuffed the material and bullet into the muzzle and used his knife to slice the material. "Well, maybe you don't know me."

A drumbeat sounded in the distance. Men hollered.

"Fall back," someone nearby called. "We can't win this. We're done here."

Dedrick grabbed my arm and helped me to my feet. The ball fell from the muzzle of my rifle and bounced on the ground.

My temper spiked. I yanked my arm from him. "You run if you want. I'm taking my—"

A gunshot rang out. A bullet struck a rock on the wall, sending flecks to my legs.

Dedrick grabbed me around the waist and yanked me down. We landed side by side on the grass near the stone wall. More shots. Dirt and gravel sprayed from the wall, cascading onto us with a surreal feeling. I could hear and see it, but I only felt it on my hands.

Dedrick threw himself over me and ducked his head, bringing it close to mine. He squeezed his eyes shut and winced the way he might in a real situation. His mouth moved as if he were praying.

I don't know why this struck me as funny, but I laughed. With eyes closed and mouth wide open, I laughed so hard that my side hurt. Then I pushed his shoulders. "Get off me. It's just a game. It's not real."

He lifted his head and looked at me, blinking. "I . . . it feels real." The intensity of his expression softened, the protector becoming the playful boy again. His gaze dropped to my mouth. "It's just a game, so you won't mind if I—" He pressed his lips to mine.

My heart stopped. Warmth. A manly scent. A tingling sensation. He did not kiss me the way Aldonians kiss each other, hungrily and with lustful passion. His kiss was simple and sweet. Still, the tingling sensation that started at my lips spread to my whole body. My hands on his shoulders relaxed. I could see myself wrapping my arms around his neck if this lasted a moment longer.

He pulled away but hovered over me for another second, his huge avatar eyes staring with a look that said he couldn't believe he just kissed me. Or maybe that he regretted it already. He popped up to a squatting position and grabbed my arms. We stood up together.

Bot strolled toward us, his attention on the controller. "So you both stayed alive. That's about all you can hope for. The colonial militia, that's us, we didn't win this one. We were really outnumbered, lost eight men. British lost none. But this all turned around once the British reached Concord. Groups of colonists came from behind every hill, fence, and barn to attack. The British fled. By the end of the day, they lost 273 to the colonists' 94. The American Revolution had begun."

Bot grinned, then dropped his gaze. "Oh, hey, look at you."

The impression of Dedrick's lips on mine lingered, giving me the unreasonable thought that Bot could tell we kissed from glimpsing my mouth. I looked down to see what Bot stared at and gasped. He *could* tell we kissed. I had a rounded belly.

In the next second, Dedrick's hand pressed against my abdomen. Not the rounded belly of my avatar. *My* belly. "What are we gonna name it?"

I flung his hand aside and looked him in the eye. His big avatar eyes made me want to scream. "Stop it. I'm not your wife. And you're with the Mosheh."

We stared at each other.

My mind took me back to the goat farm. Sunlight had bounced off his brown irises as he gazed at the sky. I had tried to kiss him. He'd pulled away, shock written on his face. "I'm sorry," I'd said, wanting to flee. I had totally misread him. "No, I'm sorry," he said. Then he proceeded to tell me about the vows he had taken when he joined the Mosheh.

What possessed him to kiss me now?

I whipped the helmet from my head, the 3D images vanishing. No Bot, no field, no big-eyed Dedrick. I stood alone in the 3D room with real-life Dedrick. Even Alix was no longer here. That gave me some relief. I wouldn't have wanted her to see Dedrick kiss me.

"Liberty, wait," Dedrick said. He still wore the helmet. Probably didn't want to leave Bot hanging. Did he see my avatar or the real me?

I removed the gloves and clawed the sensory pads from my knees and elbows.

Dedrick spoke to the air, mumbling, glancing at me.

I tossed the accessories in the general direction of the shelves and bolted from the room.

CHAPTER 29

Dedrick stood with his back and the sole of one boot against the wall, contemplating the charge in the air. He had never seen the meeting room this crowded, but then they had never prepared to break into a high-security facility before either.

The door to the meeting room burst open and Camilla bounced into the room, her ponytail swinging. She looked to either side, scanning the Mosheh members that stood in the shadows along three of the meeting room walls. With the exception of a skeleton crew, practically every member who lived under Aldonia was here.

Dedrick nodded to greet her.

Camilla smiled and then faced the elders at the long table in the middle of the room. Elders Rayna and Lukman had been speaking in hushed voices and going over charts and files that glowed on the tabletop. Elder Dean sat with his bald head hung and eyes closed, looking exhausted. More than likely, he was going over details in his mind, and he'd wake any minute and say something vital to the mission. It was amazing that he had even made it here, him in his wheelchair. Traveling through the tunnels couldn't have been easy.

"Sorry I'm late," Camilla said. A single chair at the table remained empty. She glanced at it and bounced over to Dedrick.

He slid to the side, giving her space on the wall. "Sorry, huh?" he whispered. "I think you like being late."

She opened her eyes wide and gave a sneaky grin. Growing up in Maxwell, she came late to everything. Half the time her mother had *one more* chore for her to do. The rest of the time, Dedrick thought she did it on purpose.

He could still picture the gleam in her eyes the day she'd come late to the river. A group of them had built a makeshift bridge over the deepest part of a stream and crossed, one by one. A number of boards and stones had shifted out of place by the time she got there. Maybe she liked more of a challenge.

"Okay, not everyone is here yet," Elder Lukman said, his grandfatherly voice commanding attention. "But I think we'll begin." His gaze shifted from face to face.

Dedrick almost wished he stood against the far wall, out of the ancient elder's view.

"We have with us today an elder from the Jensenville area." Elder Lukman lifted a hand to indicate the face that appeared on one of the wall monitors. "Elder Klein."

Elder Klein nodded. He may have smiled. The crease that slanted down from his nose deepened, but his beard, full and dark with white flecks, hid his mouth.

"We'll go over preliminary information." Elder Lukman's gaze went to Dedrick, piercing him through. "We have our children back from Primary." He nodded to Dedrick, his way of saying *thank you*.

Dedrick nodded back to say *you're welcome*. Paula's brown eyes, peering up at him, popped into his mind. "Why can't I come?" she had said when he told her he had to leave Gardenhall. "You have to stay here, keep an eye on those two." He threw a glance to indicate Simon and Zachary. After playing Bot's 3D game, Liberty had crawled into one of the capsules to sleep. He went to Paula. He watched her play, read to her, then fell asleep with her on a couch. Finally, he told her he had to go. It felt like trying to sever a limb. He hated leaving his little sister so soon.

Elder Lukman's gaze glided across the members that stood along the walls, seeming to skip over Dedrick this time. "And our youth are free from the Secondary Residence."

Dedrick bristled at the choice of words. Yes, they were free, but they weren't all safe. They weren't all here. What would happen to Andy? Would Dedrick ever see him again?

He pushed the rest of his worry back. He had to focus on getting Mom and Dad and the others out of Re-Ed.

Alix leaned on the wall adjacent Dedrick, her legs stretched at an angle. She flung her arm out and left it hanging diagonally, her way of announcing she had a question. He'd been told they never raised their hands to speak in Secondary. They interrupted.

Fulton squatted beside her, fidgeting with something on his TekBand, probably texting the kids on the skeleton crew, worried he'd miss something.

Elder Rayna signaled Elder Lukman with her eyes. Elder Lukman scooted his chair back and twisted to face Alix. "You have a question, Alix?"

"Yeah. Some of those kids from Secondary were Aldonians, and now they know about our operation." She threw an accusing glare to Dedrick.

He gritted his teeth.

"I saw them in the dining hall," she said, "whispering together. Are you sure we can trust them?"

A wave of murmuring passed through the room.

Elder Dean's chin lifted from its resting place on his chest, a beam of light from an overhead fixture tracing a path on his bald head. "They wouldn't be here if we didn't trust them. Dedrick acted with our permission."

He turned his piercing eyes to Alix, seeming to peer into her soul. Alix straightened up from her casual position and stepped back. "We've been watching those particular teens for some time. A pocket of rebellion has been growing among the Secondary children. They question what they've been taught. They think for themselves, develop their own ideals. Worthy ideals. They suspect the Regimen has deceived them." Elder Dean gave a crooked grin, his eyes sliding to Dedrick. "Andy is a good judge of character. Those Aldonians you brought, those are our people."

After a pause, Elder Lukman said, "We are left, now, with our most challenging rescue." He nodded to Elder Rayna and tapped the tabletop to interface with the computer.

Elder Rayna said, "We now have our surveillance Intel, so we should have little problem avoiding surveillance when we need to."

"That's good," Dedrick mumbled to himself. Finley must have made the trade for the illegal 3D game. How did he like it? How fast would the game spread? Was Bot right? Would it change things?

"We are able to tap into the Regimen's video feeds," Elder Rayna said, "and intercept their communications, although they have a few secure lines we have yet to break into. Regardless, we will know what the Citizen Safety Station knows."

The door creaked open. Elder Rayna's face scrunched up. All heads turned.

Liberty strolled into the room. She wore an oversized button-front shirt and black jeans, clothes she probably got from the women at Gardenhall. She glanced at the elders and the empty chair, glanced at Dedrick and the empty wall on his side, then proceeded to walk to the adjacent wall. Alix glared but made room for her.

The door clicked shut. Bolcan had come in, too. He released the door handle, nodded at a few kids, tapped fists with a few others, and swaggered over to Liberty. He jabbed his thumb in the air, indicating for Fulton to move out of the way. Fulton stood and tripped over his own feet as he complied.

Dedrick took a deep breath and let it seep out of his mouth. He didn't care that they came in together. Why should he? Bolcan had probably told her about the meeting and escorted her here. She probably resented that Dedrick hadn't told her. Maybe he should've, but he didn't want her on the mission. She didn't belong here. And, besides, it wasn't his place to decide who got an invite to the rescue meeting. It wasn't his call who they put on a rescue. The elders worked that out. Liberty didn't have the training, wasn't a vowed member . . . What did she expect?

She sure flipped out over that kiss earlier.

Dedrick's hand had gone up to his mouth. He made a fist and cleared his throat in case anyone had noticed.

"Do you have something to share, Dedrick?" Elder Rayna said, sounding irritated.

"Huh? Uh, no, I was just . . ." He coughed again and pointed to his throat.

A couple of girls giggled. Camilla jabbed his ribs.

"Moving on. Perhaps you are wondering why you are all here," Elder Rayna said, her dark eyes still on Dedrick. Did she sense his discomfort at Liberty's presence? "This meeting room certainly was not designed to accommodate the entire Mosheh." A few giggles. "As Elder Lukman mentioned, this is our most challenging mission to date. Each of you has talents and gifts, and we want each of you to use them. If something doesn't sound right, you don't agree with the way something will be handled, speak up. We can't mess this one up."

Dedrick stared, too stunned to speak. Those were not the words of an elder. Was this change the result of Miriam? Somehow, she had convinced them that his spontaneous decision to rescue Liberty was a result of his gifts rather than something for which he should be disciplined. Miriam, apparently, had the gift of persuasion.

A monitor on the wall showed that Elder Klein, the elder from Jensenville, had been speaking, his mouth moving secretly behind his beard. ". . . stirring things up at the Jensenville border. This has convinced Aldonia's CSS that the Secondary kids are in Jensenville. They don't, however, know what to make of the Primary children . . ."

Dedrick risked a glance at Liberty.

She did not lean on the wall, the way most of the others did. She stood with one leg bent and her hands in the back pockets of her jeans. She licked her lips and pressed them together.

He looked away. He shouldn't have kissed her. He was never playing another 3D game as long as he lived. They messed with his mind, made him one with his character or something, turned him into some kind of out-of-control, driven-to-win, obsessed freak. It was ridiculous. Give him all the latest in weapons and let the rest of technology pass him by. He didn't need it.

". . . has eroded trust between the two cities," Elder Klein said, "so they've put a high level of importance on this transfer of our colonists."

Dedrick straightened up and tried to focus. Everyone else had his or her eyes trained on the elder. He needed to tether his mind. What transfer?

"Unfortunately, Jensenville called for an investigation. Aldonia responded in kind, calling for their own investigation. This may cause problems for us in the future. We'll need to stay on top of it and direct their conclusions."

"That's only half the colonists," Bolcan said in true Aldonia fashion, interrupting an elder. Of course *he* had been paying enough attention to ask a question. He had been leaning a shoulder against the wall, but now he stood with his hands on his hips and his feet apart. Bolcan, a hulk of a man. Did he and Liberty like each other?

"That is true," Elder Lukman said, showing no irritation at the interruption. "Before we go over the full plan and assign roles, we have something else to discuss." The elders glanced from one to the other. Elder Lukman lifted his gaze to Dedrick. "We have lost contact with Miriam and the Maxwell colonists."

Dedrick's world shifted for a moment. A knife threatened to split it in two. He felt the gaze of several in the room. What happened to Miriam? Was his sister Ann safe? Had the Torva interfered with the transfer?

"We need to send someone or maybe a team out there," Elder Lukman said. "We've had some bad weather. This may have caused a communication problem, or we could be looking at something more dangerous."

"I'll go," Dedrick said. "Tonight. As soon as we're done with this mission."

The elders stared. No one replied. They didn't like his answer. Did they want him to leave now? He couldn't do it. He needed to get his parents out of Re-Ed.

"I would have to leave at night anyway," Dedrick said. "A few hours won't make a difference. I have a dirt bike hidden just inside the Boundary Fence. I'll find the colonists in no time."

Elder Rayna exchanged a glance with Elder Lukman.

"If you're worried about my ability to focus—"

Elder Lukman raised a hand, palm up. "Then it's settled, and we'll get on with the details of the Re-Ed rescue."

Elder Dean moved his hands along the tabletop and tapped it a few times, interfacing with the computer. A map appeared on a wall monitor. "This is where we begin." A red dot popped up on the map. "The rescue team's access point is here. They will surface and follow a specific route to avoid surveillance. They will intercept the transfer bus here." The route lit up as he spoke. He explained that a member of the team would stage an injury in the road to stop the bus. The rest of the team would board the bus, sedate the Regimen workers, and clone their implants. One member would drive the bus and watch over the sedated RCT employees while the others entered the facility.

"We have already arranged for the transfer to take place late in the evening," Elder Rayna said. "This reduces the number of staff at the facility."

Elder Dean continued. "The bus will approach the gate and slow at this point here." A green "x" appeared on the map. "This is very important. There is a dead zone between surveillance cameras. This is where Dedrick and Liberty must exit the bus."

Dedrick's eyes snapped to Liberty. Her eyes snapped to him. "She's going on this mission?" he said before he could stop himself.

"There is a breach in the fence here. You will run to the backside of the facility." A green line showed the path on the map. Elder Dean had not heard Dedrick or else ignored the interruption, but Elders Rayna and Lukman now looked at him. "Cameras may be on you as you go, but you will be dressed in black and, hopefully, go unnoticed."

"Excuse me," Dedrick said, raising one hand, then the other. He was going to take hell for this, and probably from all sides, but he had to protest.

Elder Dean turned his eagle eyes to Dedrick and burned a hole through his soul. "Is there a problem?"

Everyone now faced Dedrick. Including Liberty. And Bolcan. Bolcan had a cocky grin.

"I-I don't have anything against her. Her, I mean, Liberty. But come on, she's new here. I mean, she's not part of the Mosheh, not trained or—"

"I gave her some training," Bolcan said, a challenge in his golden eyes. "She's capable."

"Yeah, me too," Alix said. She straightened up from the wall and gave Liberty the once-over. "She's not bad compared to some I've trained."

"Yeah," Bolcan said, "she taught me a thing or two." His gaze swung from Alix to Dedrick and then to Liberty. "About picking locks."

Liberty sneered at him and folded her arms across her chest. The dim lighting of the meeting room didn't hide the red that now colored her cheeks.

"One thing you'll notice about our diagrams, Dedrick," Elder Dean said as a holographic image of the Re-education Facility materialized above the table. "We do not have detailed information about the cellblock. Liberty, however, has been inside the facility."

"Bolcan's been inside the facility," Dedrick blurted out.

Bolcan sniggered and then exploded with laughter. Still laughing, he turned to the wall and raised a hand as if asking everyone to wait while he composed himself.

The blood rushed to Dedrick's face. His head threatened to explode. "That's funny?"

"Dedrick, I understand your concern," Elder Lukman said, the calmness of his voice like an insult. "You don't want Liberty anywhere near that place, but she'll have you to protect her. And Bolcan has a job he's more suited for." He scooted his chair out and turned to Liberty. "Dedrick is right to be concerned. There is a big risk here. Are you certain, Liberty, that you want to do this?"

Liberty stepped forward and dropped her hands to her sides, standing tall like a Mosheh in training. "I am, sir. I can do this. But even if something goes wrong, I'm willing to risk my safety." She pressed her lips together, and a look flitted through her eyes. Dedrick understood. She wanted to say more, but she wasn't sure she should.

She took a breath and glanced from person to person. "I share something in common with the Maxwell colonists here." Her sea green Aldonian eyes turned to Dedrick. "I blame myself for what happened to Maxwell."

Dedrick recoiled inside and dropped his gaze. He did not blame her. Or maybe he did. No, he blamed himself. He was one of the Mosheh, and it should've been his responsibility to stop her.

"I understand that it's not entirely my fault," she said, "that the Regimen made some discoveries on their own. But if I hadn't been trying to return that night . . . If I hadn't been so impatient, if I had tried to go about things the right way, this wouldn't have happened."

That night. She'd strode with purpose, away from Maxwell, her silky hair bouncing with each step and reflecting the moonlight. He grabbed her by the arm and forced her to stop. "Would you risk us all?" he said. He doubted she'd even find the way back. Wild animals, wild men would likely get to her first. Nothing he said had any impact on her. She was determined to go. He had no choice but to go with her or let her go to her death. Right? Or no, maybe that wasn't his reason.

Elder Lukman's hand went up. He wanted to interrupt.

Liberty shook her head, not permitting the interruption. "This wouldn't have happened in the way it did, with your family members taken and your homes burned. So let me do this.

"I share something in common with the Aldonians here, too. I know Aldonia and the way Aldonians think. I also know how to do the job you've given me. I know this facility."

Dedrick's gaze had returned to her. He couldn't look away. Maybe he went along that night because of the irrational feelings he had for her. He'd never known a more beautiful girl. Granted, scientists manipulated genes or whatever to create the perfect girl. But what did that matter? Outside appearances meant nothing in truth. He shouldn't be so taken by a girl's beauty.

"So, yes, I want to do this." Liberty stepped back, folded her arms, and leaned against the wall.

Dedrick couldn't take his eyes off her.

CHAPTER 30

"What transfer? Why was I not informed?" Dr. Supero shouted at Sage through his flexi-phone. First, the Secondary teens slipped away, then the children, now half the adults in Re-education. Soon he would lose everyone and every chance of finding a surgeon. He shouldn't have waited so long to re-interview the adults in Re-Ed.

Sid stepped into his peripheral vision, smirking and chewing on something. The boy did nothing but eat and experiment with gadgets in Dr. Supero's apartment. Dr. Supero should've insisted he leave this morning.

"What makes you think you belong in the loop?" Sage said. "This is Regimen business."

"As you are likely aware, I have been promoted to Head of the Department of Genetics at Aldonia's RCT University. The very foundation of our society depends upon the advancements of my work. You cannot transfer the new citizens until I conduct tests and interviews. Their DNA and other test results are vital to my research."

"Sorry, Dr. Supero, staff at the Re-education Facility received the requisition from higher Regimen officials. They have no choice but to release them as scheduled. Maybe you can conduct your tests and interviews in Jensenville."

Dr. Supero squeezed his hands into fists, his entire body trembling. He kicked a barstool to the ceramic tile floor. "Contact whomever you must. Delay the transfer. I am going to Re-Ed now. You will meet me there. Make a room available to me and ready one of the adults scheduled for transfer." He disconnected the call.

"What was that about?" Sid said, gazing through lazy eyes with lids half-mast. He held a plate of cheese, hot peppers, and dried meats. "Where're you going?"

"I am going to the Re-education Facility." Dr. Supero snatched the plate from Sid. "You are going home." He flung the plate to the marble countertop and it crashed to the floor, creating a mess he could not see from where he stood. What did he care? The apartment was no longer his.

"What the earth, man?" Sid lurched to one side and formed a fist, looking ready for a fight. "How does this help me find Liberty?"

"You wish to find Liberty. I am looking for something else." Dr. Supero stomped past him, heading for the door.

"You told me CSS ain't watching that Gray Zone, that we could get in there easy. What do you need with the people at Re-Ed?"

"That is none of your business." He opened the door, snapped his finger, and pointed to the hallway outside the apartment.

Sid slunk over and stood face to face, revealing the stubble on his jaw and upper lip. "This has to do with your brain tumor, doesn't it? You're afraid you're gonna die. You think one of them backwoodsmen can help you? Where's the sense in that? Maybe one of the people I know can help you. There's a doctor there, I'm pretty sure."

"You are wrong, Sid." Dr. Supero moved even closer so that their noses almost touched. "There is no secret community in the old city center."

CHAPTER 31

"Take that and that and that," a skinny teenage boy said. The freckles on his nose, his plain blue eyes, and his crooked teeth held my attention. He was from Maxwell or some other colony. He wasn't Aldonian.

He slid a flashlight, ID implant remover, and compact mace across the plywood crate that served as a low wall to the Weapon and Gadget room. Alix had called it the WAG room.

"Thanks." I clipped the flashlight to my belt and stuffed the mace into a holder. Bolcan had already given me a lock-pick kit, and Alix had outfitted me with black and gray camouflage pants, a ballistic vest, black boots, and a modular belt.

My skin pricked with excitement. This was really happening.

From my cell in Re-Ed, I often thought about the damage I had done to Maxwell. It seemed irreparable. I had taken apart an engine, and the parts lay scattered on the carpet. I had little hope of getting them all in the right places. Now it was coming together. We had rescued the children. The teens were free. Today we would have the adults.

We. I could say *we.* The elders had confidence in me. A part of me still couldn't believe they agreed to let me help. Maybe this was a test, a deciding factor for whether or not I could join the Mosheh. They would see that I was worthy. The weeds of selfishness and impatience would no longer rule me. The seeds of selflessness and obedience would grow instead.

"I already explained that to you." Farther down the low wall of crates, Dedrick stood with a hand on his hip and head tilted to the side. He wore black and gray camouflage, too, but the Velcro flaps hung open on the sides of his ballistic vest. "I decided to leave it with them."

The skinny teen stared at the computer notepad in his hand. "Well, unless you have permission, you can't just take things out and not bring them back. Implant removers don't grow on trees, you know."

Dedrick rolled his eyes and turned away from the kid, our eyes meeting.

I slid the ID implant remover into a holster on my belt, gave Dedrick an indifferent nod, and turned to go.

"You gave her one," Dedrick protested. "I can't do my job without . . ."

~ ~ ~

"You have a twenty-five-centimeter scar on your chest, and your sternum's been broken. You've had open heart surgery. Tell me, Michael, who was the surgeon?" Dr. Supero sat at a small cold table in a dimly lit death-gray room the size of a casket, the lifelessness of it all a precursor to his future.

"You assume I've had open heart surgery. Maybe I cut myself climbing a tree. Maybe a wild animal scratched me." Michael smiled though the ashen color of his skin and his sunken eyes showed the strain he experienced here at Re-Ed. He sat slouched back in the chair and rested his hands in his lap.

"Do not toy with me!" Dr. Supero's blood simmered. He could not let it boil over. He needed answers from these people. "I do not *assume*. I *know*. I ran tests on you the day you came to Aldonia."

"I did not come to Aldonia. Men with guns forced me here."

"Regardless, I have a 3D hologram of your entire body, inside and out."

Michael smirked. "Sounds like you've got some pretty advanced equipment there, doctor. Why do you care who operated on me?"

"I have my reasons. If you won't give a name, at least tell me if the surgery was performed by an Aldonian or by one of your own?"

He chuckled and rubbed his smooth jaw.

The last time Dr. Supero had viewed live images of the new residents in the Re-Ed Facility, the men had had full beards. The staff would not have allowed him to shave himself. Someone must've done the job for him, for all the men. They exchanged the hospital gowns for regular clothing, washed faces, and brushed hair, attempting to make the eight transfers with murky brown and blue eyes appear healthy. They would not want the Jensenville Regimen to doubt Aldonia's good faith.

"It is a simple question," Dr. Supero said. "I want an answer."

"I don't get you guys. Why are you so adamant that we tell you everything we know and that we believe everything you tell us? Doesn't anyone in your society have an opinion of their own?"

Dr. Supero's lip curled. "They are all here, in Re-Ed." He glanced at the time on his flexi-phone. He had ten more minutes and two more people to interview. The other five had given him nothing. Perhaps he had been going about this all wrong. He began by asking each person a few questions to avoid arousing the suspicion of the Re-Ed staff, questions that might be relevant to the study of genetics. "Tell me about your diet." "How did you treat your water?" "What natural remedies did you use?" The staff may or may not have been watching, but the green LEDs on the wall showed that they did record the interview. As the minutes ticked away, he grew less concerned about the staff's opinions. "How many doctors have treated you over the years? Where did they receive training? Give me the name of your doctor."

Regardless of the questions, he received similar replies: "I'm not answering your questions." "I can't answer that." "Why do you care?" And his favorite response: silence.

By the fourth interview, he had adjusted his technique.

"We only want to learn from you," he lied, but got little in return.

"If you want to return to your life in the wilderness, you can. You only need to answer my questions." Bribery had no effect on them.

"If you do not give me the name of your doctor and tell me how to reach him, I will see to it that you and your friends never leave this place." Threats accomplished nothing.

Sage had interrupted once. She pulled him from the room. "I'm done with the tests you requested."

"That is good," he said even though he did not care in the least. The tests were a cover. Something to keep her busy. He turned away.

She stopped him, grabbing his arm. "Your time would've been up now, but the transfer bus is running late. You'll have time for one or two more interviews."

"Very good." He tried shrugging her hand from his bicep.

"But I'm wondering . . ." She pursed her lips. "Your line of questioning seems inappropriate for genetic research. Care to explain?"

"No, I do not. Allow me to conduct my interviews, and I will send you my research. It will all be made clear." More lies. But what did he care? He hadn't the time. The medical evaluation panel cast a verdict and left him for dead. Any day now could be his last. Any minute he could cease to exist, or he would become one with the cosmic infinity. He wanted neither fate. No one knew the answer to the question: *What comes after death?* He did not want to know. He was not ready. He wanted to live. These people lived without the aid of the Regimen. One of them would show him the way. Maybe he had to convince them he was worth saving.

~ ~ ~

Within the hour, I sat next to Bolcan on the back of a tunnel kart on our way to the access point. Dedrick drove and Alix rode shotgun. Camilla drove a second kart in front of us. Three guys rode with her. I only caught the name of one: Arc.

He was another member of the external rescue team. The other two would remain underground and drive the tunnel karts to the access point we planned to use later. They would give rides to the colonists who couldn't walk the distance back. I hoped it wouldn't be many who needed the ride, that they would all be in good shape, but I feared the worst.

"Regimen troopers and security officers carry toys," Bolcan said, peering at a cartridge of rubber bullets. He and Arc wore midnight blue Citizen Safety Uniforms and carried the standard weapons: a rubber bullet gun, a taser flashlight, and pepper spray. "If anyone took a stand against the Regimen, they'd only need a gun with real bullets. Aldonians should rise up."

"Aldonians don't own weapons," I said. "They send you to Re-Ed for possession."

"I know." His eyelids flickered over his golden eyes as if an unwelcome memory had struck him. "But you can get them on the black market."

Alix turned around. "Are you worried, Bolcan? Don't be. I'll do the talking. This will go smoothly. But if it goes bad, I'm armed." She grinned. Alix wore an olive green shirtdress and black boots with buckles, studs and—my guess—weapons hidden somewhere inside them.

I had to look twice when I first saw Camilla. Her outfit consisted of an oversized, psychedelic pink-and-yellow shirt draped over a white undershirt and white leggings. Bizarre. But she did have to stop a bus. Elder Lukman had asked for a volunteer and her hand had shot up. "Oh, let me!" She jumped in place.

Both she and Bolcan had changed their hair colors. Bolcan had black hair, which looked odd on him, and Camilla had pink hair. I didn't think colonists colored their hair. What would her family think of her now?

"Are you checking out my hair?" Bolcan said.

Dedrick glanced over his shoulder, the kart swerving.

"No," I said. "Well, I guess I was. Why the black hair?"

"I don't want anyone to recognize me." Bolcan smirked.

"How long ago were you there?"

He shrugged. "The last time? A couple years. I'm sure it's the same workers, but they see so many people come and go. They won't recognize me with the dark hair. Besides, I have these." He pulled shades from a chest pocket and waved his brows. Then he frowned. "When you were there, did you get to the History Lessons?"

"No."

"That's good." He turned away, putting a curtain of black hair between us.

We took long tunnels that seemed to stretch on forever, covering a distance twice the size of Aldonia. Of course, my anxiety for the mission may have distorted my perception of distance and time. A sour stench wafted on the air, growing stronger by the minute.

The kart squeaked to a stop.

My heart skipped a beat.

Camilla had parked her kart at an angle that allowed the headlights to shine on the wall. Damp streaks covered the wall, probably from the recent rain. A metal ladder, painted yellow on the bottom rungs, rose up into darkness.

Bolcan jumped to the ground and swaggered toward the ladder, passing Dedrick. Now they both headed for it.

I came around the kart and stood by Alix.

She tapped the screen of the Aldonian flexi-phone that she wore as part of her disguise. Her eyes lifted to me. "You know what your role is, right?"

"Yeah." I sensed her lack of confidence in me.

"I'll go up first," Dedrick said to Bolcan. "In case anyone's around."

Bolcan laughed and patted Dedrick's shoulder. Dedrick winced. "No, Dedrick, you won't. I'll go first. If anyone is around, what're you going to do that I can't do better?"

"I can remain unseen." Dedrick stepped past him and grabbed the vertical bar of the ladder. Bolcan shoved Dedrick, breaking his connection with the ladder. Dedrick shoved back, mumbling something through clenched teeth.

"You wanna try me?" Bolcan said, flipping black bangs from his face. He formed fists and curled his bulging arms.

Dedrick, muscled but lean in comparison to Bolcan's build, took a fighting stance and opened his mouth to reply.

"You guys are idiots," Alix said. "I'll go first. The bus is three minutes out. We don't have time for your pissing contest." She pushed between them and clanged a boot to the rung ladder.

Bolcan gave Dedrick a grin and climbed up after Alix. Dedrick's eyes shifted to me with a look I couldn't read, though I sensed he, too, lacked confidence in me.

My palms were damp with sweat, and I felt like the sour stench of the tunnel clung to my skin. Impatient to get above ground, I made a move for the ladder.

Camilla cut me off and climbed up next, Arc on her heels. Dedrick motioned for me to go next. I guess he decided if he couldn't go first, he'd go last.

The rungs felt cool and slick, slippery under my boots. I climbed quicker than I probably should've on a wet surface, my eyes on the next rung up, my mind on Dedrick climbing a few rungs below me. The open manhole soon became visible, showing a royal blue night behind Bolcan's muscular figure.

When I reached the last rung and poked my head above ground, Bolcan stooped and offered his hand. I felt Dedrick watch as I took it. It was strong, callused, and warm. In an instant, I stood on solid ground, a paved road between buildings.

"Over here," someone whispered, Alix, I thought. I went to the voice, studying my surroundings.

We were on a quiet, dead-end street, a recycling center on one side and three-story buildings on the other. Security lights gave the dark buildings shape. A row of dumpsters lined the street, the foul smell coming from them an improvement over the stench in the tunnel. Alix and Arc stood between dumpsters, whispering.

"Where's Camilla?" I said, joining them.

"Doing her job," Alix said.

I peeked around the corner of the dumpster and squinted to see the crossing street. Sure enough, a girl sat in the road, the colors of her shirt and white leggings standing out in the darkness.

"She's sitting in the road," I said. "What if the bus runs her—"

A scraping sound caught me by surprise. Bolcan and Dedrick stood over the manhole, one of them having closed it. They both stood with their feet wide apart. Did they fight about who would close the manhole?

"Didn't you ever go on fieldtrips?" Alix said.

"What?" I said.

Dedrick and Bolcan jogged over and squeezed in between the dumpsters with us. Bolcan had the hint of a grin, Dedrick a sneer.

"Where'd you sit?" Alix said. "In the back of the bus? Buses have sensors and warn the driver of obstacles in the road."

"Are you calling Camilla an obstacle?" Arc said. He and Bolcan snickered.

"She is today," Alix said.

A screeching sound tore my attention. I peeked again. The bus had stopped a few meters from Camilla, its headlights now making her glow with color. The bus door opened.

Someone grabbed my shoulder and pulled me back. Dedrick. He stood close. "Count to ten before running to the bus," he said, then he, Arc, and Bolcan took off.

I guessed he meant for me to start counting now. Why ten seconds? *One, two, three* . . .

"Better turn your earphone on," Alix said.

I nodded and flipped the tiny switch. *Seven, eight, nine* . . .

"Let's go," Alix said. She dashed past me, racing for the bus.

I ran, too. Movement showed on the bus. Camilla walked backwards and Bolcan walked facing her, as if they carried something between them. Arc and Dedrick's heads showed through the windows. They seemed focused on whatever they did. Maybe they were cloning ID implants.

Alix pounded up the stairs and swung into a seat.

I grabbed the railing by the door and climbed in after her.

"Excuse me," Camilla said, pushing past me. Her polite words didn't match her cold expression. She slid into the driver's seat and closed the door behind me.

I stepped into the aisle and had to stop to regroup. I knew that the team needed to subdue the people on the bus, but it still shocked me to see three unconscious bodies. They lay with their knees pressed to seatbacks and their torsos on the seats. Two were security guards dressed in the midnight blue Citizen Safety Station uniforms. One was a woman, the Jensenville representative. Her short dark hair resembled Alix's, but the similarities stopped there. She appeared to be ten years older and twenty pounds or so heavier.

Dedrick had been leaning over one of the security guards, but now he straightened up and looked at me, or maybe past me. He stepped into the aisle, in my path, as the bus lunged.

I lost my balance and fell forward, my face slamming into his chest. I regained my balance in a split second, feeling stupid and awkward and wondering who saw. "Sorry," I said, squeezing past him. I dropped into a seat halfway back and stared out the window. The entire team probably doubted my coordination and skill.

Why do you let me mess up? I asked *My Friend.* It didn't make sense that I blamed him. He guided me, warned me, and even counseled me, but he didn't control my movements. Maybe I wanted someone to blame other than myself.

Office buildings and towering apartments crept by, a light in a window here and there. I didn't see a single person. Dedrick had moved to the front of the bus. He stood behind Camilla, saying something to her about her ability to drive a bus. Camilla answered with wide eyes and a huge smile, but no words. He continued talking to her. She mostly answered with facial expressions and shrugs. Maybe she didn't need words with him.

"You got a problem with her or him?" Bolcan slid into my seat, his leg bumping mine. He had been sitting two seats behind me, on the opposite side of the aisle, stretched out with a shoe hanging over the side.

I scooted toward the window. "I'm trying to see where we are. I saw a solar farm the day I left Re-Ed."

"You mean like that." Bolcan stuck his arm in my face and pointed out the window. The light from the bus reflected on the row of black panels nearest the road. They stood at sharp angles facing east, ready to suck the energy from the morning sun. The farther rows appeared as a strange geometric landscape, unnatural but artistically appealing at the same time.

"So does it feel like going home?" Bolcan said.

I felt my brows twitch as I faced him. "Going home? To Re-Ed? How long were you in there?"

"Which time?" He gave a crooked grin but his eyes held sadness.

Movement at the front of the bus caught my attention. Dedrick had turned around. Our eyes met, then he slid into the seat with Alix. She had been talking over a security guard's body, going over the mission with Arc. Arc sat two seats back and kept bobbing his head and saying, "Okay, I got it already."

"If I had my way . . ." Bolcan stared at the seatback as he spoke. ". . . we'd shoot the Regimen workers and free everyone in Re-Ed. No one should have to go through that. Especially not the History Lessons."

I wanted to ask about the History Lessons. What made him hate them more than the other aspects of Re-Ed? I was supposed to have begun the lessons the day Sid busted me out. He saved me from that fate. Maybe I should've thanked him.

My gaze rested on distant wind turbines, skeletal forms clawing at a black sky.

"We're approaching the dead zone," Camilla shouted, glancing in the rearview mirror. "Better get ready."

Dedrick stood behind Camilla again, hunching over and peering out the window. I caught bits of what he said to her, something about guards at the main gate.

Bolcan slid out and walked ahead of me to the emergency door in the middle of the bus. Dedrick soon joined us, avoiding eye contact with Bolcan.

I stood, clutching a seatback for balance.

"She's not going to stop," Dedrick said to me. "She'll slow and we'll have to jump. Jump hard to clear the bus and then plan to roll."

I nodded and moved closer to the door. I wanted to ask why she couldn't stop, but Dedrick had a thing about me showing trust. I decided it had to do with the view from the main gate. Maybe the guard would notice a full stop.

Dedrick stared at a map that glowed on his TekBand. A red dot marked our location. Lines showed the dead zone. He lifted the lever handle on the top side of the emergency exit and pushed the door open. A green-scented breeze rushed in and played with my hair. Tall grass and weeds whizzed by.

The bus slowed.

Bolcan moved toward me, drawing Dedrick's eye, and whispered in my ear, "See you on the other side."

I bent my legs and leaned forward, my heart racing and palms sweating at the thought of hurling myself from a moving bus. Could I do this?

Dedrick glanced at his TekBand. "Now!"

Did he mean for me to go first or that we would jump together? *No time to think. Just do it.*

I leaped. My body sailed through the air. The ground came up to meet me. My feet landed hard, sending a shock through my legs. I ran a few steps and fell forward onto my shoulder. Grass in my face, black sky, grass, sky . . . . I came out of the roll on my back and uncurled my body, struggling to breathe.

Dedrick grabbed my arm and yanked me to my feet. "Run!"

With steps in sync, we ran through tall grass under a clear night sky towards a row of dark trees. The taillights of the bus disappeared around a bend. The trees took us into their cover. Branches lay strewn everywhere, the aftereffect of recent storms.

We changed directions and now ran between the line of trees and the high razor-wire fencing. Distant lights showed the outline of the sprawling two-story Re-education Facility.

The bus had probably cleared the gate. We wouldn't see it from here. I pictured Alix between security guards, Bolcan and Arc, strutting up the long sidewalk to the facility.

Dedrick's TekBand flashed. He jerked to a stop, darted to the fence, and dropped onto one knee. He grabbed handfuls of grass and yanked, leaned and grabbed more grass.

I dropped down two meters away and did the same. Arc and another kid had come out here days ago in preparation for today. They'd cut a hole in the fence to allow our access and hid it with tall weeds. We only needed to find the loose turf.

We grabbed handfuls of weeds and tugged, moving closer to each other. Weeds slipped and sliced through my palms, but the dirt had no give. I threw a huge branch out of my way and grabbed more weeds.

"Here," Dedrick said. He lifted a wide hunk of weeds and dirt. The dirt held together like clay.

"They're in." The voice came through my earphone. "Team One is in the facility." Team One: Alix, Bolcan, and Arc. Dedrick and I were Team Two.

Dedrick and I exchanged a glance, then we shifted into overdrive. We yanked clump after clump out of the way and scraped dirt out with our hands, exposing the hole in the fence. It looked small. Maybe too small. Were any of the colonists big? Reaching through the hole, we grabbed more lose turf, more clumps of dirt. It took two hands to move each one. We pulled them through to our side and stacked them, creating mounds of dirt and weeds on either side of our crawlway.

~ ~ ~

"Somewhere in my mind," Michael said, "I always knew this day would come."

"What day is that?" Dr. Supero rubbed his head.

"The day I would lose my freedom." He smiled, his murky blue eyes calm as a stagnant pond.

"Perhaps I can regain your freedom for you."

Michael huffed. "I only need to sacrifice a friend, huh?"

Dr. Supero blinked. Minutes clicked down. He wished the conversation were not being recorded. He needed to speak candidly. "Are you aware that you are being transferred to another city?"

"I heard it said. Don't know if I believe it. I've been questioned, threatened, and given an education, if you can call it that." He smirked. "I don't believe I have received an ounce of truth since I've been here."

"Well, you can believe me. You are being transferred, but your wife is not." It was a lie. He would interview the woman next. The Regimen was foolish to keep the two in the same city. If they ever graduated from Jensenville's Re-Ed, they would seek each other out. They would tell others they were married. Questions about marriage and family would arise.

The man's expression fell. This was his weakness. The woman.

"I can change that," Dr. Supero said. "We have advanced beyond the outdated practice of marriage, but I see no reason why the two of you can't remain together."

Dr. Supero leaned across the table. "Give me the name of your surgeon."

The door creaked open and Sage stuck her head into the room. "Excuse me, Dr. Supero. The transfer bus is here. You need to wrap up this interview and make arrangements with Jensenville for the last two." She disappeared and the door clicked shut.

"See? She is referring to the transfer bus. You are going to Jensenville. I am not lying. This is your last chance to stay together." Desperation drove him to his feet and to Michael's side of the table.

Michael closed his eyes, and a tear rolled down his cheek.

Dr. Supero grabbed his shoulder and stooped to whisper in the man's ear. The one thing he had not done was attempt to evoke pity. "I have personal reasons for needing this surgeon," he said, his voice a whisper. "Without him I will die. Please. Help me."

Michael's eyes snapped open. He jerked his face to Supero, questions in his eyes.

The door flung open and two guards burst into the room. "Time for the transfer," one of them said.

"You cannot simply barge in here. I am conducting an interview. I will bring him when I am through."

"Can't wait. Bus is late already." The guards grabbed Michael, one on each arm, and yanked him to his feet.

Michael stared at Dr. Supero, his eyes still questioning as they dragged him from the room.

~ ~ ~

We had done it. The crawlway was clear.

"You first," Dedrick said, ripping open the Velcro on the sides of his ballistic vest. "You should have no problem."

I flung myself facedown onto the cool dirt and eased my head under the cut chain links. Then I crawled, pulling with my forearms, pushing with my knees and feet. Left arm, right arm, pulling and pulling, knees and feet digging in, dirt squishing and rolling against my hands and clothes, dirt in my face.

"Clear," Dedrick said.

I rolled out of his way and got up, wiping at the mud caked to my clothes.

Dedrick tossed his vest under and climbed through the same way I did, only faster. He popped up, snatched his vest, and dashed for the nearest outbuilding.

The backup generator was stored in an old brick building that had a high window on the back wall and a door on the side. Dedrick yanked something from his belt without breaking his stride.

I groped the pouches and tools hanging from my belt, trying to find my lock-pick kit. It would take no time for me to get into this building. The Re-education Facility would take longer. But I was ready for it. I had trained with Bolcan, practicing with the exact locks used on these doors.

Dedrick, running at top speed, reached the building first. Head ducked to one side, he leaped and slammed something through the window. Glass shattered and rained down. He landed with a thud and stooped for something. He stood up holding a leafy branch, longer than he was tall.

"Pass this through to me." He shoved the branch at me, then leaped up to the broken window.

"What are you thinking?" Irritation made my voice harsh. "It would've taken a second for me to open the door."

He opened the window by tilting the bottom outward. Then he pulled himself up and swung his legs inside.

I wanted to scream. This was stupid. Why didn't he let me unlock the door?

"The branch." His voice came through the dark window.

I stomped to the building, lifted the branch overhead, and thrust it through with undue force. Then I leaped. My hands slapped onto rough brick and the hard plastic edges of the window frame. Fortunately, I touched no glass shards. I pulled myself up the way he had done and swung one leg up to the windowsill.

"You got it?" he said.

"Yes, but this is stupid." I swung my other leg up and eased myself into position, plastic edges digging into my arms and hands. Then I dropped to a floor covered in glass and my feet slid. My stomach jumped. Everything tilted. I threw my arms out for balance and fell back against his chest.

"I got you," he said, sounding amused. He held me from behind, around the shoulders, the ballistic vest a buffer between us.

"I'm fine." I straightened up and stomped away from him and the shards of glass. I wanted to shove him. "You know I can pick a lock."

Tiny green, yellow, and red lights glowed on a control panel on a boxy generator. Conduits ran along the ceiling and one wall. Dedrick's flashlight lay on the floor, its beam making the broken glass sparkle.

"Yeah, I'm aware of that." He closed the window and shoved the branch halfway through it, bits of glass sprinkling the floor. "There." He stood arms akimbo. Half the branch dangled into the room. "Does it look natural?"

I huffed, disgusted. "I guess so. But why couldn't we have used the door?"

He snatched up his flashlight and strolled around the generator, studying it. "There's a surveillance camera that can see the door. It's activated by a motion sensor." He blew dust off something under a lever and then wiped it. "We can go out that way once the power is down." He looked at me and smiled.

I turned away, still wanting to shove him, and glanced around the room. An unusually small door came off the far wall.

"That leads to the hydropower plant out by the waterfall. There's an underground tunnel," Dedrick said, answering a question I didn't ask aloud. "The backup generator gets power from the waterfall. It was meant to be a primary power source, but it turned out to be unreliable."

He came up beside me staring, his vest hanging open at the sides. "I've often thought we should tap into that tunnel, make a route for rescues out here. We don't have anything out this far. It'd be a job, but worth it."

I glanced. I liked the idea but didn't want to have a conversation. I only wanted to hear Fulton's voice through the earphone, telling me the power was down and that we could move. What was taking so long?

"Hey . . ." He waited until my gaze connected with his. "What I said in the meeting room, about you on this mission . . ."

I had to force myself to hold his gaze. Why was he talking about this now?

"I don't have anything against you. I just don't want you hurt." His Adam's apple bobbed. "Or back in there."

I nodded. I could tell he held something back. He hadn't wanted me on any mission with him so far. I doubted that would change, even if the elders accepted me. Helping to rescue the colonists didn't make up for the trouble I caused. Some mistakes required a lifetime of atonement.

~ ~ ~

Dr. Supero strode through the hallway, his eyes locked on the backs of Michael and the two security guards. He had to stop them. The Jensenville team could not take the transfers yet. He needed a few more words with Michael. The look in Michael's eyes . . . . Yes, he cared.

The hallway opened to a spacious reception area. Black, spidery chairs lined one wall. Astringent lighting from square overhead fixtures threw squiggly white lines on the linoleum floor and gave everything else an unhealthy glow.

This facility had been built many years ago as emergency housing for communities displaced by war or other disasters. Government leaders soon realized the most destructive force to society was the non-compliant individual. Those with opposing views were the terrorists. With the good of society in mind, the facility was modified to accommodate those in need of re-education.

A security guard sat behind bulletproof glass surrounded by monitors and a high wraparound counter. His gaze snapped to Dr. Supero.

On this side of the counter, the shift warden, a mature man with the solid body of a hippopotamus, hunched over a computer station. A young woman Supero had not yet met stood beside him. She must've been the Jensenville representative. They took turns pointing to the screen and glancing at the transfer lineup.

The seven transfers stood in a row, their hands cuffed in front of them, a cord connecting one person's cuffs to another. Michael was added to the end of the line. Two Jensenville guards in dark blue uniforms flanked them, one with black hair that looked odd with his tan complexion and golden eyebrows. Another guard, one of the Re-education Facility staff, stood near the door. The evening shift had ended. He was one of the few on the night shift.

"Are you the Jensenville representative?" Dr. Supero said to the young woman.

She wore an olive-green shirtdress and studded black boots. Her short, black hair fanned out when she turned her head. She had a scowling mouth and striking tiger-eyes.

"I am." She tilted her chin up and narrowed her eyes. The girl was all edges and attitude.

"I was not informed about this transfer until too late," Dr. Supero said. "I have two more transfers to interview. Should take me less than an hour."

"Not gonna happen," she said, peering through black ringed irises.

Her eyes . . . . Twenty-five years ago, Aldonia's geneticists stumbled upon a genetic code manipulation that resulted in irises of gold with black edges, tiger-eyes. They shared that finding around the world. Every scientists, doctor, and engineer shared with the global community. In theory. So there was no reason a girl from Jensenville couldn't have tiger eyes. But still. How old could she be?

"What is your name?" Dr. Supero said.

She gave a little headshake, not looking irritated so much as thrown off. "I'm Waverly of Jensenville." Her commanding attitude returned. "And who are you?"

"I am Dr. Supero. How old are you, Waverly?"

The lights flickered.

Waverly's pupils dilated. Her gaze clicked to the overhead lights, then to one of the guards. "We're late already. We're on a schedule. People are waiting on us." She turned to the shift warden.

The warden tapped commands on the computer screen, shifting his solid body from side to side. He said something about the power supply giving them trouble lately.

The prisoners shuffled and muttered, tension zipping between them. The Jensenville guards had drawn taser guns but leveled them at no one. The black-haired guard eyed Dr. Supero.

Something did not feel right. "Did you verify this woman's ID?" Dr. Supero came up behind the warden.

He glanced over his shoulder. "This is a high-security facility. We've got implant readers on every door. No one gets through if their IDs aren't verified." His expression softened as he faced Waverly. "You're all set. The transfers are yours."

She gave a nod and turned to the lineup. "Transfers are ready," she shouted, raising a hand overhead. "Move them out and get them on the bus."

The first guard took a step, leading the transfers by the cord connected to their cuffs. The entire row shuffled forward.

"Stop!" Dr. Supero shouted. "Something is wrong here. Stop them!"

"Nothing is wrong." The hippopotamus warden emerged from the computer station. "I understand you want to continue your interrogations, but everything checks out. You will have to contact Jensenville—"

"No. Don't you see?" Minutes ticking down. Doors closing. Blood rushing to the tumor. "Something is wrong here. The rest of their people, the teens and children, they have escaped the Primary and Secondary facilities. The only ones in custody are the adults." He glanced from face to face, looking for someone to understand him.

Waverly stood by the door as the procession filed through. She brought her flexi-phone to her mouth, communicating with someone.

"Don't just stand there!" Dr. Supero flung his hands up, wanting to grab the warden and shake him. "Send guards to the cellblocks. Make sure the other new residents are still there."

The warden jerked his face to Waverly.

She shook her head and rolled her eyes. She wanted the warden to think Dr. Supero was crazy.

The lights flickered again, then they went out.

~ ~ ~

"Team Two . . ." Fulton's voice blared in my ear.

I sucked in a breath.

"Power's down. Shut off the backup generator. It's time to move." Did this mean Alix had half of the colonists on the bus, safe? This was good.

"Copy that." Dedrick pulled a lever down and bolted for the door. He had to be wondering which colonists Alix had and which ones we'd be rescuing. It didn't matter. They'd all be free today.

"That's it?" I said. "You shut the generator off with the switch of a lever?"

"The hard part comes next." He manually unlocked and opened the door.

The facility stretched out before us as silent and dark as the abandoned buildings in the old city center. We raced toward it, our legs and the swing of our arms in sync. The security guards and staff should be in the front half of the facility or even outside by the main power generator, wondering what went wrong. They might blame the rough weather we've had these past few days. They had no reason to suspect foul play.

The back door came into view, the door the security guards used when stepping out for a smoke. An implant reader hung on the wall beside it. I put my hand on the lock-pick kit on my belt. A scan of the ID implant of an approved staff member would normally open the door. In case of a power outage, the fail-secure system would lock all exterior doors. My pick and tension wrench would get us in.

We reached the door and I dropped onto one knee. Dedrick shined his flashlight on the doorknob. Once through that door, we'd follow one hall to another and enter the cellblocks. No surveillance would pick up our movements. No alarms would sound. We'd simply open the doors and let them out. I saw the doors in my mind. I knew exactly which ones held the colonists.

I slid the tension wrench into the keyhole and turned the cylinder one way and then the other, trying to see which way a key would open it. It had more give turning clockwise, so I held the tool there and inserted the pick.

~ ~ ~

Beams from flashlights sliced through the dark. The last transfer crossed the threshold, the rear Jensenville guard pushing him along. The warden and the guard behind the bulletproof glass mumbled back and forth. "The backup generator should be kicking on."

"Has anyone done maintenance on that thing lately?"

"It'll work. Just give it time."

"You are fools!" Dr. Supero shrieked, spit flying from his mouth. "Open the doors in the cellblock and I will check!"

The warden glanced at the guard behind the bulletproof glass and gave a nod. The guard left his station and bolted down the hallway.

Dr. Supero raced after him.

~ ~ ~

"Team Two, abort." The command came through my earphone.

I didn't have time to process it. I raked the pins with the pick, trying to get a feel for them. This job would only take a second or two.

"Team One says there's trouble." The voice came again, blaring in my ear and breaking my concentration. "Abort now. Abort now."

"Copy that," Dedrick said, withdrawing my light.

"What are you doing?" I said. "We're here. We're in." I thought I'd found the stubborn pin. A simple push and a twist—

"Liberty, now." Dedrick grabbed my arms and yanked me to my feet.

I gripped the tools but they slid from the lock. I'd have to start over. "Look what you did!" I shrieked. "I can do this."

He jerked me around to face him, but the cover of night kept me from seeing his expression. "This isn't about you. For the safety of all, we have to obey orders." He grabbed my wrist. "Put the tools away. You can't risk dropping them, someone finding them. We've got to abort the mission."

"But the colonists . . ." My throat closed and the words came out strangled. I stuffed the tools into the kit on my belt and ran with him.

Half of the colonists were safe. The other half waited for rescue, waited for me.

But I ran.

I ran with Dedrick toward a fence I couldn't see through the darkness and my teary eyes. The colonists had probably watched from the tiny windows of their cells as one and then another transfer were led down the hall. They would wait and wait to see them return. They would not return. The remaining colonists would not know why.

We reached the fence. I fell to the ground and crawled through the mud, chain links scraping my back.

"Stay down," Dedrick said.

I crawled through to freedom and staggered to a tree. I had failed. I was leaving colonists in Re-Ed. They no longer knew how many days had passed, whether it was morning or night. They had probably begun the History Lessons, begun watching the bloody scenes of the cruelty of humankind. They hadn't known. They hadn't been told. They hadn't imagined such things from their peaceful life in Maxwell.

"We have to go." Dedrick appeared before me. He wrestled with his ballistic vest, twisting it around as if trying to find the right end.

"We were right there." My throat was still tight, my voice still strangled. My arms flailed as I spoke. "I only needed another second."

"I know." He dropped his vest, seized my arms, and yanked me to himself. His hand cupped my head, his fingers sinking into my hair. He eased me to into an embrace and buried his face in my hair. "We could've had them," he whispered, his lips brushing my ear. "We should have. It's not fair. It . . . it rips at your core." His words reflected everything I felt, words I couldn't get out.

Sobs started deep in my chest and spilled out onto his neck. I couldn't control it. I should've pulled away. I wanted to pull away. I didn't want to look weak, not with him, but here I was convulsing in his arms.

One minute, five minutes, I don't know how much time passed before we both heard the voice. "Team Two, what's your location? Team One is waiting in the dead zone."

I sniffed, trying to stifle the tears that kept coming, and eased out of his embrace.

Dedrick raised a hand, unsteady at first, and brushed tears from my cheeks. His red-rimmed eyes glistened. "You okay?"

"Team Two? Your location?" Fulton's voice boomed through my earpiece, his tone more urgent this time.

I nodded. No, I wasn't okay, but we needed to move. Now.

Dedrick tapped his earphone and cleared his throat. "On our way."

Steady breaths calmed my heaving chest. The sobs subsided, but I feared the slightest disturbance would set them off again. I turned away and hugged my arms to my chest, trying to regain self-control.

With a hand to my elbow, Dedrick turned me toward him. His eyes had dried, but his jaw clenched as if he, too, struggled to master his emotions. "We gotta . . ." He nodded toward the dead zone. "We gotta run."

We raced back side by side, ripping through tall grass, staggering to avoid clusters of thorny weeds. Cool sweat blanketed my neck, back, and chest. My heart pounded in my throat. I gasped for air.

Weeds jiggled in my field of vision. The evil man in my dreams laughed. The weeds had won.

I thumped onto the bus, panting hard. The bus rolled forward without warning and I fell back, into Dedrick's arms. Again. Righting myself, I glanced at the faces of the colonists Alix had rescued. Then I swung around to sit down, taking the first available seat, one between an unconscious security officer and Bolcan. I turned to see where Dedrick would sit.

He strode to the back of the bus, his head swiveling from side to side. The faces of the colonists lifted when they saw him, invisible weights rising. His parents were not among them. He went to the very last row and collapsed into the seat, doubling over.

What went wrong? I wanted to ask but my throat had closed. I rested my head against the window and closed my eyes.

CHAPTER 32

Gripping the handlebar with two fingers on the clutch, Dedrick climbed a hill. The dirt bike buzzed like a hive of bees. The beam of its headlight grazed the rugged terrain before him, revealing blades of grass on a muddy deer trail, leaning trees, and an occasional pair of glowing eyes. A tangle of roots stretched across his path ready to dump his bike and send him thrashing down the hill.

He needed to use caution. His first mission tonight had failed, but he could do this. He would find Miriam and the colonists.

Dedrick leaned a bit, redirecting the bike and deciding to hug the tree trunks. The roots were bigger there but less in number, and they grew at consistent angles. Nearing the first root, he tapped the throttle. The front wheel cleared it. He rolled off the throttle to get the rear wheel over, hoping to avoid spinning the wheel. Two more roots, same process. Then he was back to a straight path and into race mode, still on an incline but not one as steep.

Last time he'd been on two wheels, Liberty sat behind him, her hands on his hips.

Liberty . . . . He'd left her—them—over two hours ago. She'd have reached Gardenhall by now and was probably crawling into a sleeping capsule at this very moment. All of them would be. They deserved the rest.

Images popped into his mind, colonists in hospital gowns. That's all they wore in Re-Ed. The older men had grown beards; the younger men had wispy sideburns and random patches of facial hair. Dedrick couldn't shake the images loose. He had tried to avoid looking at the monitors in the Mosheh control center and spend his time on tunnel work. But there they were anyway, burned into his mind.

It came as a shock seeing the colonists on the bus all dressed in eco-friendly shades of green and gray, their hair combed, clean-shaven. They looked Aldonian. He'd had to look twice as he staggered to a seat in the back.

The colonists hadn't recognized Camilla with her pink hair, and the rest of the team was Aldonian. They probably hadn't realized they were being rescued until they saw Dedrick. What did they think about the unconscious bodies on the bus?

"Dedrick?" Several of them had called his name in a dream-like way as if he might be a mirage.

He nodded to reassure them, but he didn't want to talk. Couldn't talk. His parents had not been rescued. They remained with the other half of the colonists in the nightmare of Re-Ed.

Once the bus had arrived at the Mosheh access point, everyone had gotten off except for Camilla and Arc. It wasn't the same point they'd used to come up. Camilla and Arc needed to keep the bus moving toward Jensenville to avoid suspicion.

Dedrick directed one colonist after another down a manhole into a sewer that smelled so bad his eyes watered. He still had a hard time saying more than commands to the colonists. He couldn't answer any of their questions. The questions barely registered.

"You and Liberty lead them to Gardenhall, okay?" he had told Bolcan. Bolcan and Liberty had sat in consecutive seats on the bus ride back, talking to each other the entire time. Why not keep them together? Alix would bring up the rear.

Dedrick didn't have time to worry about the affections of Aldonians. He needed to take the quickest route to the border between Aldonia and the woods, or what Aldonians called the Fully-Protected Nature Preserves. He needed to get out of Aldonia. Earlier, he'd made a survival pack and had someone take it to a specific location so he could pick it up on his way out. He'd also heard that one of the Mosheh discovered a sinkhole under the Boundary Fence on the Breeder Facility's yard where surveillance didn't reach. That was good news. CSS had doubled border surveillance and modified the electrical current that ran through the fence. If not for the sinkhole, Dedrick might've had a problem getting out alive. But it was easy. He only had to wade through weeds, then lie down and roll. Anyone who saw the sinkhole could do the same. Maybe someone else had.

A big rock appeared in his path. Dedrick swerved to avoid it, his boot skimming it and his stomach leaping to his chest. He needed to stay alert. He had a job to do.

Miriam's last communication with the Mosheh came over a day ago. She had just set out with the colonists. The Mosheh said she had everything organized and under control. But she failed to make contact that night.

She would've headed for and maybe followed the West River or at least planned on reaching it to make camp. They'd be crossing good hunting ground, a favorite area of the Torva. Could the Torva have stopped the colonists, raiding them for supplies? Or worse, stealing the women? They would want Jessen. She had to be close to delivering her baby. They'd want Ann, too, and every other girl old enough to marry.

How would he live with himself if anything happened to them?

He didn't need to think like that. Miriam would've armed and organized the men to guard the travelers. It would take a good number of Torva to take down colony men protecting their families.

Still, Dedrick should've been there. The elders were right. He was best suited for the job. He knew the land. He knew the Torva. The Mosheh had enough trained members capable of any rescue operation in Aldonia. They didn't need him. Maybe he had only stayed to keep Liberty out of danger. He worried about her because her emotions influenced her decisions.

He sighed. Who was he to talk?

The ground leveled out. Trees with bare branches stood like skeletons with their arms up, a carpet of yellow leaves at their feet. A cool, damp smell hung in the air. Mountains rose around him. He neared a creek that looked narrow enough to jump.

He directed the bike to a clump of grass on the bank, something to give him an extra bit of lift. Almost there and . . . .

He backed off the throttle and pulled in the clutch. Nearing takeoff, he released the clutch and gave the throttle a blip, pushing the suspension a little further. Liftoff. He released the suspension, maintaining visual on the line between trees on the other side. Rising up in the seat, adjusting for landing . . .

The bike touched down. He howled. A perfect landing! And no one to see.

A flood of euphoria cleared his mind of other thoughts. A moment of peace. Bugs glittered in the beam from the headlight. An animal darted from an area of skinny trees to an overgrown bush.

He knew exactly where he was. Soon he would reach a flat track of land, an easy ride where he could make better time. He guessed that it used to be farmland. If he strayed off his intended path, he'd pass through the ghostly remains of a farming town. He didn't have the time for that detour. He needed to reach Miriam and the Maxwell colonists. Whatever the problem, he needed to be there. Miriam had volunteered in his place. She probably assumed he couldn't get himself to leave Liberty's side.

Liberty . . .

Her image came to his mind. Her body trembled. She clung to a tree as if she needed it for support. He couldn't move fast enough, putting the clumps of dirt and weeds back in place under the fence. They couldn't risk anyone finding their way onto the property of the Re-Ed Facility, or they'd never be able to use it again.

Job done, he came to her. She didn't look at him. She had taken the setback hard, harder than he had. She didn't need to prove herself. She didn't need to fix things. *One must not take the success or failure of a rescue personally.* That was a Mosheh rule. Then again, she knew firsthand about life in Re-Ed. It probably tore her up knowing half the colonists still had to suffer through it.

It tore him up seeing her like that.

The path leveled out. Dedrick squeezed the handlebars.

He'd had a deep, uncontrollable desire to comfort her. Kind of hard to do with a layer of Kevlar between them. He'd had to resist the urge to rip the vest off her. Had to resist the urge to kiss her hair and forehead the way he comforted Paula after a nightmare. It wouldn't have been the same. He might not have stopped at her forehead.

Dedrick sucked in a breath of air. He needed to erase Liberty from his mind. In another hour, he'd reach the river. He would find the trouble and take care of it. Maybe the distance would help him get his mind off her, help him refocus. He would spend the next week aiding in the transfer, hanging with friends and relatives, feeling useful, accomplishing something. He would remember the goals he'd held dear and stop thinking about the Aldonian girl with eyes the color of forest mist.

Dedrick snapped to attention. He had reached the flat track of land without realizing it. How far west had he traveled? He needed to turn north to stay on route and avoid a steep drop off that he might overlook in the dark.

The land lent itself to a hard-packed turn. He got up on the pegs, squatted with his head over the handlebar, and used both brakes. Then he sat toward the front of the seat, weighting the front end for optimum steering. He started the slide, pressing his outside knee hard against the tank, leaning the bike. Elbows up for maximum leverage on the handlebar, he swung his inside foot forward for balance and tapped the rear brake. He gave it a bit of gas and sat up midway through the turn, controlling the drift with the throttle and his body. His inside foot skimmed the ground. Coming out of the turn, he put his boot to the peg and the bike righted itself.

Oh yeah, he could handle a bike. He could negotiate through almost any obstacle. On a flat stretch of land, on a hillside of roots, on a—

The buzzing sound of the dirt bike weakened to a deep snarl. The bike slowed even though he had it gunned. Then it stopped.

Dedrick sat stunned for a moment. He huffed. No, he hadn't checked the gas.

He slammed his palms against the handlebar, grunted in anger, and jumped off the bike. He'd have to hide the thing and go the rest of the way on foot.

CHAPTER 33

I thrust a knee up and snapped my leg out, intending to crack my opponent on his ugly chin. My foot whizzed through air.

My opponent, a character that resembled the guard I hated most in Re-Ed, sidestepped and attacked with a roundhouse kick. A red light flashed in my 3D helmet. Glowing numbers showed a drop in my health points. I had taken another hit. My avatar fell to the floor, so I had to fall down, too, in order to take my next shot. The game wouldn't allow me to fight otherwise.

I dropped and rolled.

Red lights flashed. The status report and sound effects indicated hits to my back and head.

I used the momentum from the roll to sit up, planning to hop to my feet.

My opponent fell upon me and pinned me to the ground, fists swinging. Red lights burst on my right, on my left, on my right . . . . The strikes came without pause. My health points counted down.

I drew my arms up as a shield but couldn't stop him. What could I do next? How could I get out of this?

My opponent vanished.

"You lose," the game said, the voice feminine and cheerful.

I lay on the mat, breathing hard, sweat dripping to the back of my neck. I pushed myself up and hugged my knees. I'd failed. I failed to free the colonists from Re-Ed. I failed to follow orders in the last moment. If I had it to do over, I would've failed that one again. Why couldn't we have gone in and fought the guards? We would have our people now. Correction: they would have their people. I was not really one of them. I belonged to no one.

Images came to mind: Dedrick holding Paula in his arms, Dedrick with his entire family, random families from the Maxwell colony. I wanted to pretend Abby was my family, my grandmother perhaps. I could think of the other Aldonians in the Mosheh as family, brothers and sisters. But it felt sloppy, like something held together with the wrong-sized screws and bolts, ready to fall apart. Would I ever know the comfort of a real family?

236

Dedrick had had to drag me away from the door. He was probably angry about my failure to obey a command. Disgusted with me. He never wanted me on the team in the first place. He wouldn't even speak to me on the return bus trip. Sat way in the back. Once we reached the Mosheh access point, he had given me a look that I didn't understand. His face like stone, his eyes black. Then he took off.

The words *Play Again* and *Exit Game* flashed overhead.

I climbed to my feet and swiped the air, choosing *Play Again*. I selected *New Opponent* and *Random Opponent* instead of creating one as I had done last time. Then I brought my fists up and took a step back. If I wanted to strike first, I had three seconds from the sounding of the bell.

A girl about my size materialized before me. She wore the same black boxing shorts and tank top as my avatar. Unlike me, she had bulging biceps and muscular thighs.

The bell rang.

The girl assumed a more aggressive stance, her feet farther apart and arms higher.

Maybe I could use that against her. I threw a feeler jab to her left shoulder and blocked a jab to my head. We exchanged a few more jabs, both of us moving in a circle, neither dominating. My next throw brushed her chin but not hard enough to affect her health points.

Her next attack came before I was ready. A fist flew from her chin to mine. A hit to my gut. Red lights flashed. My numbers dropped.

I pivoted, blocked a third punch, and backed off.

At the same instant, her leg swung out and cracked the side of my knee.

My avatar fell to the mat, so I had to do the same, but I would come up fighting this time.

Before I got a sliver of light between my back and the mat, my opponent flung herself onto me, grabbed my wrists, and pinned me to the mat.

I pushed against her hands. I couldn't let her attack me with my back to the mat. I shot my hands off to the sides, straightening our arms and bringing her head down. Then I cracked my head against hers.

A dramatic pop sounded in the 3D helmet. Red and blue flashed in my vision. Points dropped for both of us. I retracted my left arm and twisted my body, right foot planted and right hip driving high. I threw my opponent off me and onto her back.

Then I climbed onto her and pinned her to the ground. I threw a punch to her face once, twice, three times. She tried to block but my fists found their mark.

Her points counted down, down, down . . .

A bell sounded.

"Winner!" came the feminine voice. My opponent vanished.

Heart racing, I collapsed face first onto the mat. It should've felt good to win. But it didn't.

What had gone wrong with the rescue? Alix said a man had been making trouble, trying to tell the staff not to trust her. Who was the man? How did he know? Alix convinced the staff that they were legitimate, but they'd still sent security back to the cellblock.

When we'd returned last night, the elders welcomed the eight colonists and told us all to get some rest. Nothing more could be done at the moment, so we'd meet in the morning. The elders would've known that I hesitated to follow the command to abort. My communication device had been on. If they had been considering my entry to the Mosheh, they wouldn't want me now.

I pushed myself up, got onto my knees, then forced myself to stand. My hand flew up and swiped the *Play Again* command, little thought going into the action. I'd been fighting for over an hour. Upon returning to Gardenhall last night, I had settled into a capsule. Sleep hadn't come easy. I woke four hours later with a restless mind, so I'd come here.

A tall dark-skinned man with dreadlocks materialized before me.

I lifted my fists and peered into his large red eyes. He gave a crooked smile, one thin brow lifting.

The bell rang.

Forsaking the feeler jabs, I swung hard. I failed the Mosheh's test. I wasn't worthy to join them.

Blue light flashed on my opponent's chin. He sneered and swung for my face.

I blocked and twisted, my leg swinging out. I had no mastery over myself.

A flash of blue light on his torso. He staggered back but then lunged and threw a combo.

I sidestepped and a fist skimmed my abdomen. I ducked. A breeze tickled my ear. I threw a jab to his side and an undercut to his chin. Blue light showed the success of my moves.

I no longer lived as a prisoner in a cell, yet I had not found true freedom. I was a slave to my passion and impulses. *My Friend* had tried to warn me of my impatience and impulsivity.

My opponent pivoted and kicked.

I dodged to his blindside and struck his neck with the side of my hand. Blue flashed. I needed gentleness . . . A crack to the face. More blue. . . . patience . . . A fist to the gut. . . . trust.

The wheat seeds had not grown. The weeds triumphed. I had failed *My Friend.* Or maybe I'd never understood him.

My opponent hit the mat. "Winner," the game announced. Cheers and applause roared in my helmet.

One voice rose above the others, a man's voice. "Hey, girl."

I spun to face the intruder.

Bot's avatar stood ginning at me with a hand on his hip and shades of blue swirling in his irises. He glanced at the controller in his hand. "It's like 4:00am. What're you doing up?"

"Are you here to fight?" I smiled and raised my fists, still trying to catch my breath.

"No way, man. I'm checking out your score here. You've really improved." He looked up from the controller. "I'm just early to work, noticed someone in a 3D room. I came to say *hello* and see what's up." He ran a hand through his spiky red hair. "Looks like you could use a friend. Wanna talk?"

"Talk?" My face flushed. I averted my gaze. I didn't like that people read me so easily.

"Sure, why not. Sometimes we all need a sounding board."

I shook my head and paced to the far wall.

He strolled toward me. "Come on. I'm not gonna tell anyone anything. I'm way out here in Maxwell, tucked away in the CAT cave. I don't see the same people you see anyway."

His offer convinced my heart before my brain had a chance to consider it. "I . . . we failed. We didn't get them all. Eight colonists are still in Re-Ed."

"Yeah, I heard. Crappy place to be, huh? I'm sure it wasn't your fault."

Emotion made my face scrunch up, but I refused to cry. Instead, I let down my defending wall and my thoughts spilled out. I paced the mat and told him everything that had gone through my mind as I battled imaginary opponents, without mentioning *My Friend.* After the last word came out, I shut my mouth, sat cross-legged on the floor, and hid my face in my hands.

Bot sat down in front of me, our avatar's knees touching. "Dedrick took off to help Miriam and the Maxwell colonists. There's no way he's mad at you."

"Oh, yeah." I met his avatar's gaze. "I guess I remember Dedrick volunteering to do that."

"You can't blame yourself for everything. And you sure can't give up. You're an American."

"What does that mean?" I knew we lived on the North American continent, but we had been taught to see ourselves as citizens of the world. What difference did the continent make?

"I know you don't get it, but you've got the American spirit. We've all but destroyed the country the founders built, but the spirit lives on in individuals. Americans, sure they made mistakes, but they had a higher standard and they moved toward it. They didn't give up. You'll find a way to get those last eight colonists."

He placed the controller on his thigh and touched the screen with a finger. "Aldonians need the spirit of the early Americans. That spirit can change things for the better." He stood up and offered his hand. "Come with me. I'm gonna take you somewhere."

I reached for his hand. My glove gave the impression of physical contact, but I had to get up by my own efforts.

Our avatars' clothes morphed into dirty uniforms: long brown jackets, scarves, form-fitting breeches, and white stockings. I wore a long cape. Neither one of us wore boots or even shoes. We had dirty rags wrapped around our feet.

"What's with the rags?" I lifted a foot. Blood stained the bottom of the wrappings.

"Oh, yeah. Some guys went without shoes. It was 1776, Battle of Trenton during the Revolutionary War." Thumbing the controller, he glanced at the ceiling.

A sky with heavy gray clouds unrolled above us. Bare trees laden with snow appeared on every side. The sky darkened. A campfire and crowd of men materialized. Snow began to fall.

The men turned their palms and faces up and let out a collective groan.

"At least it stopped raining," one man said, his teeth chattering. He sat with four others on a log by the fire.

"Snow is better than sleet," another said, hugging himself and trembling.

"Either way, I'm freezing to death."

"We'll all die one way or another."

"Morale was low," Bot said. We stood a short ways off and two men glanced when he spoke. "The army had suffered defeat after defeat, and they'd been forced to retreat. It was a cold December and the commander-in-chief didn't want to end the year with failure, so he devised a plan." Bot pointed.

A man in a long blue coat stepped into the group. Snow fell on his triangular hat. The firelight revealed pitted scars on his face, pale gray eyes, and a straight line for a mouth. His posture and the tilt of his chin made him seem important. He commanded the attention of the others without speaking a word.

"It is time to move if we hope to have victory by dawn," he said.

The men grumbled. One adjusted the rags on his foot. A few stood up.

The commander-in-chief inhaled, his chest puffing up. He stuffed a hand into a jacket pocket. "Before we go, I should like to read something to you." He withdrew a thick paper and unfolded it with careful movements. His eyes turned to every person in the group, even me. "This comes from the pen of Thomas Paine."

He angled his body to get the firelight on his paper. "These are the times that try men's souls. The summer soldier and the sunshine patriot will, in this crisis, shrink from the service of their country. But he that stands by it now, deserves the love and thanks of man and woman . . ."

As he spoke, the men gazed at the fire. Eyes watered. Mouths twitched. Some men sat up straighter, others hid their faces in their hands.

"Let it be told to the future world," the commander read, "that in the depth of winter, when nothing but hope and virtue could survive, that the city and the country, alarmed at one common danger, came forth to meet and repulse it."

He finished reading and folded the paper with care.

"Here, here," a man shouted. He jumped to his feet and grabbed a musket from under a tarp.

The others stood up, too, and armed themselves. Men shouted, encouraging one another.

The commander turned his gaze to us. "Are you with us?"

"Victory or death!" Bot said, pumping his fist in the air.

The commander smiled. "Victory or death!" He turned and stomped through the snow, following the others.

Bot looked at me, flames reflecting in his big avatar eyes. "So, anyway, they've got to get the troops across the Delaware River. If we were actually playing, we'd go with them now. Some of the men fall overboard, but no one dies. Everyone makes it across, just takes longer than old George wanted and spoils their plan for a predawn attack."

"Who's old George?"

Bot glanced and snickered. He slid his finger along the controller's screen. "Well, he's gonna be the first president, but that's farther down in history. He's the commander of the Continental Army right now."

The scenery changed, a gradual morphing where trees shifted, the fire faded, and a river appeared.

The process made me queasy, so I closed my eyes and took a deep breath. The air smelled cold and damp.

"Hurry, men," someone shouted.

Wind blew in my ears, water sloshed nearby, and anxious voices carried. Heavy footfalls, creaks, and banging sounded.

I opened my eyes.

A man stood on the riverbank, one foot propped on the end of a long wooden boat that rolled and swayed. Chunks of ice bounced on waves in the river, sloshing against the boat. Eight men stumbled about on the boat, trying to arrange themselves and their weapons. Several other boats floated in the river, fading into the night. Something splashed in the water and someone out of view shouted for help.

"Come, time is a-wasting," the man on the riverbank said. He waved us over. "We wish to reach town before the day is fairly broke."

Bot stepped forward.

I stepped back. "I don't think so." A cold sensation had begun in my head from my 3D helmet and now spread to my body. I shivered and rubbed my arms.

"Why not?" Bot said, grinning. "It'll be fun. What else you got to do this early in the morning?"

"I can't swim."

Bot groaned and sunk a hand into his spiky hair. "All right." He turned his back to the man and fidgeted with the controller. The man and the river disappeared, leaving us alone in a snowy wood.

"So the Battle of Trenton is a small victory in the Revolutionary War, but it came after much failure. The army was on the verge of collapsing. They were cold, hungry, lacking in supplies, dragging themselves through harsh weather to do battle against the well fed, well rested Hessians." He smiled. "But they won. They took the Hessians by surprise. The battle was bloody, chaotic, and quick. It was over in two hours. Most of the Hessians surrendered. General George Washington had led them to victory.

"News of this battle spread and gave hope to all the Americans. Soldiers pledged to serve longer. New recruits came. These people, they risked their lives for the sake of their fellow Americans, for the sake of freedom."

The blue in Bot's avatar eyes deepened.

I remembered how he used to look through me when he got going on a subject. I imagined he had that distant look in his real eyes.

"Aldonians have no one to fight for," he said. "And nothing *to* fight for. They don't know what they're missing. They don't even know they have rights. We need to get our people fired up for freedom. And you, Liberty, things don't always work out the way we want, but that's no reason to give up. Dig deep and find your American spirit. Then go out and do what only you can do."

Bot continued to show me periods of American history. He took me to the Civil War era. We had been taught that people throughout the world, before the world government, had bought and sold slaves from Africa. We hadn't been told that slaves came from other countries and that many were white. Over half the first settlers in this land were white slaves. They were war prisoners from other countries, or the poor and unwanted, even kidnapped people. We were never told that one country alone fought to end slavery. Two million Americans fought and three-hundred, sixty-five thousand died to end slavery in their country, our country. America.

America was founded on the principles that all people are created equal and have certain inalienable rights, including life, liberty, and the pursuit of happiness. None of those principles guided our society today. How did we get to this point?

"We are again enslaved," Bot said, grimacing and shaking a fist, "controlled by a government that does not value life or recognize our freedoms."

He took me through other stages of history.

And I began to realize what I must do.

CHAPTER 34

Dawn came at last. Black gave way to greens and grays. Sunlight stole through the branches and leaves, making misty search beams. Dampness hung in the air and clung to Dedrick's skin. Birds carried on in the trees, creating a cacophony of tweets and chirps, probably warning each other that a deranged man headed their way.

Dedrick dragged his feet, left foot, right foot, left . . . his thighs begging for rest. He had pushed through all night, ever since the dirt bike gave up on him. He'd kept an admirable pace in the beginning, jogging two miles for every one he walked. Now he felt lucky to stay upright.

He liked that bike. Would he ever find it again? He'd stashed it behind a bush in a group of trees that resembled every other group of trees on his journey. Maybe somebody else would stumble upon it. Maybe one of the Torva. He couldn't bear the thought of losing it to those Torva boys. They didn't have access to gas, though. What would they do with it? They could always steal a gallon or two, the way they stole everything else they wanted.

They better not have messed with the colonists.

Dedrick took a deep breath of cool air and staggered a few paces with his eyes closed. He'd been following a deer trail that overlooked a cliff. He planned to descend when he found a suitable path and a little more sunlight. The river ran parallel with the cliff. Sort of. Once he got down there, he'd probably see signs of the colonists' travel.

He took another deep breath. The air smelled good. It reminded him of lazy days at home, or sitting with friends around a campfire, or long hunting trips. He liked hunting with Dad, especially when he was a boy. Dad taught him how to shoot, about wind direction, and how to read signs. It made him feel like a man, ready to take on anything.

Campfire?

Dedrick stopped, tensing. Whose camp? Colonists' or Torva? He jogged through a line of trees, to the edge of a steep slope, and peered into the woods below.

Trees still clinging to their leaves grew from the side of the hill, blocking his view. The gray morning concealed whatever he might've glimpsed through the branches. He'd have to get closer.

He took a few steps down the slope, sliding on leaves, stopping himself on clumps of grass. One clump of grass refused to hold him and he landed hard on his back. Something in his pack dug into his side. He'd probably smashed his granola bars. At least he hadn't slid all the way down. He'd have broken more than the contents of his pack.

Dedrick pushed himself up and reached for the nearest tree, a smooth-trunked beech that grew diagonally. He flung himself onto it and, hugging the tree with one hand, unclipped his binoculars from his belt.

He focused and caught sight of a boy crouched by a woodpile and playing with a bug or something. The boy lifted his head and smiled at whatever was in his hand. It was a kid from Maxwell. Joey!

Wanting a different view, Dedrick shifted the binoculars. Orange flames twisted through twigs and freshly cut wood in a ring of stones. A dozen people milled around it: a woman in a long homespun sweater, an old man in suspenders with pant legs sticking out of his boots, a longhaired woman holding a baby to her breast, a group of three knee-high children.

Dedrick's spirits lifted. He'd found the colonists.

A tall man crossed Dedrick's circular view. Dedrick adjusted the lenses to see him. Dressed in a yellow deerskin jacket and boots that had seen better days, he sat down on a camp chair and packed a pipe. His head was down and face was hidden. A woman approached with a steaming mug. He looked up.

Dedrick's breath caught. His body tensed. He was one of the Torva.

He turned the binoculars, gaining random glimpses and sighting at least ten Torva men and two of their women among the colonists. Where was Miriam? And Ann? Why did the colony men not defend themselves? What did the Torva want from them? It didn't seem typical of the Torva to fall upon an entire community of families. They attacked individuals or isolated groups, and usually at night.

Dedrick scanned for the chieftain, Takomo. A man with unusual bulk and a grisly beard, he should be easy to find. If Dedrick were closer, he'd be able to hear him. He liked to talk and he had a booming voice. Dedrick could almost hear him in his mind, a conversation from the first time they met. "You think that by bringing medicine we will leave this area. We have lived in these lands for a hundred years. You have set up homes here, but it gives you no exclusive rights." Dedrick knew that they wouldn't leave until fall and that they'd return next spring.

He only wanted to make sure the little Torva boy didn't die from an infection that medicine could cure.

Dedrick shifted his position on the tree, securing his balance. He would have to take Takomo, an impossible task if attempted hand-to-hand. Fortunately, he'd brought his capture gun in his jacket pocket. He'd have to move in close enough to take the shot.

Maybe Takomo hadn't come on this raid. Maybe this was his eldest son's doing. Dedrick continued searching with the binoculars, pausing on every man. What was his name? Something that started with a *k* or maybe a *g*.

"You there." The baritone voice came from behind him.

Dedrick jerked. The earth tilted. The binoculars and tree trunk slipped from his grip at the same time. He slid off the trunk sideways, hands and chest tingling, ground racing toward him. Arms flailing, he managed to latch onto a thin tree trunk before hitting the ground. He swung around to face his discoverer.

Grenton. That was his name. The firstborn of Takomo, chieftain of the Shikon Tribe. Big like his father, he carried a good two hundred pounds—all of it muscle—and towered over most men. His hair, the color of sunspots on bark, stood up in tufts. He peered down at Dedrick, angling his head as if to show off the battle scar over his left eye. A smile slithered across his face. Then he laughed. Three of his men stood some distance behind him. They laughed, too.

"Dedrick, this an odd place to find you," Grenton boomed. "There are better ways down to the river."

Dedrick gripped one tree trunk, then another, climbing back up.

Grenton stuck out a muscular hand, offering to help Dedrick up the last steep edge.

Rejecting the offer, Dedrick used a knee to climb up instead. Then he stood as close as he dared and glared at Grenton. He'd have to come up with another plan. He couldn't take the four of them. Weary as he was, he'd struggle taking even one.

"Why can't you leave our people be?" Dedrick said, his tone and gaze unflinching. "You know their homes have been burned. They've got nothing."

"Yes, we know." Grenton reached into Dedrick's jacket and snatched his capture gun. Then he nodded to indicate the direction Dedrick should go. His men fanned out behind him.

Dedrick walked, not watching his step and twisting around to glare over his shoulder. "So let them be. They're just trying to reach another community. Why do you see their vulnerability as an opportunity to take advantage?" He stubbed his toe and stumbled forward.

Grenton chuckled. "Stay alert, Dedrick, you might miss something."

CHAPTER 35

Windows in the common area overlooked the long rectangular garden that gave Gardenhall its name. Beams of morning sunlight angled down from a labyrinth of mirrors, cutting across the dark and walls and falling on barrels of leafy vegetables and miniature trees. An old man pulled cords that hung from above, adjusting the angles of the beams. A white-haired woman picked ripe tomatoes from lush, towering plants. A younger woman stood in an area that used artificial light amidst shelves of plants that spilled out of horizontal PVC pipes. She was probably testing the water. They took good care of their hydroponic garden. They said their system required less water than soil-based agriculture, and they didn't have to fight bugs, weeds, or diseases.

I strode through the common area on my way to the meeting room. Abby sat sipping tea at a table, too far away to notice me. I wished I could sit with her and watch her turquoise eyes light up as she told stories of her past without fear of the Regimen overhearing. That would be a long way off for me. I had weeds to fight.

Voices traveled through the open door to the meeting room.

I stepped through the doorway into a meeting room half the size of the one at the Mosheh Control Center. Members of the Re-Ed rescue team sat around an oval table. Wall monitors showed the faces of Elders Lukman, Rayna and Dean, the three who had taken the lead in organizing the colonists' rescues.

Everyone hushed. All heads, all eyes turned to me.

My face flushed. The video conference had started without me. "Meeting's at break of dawn," Alix had told me last night, not giving me an actual starting time. I felt like a Secondary girl late to class.

Bolcan gave me a nod, smiling with eyes that peeked through blond locks. I was glad he had washed the black dye from his hair. He sat between Arc and one of the inside guys who gave rides to the colonists on tunnel karts. The other tunnel kart driver sat on the same side of the table, leaving me to sit on the girls' side. I could take the empty chair beside Camilla or the one beside Alix. They both glared at me. Had I been a topic of conversation?

I grabbed the chair next to Alix.

"Welcome, Liberty." Elder Lukman's voice came through speakers under the wall monitors. He smiled, the wrinkles around his eyes deepening. "We were discussing the Re-Ed rescue mission. Our thanks go out to each of you for what you have done."

I nodded even though I didn't feel like I'd accomplished anything. More like I had taken a step backwards by giving in to the weeds of disobedience. Did they know of my delay to abort the mission?

"Our eight rescued colonists are recuperating," Elder Lukman said. "They will remain under a physician's care for a few days. Later today, we will interview them."

"They'll be all right," Bolcan said. He leaned back and clasped his hands behind his head, making his biceps bulge. "I mean, the lack of sleep and food takes its toll, but a few good days, that's all they need. It's the brainwashing that does the most damage." His eyes skated to me. "That lingers."

"Yes, sadly." Elder Lukman glanced to either side, probably at the other two elders who were likely at the same location: the Mosheh's Control Center. Their gazes shifted, too. Elder Rayna nodded, then Elder Lukman said, "We are hoping one of the colonists can tell us something about the man who forced us to abandon the other eight. Who is he? Does he do interrogations? What does he know?"

"Whoever he was," Alix said, "he suspected something was up. He questioned my identity. No one listened to him at first, like he was only some rambling idiot, but they finally gave in and sent security to the cellblocks." Her leg started bouncing.

"Which brings up another concern that we need to focus on as we plan the final rescue," Elder Rayna said, her dark face turning grim. "Have the colonists mentioned us in their interrogations? Are we safe? Or is the Regimen now aware of us?"

"The Regimen," Elder Dean said, "or maybe an individual."

"Whether they know about us or not . . ." Bolcan slammed his fists to the table. ". . . we need to get our people out. We ought to clear that place, blow it up. No one deserves to live in there."

"That facility has forty cells," Elder Lukman said. "We could never pull off a rescue of that size. Keep in mind we've only rescued one person at a time before. It has kept us safe and able to continue our work in Aldonia. The eight remaining colonists will be enough of a challenge."

Bolcan's gaze slid to me. He wasn't satisfied with the elder's statement.

"So how do we get in this time?" Alix said, her leg bouncing faster.

"Is our hole by the fence still hidden?" Arc looked at me.

I didn't know if Dedrick had concealed it or not. I'd been distracted crying my eyes out.

"We could take out the backup power generator again," Bolcan said.

"It will not do any good to come in that way," Elder Lukman said. "They have most likely increased security. Were we to break in the back door without something to distract the guards, we would risk security finding out."

"So what?" Bolcan spoke with the tone of a fighter. "We come in the front? We come in ready to fight?"

"No, Bolcan," Elder Rayna said. "Any obvious attack would be met with force. Unity Troopers would be upon you in minutes."

"Good. So we fight," Bolcan said, fists curling, biceps twitching. He was a wild animal ready to attack. "Unity Troopers don't use real bullets. We could take them."

Elder Rayna shook her head, the silver strands in her black braids catching the light. "We do not kill others in order to free our own."

"As with all our missions," Elder Lukman said in a calming voice, "we need secrecy. We need to sneak the colonists and keep it secret for as long as possible. Unfortunately, the motion-activated security cameras prevent a secret approach."

Bolcan slammed his back against the chair and folded his arm across his broad chest. "Are you gonna tell us the plan? You've shot down our ideas. How do we get in?"

"We do not have a working plan yet." Elder Lukman stroked his beard. "However, since we took their transformer out, the Re-Ed Facility has been powered by the backup generator."

"So?" Bolcan shook his head.

"So," Elder Dean said, "they need a crew out there to fix the transformer."

Bolcan's golden eyes gleamed. "So we come out as workers, create a disturbance that gets the attention of Re-Ed security, and shut the backup generator down, too." He slapped hands with Arc.

"Did someone say explosives?" Arc said with a grin.

"I am sorry to disappoint you," Elder Rayna said. "No one on Team One will have that job."

The guys moaned. Alix and Camilla chuckled.

I remained quiet, anxious to hear the rest of the plan. I didn't care what specific job I got. I wanted to help.

"We can't afford to have anyone recognized," Elder Rayna said. "We need different faces on this mission."

"We won't help at all?" I blurted out, unwilling to accept that.

Groans circled around the table. Alix dropped her head into her hands. Her leg stopped bouncing and bumped mine by accident. Camilla shook her head and muttered something. Bolcan flung himself back in his chair, tipping his face to the ceiling. The other three guys whispered to each other.

"Now, now," Elder Lukman said, raising a hand. "Some of you can provide transportation for the colonists once they're out. What we need from you, Liberty, is a detailed diagram of the cellblock. We can't be sure the colonists are in the same cells, but we'd like to know where they were when you were there."

"That's it? That's all I can do to help?"

Everyone at the table started talking at once, frustration and anger in their tones.

Maybe I shouldn't have, but I blamed Dedrick. He had probably given a report on his way to the wilderness. He'd probably told them about my hesitation to obey the command to abort. Now they doubted they could count on me. But they could. I would not let emotions rule me. I was ready to sacrifice myself for these people.

In the next instant, the solution came to my mind with clarity. The elders wanted a plan with minimal risk, so they couldn't see it. But I could see it. It was the only way.

"Wait. Listen." I pushed my chair out and stood.

Everyone silenced and looked at me.

"We need someone on the inside," I said. "Someone who knows the place and knows the rescue plan. Me."

No one replied. They all continued to stare with looks ranging from annoyance to curiosity. None with understanding.

After a moment of silence, Elder Rayna spoke. "We were wrong to have put you in danger on these past missions. You aren't trained, and you haven't made a commitment to our work. We weren't being fair to you."

"But I want to do it, and I have made a commitment, and you absolutely need someone on the inside."

"We are working on a plan," Elder Lukman said. "It is only a matter of time. It will all come together. We cannot sacrifice you to accomplish our goal."

I shuddered at the thought of returning to Re-Ed, to the cold cell, the disrupted sleep, the constant banging sounds, the guard with the potato chin . . . .

If the plan failed, I would move on to the History Lessons. I would be brainwashed, sterilized, and monitored for the rest of my life. I would be broken.

"This is the only plan that will work," I said. "The day you get the backup generator down, I jimmy the lock to my cell. Then—"

"How will you do that?" Camilla said, giving me a dirty look. "You won't have any tools."

I glared. "Leave that to me." I returned my gaze to the images of the elders on the wall monitors. "Then I can simply unlock the other cell doors by hand. The colonists, once free from their cells, could help free others. The job wouldn't take more than a minute or two, then we'd run for the back door. Of course, I'd need an implant remover placed outside somewhere."

In my peripheral vision, I saw Alix nod her head. She liked my plan.

"If the hole's still under the fence," Arc said, "I'll leave it there for you."

I nodded, thankful for his support.

"There's a tunnel in the shed that houses the backup generator," one of the boys who had driven the tunnel karts said. I wished I knew his name. "You could take them there."

"What good would that do?" Alix said, leaning forward. She was in planning mode.

"It's connected to the dam at the waterfall," he said.

"So?" Alix said. "We don't have tunnels that connect to it."

"But they'd get outside the fence by going underground. Then they'd only have to cross the dam."

"They'd be in no condition for that," Bolcan said. "The river's too deep to chance it. No, they should go the way Liberty and Dedrick went. Under the fence. We'd be waiting for them on the other side, eight of them, eight of us. On motorcycles." He moved his index finger in the air, counting everyone who sat around the table.

"Count me in," Camilla said, bouncing in her seat.

"Don't count me," I said. "I'll be on the inside."

Bolcan froze with his index finger still in the air. "You sure you wanna do this?"

"This is out of the question," Elder Rayna said leaning forward, her ebony face filling the monitor. "If something goes wrong, we have nine of our people inside instead of eight."

"We are close to formulating a plan, Liberty," Elder Lukman said. "Give us time."

I shook my head. "If I've learned anything from all of you . . ." My gaze skipped from one to the other of those around the table and then to those on the monitors. ". . . it's that a person should be free to do what he or she thinks is right, to make choices that are guided by conscience, by that inner voice."

My gaze turned inward for a moment, to *My Friend*. I hadn't seen it before, but I saw it now. He'd been preparing me for this. This was mine to do.

"Well, I think this is right," I said with confidence. "It's the only real solution. I am aware of the risk. Allow me the freedom to sacrifice for others."

Bolcan stared at me with his mouth open. Alix gave me a nod, a look of solidarity in her eyes. Elder Lukman dropped his gaze. Elder Rayna glared off to the side. Elder Dean's chin rested on his chest. Had he fallen asleep?

I waited for their answer, thinking of this stretch of time as a test of my patience.

Then Elder Dean lifted his head. "She's right. We must let her do this."

CHAPTER 36

Dedrick trudged through the woods, dead leaves crunching under his feet, Grenton and three of his men on his heels. They passed horses tied in groups as they marched to the camp. He'd have to discover the condition of the colony men and find out what prevented them from defending their own.

Four Torva men stood in a circle near the riverbank, a stone's throw from a row of tents. In the midst of them, a skinned deer carcass hung upside-down from a tree. They would use every part of their kill, every bit of skin, brain, fat, and sinew for everything from candles to bows and arrows. Grenton and his men wore buckskin vests or jackets. Hock skin sacks and knives with deer antler handles dangled from their belts. The Torva respected nature and animals. You could give them that.

Dedrick strode between a tent made of skins and another of synthetic material. He headed for one of the campfires where a group of colonists sat eating from bowls and talking in mellow voices. Beyond the campfires stood tents, rows and rows of tents, most looking large enough to sleep a family. Children sat in circles on the ground, also eating. A little girl dashed across Dedrick's path, shouting, "Ready or not, here I come." She darted around a tent. A horse whinnied.

Two colonists at the campfire turned their eyes to Dedrick at the same time, Mr. and Mrs. Phillips. They were an older couple with eight grown children who had families of their own, half of whom should be here somewhere. The couple did everything together. Finished each other's sentences. Read each other's minds.

"Well, hello there, Dedrick," Mr. Phillips said, the crosshatch on his forehead deepening.

"Fancy seeing you here," Mrs. Phillips said, smiling.

That began a cascade of greetings from every colonist around the campfire.

Too irritated over the presence of the Torva to smile, Dedrick waved. Did no one realize the threat that the wild men posed?

Grenton came up beside Dedrick and whacked his arm. "That way." He pointed to a big camouflage tarp at the end of a row of tents. It hung above a table, several trunks, and a cot. Three or more people milled around under the tarp. A tent blocked the full view, but it seemed like a work area.

Dedrick kept walking.

A Torva boy his age caught his attention. The boy was talking to a teenage colony girl, gesturing with his hands. She stood with folded arms and nodded her head. He must've finished giving her orders, because then she took off.

Dedrick clenched a fist and had to stop himself from grinding his teeth. These men had no right to the colony girls. They had no right to any woman. Women deserved better. Aldonia had stripped women of motherhood and the joy and security of lifelong relationships. The Torva men treated them like property and branded them like cattle.

"Move," Grenton said, shoving Dedrick. "Over there." He pointed to the work area again.

"I am moving," Dedrick said, though he had stopped. He assumed Grenton was taking him to Takomo, but they might have had a place for resistant colony men.

Walking again, he scanned as much as he could. He needed to understand their situation and to get an idea of the number of Torva men.

Along the riverbank, a group of teens, five boys and one girl, loitered around a bunch of wooden buckets. They might have been tasked with fetching water, but they weren't in any hurry to get the job done. Were they colonists?

Dedrick squinted to see.

The boys all wore jeans. Two had long hair and copper skin. None of them seemed familiar. The girl wore a long skirt and an oversized sweater, tassels and fringes hanging off everything. She was not dressed for work. Her hair, worn in braids and decorated with crisscrossed bands, showed she was a Torva girl. The girl turned enough for him to identify her.

Dedrick spun face forward, his heart racing. She hadn't seen him, had she? His stomach twisted into a knot. *Shaneka.* Why did she have to be here? Why did any of them have to be here? They always left in the fall. What made this year different?

"Look what I found," Grenton said, his voice light and without edge.

Dedrick snapped from his thoughts and focused on the people in the tent, two women and a man. One woman had dark hair with a few gray strands and—

"Miriam?" he said.

Miriam rushed toward him, smiling and stretching her arms out, looking like anything but a woman in distress. "Dedrick! What are you doing here?" She wrapped her arms around his waist and squeezed.

He hugged her back, his arms around her shoulders, his stomach still twisting into funny knots. "What the hell is going on here?"

Miriam gave him one last squeeze and backed up. The gleam of joy in her expression faded. She glanced around. "Oh, we're trying to recover." She returned to the work tent and hunched over a map laid out on a trunk.

A five-year-old colony boy, Xavier, came up beside Grenton and tugged on his vest. Grenton glanced but then folded his arms and looked away as if the kid were a dog. The boy tilted his head back as far as it could go, trying to make eye contact. He continued tugging.

Grenton glared. "What do you want?" His tone was harsh enough to scare a ghost.

"Can you make me a whistle, too?" Xavier said.

Grenton's gaze snapped to Dedrick. An embarrassed look? "Beat it, kid. I don't know what you're talking about." He stomped off, but he pulled a piece of whittled wood from his pocket. Xavier ran after him.

Dedrick approached Miriam and glanced at the map. It was an old state map with Regimen cities outlined in red and colonies marked in yellow. "What're they doing here?"

"The Torva?" Miriam gave him a little grin. Nothing ever rattled her. "They're helping us." She turned away and went to another table, which was loaded with boxes. She picked up a notebook of thick paper. "Hard to believe, isn't it? We didn't know what to expect when they first showed up, but we weren't in a position to fight anyone. All the rain caused a mudslide, took down a good number of our people and our equipment. We have no communications, as I'm sure you guessed. I sent a runner on ahead to Rivergrove and one back to Maxwell, to the CAT Cave, to let them know what happened."

"A mudslide? Anyone killed?"

"No, but we've got some sprains and a broken arm. A few older people were hit hard. They'll need time to recover."

An older Torva boy ran up to the opposite side of the table, panting hard. He looked at Miriam. "We've got the parts cleaned up and laid out like you said."

"Okay, let them sit in the sun for a couple hours," she said, sounding businesslike. "Did you eat breakfast?"

"No, they're almost ready."

"Okay, thanks for the help." She smiled. "Go eat."

The boy smiled back, a toothy grin, then ran off.

Miriam turned to Dedrick. Her gaze dropped. She looked him over from his dirty boots to his greasy blond-tipped hair, pausing here and there. Whatever judgment she made of his appearance, she held it back. Yeah, he probably looked a little rough. He hadn't cleaned up since the failed Re-Ed rescue. Walked all night. Slid down the side of a hill. Nothing but failure.

"You're probably hungry, too," Miriam said, now staring intently into his eyes. "I sense bad news. You want to tell me about it?"

His mouth popped open, but he didn't answer. How could she read people like that? He closed his mouth and shook his head. He wasn't ready to talk about it. "I am hungry."

Someone shouted something, a girl in the distance. She screamed his name.

He shuddered—*God, don't let it be Shaneka*—and turned.

His sister Ann, dressed in jeans and an off-white shift, stood next to Grenton in the opening of a tent. Grenton must've told her he was here. She took off running towards him, weaving around groups of colonists and tripping over a toddler. The toddler fell over and cried. She slowed and apologized.

Grenton stared, smiling. His gaze snapped to Dedrick's, and he laughed.

Dedrick's glands released a burst of adrenaline. His hackles rose from his neck to his tailbone. Grenton had better keep his eyes off his sister.

"I can't believe you're here." Ann flung herself into Dedrick's arms and squeezed the breath out of him. "You're here, you're here!"

He rubbed her back and then pushed her away. "Everything okay?"

Strands of hair hung free from her ponytail, framing her face and bringing out the pink glow in her cheeks. She laughed and exchanged a glance with Miriam. "I'm okay, but it's been terrible trying to heal wounds and wash mud, mud, and more mud off everything."

"Off everyone," Miriam said.

They giggled together, the way only two girls can. Then Ann looked him over and wrinkled her nose.

"You smell like you need a bath," she said.

Dedrick rolled his eyes. "It's great to have a brutally honest sister."

"Well, Mom's not here to tell you." Her smile fell. She made a sweeping glance toward the campfire, then grabbed Dedrick's hands and whispered, "Did you get them?"

His throat constricted. Her question came too soon. "I got Paula."

Ann squeezed his hands and sucked in a breath.

He faced Miriam. She'd want to know, too. "We got the Primary children. They're staying at Gardenhall for now. And the Secondary kids are out." He couldn't explain about Andy and the ones who didn't want rescued. Not right now.

"And Mom and Dad?" Ann said. "Why aren't they with you?"

Dedrick licked his lips, tasting salt and dirt. "We got half of Re-Ed."

"What does that mean?" Ann whispered. Hope drained from her eyes.

Dedrick averted his gaze. He couldn't look at Miriam either. "It means we didn't get everyone. We don't have Mom and Dad. But we, I mean they, the Mosheh's not done yet. I'm sure they're working on it right now."

Ann released his hands, her expression and movements turning cold. "Then why are you here?"

He shook his head, biting back a rude reply. Why did she think he was there?

"You don't need to be here." Ann took two steps back and nearly bumped into Grenton. When had he come over? And why?

"Well, I am," Dedrick said. "There's nothing I can do in Aldonia, so I might as well help with this."

Miriam rubbed his arm and smiled. "I'm glad the children are safe. The others will be out soon."

He nodded, anger and guilt strangling his vocal chords. He appreciated her not saying more about it. She knew the rescues were supposed to occur simultaneously. She knew something went wrong. He'd give her the details later.

"Why don't you clean up in the river," Miriam said, "then come get something to eat. We've got coffee and hot cereal."

He nodded again.

Ann walked off with Grenton. He put his arm around her. She let him.

"I'll have someone get you a towel and a clean shirt," Miriam said.

Dedrick stared at Ann and Grenton. Grenton walked with his head low, saying something to Ann. She nodded and bumped her head against his arm.

"Shaneka!" Miriam shouted. "Shaneka, come here!"

Dedrick froze. The blood drained from his face. His feet said to run. How far was the mudslide? Maybe he could bury himself in it before she reached him.

CHAPTER 37

I walked out in the open, down a sidewalk that glowed in the noon sunlight. Cotton ball clouds had been drifting across the sky ever since I poked my head above ground. People strolled by, none of them meeting my gaze. Buildings towered above me, seeming to lean in and ask, "Where've you been, Liberty?" When I lived as a citizen of Aldonia, I walked among them for hours every day, discovering their secrets and sharing mine. It felt good to be out again, but I had only a few more minutes to enjoy it.

I took a deep breath and sighed. Then I locked my sights on the towering building that housed the Citizen Safety Station. I had steeled my mind for this. Peace overwhelmed me, *My Friend* letting me know he was there.

After the first meeting today, Bolcan had cornered me. "I thought *I* was crazy," he said, tossing his mane from his shoulders.

"I'm not crazy yet," I said, "just determined." These people had families. I was responsible for them. In a way, I felt a link between my inner freedom and their physical freedom.

"Even if something goes wrong," he said, "we won't leave you in there. We'll get you back. *I'll* get you back." Then he kissed me on the cheek.

Camilla came up to me later in the morning while I was studying the route I needed to take. "Hi, um," she said, staring at the little package she held. "I just want to say thank you." She shoved the package into my hands. "I guess I kind of blamed you for everything that went wrong lately. I know the people who were taken." She gave a weak smile. "But I appreciate what you're doing. I know you didn't mean for people to get caught, or for Maxwell to . . ." A strained look came over her face. She turned and bolted. I opened the package and found three warm raisin cookies.

Alix hadn't said a word to me before I left. I caught a glimpse of her on my way to the tunnels. She stood leaning against a stack of crates, doing nothing in particular. Our eyes met. She gave me a nod and strode away.

~ ~ ~

I stepped into the shade of a covered walkway. Three other people directed their steps to the glass doors of the Citizen Safety Station. I slowed so they could pass me.

Then I stopped. This was it. In a few steps, I would forfeit my freedom. I took a deep breath and strode forward.

The doors to the Citizen Safety Station opened.

I slipped my thumb between my wrist and the fingerless glove that blocked the signal of my ID implant. I slid the glove off and let it fall, not breaking my stride. Then I strolled through the threshold, past the implant readers built into the doorframe.

The readers worked well. Ear-piercing alarms sounded. Lights flashed. All heads turned to me. Six security officers appeared. They whipped guns from their holsters and leveled them at me, each crouching in a different posture. It reminded me of the poses avatars took in 3D games.

My heartbeat quickened. I raised my hands shoulder-high and palms out. My right palm ached from having had the implant reinstalled. I resisted the urge to touch it.

One officer approached, taking cautious steps and staring at me through the sight on his rubber bullet gun.

"I surrender," I said, staring down the barrel.

The guard lunged. He grabbed my wrist and twisted it behind my back.

Pain shot through my arm, making me groan.

"We have Liberty 554-062466-84 of Aldonia," he said into the flexi-phone on his wrist.

"I surrender, okay?" I said over my shoulder.

He grabbed my other hand and slapped cuffs on my wrists. More guards surrounded me. "This way," one said, motioning with his gun. A guard shoved me.

I stumbled forward, losing my balance and bumping into another guard.

"Watch it." One guard yanked me back while another shoved me forward.

I staggered, trying to stay upright and move forward through a waiting room of gawking strangers.

They escorted me into an interrogation room and shoved me into a seat. All but one of them left the room.

I struggled to control my breathing and my pounding heart. I had expected this treatment, so I don't know why my heart had lost control.

The door slid open, and I shuddered.

I faced the man who had interrogated me the first time I was caught. Chief Varden.

He smiled as he sauntered into the room. "We meet again." He pulled out the chair across from me, turned it around and straddled it. Then he smirked. "So you surrender, huh?"

"Yes. I want to finish my re-education. I want back in society." Words from Primary came to mind. I used them. "I want to do my part for the world, for Aldonia. I don't want to hide anymore."

CHAPTER 38

Sid banged on the door for the fiftieth time.

Dr. Supero shined a flashlight on a mangled spider's web that stretched across the corner of an ancient air conditioner unit. The skeleton of a leaf and a milkweed seedpod clung to the web. The spider lurked, half hidden under a corroded metal flap. It had not gotten what it wanted. It was determined to wait.

They stood at a door inside a retaining wall on the backside of a three-story building, perhaps the old courthouse.

"Man, I don't get it." Sid leaned a shoulder against the door and stuffed his hands in the front pockets of his jeans. Like his jacket, his jeans were slim and faded, made of material reclaimed too many times. "We gave them the signal."

Dr. Supero grunted. They'd supposedly signaled the hidden group of miscreants by hanging a noose they found on the ground over the branch of a specific bare tree. They did this after climbing a barbwire fence to get into an area of Aldonia that should've been leveled decades ago and then jogging several blocks over weeds, rubble, and broken pavement. It was the same area they had driven into with the Unity Troops some nights ago. He had ripped his cotton twill pants on the barbed wire and cracked his knee on a chunk of cement. The dampness told him it was bleeding, but he hadn't checked. The fingerless glove Sid had forced him to wear protected his right hand when he fell, but his left palm had suffered scrapes and collected gravel.

"Maybe the signal has been changed?" Dr. Supero picked at a granule embedded in his palm. "Or maybe they do not wish to grant us entry." His voice rose, his patience waning. "Or maybe there is no secret community, and we are two fools standing in a condemned section of Aldonia waiting for Mother Earth to freeze over." He kicked the air conditioning unit, flexing the sheet metal and making a loud popping noise.

"Shut your flap, man. They're probably wondering why the earth I brought you along. We gotta follow their rules, give 'em time."

"I don't want to give them time. What is the point in waiting? We are on a fool's mission. Neither of us will find what we want here." Dr. Supero lunged for the door and pounded on it with both fists. "Open the door, you outcasts of society."

Sid jumped out of the way.

Dr. Supero pounded harder. "Who other than a group of criminals and degenerates would hide in a decrepit building in a condemned area of town?"

"Man, you need a psychiatrist."

"Yes, I do believe you are right. What man in his right mind would be out here with you?" He pressed his forehead and forearms to the door, resting a moment. "Did I actually believe you would be able to lead me to someone who could help?"

He had few options left. Desperation alone had made him go along with Sid's idea. Last night, once he convinced the idiots at the Re-Ed Facility to check the cellblock, he had busted through a service door. He thought he might catch the other adults escaping, but the door swung open to a quiet night. The movement he thought he saw near the fence must've been his imagination. Before he could investigate, he heard the guard call, "All residents present or accounted for." Dr. Supero had let the door slam shut and gone home. He'd gained nothing from interviewing the transfers, and he'd been wrong about the escape.

Chief Varden had called him in the morning with curious news. "Jensenville claims they never received the transfers. Their transfer team woke up on an empty bus with no idea what happened." He wanted to know what information Dr. Supero gained from his interviews.

"Nothing that can help you," Dr. Supero had said. "You told me there was friction between Aldonia and Jensenville. Maybe Jensenville is lying."

"My thoughts exactly," Chief Varden said. "I think they're pissed about losing out on their share of the children and teens. They don't believe the children were kidnapped or that the teens ran away."

Dr. Supero no longer looked at the new citizens as a source of help. That path had become a dead end. He now hoped, probably in vain, that the miscreants would help him.

Sid grunted and cussed, his words sounding muffled.

Dr. Supero lifted his forehead from the cold door just as hands latched onto his wrists. He spun his face to one side, catching a glimpse of movement. A cloth bag, maybe a pillowcase, came down over his head. He could see nothing more than the ground under his feet. Someone tied his hands behind his back, the cord cutting into his skin.

He had played this game before. He did not like it.

"This way," a boy said. "Pick up your feet, freak." Someone tugged Dr. Supero's arm and turned him around. Something, maybe a gun, jabbed his side.

Dr. Supero's mind careened as he was pushed along a broken sidewalk and into the grass. The pushing, pulling, jeering . . . . Memories flooded his mind. He had lived through this as a teen in Secondary.

"Sparrow, Sparrow, sing for us." No one had called him by his name in Secondary; they called him Sparrow. The boys had eased a pillowcase over his head while he slept and then tied his hands behind his back with a long-sleeved t-shirt. Now they pushed him from boy to boy, laughing and taunting, initiating him into a group to which he did not want to belong. "Sparrow, Sparrow, fly to me, fly to me." A shove to his back sent him face first into a boy's bare chest. Laughter. Hands everywhere. Pulling, pushing, mauling . . .

"Watch your step, dude," a boy said. He tugged Dr. Supero to one side, preventing a collision with debris, perhaps the remains of a wall. Then he shoved him forward.

Dr. Supero stumbled over a clump of weeds that had forced its way through a disintegrating foundation. He regained his balance, but then hands landed on his shoulders and shoved him to his knees.

Someone whisked the bag from his head.

Flames lapped at darkness. A surge of heat and the odor of burning wood blasted him.

He recoiled and blinked, trying to get his eyes to adjust.

"Why the treatment, Guy?" Sid whined. He knelt beside Dr. Supero, leaning back on his heels and squinting over the campfire.

On the opposite side of the fire, a man and a woman sat perched on a high stack of wood beams and cement slabs. Partial brick walls, jagged at the tops and open to the night, rose up around them. The leaping flames created shadows that morphed the man and woman's expressions, making them appear harmless one moment and fierce the next. The man, scrawny and with stubble for hair, wore a dingy white shirt under a gray Regimen coat. He must've stolen it. He was not a Regimen official.

"Who are you?" the woman said. Shadows made her eyes into black holes, but she appeared to be speaking to Dr. Supero. "What do you want?"

"I am Dr. Supero," he snapped. "Who are you?" He twisted his hands, making the cord cut into his skin, and shifted his weight off the knee he had cracked earlier. More dampness assured him that it bled.

"Look, man, you've dealt with me before," Sid said. "I've come trading. Don't pretend you don't know me."

A boy came from behind and whacked the side of Sid's face. Sid jerked toward Dr. Supero and grunted. "Shut up," the kid said. "You can't just bring anyone around."

The man in the Regimen coat, Sid had called him Guy, put up a hand. "Relax. We are all friends here. Tell us what you want."

Sid glanced at Dr. Supero, a crazy look in his eyes, and then turned to Guy. "I'm looking for a girl. I know she's with you guys. Her name's Liberty. We saw her here two nights ago."

Guy and the woman exchanged a glance. The kids behind Dr. Supero and Sid shifted, their feet scraping. Hands grabbed Dr. Supero and Sid from every side, gripping them like vices.

"They're spies."

"They're working with CSS."

"Mother Earth, man, get off me." Sid twisted and glared over his shoulder. "We aren't working with anyone. I just want to find the girl. Her name's Liberty. I know she's here. I saw her."

"And why are you here?" Guy said to Dr. Supero.

"I have made a mistake coming here." The slightest shift in wind direction blew smoke into his face, stinging his eyes and making him cough. "You cannot help me." He had been a fool for listening to Sid. He would call Chief Varden first thing in the morning and report the hidden community. This would be their last night of freedom.

"He's dying, man." Desperation oozed from Sid's tone and movements. "He's got a brain tumor. I told him you might know of a brain surgeon or something. I know people have come to you when the MEPs turn down care. You can help him."

"A brain surgeon?" the woman said, turning to Guy.

Guy held her gaze for a long moment. Then he nodded and faced Dr. Supero. "We can make you a deal. But first you need to prove we can trust you."

CHAPTER 39

Flames leaped and twisted around Dedrick's feet. Smoke snaked up into a black sky. He couldn't move, but the fire didn't burn him.

A longer look told him it was an optical allusion. He lay on the ground, his feet toward a campfire. Something screwed with his mind.

Laughter and crude talk came from every direction. Teenage boys and young men moved into and out of his peripheral vision. Five? Six? How many?

A girl appeared by the fire. Long braids. Long legs. Light from the flames made her brown skin glow orange. Did he know her?

He tried to push himself up onto his elbows, but he hadn't the strength.

The girl smiled at him. He'd seen her before. Never knew her name. She was one of the few Torva girls. What did they want with him?

Sparks swirled up from the fire. Tongues of flame reached higher. The girl's face appeared over him. Black eyes and a wicked smile. She touched him.

Searing pain ripped through his arm. He tried to pull away . . . tried to swing his arm in defense. He couldn't move.

Dedrick grunted and sat up, panting and drenched in sweat. Where was he?

Darkness surrounded him. Voices and laughter came from nearby.

He wiped his face, reality setting in. He was in a tent at the colonists' campsite. Shaneka had brought him a clean shirt and a towel that morning. Threatening her with his eyes, he'd said, "Don't follow me." After washing up in the river and drying in the sun, he had collapsed in the tent and taken a nap.

What time was it? He must've slept the day away.

The stuffy air in the tent stifled him. He rolled off the mat, groped along the tent wall until he found the flap, then stumbled out into the night.

Cool air hit his sweaty face and neck. He inhaled a breath of campfire-scented air, sucking it deep into his lungs. A dark sky showed through a shadowy canopy. A group of mostly men sat around the nearest campfire. The farther campfire had burned down to embers. Two adults and a child sat by it. Across the way, a few tents glowed orange. Shadowy figures moved inside one of them.

Dedrick stretched and then strolled to a tree to relieve himself.

~ ~ ~

". . . it's not only them. It's the way of the world," Miriam said, her eyes on the campfire. She sat on a blanket with her knees up and her back against a wooden chest.

A dozen or so men and four women, including Ann and Miriam, reclined around an oblong ring of rocks. A black pot sat in glowing embers on one end. A waist-high fire crackled on the other end, its flames twisting and snapping in the air.

"The Regimen should be overthrown," Grenton said.

Dedrick glared at Grenton's back as he approached. Why was Ann sitting next to him?

"Our tribes would come together to help." Grenton spoke with force.

"The Regimen is too big," Miriam said. "And too strong. And even if you brought the government down, the citizens are too content with their easy lives."

Dedrick stepped into the firelight and neared the group, noticing two things that made him curious and irritated: Grenton clenched a fist, and his thigh rested against Ann's knee.

First off, the Torva never seemed to care what went on in Aldonia, so why the anger? Second, Ann had always ridiculed Dedrick for helping the Torva. What made her so tolerant of Grenton, the soon-to-be leader of the Torva?

"There you are." Miriam smiled and patted the blanket beside her.

He sat down between her and Ann.

"I can't believe you slept all day," Ann said, repositioning herself. She'd been sitting with her legs bent, both knees pointing at Grenton, but now she sat cross-legged.

Dedrick locked eyes with Grenton. "What do you care about the Regimen? They live behind a fence, never step foot out here. They know nothing of you. They've done nothing to your homes, your people."

A strange mix of emotions showed on Grenton's face, like the colorful swirls on an oil puddle. "Fifteen years ago . . ." He paused. Swirls of emotion twisted one way and then another. "The Regimen killed my mother."

"I-I didn't know," Dedrick said. Grenton's mother had been murdered by the Regimen? How? And why? Was she the only one or were there more? "I'm sorry. How did—"

Grenton's features darkened, the colorful swirls dissipating beneath a hardened mask. His meaty hand clenched and a muscle in his jaw ticked.

Dedrick shrunk interiorly, deciding to leave it alone.

No one else spoke. A branch popped and sparks shot up. The chirping of the bugs seemed to amplify as the moment stretched an unbearable length. Grenton shared nothing more. He probably regretted bringing it up.

"I'm sorry, too," Miriam said.

Dedrick breathed.

"We are few compared to them," Grenton said. "So we have never retaliated. But sound the battle cry and we will fight at your side." He raised a mug.

The other men around the fire cheered and grunted, some raising mugs. Two of the men were colonists, both in their early thirties and older brothers of Dedrick's childhood friends. The others were Torva. Five of Shaneka's seven brothers sat across the campfire from Dedrick. One of them, a kid with rectangular eyes and wild strands of hair growing from his chin, met Dedrick's gaze and grinned.

The look returned Dedrick to the night he met Shaneka's seven brothers. Dedrick had been jogging alongside a dry creek, watching his steps in the failing light on the way home from a friend's house.

"Hey, Dedrick." The kid with rectangular eyes had come from out of nowhere and stood in Dedrick's path. He wore a buckskin vest and had his hair tied back. An assortment of tools and pouches hung from double belts.

Dedrick bristled, not recognizing the kid but knowing him to be Torva. Torva never traveled alone, and the young men had a reputation for wild behavior.

In the next second, three more boys had stood behind Dedrick. "Thought you might want to join us. We got a campfire over there," an older one had said, grabbing Dedrick by the arm, making it clear that he had no choice but to join them.

More boys and young men had crawled out of the woods. A few of them shook deer hoof rattles and chanted strange words. They weaved across the path, in and out of Dedrick's view, making their number hard to count. By the time they reached the fire, Dedrick had counted seven of them.

~ ~ ~

"You're probably hungry," Ann said, pushing herself up.

"Yeah, I am," Dedrick said.

"I will give him something to eat." Shaneka materialized from the darkness, a tray of drinks in her hands.

Time froze for a second. Dedrick wished himself somewhere else.

Shaneka wore a shorter skirt and a lower top than the one's from earlier despite the chill in the air. She handed mugs to one person after another, her gaze flitting to him.

A flame shot out, reaching for Dedrick's feet. It snapped back, undulated like a wave, and reached again.

Dedrick's face and chest warmed. He scooted back and bumped the wooden chest behind him.

Shaneka squatted between two of her brothers and whispered. Her brothers' eyes pivoted to Dedrick.

He tugged at the front of his shirt, trying to get air. He wished the Torva had gone south already. Why hadn't they?

Dedrick faced Grenton. "I'm having a hard time understanding why you guys are still here? Don't you head south every fall?"

A smile flickered across Grenton's lips and disappeared. A shadow, moving with the flames, magnified the scar over his eye. "I believe you know the answer to that."

Several, maybe all of Shaneka's brothers snickered.

Dedrick shook his head and stared at his feet. A film of sweat now covered his chest. He shouldn't have asked.

Bronze legs appeared before him, making him look up.

"For you." Shaneka extended a slim arm, a mug in her hand.

"I don't want it," Dedrick said.

Ann's face snapped to him. Miriam looked, too. Shaneka's brothers mumbled to each other. Was anyone not watching him?

"Do you think I poisoned it?" Shaneka said, her eyebrows reaching for her hairline. She continued to hold the drink out to him.

"I don't know. Did you?"

More snickers came from her brothers. More mumbling.

"Oh, for real." Ann huffed. She snatched the cup and took a big gulp. Then she sat the cup on the ground near Dedrick. "It's tea with berry juice. It's delicious." She smiled at Shaneka. "Is there any leftover stew?"

"I will get him some." Shaneka leaned over Dedrick, making him tip out of her way, and set the tray with two remaining drinks on the wooden chest behind him.

"Sit up," Ann said, sounding disgusted. "Stop being weird. Why don't you tell me about Paula and Andy?" Her voice softened. "I miss them terribly."

Dedrick propped a knee up and leaned back, trying to relax. "Paula's fine. She's with Zachary and Simon at one of our underground communities."

"What's it like there?"

"It's a good place. A lot of old people there, Aldonians who've been rescued but can't make the journey out to a colony. It's a happy place. They have an underground garden and a lot of games. I'm sure she misses you, too, but she's fine there."

"And Andy? Is he with her?"

Miriam leaned forward, no doubt eager for the details. She liked to know everything about the rescues.

"Uh . . ." Dedrick still didn't want to talk about it. He had failed that one. No one in the colony would be happy with the results. "Andy didn't want to come back with us."

A look of concern that bordered on anger flashed in Ann's eyes. "What do you mean? He's still in the Regimen facility?"

All eyes turned to him, including those of the Torva. Shaneka even watched him while she scooped something from a black pot on the opposite end of the fire ring.

Dedrick had to force himself to explain. "I . . . We didn't actually rescue Andy. He and a group of teens, ours and Aldonian, escaped on their own from the Secondary Residence. Some of them decided to remain in Aldonia. They want to change things for everybody. They think they can make a difference."

Ann's eyes popped. Reflections of flames danced in them. She was ready to scream. If they were back home in Maxwell, she would scream. She might even have grabbed something and whipped it at him. "And you let him stay there?"

Shaneka appeared between Ann and Dedrick, slinking from the shadows. She lowered herself onto one knee and offered Dedrick a steaming bowl of stew.

Dedrick snatched it from her, taking it only to avoid making Ann angrier.

Shaneka remained on her knee by his side.

"I got it," Dedrick said, sparing a glance. "You can go."

She lifted her eyes to him and offered a flirty smile. Then she traced her finger up her arm, to her shoulder, and made the letter *s*.

Dedrick blinked. His heart pounded in his ears. "Get up," he said through gritted teeth. "Go." He shifted his gaze back to Ann, determined to ignore Shaneka. "What could I do? Andy's sixteen. I can't throw him over my shoulder and carry him home."

Shaneka stood and slithered back into the shadows.

Dedrick set the stew on the ground, unbuttoned his shirt cuffs, and pushed up his sleeves. Then he tugged at the front of his shirt, trying to cool off.

"Well, you can't just leave him there," Ann said, her voice high. "He's *only* sixteen, and he's always been rash."

Grenton touched her arm and rubbed it, then whispered in her ear.

Dedrick's jaw tensed. Grenton had plans for his sister. "Besides, there's a priest with him. He has a small flock there. Andy won't be alone. He'll have an adult to guide him."

"How does he intend to make a difference?" Grenton said. "Will he build a resistance?"

"No, Andy doesn't think in terms of violence. He wants to spread the truth."

Ann huffed. "Like Bot and his stupid game."

"The truth about what," Grenton said, "the corrupt government?"

"That and moral truth, for example, the connection between love and life. You . . ." Dedrick sneered at Grenton. ". . .the Torva have strayed from the truth. You could learn a thing or two."

Shaneka crouched between two of her brothers.

Over leaping flames, Dedrick's gaze connected with hers. "Who knows where you'll end up if you continue with your distorted version of truth?"

"You call us the Torva, wild men." Grenton's voice boomed. "We call ourselves the Shikon. It means wanderer. There is no moral wrong in choosing a wanderer's life."

"There is when you take things from others."

"We do what we must to survive. I will not see the ruin of our people."

"You could always ask for help."

"Our reputation goes before us." Grenton gave a crooked smile. "How many would say *yes* to us? No, we will not let our people die out due to lack of goods or wives."

"Trust the charity of others and learn how to court a woman. You treat them like objects for the achievement of your goals, like animals." Dedrick's gaze caught a Torva couple who sat curled up together, a bearded man and his yellow-skinned wife who, no doubt, had been taken from another region.

Ann's eyes narrowed, but she had made the same observations in the past.

"That is not true," Grenton said. "We bring women into our tribe by force, but they stay because they want to. They learn who we are, they see how we treat them, and they are satisfied."

"Besides," one of Shaneka's brothers said, "we could die out before we master this courtship you speak of."

Everyone laughed, including Miriam and Ann.

"You prove my point." Dedrick looked at Miriam. "Andy will have no more success teaching truth to Aldonians than I would have teaching these guys that it's wrong to steal women."

Miriam shrugged, amusement flickering in her eyes. "Perhaps." She reached across him and grabbed his bowl of stew, took a bite, and handed him the bowl. "Tell me what happened at Re-Ed. You only rescued half of our people?"

Dedrick watched her swallow the stew and take a drink from her mug. She looked fine, so he took a bite. Savory flavors threw his taste buds into overdrive. Venison, onions, potatoes . . .

"I don't know what happened," he said, his mouth full. He swallowed and took a swig of the tea.

The others around the campfire carried on quiet conversations, no one paying attention to him.

"A team went in the front door," he said, "posing as Jensenville reps, and brought out the half meant for transfer. The power went down and we were supposed to go in the back, but we got the call to abort."

His stomach twisted, the devastated feelings rushing back to him. He could still see the pain of failure in Liberty's eyes. "I- I never found out what went wrong. I came here." He shoveled more stew into his mouth.

"Do the elders know you're here?" Miriam said.

"Of course. That was their plan for me. To help there, then come here."

"How did you get out?" she said. "CSS tightened security by the fence."

He wiped his mouth on the shoulder of his shirt. "Yeah, it was easy. There's a sinkhole behind the Breeder Facility. I crawled right under the fence."

She grinned. "That's how I came. I hope no one discovers it until we've got other ways in and out."

"What do they breed?" Grenton broke into their private conversation with his baritone voice.

Miriam and Dedrick looked at him and exchanged a glance, Miriam smirking. This wouldn't be easy to explain.

"They breed people," she said, no longer smiling.

The group quieted.

"What do you mean people?" Grenton said.

"It's not what you're thinking," Miriam said. "It all takes place under a microscope and in a Petri dish."

The colonists knew this already, but the Torva shook their heads and their faces wrinkled with confusion.

"Aldonian girls are sterilized," Miriam said, "except for the breeders. Those girls live in a facility. Doctors take their eggs, fertilize them in a laboratory, and manipulate genes. Then they implant the best in the girls and dump the rest."

Grenton rubbed the scar over his eye and twisted his mouth. "You mean the girls do not know a man's love?"

Miriam and Dedrick exchanged another look, Dedrick almost laughing.

"Oh, they know about making love," Miriam said. "If you can call it that."

"They don't know the connection between love and life," Dedrick said. He finished the last of the stew and set the bowl on the wooden chest behind him.

Shaneka peered at him through dancing flames, then stood up.

Grenton played with a tuft of his hair, one directly over the scar. "You say there's an easy way into this Breeder Facility."

Miriam shook her head. "Don't get any ideas. They've got surveillance and security. You'd never be able to steal a girl from there."

"We wouldn't steal *one*," he said. "We'd take them all. They shouldn't live like that. It's inhuman."

"They have babies," Miriam said. "You can't take the girls and leave the babies with no one to care for them."

"Then we will take their babies, too."

"Forget about it," Miriam said. "Your weapons and numbers don't compare to the strength of Aldonia. And their girls like it in there. It's the most desired vocation."

"They have never met us," Grenton said, "us wild men."

The Torva men roared with laughter and began talking all at once. They liked the idea.

Something brushed Dedrick's arm. He wiped his arm and then he saw her.

Shaneka stood between him and Ann, looking like she wanted to sit down. Ann scooted over.

"No," Dedrick said. "Sit somewhere else."

"Wow," Ann said, glaring at him. "Why are you so mean?"

Grenton chuckled.

"*I'm* mean?" Dedrick's temperature spiked. A voice in his head told him to chill and that he would regret this. He jumped to his feet, unbuttoned the top buttons of his shirt, and ripped the shirt over his head. He twisted his torso so Ann could see the scar on his shoulder.

Shaneka giggled and soaked him in from head to toe with hungry eyes, looking like a leering Aldonian. Whispers and stifled laughter came from several behind him. He'd never live this down. Word would spread to every colony.

Dedrick regretted stripping his shirt off.

Ann's cheeks had turned red. She gave a slight headshake, not seeing it. "What's wrong with you?" Then her eyes found it, the s-shaped scar on his shoulder. "What is that?"

"It's a brand. Her brand." He threw a glance to indicate Shaneka.

Shaneka gave him a snake's smile.

"These people are helping you," Dedrick said. "But you know it isn't their way. Take the advice you've given me over the years: don't trust them. They take what they want and give nothing in return."

Ann shook her head. "I thought the Torva only branded women."

Dedrick winced at the slap to his manhood.

Men chuckled behind him and made rude comments.

"When did this happen?" Ann said.

"What difference does it make?" Dedrick snatched his shirt from the ground and struggled to locate the bottom hem.

"You're telling me this fifteen-year-old girl did that to you? You're a trained Mosheh." Ann's eyes narrowed. "What were you doing with her?"

He figured his shirt out and stuffed his arms into the sleeves, using the diversion to keep himself from cussing his sister out for her accusation. "Shaneka has seven brothers. I was returning home, alone, when they surrounded me." He pulled the shirt on over his head and glared at Shaneka's brothers. "They drugged me. All I could do was watch while they stripped my shirt off." His gaze slid to Shaneka. "And she seared my flesh with her mark."

Shaneka smiled and touched his arm.

He jerked back, raising his hands to keep from shoving her. "I'll never marry you. Find someone else."

Shaneka lifted her chin. "You will marry me, or you will marry no one. You are marked. No girl will have you. It would be an offense against the entire tribe."

Dedrick stood stunned. He hadn't thought about that.

With the side of his arm, he pushed Shaneka out of his way and stomped through the camp towards the riverbank. The cool night air collided with his hot temper. A storm brewed inside him. Someone called his name, Ann or Miriam. He hoped they wouldn't follow.

Would the mark keep him from marriage? Would it put his future wife in danger? Would it turn her away from him? Liberty . . .

CHAPTER 40

Dr. Supero lifted a backpack overhead and hurled it into the air with all his might. It sailed to the top of the fence and started over. Then it jerked out of its arc and slammed against the fence. The barbed wire caught it.

He wrestled a flashlight from a pocket and turned the light on the backpack. It hung by a single barb at the top of the fence. A single barb.

Dr. Supero shouted curses and rattled the fence, making enough noise to wake neighbors had there been apartments nearby. No one would hear him at this hour on this side of Aldonia.

Sid was supposed to have carried that backpack. They'd had everything ready by late afternoon. Dr. Supero was trimming his goatee in the bathroom. Sid was clanking around in the kitchen, making something for them to eat. Without warning, the apartment door had banged open and six CSS officers barged in, waving guns. They had Sid on the floor and in handcuffs before Dr. Supero had emerged from the bathroom. "What's this about, man?" Sid said as two officers yanked him to his feet. "A girl turned herself in," one of them said. "Says you broke her out of the Re-Ed Facility." Neither Sid nor Supero wore flexi-phones lately. Sid still wore the RF signal suppressing glove. CSS must've discovered Sid's location from surveillance cameras. Chief Varden had organized Liberty's rescue mission, but he'd done it secretly. Liberty's surrender blew the cover and probably put him in a tight place. Had she really surrendered?

Dr. Supero slammed the fence a final time. A ripping sound came to his ears. The backpack fell to the ground on the other side of the fence, several medicine bottles spilling out. Dr. Supero adjusted the pack on his back and climbed the fence.

When CSS officers had busted through the door to his apartment, he had stopped breathing. He'd thought they'd come for him. That morning, he had gone to work and told Muse he needed to collect his things. Instead, he cleaned out the medical supplies and medications, taking as much as he could fit into two backpacks. He'd made certain to grab the instrument set the neurologist would need for his surgery, the retractors, probes, forceps, spatulas, and needles—most especially, the miniature robotic system that a neurosurgeon should not be without. Who knew what crude instruments those rejects of society had? Perhaps he was a fool for putting himself in their hands. If only he had another option . . .

Dr. Supero jumped to the ground, landing near the backpack. He tossed the spilled bottles into the bag.

Light flashed down the road from which he came, headlights.

He scooped the backpack into his arms, ripped side up, and stumbled farther into the restricted ruins.

~ ~ ~

Dr. Supero stood on the Judgment Step under a blinding beam of light, hugging the ripped backpack and feeling foolish.

He had left the noose in the tree and pounded on the back door of the old three-story building as Sid had done. This time the door opened to him, an invitation to darkness that reeked of mold and jeers, whispers and snickers. The ghosts of past generations and the rot of decay lingered in the damp air of the building. Dr. Supero balked at the thought of stepping inside. He took a step back but then forced himself forward.

Pale forms in the dark rushed at him. Hands grabbed his arms, yanking, and struck his back, shoving. He clutched the ripped backpack to his ribs, not wanting to lose any of its contents amidst the flurry of erratic movements. The guerilla escort moved him through darkness, his passage ending on the second step from the first landing of a marble staircase.

The light in his eyes prevented him from seeing much, but he heard the voices and shuffling bodies of people on the landing behind him. Amber lanterns revealed more kids above him, wiry figures, shadows with hostile postures. Red dots of light, probably from cameras, appeared among the figures above him. Voices turned to whispers. The whispers stopped.

"Do you have what we asked for?" a man said. It sounded like Guy. He seemed to be the man in charge.

"Who am I speaking to?" Dr. Supero said, attempting to show strength in his tone. He had enjoyed status and power as an adult. Now he was stealing and begging children for his life. How had it come to this?

The beam of light swept from Dr. Supero's eyes to the backpack in his hands. Faces became visible. Guy and the woman from last night stood on the level above, leaning their arms on a metal railing and peering down at him. Guy rubbed his wrist with a twisting motion that appeared odd.

"I'm Guy. We met last night. Do you have a problem remembering?" His expression did not show sarcasm. Perhaps he knew of the possible symptoms of a brain tumor.

"No, I do not have a problem remembering. I brought what you asked for. I want to meet the surgeon." The backpack grew heavy and slipped from the numb fingers of one hand. He hefted it up in his arms and re-gripped it. A bottle of pills slipped out and clanked down several steps, rattling to the floor.

"Help me!" Dr. Supero shouted, jerking his armload.

Guy nodded to someone over Dr. Supero's shoulder. A young man came from behind and grabbed the ripped backpack. Another young man latched onto a shoulder strap of the backpack Dr. Supero wore.

"Be careful with it. There are delicate instruments inside." Dr. Supero shrugged the backpack off and let the boy take it. He rubbed the shoulder where the strap had dug in.

The young men attached the backpacks to a rope and pulley arrangement and sent them up to the next level over a pile of marble that had once been a staircase. How did the miscreants get to the next level?

Dr. Supero rubbed his head in the location of the tumor. Why would anyone live here? These people were animals. They would not be able to help him.

Once the backpacks reached the top, a girl squatted and removed them from the rope. She brought them to the woman who had left her place by Guy's side. The woman squatted over the packs and rifled through them like a scrounger. What felt like five minutes later, she nodded to Guy.

"Well, Dr. Supero." Guy straightened up as the woman returned to his side. "You have brought what we asked, so we will perform the surgery you need."

Dr. Supero found himself sucking in a breath of air. Could it be true? "Please allow me to meet the surgeon. And I would like to see your operating room."

"If you survive, you must never tell anyone about this place. We have video of you here and of this transaction." He motioned toward others that stood along the railing. Three of them held cameras with little red lights. "If you betray us, the video goes directly to the Regimen."

"I will not betray you. As for survival . . . an experienced neurosurgeon should have little problem with this procedure, given the location and type of tumor." He pointed to the packs on the upper level. "My scans and test results are on a flash drive in my backpack. Let me speak with the surgeon."

Guy glanced at the woman who stood beside him. "This is Angel, your brain surgeon." He swung his arm out, gesturing toward the woman.

Dr. Supero drew back, cracking his shin against the step behind him. His head grew light. Guy had no hand. A bare stump stuck out the sleeve of his Regimen jacket. What had happened to his hand? And how could that young woman be a neurosurgeon? She couldn't be over thirty. This was a joke. They played him. They used him. They got the supplies and medicine they wanted and made the video for blackmail. He had nothing. What could he do?

He took a breath and grabbed hold of the handrail. "You . . . are a neurosurgeon? H-have you done this before?"

"No, but I read a lot. I've studied up on it since last night."

A weak laugh escaped him.

"I'm glad you brought those instruments," she said. "I wasn't sure how I was going to hack open your skull."

Dr. Supero shook his head, a reflexive movement. His legs turned to rubber. He swayed.

Arms reached out and caught him, steadying him.

"No," he said, his hope becoming a dream on the wind. He pushed the hands away and leaned on the railing for support. He stumbled down two steps. Who were these people? Did they really live here? He took two more steps. The man had a stump for a hand. Angel had offered to cut open his head. Had she operated before, perhaps on Guy?

Dr. Supero stumbled to the foot of the steps.

Jeers and taunts filled the air, indiscernible words. Or maybe he knew what they said. "Sparrow, Sparrow, don't fly away. Sparrow, Sparrow, come let us play."

Dr. Supero ran.

CHAPTER 41

I lay on a muddy path, tall trees whispering over me. Harsh male voices sounded nearby, then the clomping of horse hooves as my accomplices left without me. Two arrows had pierced me, one near the elbow and the other in the back of my hand. Pain pulsed through my arm.

Suppressing a whimper, I grabbed the shaft of the arrow near my elbow and pulled. Blood gushed but the arrow didn't budge. I had no strength in my grip.

"Hey, what're you doing?" a man said. His mature voice sounded familiar. "You can't do that."

I rolled onto my good arm and sat up to look around. My arm screamed.

I couldn't see the man anywhere. Did I know him?

On the ground at my feet, a young woman lay with one arm extended over her head. Her flowing hair splayed out over the sleeve of her buckskin dress. The fringes of her sleeve among locks of hair made a bumblebee pattern of yellow and black. A red splotch spread out on her dress, a rose blooming over her left breast.

She was dead. Shot.

Dead bodies lay everywhere, tangles of brown limbs, black hair, feathers, and blood. These people were native to this land.

I had come on a ship with the white men who attacked them. This was part of the history of our continent, according to the Regimen. We did not try to establish friendships. We didn't care about them. We came as conquerors and greedily took the land.

I wiped my bloody hand on my skirt and grabbed the arrow's shaft again.

"Hey, you can't do that!" The man sounded angry. And near.

I glanced from tree to tree but didn't see him. "Where are you?"

Then I remembered. I had wires connected to various points of my body and wore an advanced 3D helmet, one that read my thoughts. It couldn't read all my thoughts, but it picked up certain things that added to the realism of the 3D experience. People did not have the big eyes and exaggerated features of avatars in 3D games. They looked lifelike.

This was the History Lesson. I was witnessing the wretchedness and oppression that grows in the human heart when people are given freedom. The small-mindedness of ordinary men and women prevented them from making good choices and progressing. They needed an all-powerful sovereign like the Regimen Custodia Terra to govern their affairs.

"You shouldn't be able to hear me," the man said.

I recognized the voice now, though I still couldn't see him. I saw only trees and dead bodies, a fly buzzing around my arm.

The man, forty-something with hollow cheeks and a long ponytail, had not introduced himself when I began the History Lessons three days ago. He was the *teacher*. He avoided eye contact and spoke to the guard with the black eyes and potato chin. Maybe the distance made his job easier.

"Put her in the chair and strap her wrists and ankles," he had said.

"My pleasure." The guard had scooped me up, laughing.

I did not struggle. I had a buzz from lack of sleep, and my stomach ached from hunger. If I cooperated, I got a warm meal and extra time to sleep as a reward. Unfortunately, my dreams usually repeated the lesson of the day, waking me several times in a cold sweat.

"They working on that transformer yet?" The teacher held a control pad, bringing up my next lesson. "That secondary generator's weak, causing problems with the high-tech equipment."

"I guess the wrong parts came. Repair crew has to wait." The guard strapped my wrist to the arm of the chair and waved his brows at me, smirking.

I turned away. Their words gave me hope. I assumed the Mosheh was responsible for the delays, buying time for whatever reason. Maybe waiting on me.

~ ~ ~

My hand slipped on the shaft of the arrow, smacking into the feather fletching and renewing the pain in my arm. A moan escaped me.

The leaves of a tree rustled. Then a horse and rider approached.

"There you are," the rider said, smiling. He wore a flintlock slung over his buckskin tunic, a fur hat, and high brown boots, but he resembled Dedrick from his voice and mannerisms to his earthy brown eyes. His dark hair even had blond tips. I supposed that my mind generated the image. Many people in the History Lessons looked like people I knew.

Dedrick's gaze clicked to my impaled arm and he frowned. "Hey, what happened to you?" He leaned forward, swung a leg over the horse, and dismounted. Leaves crunched under his boots as he landed.

"We found another tribe on our land," he said as he yanked the arrow from my hand. It slid right out, unrealistically causing no trouble.

"I don't want to do this anymore." It sickened me to be a part of this. The boundaries of the land we wanted grew daily. Every day we scared off or killed more natives.

Dedrick removed the second arrow from my arm and wrapped a dirty rag around the wound. He made a knot, then met my gaze and smiled. "You're good to go." He jumped up and reached a hand down.

I took his hand and let him yank me to my feet. "This isn't how it happened." It's what I'd been taught in Primary and Secondary, but Bot's 3D game had taught me otherwise. The white men didn't come to conquer. Wanting to escape a controlling government, they left everything behind and came as settlers. They wanted a better life for their families. The natives had lived here but never claimed to own this land. They believed the land belonged to all. In fact, several tribes had lived here, each defeating and displacing the tribe before it.

"This *is* how it happened," Dedrick said. "We're here to conquer. It's what we do." His brown eyes locked onto mine, and I saw him sitting in Gardenhall, his little sister Paula on his lap. He laughed and whispered something to Paula. She squealed, throwing her head back against him.

My heart ached. The ache spread to my whole body, making me moan. I wanted what they had. I wanted family.

"What's the matter with you?" The harsh voice was not Dedrick's. "Get up. It's time for your lesson."

A jolt of pain ripped through my hip. The guard liked to wake me with the toe of his shoe. I must've been back in my cell.

"Okay, okay." I swung my arms out, reaching for something to support me as I climbed to my feet. Every time the guard came for me, I found myself mumbling the same words. "I'm sorry. I deserve this. It's okay. I deserve this." I had first said the words to the redheaded counselor during my entrance interview the day I returned to Re-Ed. Now I couldn't think of anything else to say. I only wanted it to end. My body begged for sleep, warmth, and food. My mind wanted silence.

"You get five minutes in the bathroom and then it's off to class." The guard snickered. "Must be nice to sit in a comfy chair and play 3D games all day and night."

I staggered alongside the guard down the cold hallway to the bathroom. Was it morning? Night? When would the nightmare end? Was the Mosheh watching me? Maybe they were waiting for me to find something to use as a lock pick or to give a signal.

Maybe I was wrong to come back here. Would I be free to act when the power went down? Would I even know when it happened? The History Lessons took up large chunks of the day, seeming endless. I slept whenever I returned to my cell, but it never felt like enough sleep. The lessons played in my mind, in random order, over and over.

I experienced, firsthand, the history of the world from the time white people invaded this continent to now, witnessing the destructive forces humankind brought to the earth and to each other. Music played with the visuals, the volume rising as scenes unfolded, a sad song I remembered from Secondary: *Look What You've Done to Her.* We always cried to that one, thinking about what humans did to the earth. Now I could see it happening before my eyes. Men shouted and trees fell behind me, one after another, making the earth quake and shuddering through me. The aroma of sweet sap that filled my nostrils soured as the landscape morphed into miles and miles of garbage dumps. Toxic smoke streamed from factories, filling the sky with clouds of vomit. The stench pervaded my senses, clung to my skin, and told me this was my fault. The earth would never heal from the scourge of man unless we acted quickly.

"No," I screamed at the puke-colored clouds in the sky. I fell to my knees in a puddle of warm sludge. "We can learn from our mistakes. We can change without needing an all-powerful sovereign. We have always wanted to perfect ourselves. It's in our nature."

The Maxwell colonists believed we were made in the image and likeness of God, called to holiness and destined for eternal life. Throughout history, people of goodwill had risen up against evil and destruction. Especially the people here on this continent.

Lights flashed overhead. Population numbers and natural resource numbers had appeared in glowing orange. I saw the entire earth turning like a globe on a stand and, at the same time, people on the street before me. People popped onto the scene in groups. Colors on the globe showed population increases and the resulting decrease of resources. Apartments rose up on the street. More and more people appeared, all of them looking at me. The numbers clicked up at a rapid pace, glowing red as if ready to explode. Thin, dirty-faced, shirtless children appeared. They ran to me and grabbed my hands. "I'm hungry." "Feed me." "Can I live with you?" One little girl didn't speak at all. She clung to the hem of my shirt and lifted her face to me.

I shrunk back and acid rose in my throat. I wanted to run.

Her head bulged on one side. A flap of skin hung over her eye. Rotting teeth and gums showed where an upper lip should've been. What had happened to her?

A dazzling light appeared in my peripheral vision, warmth and peace accompanying it. I wanted to look at the source, but I feared beholding it. Ever since the History Lessons began, *My Friend* had made himself known to me in this new way. Truth made himself known.

Shame assailed me. I dropped to my knees and pulled the little girl into my arms. Her deformity made her no less worthy of love and life than the rest of us. Scientists and doctors rid our world of disorders and deformations through gene manipulation, embryo selection, and abortion. This girl would never have survived our day. She would've been aborted.

Humans had no special place among other living things, we'd always been told. They taught us songs in Primary to help us understand that all living things had the same value. The tune of a silly song came to my mind, *Invertebrates Outnumber us 97 to 3*. I could almost hear my classmates singing, "I'm no better than a polypore mushroom."

~ ~ ~

"Get her in the chair and strap her down."

"My favorite job." The guard wrapped an arm around my back and grabbed my legs, laughing.

His touch made my skin crawl. "Get off me," I shrieked, jerking and twisting my body, digging my nails into his hand on my thigh.

The guard dropped me into the chair, cursing Mother Earth. He wrestled one arm to the armrest, his grip like a vise, and strapped my wrist. "Where'd my nice girl go?" He caught my other arm and leaned close, bringing his face a breath away from mine. "I thought you and I were starting to get along." His gaze dropped to my mouth.

Adrenaline surged through me. I threw my head forward and cracked his nose.

He freed my arm and coddled his nose, spitting obscenities. Then his hand flew out and struck me on the cheek, stinging my face and making my ear ring.

I grabbed the strap on my restrained wrist and fumbled with the fastener.

His hands latched onto my arm. Then he leaned over me, something dropping from his chest pocket into my lap.

I struggled against him, using my knee, my head, and my free hand.

In less than three seconds, he secured the strap to my wrist anyway. Then he pulled it too tight.

"Get her strapped in," the teacher said, turning hard eyes to the guard, not looking at me. "What is your problem?"

"I don't have a problem. It's the bitch."

I twisted my free hand from his grip and drew back to strike him, but then stopped.

A luminous being stood in the corner of the room. *My Friend.*

Every muscle in my body relaxed, my heart calmed, and peace overwhelmed me. I gazed at him, light so bright and beautiful it seemed impossible to behold. I couldn't look away. A love I had not known ebbed and flowed like waves in the ocean, lapping over and through me. I wanted to return the love. I wanted to give myself entirely to love. If I had been free of the chair, I would've fallen to my face on the floor.

Then images appeared in my mind of people and moments from the past. Jessen giving me an impish smile, her curly hair falling in her face, her hand on her pregnant belly. Abby's turquoise eyes looking sadly at me as she rejected my offer of help. The red-haired woman in the interrogation room saying, "Liberty, pick up the pencil. You have to write this." Dedrick with his arm around me after I woke from a nightmare. Flames destroying homes in Maxwell. Flames destroying everything.

Anger smothered the feelings of love, and I wanted answers. "Why have you let all this happen?" I shouted in my mind.

The dazzling light flickered like flames. *There is a reason.*

A tongue of fire leaped from *My Friend*, from the area of his heart. It stretched out as thin as a ribbon and traveled toward me, undulating like a wave, making itself known. It was freedom.

A great thirst overcame me, made me long for it to draw nearer, but I knew it would not be enough. It was not meant to be alone.

Two more tongues leaped and stretched out from the heart of *My Friend.* Goodness and truth. The three undulating ribbons intertwined and weaved together, forming a single braid.

I was land, dry and weary, thirsting for rain.

The more I pined, the closer it came. The braid embraced and wrapped around me several times without restricting or binding. Warmth and peace overwhelmed me. I grew lighter. The ribbons of flame came to my ears like three notes in a harmony, so beautiful I closed my eyes to relish it. I opened my eyes and found myself floating, gliding through the air like a bird on wind currents of freedom, goodness, and truth.

Then I stood on a vast stretch of cracked land. My dream, my nightmare replayed itself. The emaciated man in robes of purple drew a handful of tares from his sack. Inky eyes looked at me. I saw the tares for what they were: lies, wickedness, and control. Then dark clouds rolled back at an accelerated pace, time reversing.

Amber waves of grain stretched out on every side, crops tall and strong. A breeze rolled over purple mountains, causing the grain to sway and rustle in one direction and then another, rippling through the field. Deep roots made the wheat strong and able to withstand adversity. The field spread wide.

As I gazed at the amber ocean, I realized weeds grew there, too, one here and one there. So few. It did not seem possible that they would ever overcome the wheat.

My Friend appeared as the second sower, the enemy of the first. Together we appreciated the grain. I knew that I had little, if anything, to do with the golden field, that I was but a single grain myself, but he made me feel like his coworker.

Then he turned to me and communicated a message. *We will overcome.*

~ ~ ~

I no longer sat in the chair with the guard and teacher above me. I stood on the steps of a ladder to the cargo hold of a ship overlooking darkness. The odor of filthy bodies and sewage made me reel. The ship rolled and pitched. The bilious contents of my stomach surged up my throat.

My eyes adjusted and I saw them. A hundred or so pairs of white eyes looking up at me. A throng of dark bodies, men, women, and children, filled the hold. Chains connected them to each other and to the walls.

I clung to the railing of the ladder, not wanting to go down. I didn't want to visit this horrific part of history. The truth was bad enough—people were treated as property, bought, sold and beaten—but I knew what the Regimen taught about it. This was my fault. The History Lessons would not recall the thousands that risked their lives to free them.

I peered up at the dirty ceiling of wooden planks. "What is the reason?" I cried to *My Friend*. "When will we overcome?"

CHAPTER 42

Dedrick pushed an oversized garden cart, trying to keep the load balanced over its big wheels. He hadn't seen the groove in his path until too late. With a grunt and a bit of exertion, he wrestled the cart up to flat land.

He could almost say he enjoyed this. Day after day of early rising, hard work, and needed rest had given him time to think.

A cool breeze ruffled his hair, refreshing him. Good weather had accompanied them for the past six days, clouds and cool fall temperatures but no rain or direct sun. The mild temperatures helped them persevere in their relocation efforts, and the clouds shielded them from drone detection if any drones flew by.

A melody carried on the air, the voice of a woman and a choir of children. The Putman family marched nearby. Eight of the ten children lugged backpacks. The eldest daughter, a cute twenty-year-old, carried the baby in a sling. Mr. and Mrs. Putman pushed a cart bigger than Dedrick's. It probably carried all their possessions.

Most of Dedrick's possessions had burned. He would never return to his family home in Maxwell, the home his father built. He would never bring rescues from Aldonia to Maxwell or waste time in the woods he loved. He knew every inch of them, every tree stump, creek, and berry bush. Now he'd have to learn new routes to other colonies.

The throng of colonists walked before and behind Dedrick, swarming over the rolling landscape. Some weaved through a wooded area he had already passed. Others emerged onto a field, the river ever to one side though not always visible. The Torva traveled with them, leading the way with horse-drawn wagons or riding and walking behind to watch for stragglers. Older people, pregnant women, the injured, and young children rode in the wagons. A shepherd with his sheep had gone on ahead, keeping his own pace.

Every able-bodied man, woman, and child—Torva and colonist alike—pushed, pulled, or carried something. Unless they had other responsibilities. Ann wandered from family to family, group to group, person to person, searching for headaches, chafes, and sprains.

Dedrick let go of a handle and wiped his sweaty palm on his jeans. He wished he had water.

"You show signs of fatigue," Grenton shouted over his shoulder. He wore a vest over a bare chest and his muscles glistened with sweat. He pushed a three-wheeled wagon and seemed to have an easier time than Dedrick navigating over rough terrain. That was the only reason he had edged into the lead. Grenton's wagon carried more, but Dedrick had the heavier load. He had farming supplies and tools while Grenton had only household items.

Dedrick gave the cart an extra push and closed the distance between them. "I could go all day."

Grenton laughed.

"We should put all the men with carts and wagons side by side." Ann sat in the back of a horse-drawn wagon on top of a mound of tents and bedding. Jessen, an elderly couple, and five small children rode with her. She finished wrapping an eight-year-old boy's sprained ankle while lecturing him about safety on the journey. She had tended Dedrick's sprains and wounds countless times over the years. He could almost hear the lecture. "You're not invincible. You only have one body. Take care of it."

"The competitive spirit keeps you from dallying," Ann said. Medical bag in hand, she scooted to the edge of the wagon and got up into a crouch. She shot teasing looks to Grenton and Dedrick. Then she hopped out of the moving wagon and came to walk between them.

"I only need a pretty woman in a wagon before me," Grenton said. "I cannot guarantee my pace now that you have jumped down."

Ann laughed. "How ever will you make your long journey south?"

"I have been considering that. And I do not think we will go immediately."

Dedrick's hand slipped off a handle. "Wh-what are you saying?"

"We would like to remain in Rivergrove for the winter. We can help make the colony undetectable from above, from the drones you speak of." He looked past Ann to Dedrick.

"Where will you stay?" Dedrick tried to hide his aversion to the idea.

"We are ill prepared for winter in these lands. We will need accommodations. In return, we will hunt and patrol the surrounding lands."

"That sounds like a good trade," Ann said. "I think the Rivergrove colony would welcome you."

"I don't know." Dedrick kept his voice low, wanting only Ann to hear. "They've had more than a few run-ins with the Torva. Just as we have."

"Well, then I'll have to convince them," she said.

Dedrick slowed a bit, gaining distance from Grenton. "Look, I know you have feelings for him."

Ann gave him a look as if to say it wasn't his business.

"You gotta keep it in perspective," Dedrick said. "He's Torva. When his father steps down, he'll be the chieftain of their tribe. Maybe they'll stay the winter, but they won't settle down. It's not their way."

"Maybe I like to travel." She flashed a smile and put a bounce in her step.

He shook his head and tightened his grip on the cart. "You know they don't honor their women. You won't change him. If you fall for him, you'll end up like me with a brand on your arm." Bringing it up humiliated him all over again, but he might as well get comfortable with the subject. He had one more person to tell.

"You don't give me much credit. Maybe I could change him. Maybe I could change the entire tribe."

"Yeah, one girl can do that." He glared at Grenton's sweaty back. Liberty's dream came to mind. "You'd be a wheat seed in a field of weeds."

"What's that supposed to mean?" Her eyes flashed with anger. Then she jogged to catch up with Grenton. He had gotten a good twenty yards ahead.

Dedrick leaned into his job, wanting to catch up.

A horse clomped up behind him. A woman called, "There you are."

Miriam swung down from the saddle of a black Morgan and led the muscular beast by the reins. She had the carefree look of a woman in her element. "Think we'll arrive by nightfall?"

"You know we will," Dedrick said.

Miriam had planned the entire move down to the smallest detail. The mudslide hadn't even unnerved her. She'd arranged a thorough cleanup, completing it the day Dedrick arrived. The next day they woke before dawn, ate a good breakfast, and tore down the camp. By 9:00am, they'd set out. They had walked three hours in the morning, taken a two-hour break that included lunch, walked for three more hours in the evening, and rested all night. People who complained about the slow pace, teens and young adults, were given more to carry. This was the sixth day of their journey. The last day.

"Think you'll find your future wife in Rivergrove?" Miriam said. She stroked the horse's muscular neck as she walked. The Morgan peered at her through its large eyes.

Dedrick chuckled. "You heard Shaneka. No girl will marry me now."

Miriam watched him for a long moment and then said, "You'll have to find a girl with unflinching courage."

"Yeah, maybe you're right."

After another long pause she said, "Know anyone?"

He met her gaze. Did she already know the answer to that? "Maybe."

Miriam smiled. Her gaze shifted, her eyes focusing on something behind Dedrick.

He turned.

Shaneka sauntered toward them, her hips swaying and leg popping through the slit in her skirt. She and several other kids had the job of making rounds with water. They had less to carry than everyone else but farther to walk each day. They had to fill up at the food wagon, getting water they had boiled the night before, and weave through the entire group of travelers.

Dedrick stopped pushing the cart and wiped the sweat from his forehead. He preferred getting water from one of the others. He had made it a goal to avoid Shaneka and her brothers in every possible way. But at the moment, he needed water.

"Hello, Dedrick." Shaneka batted her eyes and looked up at him.

He bristled. He liked it when Liberty looked up at him like that. That girl could render him senseless with her smile, with her glance. What was she doing now? How long before he saw her again? Was Bolcan keeping her safe? Was Bolcan to be trusted with her?

"Are you thirsty?" Shaneka said. Three water skins hung around her waist, two of them bulging.

He nodded. "How's it going?" he said, keeping it civil. He could see himself drinking directly out of a water skin, could almost feel the water rushing down his throat.

She filled a cup. "I am tired of walking and glad we are almost there." She handed him the cup, brushing his fingers.

Cool water in his mouth, rushing down his throat, dribbling down his chin . . . . He gulped it greedily, took a breath, and then wanted more.

She filled the cup a second time and stepped closer to hand it to him.

Her fragrance, sweet and citrusy, made him want to draw back. But he wanted the water. He took the cup, closed his eyes, and tipped back his head. An impression came to his mind: Liberty lying next to him in the old courthouse, the smell of her hair, the feeling of closeness.

"We will stay at Rivergrove for the winter," she said.

He snapped from his thoughts and handed her the cup. It was strange that Shaneka's presence made him long for Liberty. But it did.

"I will turn sixteen," Shaneka said, "old enough to marry."

Miriam turned away, smirking. She stroked the Morgan and whispered in its ear. The Morgan bobbed its head and nickered, appearing pleased with the affection.

"Well, happy birthday," Dedrick said. "But I hope you're not sticking around on my account." He grabbed the cart by the handles and shoved it forward.

"Wait, Shaneka," Miriam said, "I'll have some water."

Dedrick kept moving. He decided right then he would not remain at the colony any longer than necessary. Tomorrow before dawn, he'd head back to Aldonia. He'd help with the Re-Ed rescue and finish his time with the Mosheh. And he'd talk to Liberty, try to dissuade her from making a commitment to serve.

"Hey," Miriam said, catching up. "You took off without me."

"Oh, sorry, just trying to stay on schedule."

"Right." She gave an exaggerated nod. "I was actually looking for you for a reason. I need someone to ride ahead and let the colony know when we should arrive. Maybe they can send a group out to meet us and take over with some of the load."

"Yeah, I'll do it." He could use their communication equipment to get the status of the Re-Ed rescue. Maybe he'd find out Liberty's status, too. Would they have let her on the rescue team? No, she was probably doing something on the inside.

"Take the horse," Miriam said, handing him the reins.

The Morgan blew air from its nose as if he understood and wanted to get moving.

"Dedrick," Grenton called. He had stopped pushing the wagon. Ann had gone off somewhere else, probably back to her duties.

"Yeah, what?" Dedrick said. He slipped his foot into the stirrup and swung into the saddle.

Grenton stood with feet apart, arms curled, and his chin held high, the stance of a warrior. "If I do not see you in Rivergrove, send word when you plan to bring the Regimen down."

Dedrick smiled and turned the horse to go.

~ ~ ~

Dedrick rode without looking back. Sitting deep in the saddle, he loosened the reins and let the Morgan set the pace. The girl liked speed. Her compact, powerful body moved to her own rhythm. With arms and body relaxed, hips moving with the motion of the horse, wind blowing his face and chest, his mind cleared. The worries of the world disappeared, leaving Dedrick alone with the horse, flying through woods and over fields.

He never had reason to worry, never needed to leave Aldonia. Or Liberty. Miriam had the transfer under control. And the colonists had made an ally out of an enemy . . . unless the Torva had them all fooled. No, Grenton seemed sincere.

This new friendship could change many things. The Torva had learned more about Aldonia and the Regimen. A good thing? Maybe. If the day ever came that the colonists had to rise against the Regimen to protect themselves, the Torva would help. Grenton already seemed eager to do more than the Mosheh did. "You save one here and there while the rest of them rot." He wanted to free the entire city, giving people the right to their own lives. Odd coming from a man whose tribe stole women.

Grenton's enthusiasm lacked realism. The colonists could not beat an army of Unity Troopers. Aldonia would gain more residents in their Re-education Facility.

Dedrick wanted no part of that battle. He wanted an untroubled life where family and community were everything. Granted, troubles went hand in hand with life, especially living out here off the Regimen's grid. Still, Mom and Dad had sheltered the family, giving them a happy, carefree childhood but also instilling in them a respect for and a desire to help others. He knew freedom and security. He was willing to sacrifice and fight for it. He wanted it for everyone. But he was ready to leave that battle to others now. He wanted to settle down and raise a family, to shelter them and give them love and security. He wanted that with her . . . with Liberty. She wanted to join the Mosheh. He needed to change her mind.

The Morgan slowed to a trot, then to a walk. They neared an overlook. A horse whinnied in the distance.

Dedrick shifted in the saddle, signaling the horse to stop. A warm feeling of satisfaction came over him as he gazed out at the view.

Less than an hour had passed, and he had reached Rivergrove.

Rivergrove nestled up to foothills. A lazy river snaked around and through it. Rooftops peeked through trees blazing with autumn colors. Dilapidated rooftops.

Every colony had a unique style and method of remaining hidden. The Maxwell colony built underground homes and imitated nature in their aboveground construction. Rivergrove used existing structures, homes, and stores, but let nature claim rooftops and porches. They built frames and created drainage systems under rotting roofs, and they grew trees to cover paths. They farmed on uneven strips of land between trees, all the while keeping watch for drones from the hilltops.

The sentry must have seen Dedrick's approach and sent a rider.

The rider, a wiry kid on a blue roan Quarter Horse, crested the ridge. He drew near, chewing on a stick and peering into the distance. He took the stick from his mouth. "Who are you and what's your purpose?"

The Morgan whinnied at the blue roan. The blue roan bobbed its head and stamped a foot.

"I'm Dedrick, courier for the Maxwell colony. Miriam sent me. The colonists will get here by nightfall. Miriam would like whatever assistance you can provide. Think you can send a group to meet them on the last stretch?"

"Sure." The wiry boy nodded and stuffed the stick back into his mouth. "Heard about the mudslide. You guys find more trouble?"

"Uh, not really." He decided against mentioning the Torva. It might delay their assistance. "We received some unexpected help. I'll let Miriam and my sister Ann explain the situation to your elders."

"Alrighty then. Let's go round up some help." He lifted the reins, making the blue roan take a step, but then slumped in the saddle and said, "Whoa. You said your name is Dedrick?"

"Yeah."

"With the Mosheh?"

"Yeah."

"Then you'll want to know. The Mosheh sent word for you and Miriam. They said something about a girl, an Aldonian they once rescued. She turned herself in."

"What? What Aldonian girl?" The Morgan stamped the ground and snorted, picking up the tension in Dedrick's body, signals he hadn't meant to send. "Turned herself in to who?"

"She surrendered to the government, I suppose. That's all I know. Come on to the communication center for the details."

Every muscle in his body had tensed. "Her name, what's her name?"

"Oh, yeah. That I remember. Kind of unusual for a name." He smiled. "Her name is Liberty."

CHAPTER 43

The blades of the wind turbines sliced the air under moody clouds, knives in Dr. Supero's peripheral vision, knives slicing at his head. He adjusted the window tint to high, but the sight still tormented him as he drove the last stretch to the Re-education Facility.

He needed a skilled surgeon, not a hack who lived among miscreants in a decaying building.

Dr. Supero closed his eyes and rubbed his head. He fingered the lump from the tumor, going from edge to edge to determine the size. A dull headache had plagued him all morning. The headaches had increased in frequency and duration. He also struggled to stay awake most afternoons. Was he worn out from defeat or was it a symptom of the growing tumor?

Perhaps the open floor plan of his new apartment made him sleepy. He could view the oversized bed from everywhere except the bathroom. A raised floor and thick columns set the bedroom apart from the dining and living area. Previous occupants may have installed a curtain or screen. He did not have the drive to pursue either option. He hadn't even hung a curtain over the balcony window that overlooked the college campus. He would wait until his credits accrued and have someone else do it. He had lost a considerable amount of credits due to the damage he'd done to RCT property. It had invigorated him, trashing his old apartment and his office.

The new apartment was smaller than the previous one, the one afforded the Head Physician, but at least he still roomed alone. His possessions, all but the necessities, remained in boxes, always in his way. Perhaps he would die before he unpacked a single box.

The steering wheel tugged to the right, the anti-sleep alarm sounded, and a feminine voice said, "Warning, you are drifting between lanes."

He snapped open his eyes and shut off the alarm. He neared the main gate of the Re-Ed Facility.

A guard watched his approach from a cement-block tower inside the gate. He would soon verify Dr. Supero's identification, an automated process that

293

required a tap of a computer screen and used Dr. Supero's flexi-phone to read the radio frequency of his ID implant.

Dr. Supero eased off the accelerator and braked at the gate. He glared up at the guard, though he only saw heaping cumulonimbus clouds reflected on the tower windows.

His flexi-phone rang.

He answered it. "Yes, what is the problem?"

"You are not on the visitor roster."

"Of course I am."

"No, Dr. Supero, you are not. You will have to schedule an appointment for another day."

Blood rushed to his face. White gnats darted before him. He slammed his palms to the steering wheel and let out a string of obscenities. Then he breathed. "I was here yesterday, and I will likely come again tomorrow. The appointments have been approved. If I am not on the roster, it is due to the incompetency of others. Make what calls you need to. I am visiting today."

He ended the call and gripped the steering wheel with both hands. He would sit here until the gates opened. His list of people available for questioning grew smaller every day.

Liberty did not surrender out of a desire to regain harmony with society. No, she had an ulterior motive. Just as someone had kidnapped the children and aided the teens, somehow she would free the adults from this place. He would have no one left to question, no other path to take. Desperation would find him under the knife of the miscreants. He would likely wind up lobotomized or dead.

He found himself gritting his teeth. His jaw popped. Why wouldn't anyone give him the surgeon's name? They should be thankful for Regimen assistance. They no longer needed to struggle in the wild. They should be cooperative.

The Regimen rescued these people—rescued the Nature Preserves *from* these people—and cared for them as her own. In return, they spread their poison to every level of society. Primary children had formed groups, calling each other brother and sister. Some referred to one nanny or another as Mommy. The teens in Secondary had grown increasingly restless. They listened with eager ears and impressionable minds to the stories of life off the grid. Now they questioned everything. They doubted the ways of the Regimen. They wanted freedom to think and live as they saw fit. The infection had spread even to the counselors and psychiatrists. Report after report had come in showing the positive effects the antiquated nuclear family had had on these people. They saw motivation and strength of character, achievers and not receivers. They failed to consider the danger that society and the earth faced when the individual was allowed to grow strong with freedom.

The gate clicked and then creaked open. A voice came over a loudspeaker. "You may go in."

Supero put his foot to the accelerator pedal. He lacked the power to crush this plague in Aldonia, but he would not let his last opportunity slip by. He would speak with every one of these strangers. Even Liberty.

CHAPTER 44

I've watched movies where a character dives underwater to rescue an endangered species or gather toxic materials before it harms the aquatic ecosystem. Sometimes the character dove in unprepared, without an oxygen tank. I used to hold my breath as I watched, but I'd run out of air before the character completed his or her mission.

I felt like that now as I paced and waited with folded arms and a swatch of the wrapper from a pack of cigarettes in my hand. Today was the day.

This I discovered earlier as I staggered back to my cell from History Lessons. Two guards were talking, their voices echoing in the hallway. "Service crew's finally here. Maybe we'll get our power back today."

"About time. I'm sick of the lights dimming every half hour."

"You just want TV and game privileges back."

"Oh yeah? Well, I know what you want." The conversation turned lewd.

Once I returned to my cell and the door slammed shut, I shifted into high gear. I had to get the door ready, so I sat on the mattress and leaned back. Aware that a camera watched me from its perch on the wall, I reached into the slit I had made in the corner of the mattress and drew out the swatch that I had made from the cigarette pack. The guard had *given* the pack to me.

During one of my History Lessons, he'd had to wrestle me down. In the process, something fell from his chest pocket and landed on me. It slid over my abdomen and onto the chair, lodging itself under my hip. No one had noticed except for me. After the lesson, the guard unstrapped me and yanked me from the chair. I snatched the object—a pack of cigarettes—without anyone seeing. Then I walked with folded arms, sneaking it back to my cell. It took a bit of work to make the size of swatch I could use and to make a slit in the plastic mattress for a hiding place, but I didn't have anything better to do.

The door clicked.

I stopped pacing and tightened my grip on the swatch, making sure it remained hidden between my folded arms.

The door flung open and banged against the wall.

I jumped, not because it startled me—I was ready for it—but because the guard expected me to, and I didn't want to arouse suspicion.

He chuckled. "Hey, Breeder." He carried a tray that held a plastic cup, a slice of bread, and a steaming pile of something unrecognizable.

"You were a good girl today, so I brought you something special." He set the tray on the floor, inside the door, and pushed it with the toe of his shoe.

I sneered at the food. "I don't want that. It looks gross. I want something else."

He laughed, making a goat-like sound. "Is that right? The breeder wants something else?"

"You said if I cooperated with lessons I'd get something special to eat. So far I've gotten soup and bread. Every day. And now this?" I stepped forward and pushed the tray with my toe. I didn't want to provoke him, but I needed to appear upset over something for my plan to work. And the meal did look disgusting.

"Hey, that's good stuff," he said, grinning. "It's made with cornmeal. Got some kind of meat in it. It's real spicy."

I huffed and curled my lip to show disgust. "Some kind of meat? I don't want it."

He snickered and backed out of the room. "So sorry, breeder girl, eat it or don't."

The door began to swing shut.

I lunged for the door, reaching it in time to slip the swatch between the latch bolt and the frame before it clicked shut. Then I pounded on the door and threw a little fit for the camera. I couldn't help but smile. It was almost too easy. The swatch now bridged the strike opening, preventing the deadlock mechanism from setting but allowing the latch bolt to partially engage. Once I put a little pressure on the door and retracted the swatch, the latch bolt should ramp out of the strike.

I only needed to wait for the power to go down.

~ ~ ~

Dr. Supero popped two painkillers into his mouth, threw his head back, and swallowed the pills with his saliva. He leaned over, propping his hands on the smooth touchscreen of the computer stationed in the reception area of the facility. Colors swirled on the inside of his eyelids. Pain throbbed in his head. Four hours of questioning these people had taken its toll.

"Warden wants to know . . ."

Dr. Supero jumped. His breath caught.

The guard, Iden, chuckled, making an odd sound that one might expect from a farm animal. "Sorry, Doctor. I didn't know you were so jumpy." He gave a crooked grin that emphasized the odd shape of his large chin.

Dr. Supero returned his attention to the list of residents. He had interviewed seven of the eight adults acquired from the Nature Preserves. They had forbidden him from speaking with Liberty.

"So Warden wants to know," Iden said, "if you're done here. We got people working on the power supply, and we got shift changes. So he thinks you should go."

"I have not interviewed the eighth person on my list." Dr. Supero pointed to the name on the screen. "I will go when I am done. If allowed to finish, I do not foresee a reason to return here."

"Well, who is it?" Iden leaned over the screen, bumping shoulders with Dr. Supero. "Oh, him. You can't see him." The astringent overhead lighting and the protrusion of his forehead made his eyes resemble polished obsidian stones.

"What is the reason for that?"

"He's a priest. He has a different curriculum."

"I will speak with him."

Iden snickered. Licking his lips, he glanced in the direction of the guard who sat behind the counter and the bulletproof glass. "I could get you back there, take you to him, but you're not really allowed."

Dr. Supero grinned. He could work with this man. "And what is your price?"

A few minutes later, they stood in one of the lesson rooms, gazing down at a pale, bruised body with hirsute arms, legs, and chest. Damon lay reclined in a chair, a 3D helmet masking his eyes and sensors attached to various parts of his body. He wore only undershorts.

"Do you not have to monitor this procedure?" Dr. Supero said, disgusted at the obvious barbarity of the staff toward the resident.

"Not really. The Teacher just sets them up and goes about his business. Oh, I guess he monitors them for a little while, but once you get the lesson started, there's not much to do."

Dr. Supero ran his finger over a purple bruise on the man's side. "Do you treat all the students like this?"

Iden chuckled until he met Dr. Supero's hardened gaze. Then he wiped his mouth. "Not really. He's a special case."

"Why?"

One eye narrowed. His lip curled up on the side. He huffed as if he thought Supero should know.

"Never mind." Dr. Supero said. "How do you shut this off?" He motioned to indicate the 3D helmet.

"Oh, that's easy." Iden popped over to a screen that sat in a nook in the wall. He tapped a few controls. "Sometimes it takes awhile for them to adjust, but you can probably talk with him now. He might be a bit out of it. Some lessons have more impact than others." He glanced over his shoulder and grinned.

"Very good. You may go. I will speak with him alone."

Once Iden had vacated the room, Dr. Supero peeled the helmet off Damon's head.

Damon stared at the ceiling without blinking. His grisly beard and bushy brows aged him, but a second glance took years off the estimate. He was probably in his thirties.

"I am Dr. Supero." He transferred the helmet to one arm and scraped a sensor from the man's chest, finding a patch of pale skin and stubble.

Damon had not blinked once.

Dr. Supero snapped his finger in Damon's face.

Damon blinked.

"Good, I assume you can hear me, but I need more than that from you." He continued to scrape the sensors off, letting them fall to the floor. "I need you to respond. I need you to answer my questions. Do you understand?"

He peeled the last sensor off the man's ankle and tossed it. Some of the wires connected to the sensors did not lay flat and they rubbed against Dr. Supero's legs.

Damon stared. It took a minute of observation to witness the rise and fall of his chest as he breathed. The lesson had thrown him into shock.

Dr. Supero backed up and whipped the helmet to the floor. It banged against the frame of the chair. This was another dead end.

"I do not have the time for this." He returned to Damon's side, put one hand under his neck and the other on the outside of his furry thigh. "I need answers." He pivoted him around and forced him into a sitting position. "You will be the one to tell me what I need to know."

Damon tipped forward.

Dr. Supero leaned into the man and grabbed his shoulders, preventing him from falling over. Then he wrapped his arms around his torso and heaved his body of dead weight from the chair.

"Try to stand." Dr. Supero spoke into the back of Damon's neck as he struggled to move him to the wall. The earthy odor of a man who hadn't bathed in days came to his nose, making him breathe out of his mouth.

Damon collapsed, slipping through Dr. Supero's arms and landing on the floor, a leg on Dr. Supero's feet.

Dr. Supero felt the urge to draw a foot back and punt the body, but he needed to try a more gentle approach. Perhaps Damon's teacher met with resistance because of his use of force. Force and threats had not worked on any of the people from the Nature Preserves.

He squatted near Damon's head, grabbed his dry hands, and dragged him to a corner where the surveillance camera couldn't see. He continued pushing and pulling the body until he had it propped up in a sitting position in the corner.

Damon sat hunched over straight legs, his arms loose at his sides, his head tipped forward. His head moved! Then it lifted. His gaze connected with Dr. Supero's, and he almost seemed to smile. His eyes, brown as dirt like the majority of these people, held no anger or resentment.

Dr. Supero sat on the floor facing Damon, studying the eyes and weighing questions in his mind. He felt vulnerable, like a begging child as he leaned and whispered, "Please. I need your help."

The priest nodded and lifted a hand, maybe to sign something or touch Supero, but his hand fell to his lap.

"I know that the off-grids, I mean the rest of you, you were not the only ones out there. Some of your people have had advanced medical care. You have a physician, a surgeon, facilities. I need your surgeon." He whispered the last sentence with force.

The man continued to gaze at him, unblinking, but not with the distant look he'd had in the chair. "I can't help you in that way," he said in a dry, weak voice.

Dr. Supero sucked in a breath and grimaced. "Then you can help me in another way. Give me direction. Who can help me? Who will lead me to the answer I seek." He leaned into his face, gaining a close-up of the strange brown irises, the pores on his nose, and the unkempt beard. "My time is nearly up."

Damon made no reply. Nothing.

"I know that you care about others. I saw the video of you when the Unity Troopers came for you. You stood between armed men and that boy, what was his name?" He searched his memory. "Ah yes, Rick. His name was Rick. You would've taken a bullet for Rick. Take one for me. Without your help, I will die."

Silence.

The man's eyes flickered and his mouth opened. "Do you believe in God?"

"Will that help me?" He would profess whatever the priest wanted if it would get him a surgeon.

The priest smiled and lifted his hand, successfully bringing it to Dr. Supero's shoulder. "It will help you in the next world."

Dr. Supero brushed the hand from his shoulder. "I do not want to see the next world. My life is here. I want to stay here."

"You were not made for this world. You were made for something better. We must all prepare."

Hope slipped away. Dr. Supero grabbed Damon by the shoulders, perhaps squeezing too tightly. "Give me the name of your surgeon."

Damon's head rolled forward.

Dr. Supero released his grip and stood up, wiping off the man's sweat on his trousers. "You are a waste of my time." He sneered and backed to the door. "Iden will show me to Liberty."

~ ~ ~

The light in my cell turned brown.

I sat upright. My senses heightened. My breaths came short and fast.

The light went out.

I jumped up, reached into the dark, and dashed to the door. No light showed through the little window. The power was down. The cameras would no longer work. Neither would ID implant readers. And the fail-safe system should've opened the primary cell locks. I would have only the deadbolts to worry about.

Seven of the eight colonists had cells in this block, and I knew where they were. I hoped one of those seven knew the location of the eighth person's cell. We would not leave anyone behind. I saw the eighth colonist's face in my mind. He was the priest who wore the straw hat. I could still picture it tossing and turning in the wind from the Unity Trooper's helicopter.

Unable to see, I ran my hand up the edge of the door until I brushed the end of the swatch. Then I gripped the swatch and leaned against the door. "Please, oh, please work," I said to *My Friend.* I didn't see him but I believed he could help me. Was it unreasonable to think He could do anything?

The lock clicked. I turned the knob and the door opened.

My heartbeat quickened. "Thank you," I whispered. Then I stepped into the hallway.

Emergency lights illuminated the double doors at the far end of the hallway, giving me a hint of light. If guards came, they would come through those doors. I would see them before they saw me.

I ran barefoot across the floor and slammed into Mr. Ryder's cell door. The whites of his eyes appeared in the tiny window. I turned the deadbolt lever, unlocking the door. He opened it.

"Liberty," he said, smiling down at me and grabbing my shoulder. He wore a gown identical to mine. All of us wore them. It would be cold outside. I hadn't thought to mention that detail in my last meeting with the Mosheh. *Oh well.* An unpleasant bike ride would be better than remaining here, and warm blankets would await us.

"Get those doors." I pointed to the particular ones. Two of the cells held other people, not colonists. My heart ached for them. I understood Bolcan's intense desire to free everyone. The History Lessons had given me insight. Maybe someday we could close this place.

"I know which ones." Mr. Ryder turned to his wife's door.

"I need to find someone. One of ours isn't here."

Mrs. Ryder, a thin, trembling figure, emerged from her cell and flung herself into her husband's arms. He wrapped his arms around her and glanced at me over her head. "You mean Father Damon. He's in one of the lesson rooms. They keep him there longer than us." He released his grip on his wife and broke their embrace. They dashed for other doors.

"Meet me by the service door," I said, walking backwards. "There's a hallway just past the cellblocks." I pointed.

"Got it," Mr. Ryder said as he opened another door. Four colonists stood in the hallway now, shadowy figures of people waking from a nightmare.

I bolted for the lesson rooms. Emergency lights glowed at the end of most hallways, but not this one. Blackness lay ahead. A dim light showed an intersecting hallway behind. How long would the power remain down? How long before guards checked the cellblocks?

I ran my hand along the wall until I came to a door. I unlocked it and cracked it open.

"Hello? Anyone in here?" I strained for a glimpse of something. If the priest sat on the chair hooked up to the sensory equipment, would he be able to respond?

I opened the door all the way and took a few steps in. If the door closed, would it latch?

"Hello?" I listened for breathing. Hearing nothing, I dashed from the room.

No one answered me from the next three rooms. I heard no sound at all. I was certain I was in the correct hall. How many lesson rooms were there?

As I gripped the lock to the next door, voices and footfalls traveled to my ears.

"You cannot expect me to waste my time simply because you have a power failure."

My mouth went dry. I knew that voice. I cranked the lever to unlock the door. My fingers felt numb as I searched for the knob.

A light appeared—the beam of a flashlight coming from around the corner. It swung to my face.

"Well, what do ya know?" It was the guard with the dark eyes and potato chin. He reached for something on his belt. "The Breeder's left her cage."

Another man stood beside him, a man with a strange goatee. Even in the dark I recognized him. I had recognized his voice. *Dr. Supero.*

"Liberty," he said, his voice almost a whisper.

I was a child in Primary, playing hide-and-seek. I was a girl running for my life. I was the key to the freedom of the colonists, a key about to be lost.

They'd found me.

They would throw me back into my cell, starve me, deprive me of sleep, and brainwash me. I would graduate from Re-Ed a new person. Sterilization and job training would prepare me to re-enter society. They would monitor me for the rest of my life.

A surge of adrenaline coursed through my veins. I could not run, so I would fight. With a low, guttural scream that I couldn't believe came from me, I charged the guard.

The guard dropped the flashlight and lifted a weapon, bracing it with both hands. A stun gun, a taser, a rubber bullet gun?

I rammed my shoulder into his arms, into his chest.

He staggered back and the weapon clattered to the floor. In the next instance, he lunged. He grabbed me by the hair and throat and slammed me to the wall. "Don't even think about it, breeder girl."

I thrust my knee into his groin and sliced my arms up through his, breaking his grip. "I am *not* a breeder!"

He doubled over for a split second and then jerked upright.

A crackling, clicking sound tore through the air. A line of blue light zipped to the guard's side. He groaned, fell to his knees, and dropped like a sack of potatoes.

Dr. Supero stooped over him, pressing the stun gun to the guard's side. The clicking sound stopped. He dropped the gun, grabbed the flashlight, and straightened up. His gaze slid to me.

I gulped in air, trying to catch my breath. "Why did you . . . ?"

"The man you are looking for . . ." He directed the beam of light to the first door I had tried. "He is in there."

I shook my head, stunned with disbelief. Then I regained my senses and rushed to the door he indicated. I wished I had something to block the door in case it locked automatically, but I took my chances and let it close behind me.

"Father Damon? Are you in here?" I swung my hands out before me and to each side as I stepped along, like an actor under water trying to save the day. Several steps into the room, I slapped something with my hand and kicked something else. Wires brushed my legs. Further inspection told me I had found the chair, but it was empty. The object on the floor was a 3D helmet.

My stomach sunk. Had Dr. Supero lied?

The door swung open and light spilled into the room. Dr. Supero held the door open with his back, the guard's shoes and clothing in his arm. He shined the flashlight's beam at a corner of the room.

A man in nothing but undershorts sat slumped in the corner, his arms hanging loose at his sides, his chin resting on his hairy chest.

I ran to him and fell to my knees. "Father Damon?" I hesitated to touch his bare skin but then grabbed one shoulder and shook him. "Are you okay?"

The priest lifted his head and blinked.

Something squeaked and scraped along the floor.

Dr. Supero dragged the guard's half-naked body into the doorway, preventing the door from closing, and joined us in the corner of the room. He stuffed the priest's foot into the guard's pants.

The priest looked at him and gave a weak smile. "We must all prepare."

Dr. Supero glanced at me. "We must hurry."

I grabbed the guard's shirt and found the armhole. "Why are you doing this?"

"I . . ." He paused, seeming focused on wrestling a shoe onto Father Damon's foot. Then he turned his eyes to me. The flashlight on the floor threw hard shadows on his face, making him resemble a vulture. "I want you to remember this because I need your help."

With the priest half dressed, we each grabbed an arm and lugged him to his feet. I yanked his pants up.

"May God bless you," Father Damon said. "You are both very kind." He reached for a button.

"That'll have to wait, Father Damon," I said. "We have to get out of here." I drew his arm over my shoulders, wrapped an arm around his waist, and started for the door.

Dr. Supero dragged the guard farther into the room and caught the door before it closed. He held it while we stumbled through. "I will blame this all on you, but please remember me."

I glanced back, not sure what to make of him. "Thank you."

The eight colonists, all in flimsy gowns, met me at the end of the hall. Mr. Ryder and another man took over helping the priest, each of them throwing one of his arms over their shoulder.

Dr. Supero stood where I had left him, staring.

~ ~ ~

We stopped at the service door under an emergency light. I had learned in the last meeting with the Mosheh that the door was made of hollow metal and had a reinforcing channel around the edges and lock mounting area. It had a fail-secure lock that required power to unlock. Of course, with the power on, it would also require an approved ID implant. And if the power was on, trouble would soon find us. Surveillance cameras would show our empty cells and probably us at the service door. I wished I had a lock pick kit.

"Stand back." Mr. Ryder let go of the priest and waved us away from the door. He studied the doorframe and the lock. Then he spun around and kicked, grunting, his bare heel cracking the door just under the knob.

"Wait." The priest withdrew his arm from the shoulders of the man who supported him. He dropped to one knee. "Use a shoe."

After countless kicks by three different men, each wearing the shoe, the door swung outward.

Cool air and muted sunlight rushed in. Leaves rustled in the wind. A voice sounded in the distance, probably from one of the repair crew who worked on the transformer. Heavy gray clouds crept through the sky forming shapes of beasts and prey, stretching out in every direction except for one. A pastel blue and pink sky hung over the treetops. The Mosheh would be waiting under the clear sky on the other side of the trees, ready to ride the colonists to safety.

"Run for the fence," I said, pointing. I pushed aside knee-high weeds that grew along the building. Arc would've been the one to bring the ID implant remover, but he couldn't have come this far. The motion-detecting camera would've caught him.

I stopped my search and bolted after the colonists.

The door to the old brick building that housed the backup generator hung open a bit.

I nearly stopped in my tracks. Someone from the service crew must've gone inside. Had they heard the colonists running past? The wind might've obscured the sound.

Running with soft steps, I neared the fence and found them.

They all huddled together behind the brick building. Mr. Ryder held his wife and rubbed her back. The priest leaned against the wall with his eyes closed.

I glanced at the window that Dedrick had broken and I had crawled through. It had been repaired.

"There's no one in there," Mr. Ryder said. "I peeked inside."

"Good." I exhaled. "Over here." I motioned for others to follow and dropped down by our exit point. Some of the wild grasses in the loose clumps had turned a paler shade of green. I yanked one of them up and set it off to the side. "We need to clear out a crawlway."

Several people, men and women, dropped down beside me. They would have the job done in no time.

I got back up to search for the implant remover. Arc may have stashed it near the building.

"What's this?" Mr. Ryder said, holding the implant remover like a gun, his finger on the trigger. "I found it in there." He pointed to a clump of weeds.

"I think you know what it is," I said, smiling and taking it from him. I turned his hand up and pressed the gun to the pink mark on his palm. "It removes the implant they gave you on day one."

He winced as I pulled the trigger. The implant shot up into the cartridge with the faintest clink sound. Then he smiled, reminding me of Dedrick. "I'll take care of it." He took the implant remover and his wife's hand.

The colonists had the crawlway completely cleared out, the clumps of grass all along the fence. A man, one of the hunters, smoothed the floor of the crawlway by scraping dirt out with both hands, his arm muscles rippling with the effort.

"Okay, once your implant is out, go on through," I said. "You'll run through the trees into a field. Rescuers will be waiting for you on motorcycles or dirt bikes."

The man who had helped carry the priest crawled through first. He knelt on the other side and hunched over the crawlway. "Send Father through next."

They had lived in separate cells for over a month, but they worked like a team, encouraging and assisting each other through, then jogging by twos and threes into the woods. The second the last one crawled through, I pushed the loose dirt back in and grabbed clumps of grass. I wanted to keep people from knowing we had gone this way for as long as possible.

"Liberty."

I glanced up.

Mrs. Ryder stood on the other side of the fence, her gown billowing with the breeze, her forehead wrinkling with worry. The two people she had started to leave with waited farther in the woods.

"Hurry, Mrs. Ryder," I said. "You have to run."

"What about you?"

"I have another way out. Run!" I stuffed the last bit of grass into its place and packed them all down.

She hesitated but then turned and ran, her slender figure disappearing from view.

A great weight lifted from me. Even if I didn't make it, they would. The Mosheh—Bolcan, Arc, Alix, Camilla—would bring them to safety. This did not repair all the damage my selfishness had caused, but every one of the colonists would now live free.

I brushed the dirt from my hands, picked up the implant remover, and turned to the brick building. Someone had left it open, someone with the Mosheh. He or she must've left it open for me. It only made sense. It was the best way to keep the colonists and the Mosheh safe. The Mosheh always looked for a way to throw the Regimen off their track by laying clues in other places. I knew what I had to do. The colonists would leave under the sun, but my destination lay under storm clouds.

I slipped through the open door.

CHAPTER 45

Dedrick stood on top of a hydroelectric dam on the foot-wide ledge that stretched across the river. Black clouds raced through the night sky, allowing glimpses of the moon. Moonlight fell on troubled waters on both sides of the dam. Water surged through outflow valves in half of the dam wall, rumbling beneath his feet and creating an angry man-made waterfall where a natural waterfall once cascaded to the deep river below.

On the other half of the dam stood the powerhouse. A tunnel ran from the Re-education Facility's backup generator to the powerhouse. Fulton had told him one of the colonists saw Liberty go that way.

Dedrick had searched it already. He found the door open but no one inside. Where could she have gone?

Once the staff realized their prisoners had escaped, the search began. Bolcan and the others had the colonists on their bikes by then, safely on route to the nearest underground access point. By the time the search ended, the colonists had reached Gardenhall and Dedrick stood outside the Boundary Fence behind the Breeder Facility. He had contacted the Mosheh at once.

"We've got our people, Dedrick," Fulton had said. "Every one of the eight colonists."

Dedrick's heart nearly burst. His mom's face came to mind. He wanted to hold her.

"What about Liberty?" He laid his bike on its side, dropped to his knees, and shoved the back end of the bike under the Boundary Fence.

Fulton made no reply.

Dedrick stopped pushing the bike and tapped his earphone to make sure it was working. "Fulton?"

"Yeah, I'm here. We don't have Liberty. We don't know where she is."

"What do you mean? Why didn't she go with them?"

"I don't know, Dedrick." His voice softened. He must've known Dedrick's feelings for her. Maybe Miriam was right and they all knew. "She didn't stick to the plan."

Dedrick shoved the bike the rest of the way and crawled under the fence. He needed to refuel but nothing else would stand in his way. He had to find her.

~ ~ ~

Dedrick took slow steps down the ledge of the dam. He had already searched the woods. He'd search again. He couldn't give up.

"Dedrick." Fulton's voice came through his earphone.

"Yeah, what you got?" Dedrick cupped his hand over his ear to hear over the rush of the water.

"We've intercepted CSS communications. They've stopped the search; they stopped about an hour ago."

Dedrick froze. "They found her?"

"No, they didn't find her. Well, they think they did. They picked up the colonists' ID implant readings in the river under the waterfall and claimed it was a mass suicide. Not sure how Liberty pulled that one off, but it's good she did. We're all safe because of her."

"So where is she?" Dedrick whispered, his gaze dropping. Something on the ledge, half under his foot, drew his attention.

"I didn't catch that," Fulton said. "Come again."

"Nothing. I'm out." He tapped his TekBand to disconnect the call, took a step back, and squatted.

Someone had carved words into the cement. LIVE FREE OR DIE.

Dedrick almost swooned. He dropped onto all fours and then straddled the ledge to steady himself. The wind whipped his hair into his eyes. His eyes stung and blurred. He traced his finger along the freshly carved letters in the cement. A shudder ran through him. Could she have jumped, taking all the implants with her? She would've known it would stop the Regimen from searching further. The Mosheh, the colonists, everyone would be safe.

He yanked the flashlight from his belt and scanned the troubled waters for signs of a body. Dead bodies floated, didn't they?

Thick streams blasted through the outflow valves, sprinkling his face and partially blocking his view. He shined the beam and focused his gaze on the river twenty feet below. White bubbling water rolled up over itself in a mesmerizing way. The force of the water could keep a body down, maybe even lodge it under a rock shelf beneath the dam. Or she could've used something heavy to keep her body down by tying it around her waist.

No. She wouldn't have killed herself. She was smart. She would've found a way to hide while they searched.

He pushed himself up and redirected the beam of the flashlight, peering into the woods on one side of the river.

Night stole the color and details from the surroundings, but the moonlight slipped through a gap in the clouds. Wind made the river rage. Waves crashed against the cliffs on either side. Above that, bare branches and leaves swayed and trembled, bony grasping hands among evergreens and autumn leaves. Silhouettes showed that the trees on the side opposite the facility stood taller and had the greater canopy. Two trees stood alone closer to the cliff, an old fir tree and a tree that had fallen against it.

Liberty would have needed to avoid the drones. She would have gone to the thicker woods.

Dedrick jogged back the way he came, down the foot-wide cement ridge at the top of the dam.

He reached the end of the dam and leaped onto solid ground. He had searched earlier and found only the heavy prints of the Unity Troopers' boots and fresh deer tracks. Several troopers had come this way. How much time did she have before they arrived? She couldn't have gotten far. She would've had to hide. Even now, she might not have known the search was over. Drones made no sound.

He jogged farther into the woods, toward the bush where he had stashed his dirt bike.

A gust of wind stole through the tree trunks and evergreens, kicking up leaves and bringing the canopy to life. The chrome of his dirt bike reflected under the beam of his flashlight.

"Liberty," he called. "Can you hear me?" He turned in a circle, shining the beam on every inch of ground, tree trunks, and branches. She would've headed for the nearest Mosheh access point, maybe even made it through the woods. A field of windmills and solar panels lay between here and there. Could she have reached it?

He swung a leg over his bike, turned on the headlight, and kicked the gears to neutral. He walked the bike forward a few steps, reluctant to start it. The noise would prevent him from hearing her.

"Liberty!" he shouted. Where would she hide? Where *could* she hide?

He kick-started the bike and crawled forward, weaving a bit to keep from tipping. His previous search had taken him down the middle of the woods. She most likely wouldn't have ran or hid close to the river. She would've expected the search to begin there.

He turned deeper into the woods.

~ ~ ~

Half an hour later, Dedrick circled back. The buzz of the bike competed with the noise of the wind through the trees. The air had grown heavy with the threat of rain. His attention had turned to the branches of trees. He slowed at every good climbing tree and scanned the branches.

The trees parted and he found himself overlooking the cliff. Two trees stood alone here, an old fir tree and a hardwood that had fallen against it. He had seen them earlier from his post on the ledge of the dam. Now he could see that the hardwood would've landed in the river if the fir tree hadn't blocked it. It was lodged between high branches next to a six-foot wide, three-foot high mass of sticks.

Dedrick turned the flashlight on and studied the sticks.

It was an eagle's nest. They liked to build near rivers or lakes, often in a Douglas Fir, sometimes in a Black Cottonwood. The eagles would've abandoned the nest after the hardwood crashed into it, but it looked sound.

Dedrick backed the bike up and turned it around, ready to resume the search. Then he stopped and glanced at the tree. Liberty?

Unity Troopers wouldn't have touched the nest. It was illegal to disturb one. But the sparse needles above it offered no cover, so a drone would've spotted her. She would've known that. She could've created her own cover.

An eagle's nest wouldn't be a bad place to hide.

He jumped off the bike, barely dropping the kickstand, and bolted for the tree. Liberty could've climbed the hardwood. It had a wide enough trunk and a gradual slope.

"Liberty!" he shouted. He climbed hunched over, putting one foot in front of the other and using his hands for balance.

A branch poked his head, letting him know he reached the nest. He looked up, found other branches for support, and pivoted to the nest.

Leafy branches covered it. An eagle would not have brought them here. Liberty would have. It would've shielded her from the eye of a drone.

"Liberty, are you okay?" Supporting himself with an overhead branch, he snatched one of the leafy branches from the nest and tossed it. "It's me. Dedrick."

A moan and mumbled speech came from the nest.

Dedrick kicked it up a notch, yanking branches from the nest. After tossing the last one, he grabbed the flashlight and exhaled.

He'd found her.

Liberty sat up and rubbed her pale face. She wore a long raincoat, probably over the thin hospital gown, and rags wrapped around her feet.

Dedrick wished he could reach her and pull her to himself. He extended a hand. "Are you okay? We need to get out of here."

"Yeah." She pushed the hair from her face and rolled onto her knees. "I must've fallen asleep. S-s-so cold."

"Come on, I'll help you down."

She braced herself on a branch of the tree and swung a leg over the side of the nest. "I got it." She turned around and sat on the sloped trunk, her knees in the air, her feet on the trunk. She scooted down a few inches. "It's easier . . . this way." Her teeth chattered between words. She shivered.

He backed down a few inches at a time, facing her and keeping pace, ready to grab her if she swayed. Nearing the ground, he jumped. Not expecting her to allow him to catch her, he reached out to her anyways.

She glanced at him, at the ground, and at him again. Then she gave him her hand.

He pulled her into his arms and lowered her to the ground. It took effort for him to pry his arms from around her. He didn't want to let go.

"Thanks." She folded her arms across her chest and shivered.

"Here." He unzipped his jacket and shrugged it off his shoulders. "Give me yours. That can't be warm."

She trembled as she removed the raincoat and revealed the paper-thin gown.

He ached to care for her, to make her warm, to keep her safe. "What'cha got on your feet?" They traded jackets.

"Oh." She looked down at them. "Rags. I found them in the powerhouse."

"Good idea."

She gave a weak smile as she stuffed an arm into his jacket. "I got the idea from George Washington's army."

He didn't get it at first. Then he laughed. She'd probably gained the knowledge from Bot's game. "I'm glad you're resourceful. Actually, I was wondering. How did you sink the implant remover? That thing floats."

"I didn't. It's in the pocket." She pointed to the raincoat he now wore. "You have to give those things back, don't you? Or you get into trouble with that kid in the WAG room."

He shook his head and huffed. She was teasing him.

"I dumped the implants into a canvas bag with a few heavy tools also from the powerhouse." She smiled. "Before I threw it into the waterfall, I used one of the tools to carve a message on the top of the—"

"Saw it."

"Live free or die," they said together.

"Yeah," she said. "I thought it might throw them off."

"It worked. They think you're all dead, mass suicide."

"Good." She started to zip the jacket.

He grabbed her hand. "Leave it open. You've probably got hypothermia. Use my heat to warm up on the ride back."

He straddled the dirt bike.

She climbed on after him.

"Better hold tight," he said. "I want to know you haven't passed out back there." That was part of the reason, anyway.

She wrapped her arms around his waist and squeezed him. "How in the world did you find me?"

Dedrick jumped on the kick-starter and got the bike humming. "I guess I know you better than you think I do."

CHAPTER 46

I awoke in a hospital bed with an IV in my hand and lines connecting me to a bag on a nearby pole. A nurse had told me I had dehydration and hypothermia, but that I'd be fine.

I felt fine now. A little sweaty, but fine.

I sat up in bed and pushed the damp hair off my neck.

A sheet hung in front of me at the foot of the bed. Sheets also hung on either side, separating patients, but the one on my left was pushed back.

A man lay in the next bed, curled up on his side with no blanket. He wore jeans and a slate gray shirt, a sliver of skin showing between them. He had dark hair with light streaks . . .

I did a double take. It was Dedrick. Was he okay?

I threw back the covers and swung my legs off the bed. I wore black sweatpants and thick green socks. My shirt was pastel pink. Who picked out these clothes?

A shadow appeared on the curtain at the foot of the bed. Then the curtain moved and the woman who had attended me last night came through. She had a smile that said everything was right in the world. Babies grew up in families. Nature belonged to us all. Selfishness did not exist.

"How are you this morning?" She took my wrist and looked at her watch.

"I'm fine. Is he okay?" I indicated Dedrick's sleeping body with a nod.

She glanced over her shoulder and her smile grew. "Oh, he's okay. He's just worried about you." Her eyes widened and she frowned as if trying to look serious. "I couldn't get him to leave last night."

"Oh." My cheeks warmed. Last night . . . . I remembered Dedrick arguing with Bolcan. We had climbed down through a manhole and found Bolcan on a tunnel kart. Bolcan leaped from the cart, hugged me, and whispered, "I was on my way to find you." Dedrick wanted him to go above and take his dirt bike somewhere. They'd argued over who would escort me to Gardenhall.

I watched the nurse's skilled movements as she checked my vitals, made notes, and finally removed the IV catheter from my hand. "What about the others? They're here, aren't they? Are they okay?"

She rubbed the spot on my hand with a damp pad and applied a bandage strip. "Oh yes. They all need a bit of recovery time, but they're fine."

"Hey." Dedrick came up behind the nurse and stood with his hands on his hips, looking awkward. His hair stuck to his head on one side. "How is she?" He only glanced at me.

It irritated me that he asked her and not me. I could speak for myself.

"She's fine," the nurse said, smiling at me. "In fact, you can go. Just take it easy for the next few days. Regular meals, plenty of rest. All that."

"Thanks."

She gave Dedrick a look. He seemed confused but then stepped back, allowing her enough room to squeeze past. She pushed the sheet wall aside and left us alone.

Dedrick watched her go and then pivoted to me, still standing arms akimbo but now biting his lower lip. Maybe he had something to say.

I tugged the sleeves of my shirt down over my wrists. Then I slid off the bed, coming to stand too close to him.

He sucked in a breath of air, dropped his arms to his sides, and backed up.

"Thanks for coming for me last night. I don't think I thanked you."

He nodded. "I couldn't leave you out there. What if the eagles had returned to their nest?"

"Maybe they would've adopted me."

We stood there for three beats of my heart, smiling stupidly and gazing into each other's eyes, heat sliding up my neck.

"Well, I . . ." I pointed to the sheet the nurse had gone through, ready to make my own exit. "I guess I—"

"Are you hungry?" He tapped my arm.

"Um, no. Well, I mean . . ." His behavior had me feeling awkward. Whatever he had to say, I wished he'd just say it. "I'm gonna shower and find something else to wear." I grabbed the pink shirt by the hem and stretched it out. Did he know this was not my style?

He looked me over and a smile stretched across his face. "Yeah, I got you."

I felt rude turning away from him, leaving when I knew he had something to say, but I couldn't remain in that little area with him for another second.

I showered and changed into slender pants and a silky white shirt. I wouldn't ordinarily select clothes with silky, flowing fabric. I don't know why it appealed to me today.

Dedrick joined me for breakfast. We sat with Abby at a round table under a window to the garden. Dedrick nodded a few times as Abby spoke about the pet cat she had as a child and about the walks she used to take with Richter, but the gears of his mind showed through his eyes. He still had something he wanted to say to me. I hoped something wasn't wrong, but I couldn't get myself to ask.

Last night I had agreed to meet with the elders today at nine. At ten to nine, I touched the empty bowl in front of Abby and stood up. "You done? I have to get going."

She tugged the bowl from my fingers and reached for Dedrick's. "I'll take them. I like to circle around the place for exercise."

"Where you going?" Dedrick peered up at me.

"Meeting room. I haven't given my report yet. I'm supposed to be there at nine."

He got up and came around the table to me, again standing too close. A pleasant sandalwood scent teased my nose. He must've showered when I did. "I'll go with you."

"I want to give my report alone."

"I know."

We walked in silence through rows of picnic tables, past groups of old people eating and talking, past young people on errands, past Paula playing with the two boys we had rescued, past the sleeping capsules and the training room. We strode around the corner to an area with little light. A battery operated lantern hung next to the meeting room door.

"Hey." Dedrick took my hand and stopped walking.

I turned to face him, pulling my hand free.

With a downward gaze, he opened his mouth but then pressed his lips together. He cleared his throat. His eyes went to mine. "Liberty, I know you want to join the Mosheh."

Oh, so that's what this was about. My jaw clenched.

"And you'd be good at it. You're smart, able to think on your feet, creative . . . but I don't want you to make promises to them."

Who did he think he was, telling me what I could or couldn't do? I opened my mouth to argue.

He leaned in closer, his gaze travelling my face, his pupils dilating. "Liberty, make promises to me. I love you."

316

My breath caught in my throat. I backed into the wall. Was he really saying this?

"I want to make a life with you, start a family."

My head spun. This wasn't happening. "Me? No, you don't want me."

His gaze flickered. One side of his mouth curled up. "Yes, I do." He brushed my arm.

I couldn't handle the look in his eyes, so I lowered my head. His touch made my arm tingle. I glanced up. "Dedrick, I-I . . . ." I couldn't think of how to word what I wanted to say. I didn't know how to tell him. Did he really love me? I hadn't seen this coming.

"Marry me," he said, leaning in and putting a finger under my chin. He tilted my head up and pressed his mouth to mine.

My lips burned. Heat radiated through my entire body. Magnetic energy drew me toward him. I hadn't allowed myself to recognize the feelings I had for him. I hadn't believed it possible that he cared for me this way. Now my feelings poured out every crack I hadn't sealed. They spilled out all over him. I wanted to give myself to him, to belong to him, to spread roots and branches with him, to say *yes*.

But I couldn't. I pulled away. "I'm sorry. I-I have to do this." Tears stung my eyes. I trembled. A part of me desperately wanted back in his arms.

"No, you don't." He took my hands, his brown eyes locking onto mine. "You don't have to promise the Mosheh anything."

"I do." I made a weak effort to pull my hands from his, but his reluctance to let go made me give up. "I can't live free as long as Aldonians live under the lies of the Regimen. I would feel selfish. I want everyone to have what I have."

"You did your part; leave the rest to others. My term of service ends soon. We can leave Aldonia and live in one of the colonies. We can raise children who care about others and are willing to fight and sacrifice to make the world a better place. We'll raise children who know the meaning of love."

We would be a family. Our family could make a difference. The idea appealed to me so deeply that I couldn't reply at first. But then I found my voice. I had to.

"Dedrick, I hadn't allowed myself to think about this. I hadn't known you felt . . ."

"Come on," he said with the hint of a smile. "Everyone else did. Even before I did."

I smiled, feeling shy as a Primary girl. "I like the idea of being a family with you, of having children with you one day . . ." I squeezed his hands. ". . . but I'm not done here. Not yet."

He released my hands, turned his gaze to the ceiling, and ran a hand through his brown locks with blond tips. The blond tips were leftover from when he colored his hair months ago as part of his disguise when rescuing me. Was that why he never cut it?

He turned away and then back. "Okay." A wall came up between us, one he built in a matter of seconds. "You're guaranteed acceptance in the Mosheh if you tell them one thing."

"What's that?"

The light in his eyes flickered and dimmed. His mouth opened a full second before he got the words out. "Your dream."

~ ~ ~

I stood before the Mosheh, Elders Lukman and Rayna in person, Elder Dean and the other elders via video conference, their live images streaming to the wall monitors. I gave them the specifics about my time in the Re-education Facility and about the escape, including my encounter with Dr. Supero and his unexpected assistance. They thanked me for my sacrifices and praised the success of the last mission.

Then I told them my dream. I told them about the sower of the weeds and the sower of the wheat seed. I told them how important it felt that the wheat seed take root.

Stares and silence followed. Distant clanks and creaks became audible. Elder Dean even seemed to have fallen asleep with his chin resting on his chest.

Then he woke. His head lifted and he spoke. "I am an Interpreter of Dreams."

All heads turned to him.

I held my breath.

"This dream is meant for us. We are not to remain separated from Aldonians. We are to come out of hiding and live among them."

Eyes widened. Mouths fell open. Someone gasped.

Then everyone spoke at once. "Impossible."

"They would terminate us."

"We would be powerless to help anyone."

"We would be sent to Re-education."

"How can so few have an impact on so many?"

A beep, a signal of a communication, interrupted. Voices became whispers.

Elder Lukman's hand shot forward. He tapped a control on the tabletop. "Yes?"

"Pardon the interruption, Elder Lukman." It was Fulton's voice. "But we have an intruder in one of our tunnels."

"An intruder?"

"I thought it was a guy at first," Fulton said, "but it's a woman. She's found entry at one of our warehouse access points, and she's investigating the tunnels. I'm sending her image to you now."

A flat, still image appeared on the glassy tabletop. A woman held a flashlight and squinted. She wore a bulky jacket with big metallic buttons. Wild silver hair cascaded over her shoulders and framed her face.

A knot formed in my gut. "I know who she is," I said. "Her name is Silver. And she's trouble."

CHAPTER 47

Voices and the hum of electrical equipment filled the room, creating a white noise that did not soothe but rather seemed to separate ligament from bone. Lanterns lined the wall at the foot of the operating table, the laminated office desk. Monitors and surgical equipment lay out of view on other makeshift tables. Dr. Supero hadn't seen it, but he guessed that an adjustable desk lamp would substitute for a surgical light.

Canvas fabric with a disturbing pattern of red and white stripes concealed the ceiling, drooping between nails. In one corner, a blue square of stars interrupted the pattern and took up a full sixth of the canvas. The stars blurred, came into focus, and blurred again.

Dr. Supero blinked to clear his vision. He would've believed that one of the miscreants hung it there as a decoration, misjudging their own talent at interior design. His experience in a room down the hall showed otherwise.

"I do not understand why you cannot use clippers," Dr. Supero had said. He sat on an ancient metal two-drawer filing cabinet under the light of several lanterns.

A boy who couldn't be over twenty had cut his hair with scissors and now shaved his head with a razor. "Hold still, Supero." He scraped the blade over stubble on his head, the sound echoing through his brain. "Life's pretty simple around here. We only have power in a few rooms."

"That's comforting."

"Don't worry, we're generating more just for you."

"How do you even have power in this condemned property?"

"We have our ways. Don't wanna tell you too much. Don't know if I can trust you."

"I am allowing you to run a blade over my head. I am allowing Angel to hack open my skull. Certainly, you can trust me."

"No, you can trust us. I don't know that it goes both ways."

"I should think—" Something sped past his face and landed in his lap. An audible gasp escaped him. His heart skipped a beat. He leaped from the file cabinet and brushed his shirt and trousers, his hands trembling. He did not fear spiders. He simply had no desire to get a spider bite.

The room filled with laughter.

"Take a breath, Supero, sometimes paint chips fall from the ceiling."

Dr. Supero stopped dancing and peered at the ceiling. The lack of light prevented him from seeing much. His head stung though. The boy must've sliced it when he jumped.

~ ~ ~

"Are you ready, Doctor?" Angel's face appeared over his. Her smiling eyes and arched brows peeked out from between a facemask and surgical cap.

"No, I think I may be out of my mind."

Her eyes turned into half moons. "Then it won't matter if I mess up." A pinprick to his head followed. She must've injected a local anesthetic.

A man mumbled something about knocking Dr. Supero out and then stepped into view. It was Guy. He wore a surgical gown and cap and held something in his single hand. "So I just put it over his nose?" He gestured with his stump.

"Are you an anesthesiologist?" Dr. Supero said.

Guy laughed. "I'm the closest you'll get. Besides, I've knocked a few men out in my time."

"Yes, hold it over his nose." Angel leaned above Dr. Supero's head, doing something he could neither see nor feel. "Once he's out, you'll have to monitor his vitals while I work on him."

She said this to the one-handed man. The one-handed man was going to monitor his vitals, make sure he stayed alive. Comforting.

The one-handed man approached with an anesthesia facemask.

"Turn the page, will you?" Angel said to someone out of view.

"Page?" Dr. Supero pushed the mask away. "Are you using a medical book?!"

Guy forced Dr. Supero's hand back with his stump and moved in with the mask.

Did they really intend to help him? Was this all a big joke? He would die, and who would care? Who would mourn him? No one even knew he was here. Rumors would spread to explain his whereabouts. *Dr. Supero had gone mad.* Maybe he *had* gone mad. Why else would he have entrusted himself to these people? None of them . . . had the skills . . . the skills . . . needed to . . . to . . . ah . . . per . . . . ate.

"Come play with us, Sparrow." The childlike voice came from far away but sped closer and echoed in his ear. "Come fly, little sparrow." The laughter of many children sliced into his brain.

"Come fly . . ." The voice deepened and the words stretched out like a recording slowing down. "Come, fly with us, Sparrow."

Dr. Supero lifted his wings and stepped off the branch.

ABOUT THE AUTHOR

Theresa Linden, an avid reader and writer since grade school, loves American History and the things our country has traditionally stood for, especially faith, family and freedom. She is a member of the Catholic Writers' Guild and a local writers' group where she hones her writing skills. The often-disturbing current world events inspired her to write the *Chasing Liberty* trilogy. Theresa lives in northeast Ohio with her husband, three boys, and one dog.

Made in the USA
Middletown, DE
06 November 2015